• Emotional Rescue •

T0348067

. Emotional Rescue .

The Theory and Practice of a Feminist Father

Isaac D. Balbus

NEW YORK AND LONDON

Published in 1998 by
Routledge
711 Third Avenue,
New York, NY 10017

Published in Great Britain by
Routledge
2 Park Square, Milton Park,
Abingdon, Oxon, OX14 4RN

Transferred to Digital Printing 2011

Copyright ©1998 by Isaac D. Balbus

All rights reserved. No part of this book may be reprinted or
reproduced or utilized in any form or by any electronic, mechanical
or other means, now known or hereafter invented, including
photocopying and recording or in any information storage or
retrieval system, without permission in writing from the publishers.

Library of Congress Cataloging-in-Publication Data
Balbus, Isaac D.
Emotional rescue : the theory and practice of a feminist father /
Isaac D. Balbus
p. cm. — (Thinking gender)
Includes bibliographical references and index.
ISBN 0-415-91917-7 (hb).—ISBN 0-415-91918-5 (pb)
1. Balbus, Isaac D. 2. Fathers—United States—Biography.
3. Fathers—United States—Psychology—Case studies.
4. Fathers and daughters—United States—Case studies.
5. Child rearing—United States—Psychological aspects.
6. Sex role—United States—Psychological aspects.
7. Feminism—United States. 8. Feminism and psychoanalysis—
United States. I. Title. II. Series.
HQ756.B36 1998
306.874'2'092—dc21
97-28024
CIP

The author gratefully acknowledges permission to reprint
previously published material here. Portions of this book have
previously appeared in *Private Sociology: Unsparing Reflections,
Uncommon Gains*, edited by Arthur B. Shostak (General Hall, 1996)
and *Marcuse: From the New Left to the Next Left*, edited by John
Bokina and Timothy J. Lukes, ©1994 by the University Press of
Kansas. Reprinted by permission.

Publisher's Note
The publisher has gone to great lengths to ensure the quality of this reprint
but points out that some imperfections in the original may be apparent.

for Shayla

contents

acknowledgments

I have been working on this book in one form or another for almost fourteen years. There were many points during this period when I despaired of completing it. That I was finally able to do so was in no small part due to the encouragement of Mary Holmquist, who never lost confidence in my project even when my own faith in it flagged. Ron Bayer, Rob Crawford, Miriam Dixson, and Moishe Postone were also there when I needed them. All five know how grateful I am for their support. Mary, Rob, Miriam, and Moishe also read parts of my manuscript and prodded me to clarify my arguments and polish my prose. So did Sandy Bartky, Judy Gardiner, Doris Graber, David Greenstone, Peter Knauss, Allan Lerner, Mark Lichbach, Andy McFarland, Norma Moruzzi, Michael Mitsoglu, Danny Postel, Art Shostak, Dick Simpson, Marc Stier, Sandy Thatcher, Ed Tverdek, Steve Warner, and Elfriede Wedam. Peter and David died long before I completed my project. I still miss them very much.

I also want to acknowledge the enormous debt of gratitude I owe to Selma Balbus, who will reach ninety around the time this book is published. The book tells the story of a difficult period in my life during which I overcame an idealization of my mother that defended me from my anger against her. The direct expression of that anger was a necessary part of the emotional development that I describe. But that anger has long since given way to a realistically loving appreciation of the many gifts she has given me. I hope she remembers that if she reads this book.

A number of other people and institutions deserve thanks. All too often I called on colleagues Marilyn Getzov, Gerry Strom, Tom Carsey, and Jeffrey Murer to rescue me from digital disasters. Gene Ruoff, director of the Institute for the Humanities at the University of Illinois at Chicago, was kind enough to let me keep an office at the institute long after my tenure as a fellow had ended. My fellowship at the institute during the academic year

1984–85 helped me get my project off the ground, and my two-quarter sabbatical leave in 1988 gave me the time to make a necessary correction in its course. That I was finally able to reach my destination was in no small part due to the editorial assistance of Linda Nicholson and William Germano. Their suggestions ultimately proved to be even more helpful than they were initially unwelcome.

Finally, I would like to thank my former wife for long ago making available to me journals and datebooks that helped me reconstruct the first few years of my life with our daughter. Her name has been changed in order to protect her privacy.

Chicago, Illinois
September, 1997

For the real subject-matter is not exhausted in its purpose, but in working the matter out; nor is the mere result attained the concrete whole itself, but the result along with the process of arriving at it. The purpose by itself is a lifeless universal, just as the general drift is a mere activity in a certain direction, which is still without its concrete realization; and the naked result is the corpse of the system which has left its guiding tendency behind it.

—G. W. F. Hegel

. Introduction .

$\mathcal{E}$ver since I read Herbert Marcuse's *An Essay on Liberation* in 1969 I have wrestled intermittently with the question of what it means to be a radical intellectual. It was not until I finished writing this book that I realized that it represents my answer to that question. To assimilate my answer you will therefore have to finish reading it. But even at this point I can say something about how I understand the question and how I have attempted to answer it.

An Essay on Liberation culminated in the claim that "the radical transformation of society implies [a] union of [a] new sensibility with a new rationality."[1] In a genuinely emancipated society we would not only work but also feel and think in a fundamentally different way than we do under capitalism. We will never live in that new society, moreover, unless this different sensibility and different rationality somehow already inform the struggle against the old society.

On the one hand, a successful struggle against domination can only be "carried through by men [sic] who are physiologically and psychologically able to experience things, and each other, outside the context of violence and exploitation." Any liberation struggle worthy of that name must be waged by individuals whose "nonaggressive, erotic, receptive faculties" have supplanted their "aggressiveness and guilt," individuals who are "tender, sensuous [and] no longer ashamed of themselves." Revolution presupposes a "type of man [sic] who would speak a different language, have different gestures," a person who "want[s] to see, hear, feel things in a new way."[2]

On the other hand, this new sensibility is necessary but not sufficient for human liberation. Although the "senses have a share in producing the images of freedom . . . the most daring images of a new world, of new ways of life, are still guided by concepts, by a logic elaborated in the development of thought." Reason retains an essential revolutionary role. Without "critical theory" as a "guide [to] political practice," the new sensibility can easily degenerate into a mere "withdrawal [that] creates its artificial paradises within the society from which it withdrew." By itself the new sensibility "cannot possibly be a radical and revolutionary force. It can become such a force only as the result of enlightenment, education."[3]

Thus Marcuse insists that critical theory is an essential "guide" to the "radical transformation of society." But if the "radical transformation of society" implies "a *union* of a new sensibility with a new rationality," then it would seem that an authentically radical critical theory would have to be informed by, and contribute to, the very sensibility it would "guide." What would this mean? What would be the *form* of a critical theory that would simultaneously enlighten *and* embody the new sensibility? Marcuse stops short of answering this question. In truth, he never even asks it.[4]

Neither did I ask it when I began to work on this book in 1984. At that point I thought I was merely writing a theoretically informed history of Western child rearing. In *Marxism and Domination* I had made a case for the determining power of child-rearing practices but had postponed the problem of explaining how those practices change. To make good on that omission I derived what I call a gender-struggle theory of transformations in child-rearing practices from the same "feminist mothering theory" on which I had relied in that earlier book. My theory holds that the (mother-monopolized) structure of child rearing necessarily engenders an opposition between the parenting interests of women and the parenting interests of men. My understanding of the precise nature of that opposition was refined in the course of the four years that I worked on my historical book, but my central claim was always that child-rearing practices are both the outcome and the object of a conflict between women and men that is based on that opposition. It follows that changes in child-rearing practices result from a change in the balance of power between mothers and fathers *and* set the stage for subsequent struggle between them. Thus my argument was that the mode of child rearing contains the seeds of its own transformation.

At a number of points I descended from these abstract theoretical heights and touched concrete historical ground. I examined four major changes in child rearing in the West since the Middle Ages: (1) an early modern "masculinization" of the mode of child rearing, (2) an early to mid-nineteenth-century "feminization" of the mode of child rearing, (3) a late-nineteenth- to early twentieth-century "remasculinization" of the mode of child rearing, and (4) a mid-twentieth-century "refeminization" of the mode of child rearing.

Only the explanations of the first and fourth transformations were ever developed in detail. I was never able to complete the explanations of the others. In fact I was never able to complete my gender-struggle book at all. But neither could I really let it go. So I decided to respond to this intellectual impasse by writing a book about how I had reached it. I also decided that the form of this new book would have to be very different from the form of the one that I could not complete. I would have to replace a declarative voice that made claims about others with a narrative voice that allowed me to speak for myself.

When I made these decisions in 1988 I understood that my intellectual impasse was linked to an emotional impasse at which I had arrived at exactly the same time. I was also at least dimly aware that this emotional impasse had been precipitated by the problems I encountered in coparenting my daughter during the first four years of her life. Thus I decided to explore the connection between the problems with my parenting theory and the problems with my parenting practice.

There was much about this connection that I did not understand when I first decided to explore it. But I trusted that I would figure it out in the course of reconstructing my relationship with my daughter. In the meantime I would tell a story that was eminently worth telling in its own right. I would describe my struggle to live out the argument of the "feminist mothering theorists" that the liberation of women and men alike requires that men take up the tasks of "mothering" that have hitherto been reserved for women.

This was an argument that I had already taken seriously for a number of years prior to my daughter's birth. I had been persuaded by the feminist mothering theorists that unless men begin to share equally in the care of young children inside the home, men (and women) will continue to suffer the compulsion to exclude women from positions of power outside the home. As long as women remain far more essential to the physical and emotional lives of infants and toddlers than men, the authority of women will be correspondingly far more fearsome than the authority of men, and both men and women will be driven to defend against it. Until fathers begin to feather the nest of their little boys, men will be crippled by a dread of their mothers that compels them to clip the wings of women. Until little girls are nurtured by their fathers, they will never be free from the malice for the mother within that is the source of their own fear of flying. In short, I had come to the conclusion that neither boys nor girls would ever soar without the support of their fathers.

So when Shayla was born in 1984 I was intellectually prepared to practice the feminist principle that patriarchy cannot be eliminated without coparenting. But I had no idea of the emotional difficulties I would encounter. It turned out that mothering my daughter magnified both my own unsatisfied need for nurturance and my destructive defenses against it. It also intensified the already considerable conflicts between my wife and myself. Thus my effort to put coparenting theory into practice proved to be far more problematical than I had anticipated. In fact, it precipitated a particularly painful personal crisis.

Now that that crisis has been resolved, I can recognize it in retrospect as the catalyst for an important emotional breakthrough. But at the time it seemed much more like a breakdown. This break-down-through is part of the story I told in my "second" book. I also explained how that emotional crisis triggered a therapeutic encounter with psychoanalytic theories of narcissism that were very different from the feminist mothering theory with which I began. And I showed that I was eventually able to make use of those narcissism theories to understand the source of both my intellectual and emotional impasse. My second book came to a close with a description of the way in which I worked myself out of that emotional impasse and into a better relationship with my daughter.

But I was dissatisfied with this denouement. There was no theoretical development accompanying the emotional development I had described. At the end of my second book I was no closer to a better explanation of the history of Western child rearing than I was at its beginning. I had been able to improve my parenting practice but not my parenting theory. So my second book was never published.

Theoretical development was not possible until I was able to resolve the opposition between the narcissism theories that had helped me improve my parenting practice and the feminist mothering theory on which that practice had originally been based. For many reasons I did not resolve that opposition until 1996, when I worked out a synthesis of narcissism theory and feminist mothering theory that answered questions that neither of them alone was able to answer. Working out that synthesis enabled me to write a "third" book—the one you are reading—that incorporated the central features of the two that I could not complete. Thus those two "failures" were transformed into (what Hegel would call) necessary "moments" of a process of interrelated emotional and intellectual development.

The organization of this book reflects that transformation. The first ten chapters are devoted to descriptions of both my parenting theory and my parenting practice from 1984 through 1988. Chapter Eleven describes my simultaneously intellectual and emotional encounter in 1989 with narcissism theory, as well as the efforts to improve my parenting practices that were encouraged by that encounter. Chapter Twelve outlines the 1996 synthesis between narcissism theory and feminist mothering theory that the improvement in my parenting practice belatedly provoked. Chapter Thirteen rethinks my gender-struggle explanation of changes in parenting practices in the light of that synthesis and Chapter Fourteen defends that synthesis against postmodernist objections. The concluding chapter reviews the particular path that made my theoretical synthesis possible and then considers what that synthesis has to say about the general relationship between emotional and intellectual development.

This book preserves not only the different content but also the different form of each of my two earlier efforts. I continue to couch my claims about the parenting practices of others in a declarative voice. I use more-or-less standard—although hopefully jargon-free—academic language to present the product of my theoretical practice: the various historical applications of feminist mothering theory as well as the synthesis between that theory and narcissism theory. But I use a narrative voice whenever I make claims about myself. I speak personally when I discuss my theoretical process, including the connections between my theoretical practice, my parenting practice, and my therapeutic practice.

Thus different readers may be more—or less—at home with different parts of this book. Some of my more theoretically inclined colleagues may be reluctant to follow what might strike them as an overly "confessional," excessively self-preoccupied narrative road. Many lay readers who are interested in, or even committed to, coparenting may well find my theoretical turns to be uncomfortable, unnecessarily abstract detours from what is, for them, the main road of the description of a set of experiences in which they have a profound personal interest. But in my more optimistic moments, I allow myself to believe that at least some of my readers will be patient enough to discover that the two roads are both different and the same.

This claim that the personal and the theoretical are both different and the same brings me back to the question of what it means to be a radical intellectual. You will recall that I argued that Marcuse's concept of a "union" between the "new sensibility" and the "new rationality" implies that the critical theorist must embody the very sensibility he would enlighten. I hope that this introduction has clarified how I have sought to satisfy that standard. I try to "enlighten" the new sensibility by reconstructing a theory that specifies the structures and practices of parenting on which the further development of that sensibility depends. I try to "embody" the very sensibility on behalf of which I have theorized by working both inside and outside therapy to reconstruct my own parenting practice. Finally, I try to show that the reconstruction of my theory was only possible because of the reconstruction of my self, and thus that there can be no "enlightenment" without "embodiment."

chapter one

. Birth .

Shayla was born on April 22, 1984. At last I would actually be able to touch the baby that I had imagined holding in my arms as I moved across the floor, tears streaming down my face, more than a year earlier during a particularly heavy session of dance therapy. It was not until that session that I fully felt the intensity of my need for a child. Prior to that point my awareness of that need had been much more abstract. I had always wanted a child, but more in the sense that it was a normal, expected part of anyone's life than in the sense that it would be absolutely central to mine.

When a first, failed, and fortunately childless marriage was followed by another marriage in 1979, this sense began to become a bit more concrete. Now that I was in my mid-thirties, I did not want to wait much longer; more than once Dotty would hear that I did not want to be an old man by the time my child was a teenager. But Dotty was young—eleven years younger than I—and definitely not ready to have a baby. She was just letting her voice out of the closet and needed time to discover if a larger audience would love it as much as the few friends who had already been fortunate enough to hear it. Before she could think about children, she needed to establish her career. I would have to wait. So over the next two years I busied myself in giving birth to a book instead, allowing myself to hope that by the time it was published Dotty would have made enough progress on her work to be ready for a child.

Marxism and Domination appeared at the end of 1982.[1] I had worked intensively—some might say obsessively—for almost three years, and I was definitely ready for a break. Since the book was my second and virtually guaranteed my imminent promotion to full professor, my career could afford the time off. Besides, I needed to quell the anxiety that I was beginning to feel after the end of a project that had been such an important part of my life for so long. For me it was clearly an ideal time to try for a kid.

But Dotty still wasn't ready. In fact, persistent fears about the impact of a child—even a coparented child—on her fledgling career were now compounded by doubts about the impact of a child on our relationship. She reminded me that I already resented her irregular singing schedule that left us precious little predictable evening time together. A baby would mean even less time and more resentment. And this would put pressure on her to reduce—and resent—even further the inevitably reduced time she would have for herself. Having a child would only worsen our wars over time and space.

I tried my best to be patient and understanding, but beneath my solicitous surface I was angry and hurt. I didn't realize how much until the day the dam was broken by the fantasized presence of the baby that might never be born. It was then—sometime in the late winter or early spring of 1983—that my longing for a child became a burning desire and that Dotty really began to feel the heat. I made it clear that I wanted a child *now*. Dotty agreed to join me in dance therapy to work on the problems between us (as well as her own career-related fears) that prevented her from getting pregnant. The sessions were difficult, often explosive, but eventually led to what felt like a renewal of closeness between us. Dotty reassured me that she really wanted time together and that I could count on at least one night a week with which nothing would interfere. I reassured her that I appreciated her need for time for herself and that I would encourage her to take it. Enough progress was made for Dotty to make a commitment that, if she had her druthers, she would still have preferred to postpone. We would try to get pregnant that summer!

We also agreed, as a matter of course, that when the baby arrived we would assume absolutely equal responsibility for its care and that I would arrange my teaching schedule to make that possible. I decided to teach three courses the next fall and two in the winter so I would be free from any teaching obligations during the spring of 1984, when, we hoped, the baby would be born. And I also decided to apply for a fellowship that would release me from any teaching responsibilities for the following academic year as well. This would give me fifteen months that I could organize as I saw fit.

The idea was that I would be able to take care of the baby while Dotty was singing and that she could take care of the baby while I was writing: an even fifty-fifty split. More than a decade's exposure to feminist consciousness-raising had convinced me that this was the most fitting way to do it. How could the millions of women (in or out of the labor force) of contemporary industrial societies who were committed to caring for their young children within the home ever have the time and energy for the equal exercise of public authority unless their child care commitment was shared by the men with whom they had chosen to share their lives?

It also seemed to me that a feminist movement whose devotion to the task of getting women out of the home was unmatched by the resolution to bring men into it would necessarily fail to attract the support of a large proportion of the very women on behalf of whom it claimed to speak. Many of these women would instead be likely to perceive the call for equal female participation in the public sphere as a dangerous threat to the integrity of a private sphere for which they remained disproportionately responsible. This, indeed, seemed to be what had happened since the early seventies. The perception of feminism as indifferent at best and hostile at worst to the family had fueled the fires of the Right and enabled it to monopolize the movement to defend the family. Feminist calls for dramatic increases in government support for day care—however appropriate—merely fanned these flames by enabling the Right to identify feminism with the takeover of the family by the state. And even those women who would have gladly relied on expanded and improved institutional care after the second year of their childrens' lives were justifiably ambivalent about doing so prior to that point. Thus contemporary feminism had reached an impasse.

I knew that the only way around this impasse was to reverse the perception of feminism as antifamily and to mobilize profamily sentiments on its behalf. But the only feminism that could attract such sentiments was one whose emphasis on the public participation of women was matched by an equal insistence on the domestic participation of men. Coparenting, I had decided, was an essential element of an effective feminist strategy.

I had also learned, moreover, that the dependence of feminism on coparenting was by no means merely strategic. Even if it was possible for a feminism uncommitted to coparenting to mobilize overwhelming conscious support for its public goals, I was persuaded after reading Dorothy Dinnerstein's *The Mermaid and the Minotaur* that the unconscious preconditions of these goals could not be established in the absence of widespread coparenting. Dinnerstein argued that the culturally universal dependence of young children on their mothers (or female mother substitutes) was responsible for the equally universal male hatred of the female and the male-dominant practices that both reflected and reinforced that hatred. The exclusion of women from positions of authority outside the family was carried out by men (and accepted by women) whose imperious infantile needs were ultimately frustrated by the very mothers who had satisfied them, men who thus sought to ensure that they would never again have to reencounter the female authority they so painfully experienced as children within the family.

If the subordination of women was rooted in, and reproduced by, the self-imposed exclusion of men from the responsibilities of early child care, it followed that the liberation of women required that these responsibilities be shared by men: with coparenting, children would be more-or-less equally dependent on both parents and the hostility that necessarily accompanied the enforced disruption of this dependence would no longer be directed exclusively first at the mother and later at all those who come to represent her, namely women as a whole. If mother and father were both equally loved and equally feared, then it would be possible for women "to stop serving as scapegoats . . . for human resentment of the human condition"[2]—and for men to cease serving as idealized refuges against maternal power—and for women and men for the first time to face up to, and come to terms with, the inescapably painful character of this condition. Having truly grown up, men would no longer need to dominate women and women would no longer need to acquiesce in that domination.

Having just published a book in which I embraced this argument, I was scarcely in a position to ignore its personal implications: how could I fail to practice what I preached? But a theoretically informed political commitment was not my only incentive to radically reorganize my life. I also really wanted to care for a baby: to feed it when it was hungry, bathe it when it was dirty, and cuddle it when it cried; in short, to do all the things that a mother normally does.

Exactly why I wanted to do this was something of a mystery to me. It seemed clear that the overwhelming majority of men did not. The massive movement of mothers out of the home since the 1960s had not been matched by the movement of fathers back into it. In fact, a number of studies showed that men whose wives were employed were scarcely any more involved with their young children than men whose wives were not: "maternal employment appears to have little impact on the amount of time spent by fathers on specific child-care tasks, play, or other interactions."[3]

It was also clear that these lamentably low levels of paternal involvement could not be attributed exclusively, or even mainly, to
the comparably low levels of ideological and institutional support
for that involvement in most Western industrial societies. Even
when the level of such support was much higher, as in Sweden,
the level of paternal participation remained low:

> Despite nationwide advertising campaigns [encouraging fa
> thers to avail themselves of paid paternal leave during their
> child's first year of life] . . . four out of five fathers do not
> take leave for a single day. Of the total number of days of
> leave used, 4% are used by men and 96% by women.[4]

So it seemed that the motivation of men to coparent was generally low even when the cultural and institutional support was not.

Nancy Chodorow has tried to explain why. *The Reproduction of
Mothering* is a psychodynamic account of why most men are typically inclined to avoid, and are in fact emotionally unsuited for,
the very maternal tasks I sought to embrace. In their first years,
both boys and girls are deeply identified with the mother, on
whom their entire life depends. Because the girl is identified with
someone of the same sex, this identification is experienced as
consistent with, and the source of, her emerging sense of what it
means to be a woman. The girl learns, in other words, that the
(m)other is essential to her self, and this sets the stage for her efforts to achieve intimacy with a variety of others with whom she
will relate throughout her life. Chief among these others are her
children, whose complete dependence on her unconsciously
evokes the union with her mother with which her life began:

> as a result of having been parented by a woman, women are
> more likely [than men] to seek to be mothers, that is, to re
> locate themselves in a primary mother-child relationship,
> to get gratification from the mothering relationship, and to
> have psychological and relational capacities for mothering.[5]

"More likely than men," because the boy's initial identification
with his mother (on which mothering capacities and propensities

are based) is eventually experienced as an obstacle that must be overcome if he is to become a man. The boy simultaneously wants to be like his mother and learns that to be like his mother is to be a woman is not to be a man. In the normal course of events, the boy resolves this intense, unconscious conflict between feminine and masculine identity by "dis-identifying" with his mother, that is, by denying the female within him, a denial that is facilitated by a more abstract identification with what his father (or father substitute) does.

So the essential lesson that the boy, in contrast to the girl, learns from his encounter with his mother is that the development of the self requires the repudiation of intimacy with the other. Since the other is experienced as a threat to the self, the boy will either attempt to avoid the other or to keep him or her safely under his control. Thus masculine independence typically takes the form of a perpetual struggle against any dependence that would undermine its overblown and therefore easily punctured posture of self-sufficiency. This means that the man is in no position to identify with and respond to the needs of a dependent child.

But it was difficult for me to find myself in Chodorow's picture. I welcomed, even longed for, the dependence of a young child that men are supposed to fear. I did not leave my maternal fantasies behind me but increasingly tried to evoke and indulge them. Apparently I did not resolve whatever conflict I experienced as a boy between my identification with my mother and my emerging identification as a man by simply repudiating the former in favor of the latter. If I wanted desperately to be a mothering man, this could only be (according to the logic of psychoanalytic theory) because I remained more mother-identified than the "normal" man. I was clearly an exception to Chodorow's rule.

Classical psychoanalysis recognizes an exception to this rule, but this exception no more fits my experience than does the rule. Confronted with the inevitable alternative of their manhood or their mothers, some men choose their mothers over their manhood; that is, they embrace a feminine, and repudiate a masculine heterosexual, form of self-identification. Orthodox psychoanalytic theory's heavily mother-identified man is typically a homosexual man. But I was strongly mother-identified yet straight, not gay. It seems that the contradiction between my maternal and masculine identifications was resolved—if it was resolved—without abandoning either one. But the orthodox psychoanalytic either/or of the mother-denying male heterosexual and the mother-affirming male homosexual excludes just this possibility.[6]

This description of the way in which psychoanalysis divided up its conceptual terrain curiously reproduced the way things were divided up on my childhood turf, my neighborhood in New York. In that world, too, you were either tough or a sissy, a jock or a "faggot." This practical division also left me out in the cold. I was much more sensitive than the toughs and much more competitive and athletic than the sissies. Off the court I was much too "nice" to take part in the nasty macho banter of the jocks; on the court I was a tiger who could beat (some of) them at their own game. The few friends I had were more likely to be sissies than tough. Predictably, the toughest of the tough hated my guts. They would typically try to get to me by first getting to the "faggots" I had befriended. Since they were in no position to defend themselves, that task fell to me. I learned to fight, but, more often than not, on behalf of someone else. Already I was becoming a man with a need to protect, even sacrifice for, those who were weaker or more dependent than myself.

Well before the spring of 1983 I had come to believe that there were other men of my political generation who felt the same need. Sociologists like Kenneth Kenniston and Richard Flacks had stressed the unusually intense mother-identification of mid-to-late sixties student radicals and proposed that this identification was the psychological basis for their profound personal commitment to the welfare of others.[7] At the end of *Marxism and Domination* I had suggested that these and other strongly mother-identified men might well be far more emotionally open to coparenting than their predecessors. I had also hypothesized that the enhanced mother identification of such men was the result of the more nurturant, child-centered child-rearing practices that had come to prevail during and immediately following World War II among the educated American middle class.

This hypothesis followed from the psychoanalytical assumption that maternal identification was the product of maternal gratification: young boys whose needs were consistently satisfied over a long period of time should have formed an identification with their mothers that was both more intense and prolonged than boys whose mothers could not, or did not, avail themselves of the "permissive" advice of Dr. Benjamin Spock.[8] The hypothesis certainly seemed to fit my own experience. I was strongly mother-identified, and my mother had, by her own testimony, "indulged me to the hilt." It also seemed reasonable to suppose that Kenniston and Flacks's young New Leftists had been similarly indulged, since most of their parents were precisely the relatively affluent, well-educated liberals most likely to attempt to put Spockean advice into practice.

So both personal reflection and psychoanalytically informed theoretical speculation seemed to support a connection between a male child's encounter with an indulgent, permissive mother and his subsequent commitment to "mother" his own child. But in the spring of 1983 (when these reflections on the origins of my own commitment began) there was much about this connection that I did not understand. Why did the plausibly more profound and persistent maternal identification of Spockean-raised boys persist all the way through adolescence and into adulthood? Why wasn't this intensified identification eventually experienced as an even greater threat to masculine identity than the usual one, and why didn't it evoke an even more exaggerated assertion of mother-denying masculinity than the norm? Was there something else about our relationships with our mothers that made it either unnecessary or impossible to respond to it in the "normal" male way? Conversely, why were we able to retain our mother identification without having to deny our heterosexual identity? Did it have something to do with our fathers being somewhat more physically and/or emotionally available than the stereotypically distant, uninvolved, and ineffectual father of orthodox psychoanalysis's "abnormal" male homosexual?

I knew that these were questions to which I would eventually have to return. But at this point I was confronted by a more pressing problem: to help make a baby. Fortunately, this did not take long. Shayla was conceived sometime in late July or early August, while we were in Greece. Dotty thinks that it happened in Athens, but I *know* that it happened a week earlier on the tiny, lovely island of Sifnos. A broad, flat rock bathed in bright sunshine and overlooking the crystalline blue Aegean, not a sweltering hotel room choked by the pernicious atmosphere of one of the world's most polluted cities, was the obvious setting for the union of ovum and sperm that became our daughter. Nothing but the best for Shayla, even the myth of her origin. . . .

When the dark circle in the little tube of piss provided the September scientific evidence that touched off this little bit of mythologizing, I knew that it was time to begin in earnest the search for the fellowship on which our experiment in prolonged coparenting would depend. Application for a fellowship meant the selection of a simultaneously interesting and manageable intellectual project. But none had yet formed in my mind.

I had toyed with the idea of empirically testing a hypothesis about the consequence of coparenting that was derived from Nancy Chodorow's theory. It followed from that theory that coparenting should eliminate, or at least significantly attenuate, the differences in the way that men and women relate to the world. Once the father joined the mother as a deeply involved caregiver of the young boy, the boy could experience an intense early identification with a parent of *his* sex. The formation of his masculine identity would, therefore, no longer require that he define himself in opposition to his first significant other and then to the variety of others he would encounter throughout his life. Thus we should expect that boys raised under these conditions would grow up far more "relationally oriented" than conventionally raised boys. At the same time, we should expect that the coparented girl's merger with her mother would be much less overwhelming than the mother-merger of the conventionally raised girl. Since the girl, too, would now have an opposite-sex original love object against whom to define her gendered sense of self, her identity would be much less threatened by opposition or separation than (according to Chodorow) it is now. Thus under coparenting we should expect the proverbial overdependence of women on intimate relationships to end.

In sum, the consequence of coparenting would be that men would become more like women and women more like men, each absorbing the best that the other presently had to offer.

The idea was to test this hypothesis by comparing the behavior, as well as the inner emotional life, of coparented and conventionally raised boys and girls. But, even if the formidable methodological problems (e.g., How does one measure coparenting? On the basis of what external indicators can one come to valid conclusions about the inner emotional world of children? and so on) associated with the test of this hypothesis could be resolved, the logistics of testing it were clearly beyond the capacities of a man who would be deeply involved in the practice, and not merely the theory, of coparenting. For such a project I would have to get and administer a grant that would enable me to pay for the students who would have to do the bulk of the observation and testing of the kids. Their work would have to be carefully supervised by yours truly. I would want to do some of the observation and testing myself, but how could I be out in the "field" when my baby needed a less scientific, dispassionate form of attention? Besides, I had never done anything even remotely like this before, and it would probably take me at least twice as long to do it as someone who had. However important, the "Chodorow project" would clearly be far too time-consuming for someone who planned to spend at least half his waking hours during the next academic year with a five- to fourteen-month-old kid. My first idea was abandoned.

Idea number two was to interview other men who were committed coparents in order to verify and clarify my speculations concerning the connection between this commitment, mother identification, and a childhood encounter with Spockean practices. If I lacked the time and energy to study the effects of coparenting, perhaps I had enough to develop a somewhat better understanding of its origins. At the very least I would find out if the path that had taken me to coparenting was one that had been traveled by others. And perhaps I would learn something more about my path in the process.

But talking to other people meant being at the mercy of their schedules. Most of the talking would probably have to be done in the late evening, when they would neither be working at their jobs nor attending to their (now happily asleep) kids. But late evenings were one of the times that I would usually have to be at home with my kid, since Dotty normally worked nights. Idea number two also seemed unworkable. It was rejected.

What I needed, I concluded, was a project that did not require the cooperation of anyone else and thus did not depend on any one else's schedule, a project for which the research could be done in a library that was always available when I could get there or in the privacy of my home when I could not. In short, a project for which reading was the only research: a historical project.

I had already given some thought to the problem of the origins of the Spockean child-rearing practices to which I had, both in my last book and in my personal reflections, attributed such enormous significance. I had learned that Dr. Spock had self-consciously sought to translate what he took to be the central insights of Freudian psychoanalytic theory into the "common-sense" language of his all-time (second only to the Bible!) bestseller.[9] I had also learned that there were good reasons for believing that his (and other, similarly psychoanalytically informed) advice had, in fact, eventually been put into practice by the millions of parents who absorbed it. Studies showed that the relatively educated, middle-class parents who were most likely to have read Spock's advice were precisely the ones whose practices had shifted most dramatically in the direction of that advice.[10] This was strong (although not necessarily conclusive) evidence of its determinative effect.

An explanation for the Spockean transformation would, therefore, have to answer two different questions. First, what accounted for the increasing prestige of a certain kind of psychoanalytic thought within the pediatric and child development communities just prior to, during, and immediately following World War II? Exactly why had this type of knowledge about children—ultimately about human nature—achieved (what social theorists influenced by Antonio Gramsci like to call) scientific hegemony during this period?[11] Second, why was this advice accepted by the parents who began to practice it shortly thereafter? Even the most attractively packaged pediatric agenda will not be embraced by parents unless they experience this agenda to be consistent with their own. Why, then, did the needs of the experts and the needs of these parents converge?

Shortly after formulating these questions I received an announcement from my university's Institute for the Humanities encouraging faculty doing research on the "acquisition and communication of knowledge" to apply for a fellowship that would release them from any teaching obligations during the following year. Aha! This theme was so broad that anyone with half a brain could easily explain how his or her research was a perfect fit. In my case, moreover, not much academic tailoring was required: I really *was* interested in the role of "the acquisition and communication of (psychoanalytic) knowledge" in the transformation of American child rearing. That, in fact, became the title of my proposal—or rather, the subtitle. For the title, something simultaneously pithy and profound was required, something that revealed the new theoretical ground I would break. Since both Marx and Foucault were hot (and hotly opposed) items on the current intellectual scene, I settled on "Neither Marx nor Foucault." That would grab them! I would demonstrate that not Marx, not Foucault, but *Balbus* could explain the Spockean transformation.

I learned a couple of months before Shayla was born that I had been selected as a fellow of the institute for the academic year 1984–85. Great news! And we really needed it, because lately the news had not been good. Sometime during the latter part of her second trimester, Dotty's obstetrician acknowledged that she was worried about the fact that Dotty's belly wasn't growing as fast as it should; perhaps the baby within it wasn't either. She recommended an ultrasound. The diagnosis of one of the top ultra-sonographer in town: probable "asymmetrical growth retardation." We could expect that Shayla would be less than five pounds at birth and that her head might be too large for her body. Dotty would have to stop working, spend her last trimester in bed, and increase dramatically her intake of calories and protein.

So each morning I made her special protein shakes, and every day we watched for signs that her belly—and our baby—was growing. Mine certainly was: Dotty was not the only one who was gaining weight. Never before had I had (or so I believed) so little control over something so important. Never before was I eating so much. The same was true, I discovered, of the other men in our Lamaze-like class. I reassured myself that our binging was merely the contemporary version of the primitive couvade.*

After a month of Dotty stuffing herself silly, another visit to the same ultra-sonographer revealed some, but not enough growth. With only a little more than a month to go, Dotty's obstetrician was slowly coming to the conclusion that Shayla might do better on the outside than on the inside, that it might be to prudent to induce an early delivery. We agreed that before such a drastic measure was taken we should get a second opinion from another highly respected ultra-sonographer. His verdict: there were no signs of asymmetrical growth, and Shayla would probably be around six pounds. She would be a perfectly fine, somewhat small baby. After all, he reminded us, we weren't exactly giants. Go home and relax.

We tried, but we were still haunted by the possibility that the first bastard might have been right. Our obstetrician was now prepared to allow Dotty to go to term, but felt that proper caution required that she be placed in the "high-risk" category.

_____

*a practice in some tribal societies in which men simulate the effects of pregnancy and childbirth

Minor bummer. Not the warm, homey atmosphere of the birthing room we had selected, but the cold-steel atmosphere of the labor and delivery rooms we had hoped to avoid, awaited us. But this was small potatoes compared to what we had feared we might have to face.

Shayla weighed six pounds, four ounces at birth. Except for the fact that she was pigeon-toed, her body was perfectly formed. What had turned out to be an entirely technologically produced nightmare was over. But only after a labor that more than lived up to its name: twenty-six hours of intense contractions that began at five minutes apart. Shayla's face bore the mark of her protracted struggle: her nose was down to her mouth. Being Jewish, we feared the worst. Oh my God, what a schnoz, the kid will need a nose job! That was before we realized that it had been temporarily squashed by the travails of her tight-squeeze trip and that it would unsquash itself in due time. When that time came (a couple of days later), we breathed a large sigh of collective relief. Shayla would reach sweet sixteen without black eyes and bandages.

chapter two

. Discovery .

i settled in to five months of full-time fathering. Shortly before Shayla's birth I had persuaded Dotty that we should not accept her mother's generous offer to pay for a nurse following her return from the hospital. That's what *I* would be there for. No need for another woman to do what, I was determined to show, a man could do just as well. And I knew I could. After all, this was what I had been emotionally preparing myself to do ever since before Dotty's pregnancy. During the latter part of that pregnancy, I had prepared myself "technically" as well, taking a series of classes (taught in part by Mark Podolner, Chicago's most forceful, and funny, advocate of shared parenting) in which I learned how to feed, change, and bathe a baby. Although the "baby" was actually a doll—until the very last class, when Mark's colleague Steve Bogira felt we were ready to be trusted with his own infant—I was convinced that I now knew how to do all the things that women typically learn to do simply by growing up as girls in a society that expects them to mother. I was ready to surrender to the rhythms, and fulfill the requirements of, a tiny infant. It would not be that difficult.

And, in truth, it was not, at least not in the beginning. I did not retreat from, but instead did everything possible to nurture, an intensely intimate relationship between Shayla and myself. In my arms or on my chest the better part of the time we spent together, she soon began to feel like a permanent attachment. My only fear was that this attachment might not be as close as the one between Shayla and her mother. After what had seemed like an eternity of physically and emotionally painful false starts, Shayla had finally taken to Dotty's breasts. I was ambivalent about this triumph. Half of me was delighted, of course, that something that was so "natural," yet for which Dotty had had to work so hard, had finally come to pass. But the other half had been secretly hoping that she would give up the struggle and that Shayla would be hooked to a bottle, not the breast. That way I would be able to feed her as often, and as well, as her mother. Short of that, I was afraid that Shayla would wind up more dependent on Dotty than on me.

This fear was animated by concerns that were at once personal and political. Political: perhaps breast-feeding was the fly in the feminist psychoanalytical ointment. If feeding was a—perhaps the?—principal source of an infant's parental identifications, even an otherwise entirely coparented child might turn out to be more closely identified with its mother than its father.[1] And, if the child were more attached to its mother than its father, it would suffer more pain from the inevitable interruption of the attachment with her than with him. From Dinnerstein's assumption that blame follows pain we can deduce the expectation that the child would continue to blame the mother more than the father. But disproportionately blaming the mother means disproportionately blaming women. In short, a coparented but breast-fed child might well become a misogynist adult. My daughter could grow up as plagued by hatred of her gender—and thus of herself—as any mother's daughter has ever been. The political defense of bottle-feeding rests its case.

The personal defense: I wanted Shayla to love me as much as her mother. Food, I knew, was love, and I feared that unless the food flowed to Shayla as abundantly from me as it did from Dotty, Shayla's love for me would be correspondingly less abundant than for her mother. A breast-fed Shayla would (until she turned against her) inevitably prefer Dotty to Ike, would invariably turn to her mother rather than her father in moments of crisis when she needed help most. This was something to which I definitely did not look forward.

The personal and the political were, as usual, two sides of the same coin. If Shayla loved me less, she would love Dotty more, but if she loved Dotty more, she would eventually hate her and all women more than me and all men. And so my emotional needs and feminist fears combined in my mind to produce an open-and-shut case in favor of bottle-feeding for Shayla. But this internal verdict was not to be expressed (and if expressed would have easily been overturned) in the face of Dotty's fierce determination to suckle the babe that she had already been feeding for nine months. I consoled myself with the thought that I would soon be able to feed Shayla the milk that Dotty had started to pump from her breasts.

When Dotty returned to her evening rehearsals three weeks after Shayla's birth, I did just that. For a couple of weeks it went pretty well. But Dotty was simultaneously overworked and sleep-deprived, with neither the time nor the energy to keep pumping. Since formula was out of the question and Shayla still needed frequent feedings, I would bring her to gigs for a between-sets hit of her natural immunities, then take her home and put her down for the night. But it would be many months before I would feed her again. As I held her closely against me and rocked her gently to sleep, I tried to remind myself that even if food was love, love was not just food. . . .

For the next four months Shayla and I were virtually inseparable. Yet Dotty and I were still able to spend a good deal of time together. Shayla's need for sleep made it possible for us to do many of our favorite things—like eating out or going to the movies—without having to leave her. No problems finding a sitter or worrying that it was too soon to leave her with one. We could share conversation over our favorite Thai food while Shayla slept on my lap, or space out at a flick while she nestled in Dotty's arms. The first cries of wakefulness were the signal for the magical mammary medicine that invariably restored her somnolent state. These were the halcyon days when it was possible simultaneously to satisfy her needs and our own. We had our daughter and our relationship too. No tension between them.

There was, however, a great deal of tension between my relationship with Shayla and my relationship with my work. The former completely dominated the latter. Her frequent naps during the day left me with predictable, if brief, periods of time during which it was, in principle, possible to read and write. But I was often simply too tired to take advantage of them. Shayla was not always sleeping through the night, and neither was I; she could get back to sleep but I could not. When I wasn't too tired I was (I told myself) too busy with the dirty dishes and soiled sleepers to take care of more (or less) material matters. When these tasks were completed I would persuade myself that writers need far larger blocks of time than the few minutes that remained, and I would read a newspaper or a magazine until I heard Shayla cry. And so I found all kinds of excuses not to begin my work.

In my more reflective moments I recognized that they were excuses, and that I really didn't want to work. My life with Shayla was so intense, so important, so overwhelming, that anything else seemed . . . beside the point. What could compare to the wonders of her first smile, her first flip from front to back, her first patterned sounds (cleverly decoded by her father as "da-da")? "I'll put a spell on you, because you're *mine*!" And it worked; she had me mesmerized. Screaming Jay Hawkins had met his match. Shayla had made the mundane miraculous.

But there were other, less enchanting realities with which I was now faced. Shayla was now almost five months old, it was the second week in September, and I had just moved into my handsome quarters at the institute. In just seven weeks I would have to give public answers to the two questions I had posed about the

Spockean transformation. And I was no closer to these answers now than when I had brashly announced that I—and not Marx or Foucault—would supply them. I would have to come up with the answers fast. If I worked three full days a week at the institute, late evenings and Sundays at home, I would be able to do it. If I really put my heart into it. But my heart belonged to Shayla, not Dr. Spock. How could I possibly summon up the emotional energy I would need?

This proved surprisingly easy. I reread my last book for the first time in a long while. I still liked it. Reading it reassured Ike Balbus feminist father that Isaac Balbus feminist theorist had a lot of important things to say. (Selectively) rereading the reviews it received reminded me that many of my peers agreed. I wasn't just Shayla's papa, I was a well-known and highly respected intellectual. Well-known and highly respected intellectuals do not make fools of themselves at public presentations. Get to work!

Rereading *Marxism and Domination* also reminded me that the problem of the Spockean transformation was a subset of a larger problem with which I had barely begun to wrestle at the end of that book: how can a psychoanalytic theory explain change, and changes in child-rearing practices in particular? On the one hand, I started from the assumption that the child-rearing practices of the parents of one generation are governed by unconscious orientations that were established in the course of their own encounter with the child-rearing practices of their parents. The virtue of this assumption is that it makes good psychological sense: nothing is more likely to evoke, and reanimate the determining role of, a person's past relationship with his or her parents than a person's present relationship with his or her child. It seemed to me that an adequate explanation of changes in child-rearing practices could not afford to ignore this fundamental fact of emotional life. If there is often resistance to change, this can only be because the new imperatives run up against the old, familiar ways of taking care of children. And the "old ways" are "familiar" because they are "in the family," because they are the ways that parents were taken care of by their parents: "any current interaction between parent and child is motivated by the parent's past relationship with both of his [or her] parents."[2]

On the other hand, if each generation learns its parenting practices from the parents of the previous generation, why should there ever be a change in parenting practices? The virtue of the psychoanalytic assumption, it would seem, is simultaneously its vice. In clarifying the basis of resistance to changes in child rearing, it appears to rule out the possibility of these changes in the first place. This is certainly the conclusion drawn by the eminent historian of the family Lawrence Stone, who (among others) rejects psychoanalytic theory on the grounds that it "is incapable of explaining change, since each successive generation is automatically obliged, by the very fact of its own childhood experience, to impose the same experience on its children."[3]

This is a conclusion that I had tried to resist in *Marxism and Domination*. I suggested toward the end of that book that there were at least two possible ways in which parents could become conscious of, and in the process at least in part overcome, their unconsciously determined parenting orientations. The first possibility was an encounter with some type of psychoanalytically informed therapy. But this possibility was obviously unavailable in a society that had not discovered the existence and significance of the unconscious (and not universally available even in a society that has) and thus could not be relied on as a general solution to the cross-cultural problem of how and why child-rearing practices change.

The second possibility to which I referred was Lloyd DeMause's concept of the "regression-progression" process through which parents "regress to the psychic age of their children and work through the anxieties of that age in a better manner the second time they encounter them than they did during their own childhood,"[4] and are thus able to respond to the demands of their children with more empathy than their parents did to their own. Although this "regression-progression" process (in contrast to individual therapy) was, in principle, culturally universal, the only transformations in child rearing for which, by definition, it could account were those that were "progressive" in character, that is, those that involved a change from less to more "empathic" (or child-centered) treatment of children. Regressive changes, in short, could not be explained by the process DeMause described.

This is exactly why he denied their existence and insisted, to the contrary, that parental treatment of children had (at least in the West) gotten better and better over time. But for this theory of a linear, uninterrupted improvement in Western child rearing he paid the unacceptably high price of utterly implausible, even tortured interpretations of a wide range of evidence that clearly seemed to falsify the theory. To cite but one example: he interpreted what he admitted was a dramatic decline in the duration of breast-feeding from late medieval to early modern Europe as an indication of an improvement in the quality of child care. His assumption was that prolonged and indulgent suckling is based on a projective mechanism through which "the child becomes the mother's . . . own parent," that, in other words, premodern mothers "lacked the emotional maturity needed to see the child as a person separate from [themselves]." So the subsequent decline in the duration of nursing became an indication of a decline in maternal projection and an increase in the "emotional maturity of mothers," and thus in the quality of their child care![5] It seemed to me that if we wanted to avoid doing this kind of conceptual violence to the historical record we would have to admit that this record includes changes in child rearing that (from the standpoint of a child-centered norm) have been regressive as well as progressive. Consequently I concluded that I would have to look beyond DeMause's "regression-progression" process for an explanation of that record.

So both of the "escape routes" proposed in my last book turned out to be dead ends: so far I had found no reliable way around Stone's conclusion that psychoanalytic theory is "incapable of explaining change." Perhaps psychoanalysis and history really were incompatible after all. This was a depressing possibility for someone who was committed to both. So I stopped thinking about it and busied myself with less imposing problems. There was still a great deal that had to be described, however it would finally be explained. I had learned that Dr. Spock's efforts were merely the tip of an iceberg that had included years of struggle within the professional communities of pediatrics, child psychology, and education between those who were partisans of the "soft" neo-Freudianism that Spock eventually communicated to a mass audience and those who remained committed to the "hard" behaviorism that had reigned within these communities during the early decades of this century.[6] I needed to learn a lot more about this struggle. I also needed to know more about the mass effects of Spock's communication. There were, as I mentioned earlier, good reasons to assume that this communication had been effective, but I needed to become more familiar with the many empirical studies of post-World War II American child rearing before this assumption could be transformed into a definite conclusion.

One of these studies was Robert Sears, Elanor Maccoby, and Harry Levin's *Patterns of Child Rearing*. On pages 310–11, the following passage unexpectedly caught my eye:

> With the development of wider educational opportunities for girls, and with the gradually increasing participation of women in political and other public affairs, there has been a change in values. Women knew a good deal about younger children. They were strongly motivated to improve their childrearing, too. As they became more confident in their role of participants in public enterprises, they began to demand corrections in public values. . . . They sought to correct obvious ineffectualities in educational methods, and they began to express their opinions more fully with respect to the methods of discipline used in the home. Their way was the "new way." It gave recognition to the child's nature as a child: it was tolerant of childhood and did not demand early conformity or instant obedience. . . . The "new way" . . . is feminine. It says, in effect, that

men do not know everything, and especially that they often do not know best about children. So the battle line was drawn. Between men and women. Between the old and the new.[7]

All of sudden, things began to click. My conceptual wheels started to turn. . . . The parenting orientations of women were different from and opposed to the parenting orientations of men! The new, "permissive" advice of Dr. Spock and the neo-Freudianism on which it was based was a conceptual expression of the soft, child-centered orientations of women. The older, disciplinary advice and the behaviorism it reflected was an intellectual formulation of the hard, adult-centered orientations of men. The struggle within the professions between the neo-Freudians and the behaviorists had been a struggle between a "feminine" and a "masculine" approach to children. My first question—"Why did neo-Freudian psychoanalytic knowledge about children achieve scientific hegemony around the time of World War II?"—could now be reformulated as the question "Why did a feminine approach triumph over a masculine approach within the child-related professions?"

Reformulating the question in this way went a long way toward being able to answer it. If the professionally articulated "public values" concerning children had become more feminine, this could only be the result of (what Sears et al. had described as) "the gradually increasing participation of women in political and other public affairs." Thus I would have to show that the triumph of Spockean advice was but one chapter in the much longer story of the twentieth-century feminization of the American public sphere.[8]

The assumption that Spockean advice was a conceptual expression of the parenting orientations of women was already the better part of an answer to my (second) question of why this advice was accepted. Middle-class American mothers embraced this advice as their own because it was, in effect, their own; it was what they would do if they were able to have their druthers. And they were able to have their druthers because their husbands were in no position to have theirs. The experts were now on the side of their wives. Besides, the increasingly prolonged absence of husbands from the home made it impossible for them regularly to supervise their wives' child rearing, and the assumption that child rearing was, after all, "women's work" made it difficult for them to do so even when they were present. Women were home free even if homebound.

So the shift from pre-Spockean to Spockean practices was a shift from male to female control over the mode of child rearing. This increase in female power within the home had, in turn, been made possible by an increase in female influence outside it. The change from adult-centered to child-centered practices was the outcome of a combination of intra- and extra-familial *gender struggle*. A feminist theory of the Spockean transformation! That is what I—and neither Marx, Foucault, nor anyone else—would have to offer the world. I was on cloud nine.

I was soon brought back to earth by the following concern. I had outlined the essentials of a historical explanation—and a feminist one at that—but was this a properly psychoanalytic explanation? Could the existence of a gender-based opposition in parenting orientations be derived from the basic assumptions of feminist psychoanalytic theory? Quickly reviewing my earlier reflections on Chodorow, I reached the exhilarating conclusion that the answer was **yes!** Of course! If women are unconsciously prepared for an intimate relationship with a child, this could only mean that they would be emotionally predisposed toward nurturant child-rearing practices; if their general relational orientation leads them to define dependence on the other as essential to the completion of the self, we should expect them to experience the gratification of the needs of their dependent children as consistent with the gratification of their own.

If, on the other hand, men unconsciously experience intimacy as a threat to their autonomy, they would be emotionally prepared for a distant relationship with their kids; their general tendency to oppose dependence to independence and to privilege the latter over the former would manifest itself in parenting practices that frustrated rather than encouraged the dependence of their children. In other words, the father would project his own fears of dependence onto his children and attempt, in the name of their autonomy, to disrupt the intimate relationship between them and their mother that the mother both unconsciously needs and consciously perceives to be in their interest.

I needed to explain, psychodynamically, why the father is normally not only a less indulgent but also a more punitive parent than the mother. Why, if men prized independence over dependence, were they so much more likely than women to demand (to return to the words of Sears et al.) "early conformity" and "instant obedience"? We can assume that if fathers are more insistent than mothers on obedience, they must be more threatened than mothers by disobedience. But why should this be the case? I really wasn't sure.

On the one hand, a more punitive paternal predisposition seemed consistent with the generally more "oppositional" orientation of men. It certainly seemed consistent with my recollection that my own father was a far more strict disciplinarian than my mother. I remembered how angry he seemed so much of the time. But the concept "oppositional" didn't quite seem to capture the roots of this rage. An oppositional orientation is supposed to serve as a defense against a merger with the (m)other that would threaten the male sense of an autonomous self. This would imply a father's need to distance himself from, or even denigrate, his child. But it didn't seem to explain why a father gets so furious in the face of the unruliness of his child and why he strives so strenuously to subdue it. Thus I wasn't entirely satisfied that I had, in fact, derived the father's more punitive parenting orientation directly and unambiguously from the assumptions of Chodorow's theory.

Despite these doubts I was persuaded that I had uncovered the unconscious roots of gender struggle over the practices that prevail within the conventional or maternal mode of child rearing. The foundations for a simultaneously feminist and psychoanalytic explanation of the Spockean transformation were now in place! And other things suddenly began to fall into place as well. My extrapolation from Chodorow enabled me to clarify and resolve a tension that I had identified in Freud's (rather sparse explicit) writings on parenting practices. There are, in fact, two very different, even antithetical accounts of the origins of these practices within his work. The first emphasizes the unconsciously determined inclination of "affectionate parents" to raise their children indulgently:

> They are inclined to suspend in the child's favor the operation of all the cultural acquisitions [they have] been forced to respect, and to renew on [the child's] behalf the claims to privileges which were long given up by themselves. . . . Parental love . . . is nothing but the parents' narcissism [sense of infantile omnipotence] born again.[9]

The second insists that parents are "severe and exacting" in educating children because they

> follow the precepts of their own superegos. . . . They have forgotten the difficulties of their own childhood and they are glad to be able now to identify themselves fully with their own parents who in the past laid such severe restrictions on them.[10]

The second account emphasizes the determining power of the very "cultural acquisition"—the superego—that the first account denies. Freud was confused, even contradictory. But now the source of the confusion could be clarified and the contradiction overcome. Since the superego is understood by Freud to be the internalization of paternal authority, his second explanation amounts to the claim that it is the identification of parents with their fathers that is responsible for their harsh child-rearing practices. But Chodorow makes it clear that men are far more likely to become father-identified than women. (And Freud himself argues that men normally have a much more highly developed superego than women.) Thus Freud's second explanation is really an account of the origins of the parenting orientations of men.

The first explanation, in contrast, is really an account of the parenting orientations of women. He argues that the primary narcissism that is the ultimate source of indulgent child-rearing practices derives from the infant's earliest interactions with its mother. He implicitly asserts, in other words, that it is the parents' identification with their mothers that accounts for their indulgence. And Chodorow (and other feminist theorists) have explained why women are far more likely than men to remain mother-identified. Hence they are far more likely than men to be indulgent.

Without realizing it, Freud was really talking about the very gender-based opposition in parenting orientations that I had uncovered. No doubt now that my theory was "properly psychoanalytic": it had been unknowingly anticipated by the master himself!

I was feeling cocky. Now that I had assured myself that my historical explanation was a psychoanalytic explanation, I was ready to take on Stone's claim that they were mutually exclusive. His argument, you will recall, was that psychoanalysis is "incapable of explaining change" because it assumes that "each successive generation is automatically obliged, by the very fact of its own childhood experience, to impose the same experience on its children." But now it was obvious what was wrong with his argument: it presupposed that both parents of "each successive generation" share and successfully "impose" on their children the same unconscious parenting orientation. This presupposition of a single gender-neutral orientation that governs parenting practices leads inexorably to the conclusion that this unconscious orientation must somehow change in order for the practices to change—to the conclusion, in other words, that if the children of one generation are raised differently from the children of the previous generation, this can only be because the parents of the younger generation have (somehow) become different kinds of people than the people who raised them. So both Stone's argument that psychoanalysis cannot explain change because it rules out this possibility and my effort in *Marxism and Domination* to rebut that argument by attempting (unsuccessfully) to rule this possibility back in were ultimately based on the mistaken presupposition of a single, gender-neutral parenting orientation.

Once this mistake is rectified with the presupposition of two different gender-based orientations, we can continue to assume that child-rearing practices are governed by unconscious parenting orientations—and thus to remain on psychoanalytic terrain—without having to assume that a change in those practices requires an inexplicable change in these orientations. We can assume, instead, that changes in child-rearing practices are the result of changes in the balance of power between unchanging maternal and paternal orientations. A change in practices results not from an unaccountable change in the personality of parents but rather from a change in the parent who is in charge. Voilà! So much for Stone's claim that psychoanalytic explanation and the explanation of change are mutually exclusive. I was on a roll. I had solved—or so I thought—the puzzle of psychoanalysis and history.

But this theoretical solution—like all theoretical solutions— yielded its own set of problems. To begin with, how could I explain an alteration in the balance of child-rearing power between fathers and mothers, women and men? I had already come to the conclusion that this balance had tilted in favor of mothers following World War II because a neo-Freudian theory that "legitimated" their indulgent parenting orientations had replaced the behavioristic theory that had earlier justified the harsher orientations of their husbands. And (following the lead of Sears et al.) I had also concluded that this transformation in the definition of legitimate child rearing ultimately resulted from a feminization of the public sphere, that is, from the partially successful struggle of women to gain access to, and infuse their values within, the arenas of professional and political life prior to World War II. But, as the adverb *ultimately* warns, the connections between this elementary political struggle and the often arcane theoretical debates within intellectual circles are inevitably circuitous and complex, and mapping them out, I knew, would be no easy task.

There were other problems as well. My argument was that neo-Freudian ideas served to legitimate the indulgent parenting orientation of women. Thus my claim was both that post-World War II child-centered practices were an expression of an indulgent maternal parenting orientation and that these practices only came to prevail because Spockean advice transformed this orientation into the "right way," into "common sense." But the concept of legitimation, I knew, was a notoriously tricky one: it implies that interests exist, but cannot be realized, independently of ideals.[11]

It is easy to defend this claim on empirical grounds from a crude materialism that would ignore the dependence of interests on ideals, but it is perhaps more difficult to counter the idealist insistence on the independence of ideals from interests. In the present context this insistence takes the form of the following questions: If Spockean advice was so necessary, why wasn't it sufficient? If neo-Freudian ideals were so essential to the implementation of child-centered practices, then why not simply assume that those ideals directly determined these practices? What, in short, would be lost by dropping the assumption of a maternal parenting interest?

A lot, I thought. For one thing, without this assumption it would be impossible to explain maternal resistance to the implementation of "legitimate" advice. The idealist assumption leads us to expect that mothers will merely—and gladly—do whatever the doctors order. But they don't, at least not all the time. I had already learned, both from Mary McCarthy's *The Group* and from my own mother's description of her treatment of my older sister, that prior to World War II middle-class women regularly resented and often resisted the behavioristically inspired disciplinary advice they received.[12] Torn between the tough "let them cry it out" advice of their pediatricians and their husbands' insistence that it be followed on the one hand and their own more tender, solicitous sentiments on the other, these mothers did a lot of crying themselves. And sometimes they cheated.

There was, in contrast, no evidence of such maternal resistance to Spockean advice. Nor should we expect any, given the assumption of harmony rather than conflict between this advice and the indulgent parenting orientations of women. But the problem is that there is no way to determine whether that absence of resistance testifies to the explanatory power of this assumption rather than the explanatory power of the counterassumption of the exclusively determining power of the advice. I realized that the superiority of my interpretation could not be demonstrated during the child-rearing period for which the interpretation was constructed. Thus to prove the power of my postulates I would have to expand the scope of my study. Eventually I would have to include periods during which there was conflict rather than harmony between the hegemonic child-rearing theory and the parenting orientation of women, and demonstrate that mothers resisted putting this theory fully into practice during such periods.

I was not intimidated by this prospect. In fact I had already learned a great deal about the disciplinary regime of the late-nineteenth through early twentieth century. I also knew that this regime had supplanted a much more indulgent, child-centered regime that flourished during the middle decades of the nineteenth century, and that this gentle regime had itself replaced an extremely repressive form of "family government" that prevailed throughout the colonial and early republican periods. So I knew that the Spockean transformation was merely one chapter of a much larger story. Why not tell the whole story?

Doing so would take care of yet another problem. I knew that an explanation of the Spockean transformation alone would be vulnerable to the objection that applies to any case study, namely that it is always possible to construct an infinite number of plausible explanations for a single case. Expanding the number of "cases" to include the two other child-rearing changes I just referred to would obviate this objection. It is always far more difficult to explain a pattern of events than to explain just one. If I could show that my theory could explain this pattern and that, for example, Marxist and Foucauldian theories could not, then I would be able to make a much more persuasive case for the superior explanatory power of my theory.

Of course I would not be able to flesh this pattern out in the mere two weeks that were left before my presentation at the November colloquium at the institute. For that presentation I would still have to concentrate on the one transformation about which I knew a lot more than any other, but at least I could situate Spock within a skeletal outline that included the transformations that had preceded it. Although there was much that I still had to work out, I took comfort from the considerable progress I had made. At least I would not make a fool of myself in public.

chapter three

. The Institute Lecture .

Neither Marx nor Foucault: Gender Struggle and the Transformation of American Child Rearing
(Lecture Delivered at the Institute for the Humanities of the University of Illinois at Chicago, 7 November 1984)

I. Introduction

In *Marxism and Domination* I make a case for what I call the determining power of the mode of child rearing. I argue that "the unconscious, internalized relationship of the child to its mother will play a more . . . determinative role over the [economic and] political . . . relationships of the adult than the latter will play over the former."[1] But this argument is vulnerable to the objection that economic and political factors account for changes in the mode of child rearing and thus that the immediately determining role of the mode of child rearing is ultimately overshadowed by the long-term determining role of those economic and political factors. My remarks today are designed to assess this objection.

In the next section of my presentation I outline briefly the post-World War II transformation of American child rearing we associate with the name of Dr. Benjamin Spock, and situate it within a pattern of transformations in American child rearing from 1800 through 1950. In the third section I show that neither Marxist nor Foucauldian assumptions yield a compelling explanation for this pattern. This account of the limits of economic and political explanations sets the stage for my effort in the fourth section to derive a more satisfactory explanation from the assumptions of "feminist mothering theory" and the work of Nancy Chodorow in particular.

I argue that modes of child rearing engender an opposition between an indulgent maternal parenting orientation and a repressive paternal parenting orientation and that the child-rearing practices that prevail at any given time reflect the balance of power between women and men over child-rearing decisions. In the fifth section I show that this gender-struggle theory yields hypotheses that are—in contrast to those derived from Marxist and Foucauldian theories—consistent with the pattern of child-rearing transformations I describe in section two. Thus I demonstrate that the theory of the determining power of the mode of child rearing is not undermined by, but is in fact the basis for, a satisfactory explanation of changes in the mode of child rearing.

Finally, in the sixth section I conclude with some insufficiently supported speculations on the relationship between the gender struggle that culminated in the "Spockean" transformation of American child rearing, on the one hand, and the contemporary commitment to coparenting, on the other.

II. The Spockean Transformation in Historical Context: Preliminary Outline

From the end of the nineteenth through the better part of the first half of the twentieth century, (mainly middle-class) American mothers enforced a repressive regime under which infants and toddlers were fed according to the dictates of a rigid schedule, control of their sphincters was demanded shortly following their birth, masturbation, thumb-sucking, and other forms of gratification were assiduously avoided, and the misery that regularly resulted from these frustrations of oral, anal, genital, and other physical impulses characteristically evoked the response that the baby should be allowed to "cry it out." This regime was imposed in order to foster habits of self-control or deferred gratification that would enable the child to conform to the world of *adults* for which she or she was being prepared.

Following World War II, first middle-class (and then somewhat later and less uniformly working-class) mothers began to govern their infants and young children with a much gentler hand, feeding them on demand, waiting much longer (perhaps even until their children were "ready") before expecting continence, allowing them their bodily pleasures, and even enhancing these pleasures with the liberal doses of physical affection that they themselves had been denied when they were children. They did so in the name of a felt obligation to respond lovingly to what were now perceived to be the distinctive needs of the *child*.

Thus in the space of a few short years a disciplinary, adult-centered mode of child rearing was supplanted by an indulgent, child-centered mode of introducing children to their world. This transformation, in turn, was preceded by a transformation in the "expert" consensus concerning legitimate child-rearing practices. The broad outline of this transformation in "legitimation" looks something like this:

1. Beginning in the 1930s, psychologists, psychiatrists, educators, and pediatricians mounted a professional assault on the dominant, disciplinary, adult-centered practices in favor of more indulgent, child-centered practices.
2. By the mid-1940s, this new advice achieved hegemony over its professional adversary.
3. By the mid-1950s, and largely (although by no means exclusively) through the vehicle of Dr. Benjamin Spock's extraordinarily popular *Baby and Child Care* (after the Bible the most

widely read book in the history of American publishing), the new professional consensus had been communicated to and consumed by tens of millions of (disproportionately middle-class) American mothers.[2]

It is possible to demonstrate that this transformation in child-rearing advice was the proximate cause of the transformation in child-rearing practices that followed it:

1. Before the 1950s, middle-class child-rearing practices were typically less indulgent than the practices of working-class mothers.[3]
2. During and following this decade, the practices of middle-class mothers became more indulgent than the practices of their working-class counterparts.[4]
3. Studies show that middle-class mothers are far more aware of, and reliant on, the advice of child-rearing "experts" than working-class mothers.[5]
4. The fact that the mothers who were most likely to have read the new advice were the mothers whose practices shifted most dramatically in the direction of that advice is a strong indication of the immediately determinative effect of that advice.

It is also possible to show that the transformation in child-rearing advice was based on a transformation from a so-called scientific to a psychoanalytic approach to child development:

1. Experimental psychology in general and (later in the period) Watsonian behaviorism in particular was the psychological approach on which the child-rearing "experts" relied between the last decade of the nineteenth century and the early 1930s.
2. Beginning in the mid-to-late 1930s, a particular version of Freudian psychoanalytic theory—often referred to as neo-Freudianism—replaced behaviorism as the theoretical underpinning of child-rearing expertise.
   a. There is a tension in Freud's work between the (mainly

early) Freud who deplores the subordination of the "pleasure principle" to a particularly severe, bourgeois "reality
principle" and who envisions a more pleasurable, sexually
satisfying form of life,[6] and the (mainly late) Freud who insists on the irreconcilable antagonism between *any* reality
principle and the pleasure principle and who thus concludes
that "discontent" is the inevitable price of "civilization."[7]

  b. The neo-Freudian paradigm emphasizes, and elaborates
     on, the "first Freud" and virtually ignores the second.
  c. In so doing it provides a theoretical justification for efforts
     to mitigate the repressiveness of "bourgeois" practices and
     child-rearing practices in particular.
3. Spock and other advocates of the new advice self-consciously
   sought to translate what they took to be the imperatives of
   neo-Freudianism into pediatric practice, and it can in fact easily be demonstrated that the new advice is thoroughly impreg-
   nated with neo-Freudian concepts and commitments.[8]

If indulgent, child-centered child-rearing advice informed by
neo-Freudian psychoanalysis was immediately responsible for
the post-World War II transformation in American child-rearing
practices, then a satisfactory explanation of this transformation
must answer the following two questions:

1. What accounts for the emergence and ascendence of neo-
   Freudianism in the decades immediately preceding this transformation?
2. What accounts for the rapid and widespread acceptance by
   American mothers of the new advice that was informed by this
   paradigm?

My research has also revealed that the Spockean transformation was preceded by two similarly significant, large-scale
changes in the mode of American child rearing:

1. The disciplinary, adult-centered regime of the late-nineteenth

to early twentieth century supplanted an indulgent, child-centered regime that had prevailed in most American families from the beginning or middle of the nineteenth century.[9] The dominant child-rearing advice of this earlier period counseled a practice of "Christian Nurture" that was justified by a post-Calvinist theology of the innate goodness of every child.[10]

2. This gentle early to mid-nineteenth-century regime replaced a harsh, repressive regime that had dominated the colonial and early republican periods. Calvinist theology legitimated this latter regime by interpreting the willfulness of children as a sign of their innate depravity and by demanding that parents "break the will" of their children in order to prepare them for salvation.

The following figure outlines the pattern of changes in American child rearing since 1800.[11] Although a potentially infinite number of explanations may be consistent with any one of these changes, the possibility of arbitrating among different explanations increases with an increase in the number of changes against which they can be tested. Thus I assume that any satisfactory explanation of the Spockean transformation would have to be derived from, or give rise to, a theory that yields a satisfactory explanation for this entire historical pattern.

III. The Limits of Economic and Political Explanations

A. Marxist Explanations

I have located two different Marxist explanations for major changes in American child rearing. The first explanation is based on the assumption that the structures of child rearing (and the practices that prevail within them) are determined ("in the last analysis") by the functions that must be performed in order to reproduce the dominant mode of production and that changes in these structures and practices thus reflect changes in the "func-

Figure 1

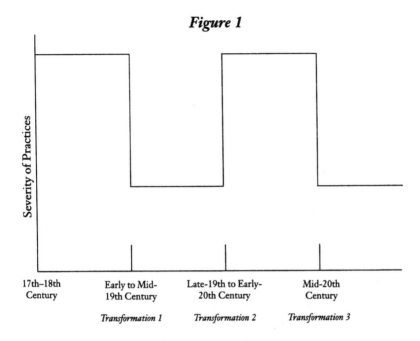

| 17th–18th | Early to Mid- | Late-19th to Early- | Mid-20th |
| Century | 19th Century | 20th Century | Century |

Transformation 1   *Transformation 2*   *Transformation 3*

tional requisites" of that mode of production. More specifically, the transition from a nineteenth- to early twentieth-century competitive capitalism whose principal functional requisite is the accumulation of capital to a twentieth-century advanced or monopoly capitalism whose principal functional requisite is mass consumption demands that an ascetic personality dedicated to the Protestant work ethic be replaced by a hedonistic personality committed to "instant gratification." This demand is satisfied by the increasing influence and ultimate hegemony of the psychoanalytically informed, Spockean child-rearing advice that legitimates the replacement of the harsh disciplinary practices of the nineteenth and early twentieth century by the indulgent, permissive practices that have prevailed in this and other capitalist societies since World War II.[12]

This Marxist explanation is empirically unpersuasive because:

1. If, on the one hand, the transition from competitive to consumer capitalism is located, as it often is, in the first two

decades of the twentieth century,[13] any transformation in child-rearing advice and practice that is assumed to be necessary for that transition should have taken place during this same period. But this period was, as we have seen, characterized by the hegemony of behaviorist advice and the austere practices that it legitimated. Thus the timing of the Spockean transformation is inconsistent with the timing of the economic transformation that is supposed to explain it.

2. If, on the other hand, the economic transition is (perhaps less plausibly) located in the years immediately following World War II, the new child-rearing practices can be synchronized with that transition, but then the fact that the new child-rearing advice, and the psychoanalytically informed professional consensus underlying it, emerged in the 1930s in the middle of the Great Depression cannot be explained. To attribute the rise and spread of this advice to the necessity of inculcating the personality type essential for consumer abundance is hardly consistent with the fact that this advice and the psychological assumptions on which it was based arose during a period of extreme scarcity and consciousness thereof.

3. Any effort to resolve these anomalies (e.g., to invoke the concept of a "temporal lag" between new functions and new structures in order to overcome objection 1) necessarily founders on the rock of the early to mid-nineteenth-century mode of child rearing. This was the period of competitive capitalism *par excellence*. A theory that links child-rearing practices to the requirements of this stage of American capitalism yields the prediction that these decades would be characterized by an extremely harsh child-rearing regime. But this prediction is entirely counter-factual, since the early to mid-nineteenth-century mode of child rearing was significantly less repressive than both its colonial and early republican predecessor and its late nineteenth- to early twentieth-century successor.

There is, however, another Marxist account for which the gentle early to mid-nineteenth-century child-rearing regime is no longer an anomaly. According to this account, capitalist industrialization requires precisely those permissive, indulgent practices that, according to the first account, only the supersession of industrialization makes possible. According to Ilene Philipson, the rise of capitalist industrialization in the early to mid-1830s undermined "the material basis" of parental authority. Because most parents could no longer "pass on land, property or significant amounts of capital" to their children, neither could they continue to rely on the threat of disinheritance or other economic sanctions to ensure their obedience. Obedience would now have to be secured by less material, more emotional, means; since parents could no longer control their children by threatening to withdraw their property, they would have to control them by threatening to withdraw their love. Hence the "use of affection and love received greater and greater attention in child-rearing literature in the nineteenth century."[14]

The problem with this second Marxist theory, however, is that it cannot account for the late-nineteenth- to early twentieth-century disciplinary regime that supplanted its early to mid-nineteenth-century predecessor. Philipson's argument that industrial capitalism demands the manipulation of maternal affection cannot be squared with the suppression of mother-love at the end of the nineteenth century. The disciplinary regime that prevailed from that time through the 1930s is every bit as anomalous for the second Marxist theory as the earlier affectionate regime is for the first. Neither theory can account for the actual historical sequence of child-rearing regimes.

Each Marxist explanation, moreover, is beset by conceptual as well as empirical problems:

1. As a species of the genus of functionalism, the first explanation tacitly assumes that practices emerge as a result of a necessity of which individuals are unaware but of which, willy-nilly, they are the agents. In ignoring the intentions of parents, it bypasses the problem of why they selected the practices that engendered the consequences that functionalism wrongly takes as

their cause. Thus the first Marxist explanation fails even to pose the second question that any adequate explanation of the Spockean transformation must answer, i.e., why was the newly hegemonic, psychoanalytically informed child-rearing advice accepted by the post-World War II generation of (disproportionately middle-class) American mothers?

2. The second Marxist explanation, in contrast, does not bypass the problem of what parents want, but its conception of parental motivation is much too manipulative. The argument that early to mid-nineteenth-century mothers offered or withheld love to their children mainly to secure their loyalty and obedience rests on the assumption that the overriding interest of parents is controlling their children, an assumption that ignores other sources of parental affection that are, arguably, equally or even more important. Since—as the example of the late-nineteenth- to early twentieth-century disciplinary regime attests—there are other, nonproperty-based ways of exercising parental control over children, the assumption that love is nothing but an instrument of control seems not only overly cynical but also empirically unwarranted.

3. Finally, both Marxist explanations are insensitive to gender. Their undifferentiated references to early "parenting practice" ignores the fact that this practice is typically carried out by women and not by men. Thus they likewise ignore the possibility that, under these circumstances, there might be significant differences between the motivations of mothers and the motivations of fathers.

B. Foucauldian Explanations

For Michel Foucault and his followers it is the "will to power" and not the mode of production that determines the fate of children. The will to power, we learn from Foucault, is (at least in the West) invariably expressed through the very will to knowledge to which it is ordinarily opposed. Discourses that speak the truth about human beings make it possible for the speakers to exercise power over the bodies and minds of those of whom they speak. One of the most recent, and dominant, forms of such true discourse is psychoanalysis, which reveals that the truth of the human being is to be found in a sexuality hidden in his or her early childhood.[15]

More specifically, maternal gratification of the libidinal needs of infants and young children is unveiled (at least by neo-Freudianism) as the source of their happiness as adults and maternal deprivation, correspondingly, as the reason for their discontent. This psychoanalytic regime of truth encourages unhappy individuals to define themselves as people who didn't get the love they needed and prepares them to enter into relationships of dependence with psychoanalytically informed experts who alone can help them understand and overcome the effects of this deficit.

From this perspective, Spockean advice might be called the prophylactic chapter of the larger book of Psychoanalytic True Discourse. In this chapter parents—especially mothers—are explicitly taught the techniques of loving their children in a manner that will maximize their happiness and minimize their need for subsequent—and more expensive—encounters with psychoanalytically informed experts. Implicitly, of course, they are also taught that if these techniques fail it is exactly to these experts to whom they must later turn. Thus dependence on the psychoanalytically informed pediatrician prepares the way for dependence on the psychoanalytically informed child psychologist, educator, social worker, therapist, etc., that is, on what Foucauldian Robert Castel has called the "psy-complex" as a whole.[16]

Earlier periods of American child rearing also seem to fit a Foucauldian framework. The colonial and early republican commitment to "break the will" of the child can be considered a classic example of what Foucault calls "repressive power," of power as prohibition. The parent lays down the law: the child is commanded not to do what he or she wants to do. Since swift and certain punishment follows any violation of the parental law, the child learns to obey this law in order to avoid that punishment. In short, the relationship between this period's parent and his children perfectly parallels the relationship between the absolute sovereign and his subjects.[17]

Thus the Foucauldian could credibly contrast the "juridical" or "negative" power of this Calvinist regime to what he or she would consider the "positive" power of the late-nineteenth- to early twentieth century protobehaviorist and behaviorist regime. H. Clay Trumball, a late-nineteenth-century advocate of the latter, concisely captured this contrast with his motto "Will Training Rather Than Will Breaking."[18] Children are not to be prevented by their parents from doing what they want but rather trained to want whatever their parents want; they are taught not to repress their desires but to develop the desires that their society—acting through their parents—considers to be normal. Hence the late-nineteenth- to early twentieth-century behaviorist regime can be comprehended as an integral part of a modern disciplinary society in which—in contrast to the juridical society that it supplants—power is exercised through the production and dissemination of "scientific" discourses that have "normalizing" effects on the human beings who are their object.[19]

Foucauldian explanations are nonetheless vulnerable to a number of empirical objections:

1. Although the behaviorism justifying pre-World War II child-rearing practices can plausibly be interpreted as part of the normalizing "strategy" of a disciplinary society, and the neo-Freudian psychoanalysis informing post-World War II practices can be seen as a later development of that same strategy (the "deployment of sexuality"), it is not, in fact, clear why Freudian succeeded behaviorist, "true discourse" rather than the reverse. Since both psychological theories were available for the legitimation of child-rearing practices throughout all of the post-War and much of the pre-War periods, reference to the demands of a disciplinary society does not succeed in explaining the actual order of their influence.

2. The Foucauldian explanation (like the functionalist Marxist explanation) cannot account for the early to mid-nineteenth-century practices that were more indulgent than both the practices that preceded and the practices that immediately followed them. Although the sequence seventeenth- to eighteenth-century will-breaking practices leading to late-nine-teenth-century- to pre-World War II will-training practices leading to post-World War II child-centered practices can (if we ignore the problem of periodization referred to above) be assimilated to the Foucauldian scheme of repressive power (law) leading to disciplinary power (norm) leading to the deployment of sexuality ("subjectification," technologies of the self), the early to mid-nineteenth-century child-rearing regime slips through the cracks, so to speak, of this scheme. Thus both the rise and the demise of this regime remain unexplained.

3. Neither is there any Foucauldian explanation for the emergence of a "soft" rather than a "hard" Freudian discourse on the truth of child rearing. Foucauldian references to psychoanalysis as a "technology of the self" fail to distinguish between the optimistic and the pessimistic Freud and thus do not explain why it was the former discourse, and the practices it incited, rather than the latter discourse, and the practices it might have incited, that achieved hegemonic status after World War II.

Thus Foucault is no more able to account for the pattern of American child-rearing transformations since 1800 than Marx. And, like Marxist explanations, Foucauldian explanations suffer not only from empirical but also from conceptual problems.

1. To his credit, Foucault does not assume that individuals will always come to practice what the discourse preaches. At least he avoids the teleology of a functionalist Marxism, which assumes that (but does not explain how) the system always (at

least in the long run) gets the practices it requires. He argues, to the contrary, that "there are no relations of power without resistances [and that] the latter are all the more real and effective because they are formed right at the point where relations of power are exercised."[20] This argument leads us to expect that parenting practice will both reflect *and* resist the dominant discourse on parenting, and thus that there will always be a difference, rather than an identity, between the discourse and the practice.

But the problem is that the extent of the difference between theory and practice is impossible to predict, because the basis for the resistance that gives rise to it remains obscure. Foucault's claim that "where there is power, there is resistance"[21] fails to clarify the conditions under which there will be more, or less, resistance to the dominant discourse. I have already suggested that whether parents mostly accept, or mostly reject, the prevailing parenting advice depends on whether this advice is consistent or not with their paternal or maternal motivations. But Foucault has no more to say about individual motivation than Marx.

Or, rather, the little that he says about it rules out the possibility of attributing to it any determining effects. To speak of an "individual" who has "motivations" is already to speak the language of true discourse rather than to "deconstruct" this discourse in order to unmask its disciplinary effects. To take seriously the theme of the "founding subject" is to fail to understand that individual subjectivity (or "motivation") is an effect of power/knowledge complexes and to fail to grasp the sense in which the constitution of the subjectivity of the individual is simultaneously the constitution of his or her subjection. The theorist who would contest, not reproduce, this subjection must "dispense with the constituent subject . . . get rid of the subject itself."[22] But eliminating the subject eliminates the possibility of answering—or even really asking—the second question that any satisfactory explanation of the post-World War II child-rearing transformation must address, namely: why did American mothers *want* to practice the advice that Dr. Spock preached?

2. In discounting motivations Foucault necessarily ignores potentially significant differences between the motivation of mothers and the motivation of fathers. Moreover, the assumption that "true discourses" enable both power and resistance obscures the fact that parenting discourses are often invented by men and usually aimed at women. Thus Foucault is as gender-blind as Marx.

IV. A Gender-Struggle Theory of Child-Rearing Change

I attempt to overcome this gender-blindness by assuming that the hitherto culturally universal responsibility of women for early child care engenders both political and parental interests that are different for women and men.

A. Political Interests

Even the most solicitous mother necessarily imposes frustrations on the infants and young children for whom she has been, in all cultures, disproportionately responsible. Dorothy Dinnerstein has insightfully argued that the rage against the mother that results from these frustrations is subsequently directed toward all those who come to represent her, i.e., to women in general, who become the universal scapegoats for the inescapable pains of the human condition. The assiduous and equally universal efforts of men to exclude women from positions of authority and status outside the family, she avers, reflect their unconscious commitment never again to experience the power of a woman to which they so painfully submitted in their earliest years.[23] In *Marxism and Domination* I show that this hypothesis is strongly supported by a large number of cross-cultural studies that demonstrate that the patriarchal exclusion of women is most extreme precisely in those societies in which male fear of female power is likely to be at its peak, namely when a prolonged and intense identification with the mother is followed by an extremely radical, enforced separation from her.[24]

Although the mother-raised woman is also necessarily ambivalent about the exercise of female authority outside the domestic domain, the "impulse toward autonomy" she shares with the mother-raised man pushes her to "keep trying . . . to shake off his tyranny over her."[25] In one way or another, women will resist the universal efforts of men to exclude them from positions of extrafamilial influence and prestige. Under cultural and historical conditions in which a belief in human equality or the "rights of man [sic]" is widely shared, this resistance will take the form of an insistence on equal political participation that men will necessarily contest. Thus does "mother-monopolized" child rearing give rise to a gender-based opposition in political interests that leads to extrafamilial political conflict between women and men.

B. Parental Interests

Nancy Chodorow has demonstrated that the nature of the child's early relationship with the mother differs dramatically depending on the gender of the child. Because the male child has an opposite-sex initial "love-object," his primary identification with this "object" is eventually experienced as an obstacle to the development of his "normal" masculine identity. Intimacy with the mother comes to be perceived as a threat to male autonomy and thus boys—and then men—characteristically come to associate intimate human relationships with the loss of self. To defend against this threat they tend disproportionately to develop an "oppositional" orientation to the others they encounter, symbolizing them as objects to be controlled rather than as subjects with whom to be involved in a caring, reciprocal relationship.

Unlike the boy, the girl can tell herself that she is like the one who nurtures her; the girl's primary relationship with her mother is not a threat to, but rather the basis of, her gendered sense of self. Thus the girl—and then the woman—characteristically develops a "relational" orientation within which precisely those intimate relationships that are so threatening to masculine identity become essential for the completion of her sense of self. This relational orientation is likely to include a need for an intimate relationship with a child:

> As a result of having been parented by a woman, women are more likely than men to seek to be mothers, that is to relocate themselves in a primary mother-child relationship, to get gratification from the mothering relationship, and to have psychological and relational capacities for mothering.[26]

What Margaret Mahler has called the "psychological birth of the human infant"[27] requires that parents everywhere confront the tasks of responding both to the infant's initially almost complete dependence on the one hand and its eventually insistent autonomy on the other. As the passage just cited from Chodorow intimates, the assumption of a gender-based opposition in social-psychological orientations leads us to expect that women and men will respond in very different, indeed, opposed, ways to these twin and conflicting demands. Whereas women's relational orientation will predispose them to an intimate relationship with their infants and young children and thus to favor child-rearing practices that nurture or indulge their dependence, the oppositional orientation of men will prepare them for a distant, controlling relationship with their children and thus to prefer strict or repressive practices that ensure the necessary distance and control. Put otherwise, fathers will project their own fear of engulfing intimacy onto their children and thus perceive indulgent practices to be a threat to their incipient autonomy, while mothers will unconsciously strive to reproduce their own more intense "preoedipal" identification with their mothers in the form of an intimate relationship with their children.

The more oppositional orientation of fathers will also manifest itself in an inclination to oppose the increasing willfulness of their children with demands for obedience, in contrast to an unwillingness of mothers to refuse the demands of children with whom they are more deeply identified and with whom they are therefore more likely to empathize.

In short, from the assumption of a gender-based opposition in social-psychological orientations it is possible to derive the corollary assumption of a gender-based opposition in parenting interests, with women preferring indulgent and men preferring repressive child-rearing practices.

Neither men nor women can rely on an automatic, or even easy, convergence of their respective political and parental interests. In fact they both face the problem of reconciling a conflict between them. Men are politically committed to maintaining their monopoly on public power and thus to confining women to the domestic domain but parentally committed to child-rearing practices that are far stricter than those preferred by the women within it. Thus the problem for men is to establish control over, without directly participating in, the early care of their children. To achieve this they will seek to secure the hegemony of a child-rearing theory that transforms their repressive parenting interest into the "right" way to raise children. If they are successful, they also can be expected to endeavor to ensure that the practices of their wives are as consistent as possible with that theory. If they are unsuccessful, they can be expected to complain consistently about those practices.

Women, on the other hand, are parentally committed to nurturing their young children but politically committed to equal participation within the public sphere. For them the problem is thus how to ensure that the time and energy they devote to the latter task is consistent with their devotion to the former. How can they simultaneously satisfy their children's needs and their own? The solution to this problem is to justify their political participation as necessary for the nurturance of their children. Only by contesting the public power of men can they contest a definition of "legitimate" child rearing that they perceive as inimicable to the interests of their children. What has come to be called "social feminism" simultaneously satisfies the parental interest of women in legitimating their preferred indulgent parenting practices and the political interest of women in inclusion within the public sphere. (Thus social—rather than liberal individualistic—feminism is likely to be the most attractive form of feminism, at least for women who are also mothers.) To the extent that the socially feminist legitimation struggle is successful, actual child-rearing practices will reflect the indulgent parenting predisposition of women. To the extent that it is not, women within the family will be predisposed to resist putting the masculine hegemonic parenting theory fully into practice.

Thus we should expect that outside the family there will always be always a struggle over the hegemonic parenting theory and that inside the family there will always be always a struggle over its implementation. Child-rearing practices, in short, are both the outcome and the object of extrafamilial and intrafamilial gender struggle.

V. The Gender-Struggle Theory Applied

Our theory leads us to conceptualize the Spockean transformation as a shift from male to female control over the mode of child rearing, a triumph of the maternal interest in nurturance and indulgence over the paternal interest in severity and control. Similarly, the transformation in child-rearing advice that preceded this transformation in practice can now be understood as the supersession of a male-oriented definition of legitimate child-rearing practices by a female-oriented definition of these practices. Thus our two central questions (see section II) can be reformulated as follows:

1. What accounts for the displacement of a male-oriented, experimental/behaviorist definition of legitimate child-rearing practices by a female-oriented, neo-Freudian definition of these practices?
2. What accounts for the rapid and widespread acceptance of this female-oriented definition by American (first middle-class and then working-class) parents?

We are also now in a position to explain the two earlier transformations in American child rearing as (1) the result of an early-
to mid-nineteenth-century victory of the maternal parenting interest over the previously hegemonic paternal parenting interest
and (2) the result a late-nineteenth- to early-twentieth century
restoration of the hegemony of the parenting interest of men. I
will preface my explanation of the Spockean transformation with
two somewhat shorter explanatory sketches of these earlier
child-rearing changes.

A. The Early to Mid-nineteenth-century Feminization of the Mode of Child Rearing

Our theory predicts that the significant softening of American
child-rearing practices in the early to mid-nineteenth century
would be associated with a shift from paternal to maternal control over the mode of child rearing. Such indeed appears to be
the case. The developing doctrine of the "two spheres"—men
naturally suited for work, women naturally fit for domesticity—
that is both consequence and cause of the progressive dissolution
of the domestic economy of the seventeenth, eighteenth, and
very early nineteenth centuries both directly and indirectly
served to legitimate the indulgent parenting interest of women.
It directly legitimated this interest by appropriating exclusive domestic responsibility for the "moral mother," undermining in the
process the claim of "less virtuous" men to speak on behalf of the
interests of their children.[28]

Equally as important, it indirectly contributed to the legitimation of the maternal parenting interest by encouraging what historians have called the feminization of American Protestantism.[29]
Studies show that women were disproportionately involved in
the Second Great Awakening of the early decades of the nineteenth century and that by midcentury women made up two
thirds of the membership of evangelical congregations.[30] This
dramatic increase in the religious participation of women can be
understood as a logical, public extension of their ideologically
defined, maternal role of "moral guardians" of the nation. The

enhanced religious participation of these moral guardians was in turn, associated with a "feminization" of the theology of the ministers who sought their support. By the middle of the nineteenth century, the bleak doctrine of innate depravity was completely repudiated by the denominations formerly attached to it in favor of the far sunnier notion of "Christian nurture."[31] Mothers were encouraged to love, even indulge, the innocent babes who were now as good as the God who had made them. Thus a successful struggle to feminize the church promoted a religious redefinition of the child's nature that successfully legitimated the indulgent parenting interest of women within the home.

The breakdown of the domestic economy also inhibited men from interfering with the efforts of women to implement this interest. Although the progressive separation of workplace and home significantly reduced the economic participation of married women, it substantially increased their everyday control over child-rearing decisions.[32] With men increasingly absent from the home the better part of the day, they were no longer able directly to supervise the child-rearing practices of their wives. Although diaries from this period are filled with the fears of fathers that their children were being "spoiled" by their mothers,[33] there was, in fact, little they could do about it. "Mothers," as one historian felicitously phrased it, were now "in command" of the mode of child rearing. Their newly gained authority was reflected in the fact that—beginning in the early decades of the century and in stark contrast to the earlier period—popular child-rearing manuals were increasingly addressed to, and sometimes written by, women.[34]

B. The Remasculinization of the Late-Nineteenth to Early Twentieth Century

The industrialization and urbanization of the second half of the nineteenth and early part of the twentieth centuries virtually completed the separation of production and consumption, workplace and home, that was already well underway during the previous period. By 1920 the majority of Americans lived in cities or towns, and the rapidly declining numbers who continued to live on farms had become as dependent as their urban counterparts on the consumption of goods and services produced outside the home.[35]

The second half of the nineteenth and the early part of the twentieth centuries were also marked by the struggle of (largely middle-class) women to overcome an exclusion from the public sphere in general, and the workplace in particular, that was the inevitable consequence of their still-mandatory monopoly on domestic duties. Although there was, of course, a radically individualistic wing of the nineteenth-century feminist movement, feminist demands for inclusion were more often couched in terms of, and supported because of, the perceived need to infuse the public sphere with sensibilities that were considered to be specifically feminine. "Social feminism" relied on the rhetoric of superior female virtue in order to justify the entry of women into teaching, librarianship, social work, and other professions that could be conceived as a logical extension of the helping role of the mother within the home, and in order to secure the political reforms—including female suffrage—designed to eliminate a host of practices (e.g., child labor, unsafe working conditions, alcoholism, etc.) that were deemed to be inconsistent with that role.[36] Paradoxically, the very doctrine of "moral motherhood" that legitimated exclusive female responsibility for the home became an indispensable ideological weapon in the struggle to escape its confines.

Under these conditions this doctrine increasingly represented a threat not only to the parental interest but also to the political interest of men. Hence the struggle of men to preserve their patriarchal privileges required both direct resistance to the feminization of the public sphere and indirect resistance in the form of an assault on the theory of the moral mother that legitimated female control over the private sphere. This assault, to be sure, was also fueled by male hostility to the indulgent child-rearing practices that were the consequence of a half century of maternal control. Thus the parental and the political interests of men converged in an effort to reassert the hegemony of the paternal parenting interest, that is, in what might be called a remasculinization of the relations of child rearing.

This masculine counterhegemonic struggle took the form of a concerted attack against maternal, in favor of "scientific," control over child rearing. The very maternal "instinct" that was formerly celebrated as the necessary condition for was now excoriated as the chief obstacle to the proper way to raise children. "Won't you ... remember when you are tempted to pet your child that mother love is a dangerous instrument?" pleaded behaviorist John Watson in his enormously influential *Psychological Care of Infant and Child*, polemically dedicated to "the first mother who brings up a happy child."[37] She will only succeed in this effort, Watson warned, if she learns to subordinate her "emotional" and "subjective" impulses to the "rational" and "objective" requirements of science: women were urged to "study the subject [child rearing] as [they] would any other scientific problem" and thus to treat it as an "experiment ... which must be worked out by patient laboratory methods."[38]

To treat child rearing like "any other scientific problem" the child must be known in the same way that the Enlightenment knows nature, namely an object of prediction and control. Just as the Enlightenment conceptualizes nature merely as raw material for human production—a purposeless object awaiting the control of the human subject—so "scientific" child rearing rejects the claim that the child has instincts or internal impulses that must be respected in favor of the assumption that its behavior is entirely determined by the external stimuli to which it is subjected.[39] Thus in order to ensure that the child responds "correctly" the parent must understand—and then arrange—the stimuli that will uniquely "condition" the correct response.

It is not difficult to demonstrate the sense in which the Enlightenment worldview is a particularly masculine worldview. Just as the boy defends against maternal engulfment by fantasizing his mother as an object from which he is entirely independent and over which he can exercise complete control, so Western man [*sic*] denies his dependence on the nature she represents by symbolizing it as a wholly external object that must be known and mastered by a sovereign subject.[40] In short, the Enlightenment separation of "subject" and "object" that is the condition for the possibility of the "objective" knowledge it pursues can be understood as an expression of the object relations of the "normal" man. The "positivist" extension of this separation between subject and object to the relationship between parent and child thus signaled an effort to "masculinize" this relationship, i.e., an effort to articulate and promulgate a child-rearing theory that both grows out of and justifies the oppositional parenting interest of men. Through the patrimony of scientific authority late-nineteenth- and early twentieth-century men attempted to legitimate a paternal interest that could no longer be religiously reinforced.

The advice that issued from this scientific authority was transmitted to American (especially middle-class) mothers through a variety of media. The almost exclusively male pediatricians parroted this new line in their increasingly frequent, influential contacts with the mothers of the children they treated. Baby manuals and articles in mother's magazines written by the most eminent of those pediatricians were produced and consumed by the millions.[41] Corporate foundations and the federal government provided financial support both for research informed by behaviorist assumptions and for the dissemination of the results of this research to a mass audience.[42] The government also provided a direct channel of communication to mothers through its widely circulated brochure *Infant Care*, which from its inception in 1914 until the late 1930s was entirely given over to protobehaviorist and behaviorist advice.[43] Throughout this period there was little or no evidence of contrary advice based on earlier, feminine assumptions, and by the 1920s the hegemony of the masculine, "scientific" theory of child rearing appeared to be complete.

Thus, as our theory predicts, the late-nineteenth- to early twentieth-century period of harsh disciplinary practices (summarized in the introduction) was associated with the reassertion of male control over the mode of child rearing. But male control did not go entirely unchallenged. As our theory also would predict, mothers regularly resisted fully implementing the theory of scientific child rearing. Diaries from the period show that they often fed their infants more frequently and treated them more lovingly than their doctors ordered.[44] Even Watson's dedicated wife and professional assistant Rosalie found it impossible to follow his rules, confessing that she was "always a little too affectionate to stick to the conditioning" and that she was unfortunately "not the perfect behaviorist wife."[45] And it was elementary that dear Watson's rules would be more easily broken by the millions of middle-class mothers who were neither behaviorists nor his lover. Thus a number of studies suggest that although twentieth-century middle-class American children were raised far more strictly before World War II than after, they were never treated as harshly as Watson prescribed.[46]

C. The Spockean Transformation: Refeminization of the Mode of Child Rearing

As we have seen, "permissive" post-World War II child-rearing practices were informed by a "female," neo-Freudian child-rearing theory that succeeded the "male" behaviorist theory that dominated the preceding period. The hegemony of neo-Freudianism, I will argue, was rooted in the "feminization" of the public sphere that resulted from the extrafamilial gender struggle carried out by women from the middle of the nineteenth through the second decade of the twentieth century.

Historians have stressed the influence of the Progressive movement of the first decades of the twentieth century on both the unparalleled popularization—and subsequent influence—of psychoanalysis in America and the transformation of psychoanalysis into its specifically "soft," neo-Freudian form. The progressivist emphasis on ameliorating the environment of the individual, and the child in particular, helped to create an intellectual atmosphere that was far more receptive to a theory stressing the primacy of childhood than the atmosphere fostered by the socialist commitment to the transformation of the mode of production that prevailed elsewhere in the Western capitalist world during this period. Because the American social reform impulse was expressed in a uniquely individualistic idiom—as a concern for the health and well-being of individual Americans irrespective of their class position—liberal doctors were able to identify with this reform impulse and the "socially meliorist" theories that sustained it to a far greater extent than their European counterparts. Thus American psychiatry became, in effect, the mental health wing of the Progressive movement.[47]

As a consequence American psychiatry absorbed psychoanalysis far more rapidly and wholeheartedly than European psychiatry. This uniquely American medicalization of psychoanalysis, in turn, has been hailed by a leading student of the subject as "the most important single reason for [the] popularization" of psychoanalysis in America. Due in large part to medicalization, the "connections between professional and popular culture were unusually intimate in the United States."[48]

The ideological influence of progressivism also accounts, in part, for the transformation of a Freudianism that was ambivalent about the possibility of psychosexual reform into a neo-Freudianism that avidly embraced it. The "socially meliorist" atmosphere of progressivism was conducive to the flowering of the "optimistic" Freud of the early essays and the withering of the pessimistic Freud of *Civilization and its Discontents*, to the growth of a Freudianism that could theoretically justify the effort to reduce repression rather than a Freudianism that counseled resignation in the face of the irreconcilable conflict between the pleasure principle and the reality principle.[49]

The "social meliorism" of progressivism was itself decisively shaped by the "social feminism" of the women's movement of the nineteenth century. As William Leach has shown, "a straight line appears to connect [mid-nineteenth-century feminists] . . . with such later progressives as Jane Addams, John Dewey, Walter Lippman, and Herbert Croly." Much of the early twentieth-century Progressive agenda—preventive hygiene, social welfare, sex education, among others—incorporated demands that had for decades been central to middle-class feminism and that reflected the struggle of women to overcome their exclusion from the public sphere by infusing that sphere with what were understood to be specifically female sensibilities and concerns. Leach's demonstration of the "remarkable . . . extent to which feminism shaped . . . the [Progressive] reform impulse," combined with the recognition of the role of this reform impulse in the transformation of Freudianism into neo-Freudianism, compels the conclusion that this theoretical transformation was, in no small part, an indirect outcome of the extrafamilial gender struggle of the second half of the nineteenth century.[50]

This struggle had more direct, immediate effects on that transformation as well. A number of prominent neo-Freudian psychoanalysts in the 1920s and 1930s—including Karen Horney and Clara Thompson—were beneficiaries of the partially successful efforts of the late-nineteenth-century feminists to open up the professions—especially the "helping professions"— to women. Horney and Thompson sought to undermine Freud's patriarchal account of women's psychosexual development with a feminist account thereof, arguing that female submissiveness was not rooted in biology and thus was not the inevitable outcome of any conceivable set of childhood experiences but rather was the result of childhood experiences peculiar to particular cultures. In the name of feminism a psychoanalysis was forged that was based on the assumption of the preeminence of nurture over nature, culture over instinct. Since society shapes the drives, it follows that a certain kind of society is essential for—rather than an inherent obstacle to—their satisfaction.

This "culturalization" of psychoanalytic theory was, in turn, decisively affected by the increasingly intimate, reciprocal relationship between psychoanalysis and cultural anthropology during the 1920s and 1930s. Psychoanalytically informed anthropologists like Bronislaw Malinowski, Edward Sapir, Ruth Benedict, and, especially, Margaret Mead, lent cross-cultural support to the emerging neo-Freudian theory by purporting to demonstrate that an intense conflict between the pleasure principle and the reality principle—libido and culture—was by no means universal. The claim that there was little or no sexual repression in many tribal societies, whose child-rearing practices were very different and typically far more indulgent than our own, legitimated the reformist impulses of neo-Freudians like Horney and Harry S. Sullivan, whose increasing intellectual prominence, in turn, helped nurture the growing influence of what later came to be called the "culture and personality" school (rather than the more orthodox psychoanalytic anthropology of Geza Roheim) within American anthropology.[51]

This mutually reinforcing intellectual (as well as interpersonal) relationship was fostered by a series of conferences from the late 1920s to the mid-1930s to which these as well as other neo-Freudians and cultural anthropologists were invited, and that were organized by Larry Frank, executive director of the Laura Spelman Memorial of the Rockefeller Foundation, himself a neo-Freudian and a close personal friend of Margaret Mead. In sum, during the twenties and thirties "anthropologists and psychoanalysts were," in the words of Marvin Harris, "allies in the intellectual revolt against the constraints of sexual and other forms of provincialism,"[52] united, according to Christopher Lasch, in the "service of psychosexual reform."[53]

The very cultural anthropology that helped to shape neo-Freudianism was itself shaped by the feminization of the public sphere for which first-wave feminism was responsible. The historical connection between American anthropology in particular and the "soft" social sciences in general, on the one hand, and mid-nineteenth-century middle-class feminism, on the other, is so tight that during the latter part of that century the social sciences were often typecast as "women's work." Some of the major contributors to twentieth-century American anthropology, like Mead and Benedict, were women whose professional opportunities were as much the result of the gains of middle-class feminism as those of their neo-Freudian counterparts. By emphasizing the pivotal role of child rearing in cultural reproduction, moreover,

Mead and Benedict brought into bright focus a traditionally female preoccupation that had previously languished in the shadows of the discipline. Finally, this focus on child rearing was often accompanied by an explicitly feminist message concerning its effects: adolescent Samoan girls were portrayed by Mead—herself steeped in the nineteenth-century feminism of her mother—as "unneurotic" in part because of their relatively relaxed, frequent premarital sexual experiences.[54]

Thus nineteenth-century feminism contributed significantly in both direct and indirect ways to the neo-Freudian transformation of psychoanalysis. By the end of the 1930s this transformation was more-or-less complete. It was at this point that psychoanalysis became serviceable as a theoretical justification for child-centered child-rearing reforms. In 1938 Benjamin Spock—who had recently been analyzed—and his colleague Mabel Huschka published a long article in the prestigious *Practitioner's Library of Medicine and Surgery* that outlined in explicitly psychoanalytic terms the case in favor of child-centered child rearing that would later be articulated in more "commonsense" language in *Baby and Child Care*. Neo-Freudians like Frank, Erik Erikson, and Margaret Ribble made similar cases for more indulgence in the professional journals of psychology, child development, and education.[55]

The neo-Freudian account of repression as the source of neurosis encouraged a relentless critique of exactly those practices that were earlier seen as essential to the development of well-adjusted children. The neo-Freudian insistence on the importance of maternal gratification produced a celebration of the very mother love against which an earlier generation of psychologists and pediatricians had waged war. Arguments in favor of more indulgent, child-centered child rearing often relied not merely on the general assumptions of neo-Freudianism but also on the specific findings of the psychoanalytically informed anthropologists: "unneurotic" primitive people were typically cited as proof that the neurotic, compulsively competitive personalities of twentieth-century American society could be restructured in healthier, more cooperative directions if more relaxed, less severe child-rearing practices were adopted.

By the end of World War II, this psychoanalytically and anthropologically justified theory of child rearing achieved hegemony within professional circles. By this time as well the channels of mass communication began to be filled with advice that issued from these circles. Although there are few, if any, indications of psychoanalytic influence in the baby manuals and mother's magazines prior to World War II, following the war such indications abound. By the mid 1950s—a decade after the publication of Dr. Spock's amazingly successful *Baby and Child Care*—the monopoly of this advice over these channels was every bit as total as the disciplinary monopoly of the previous generation. A feminine public definition had completely displaced a masculine public definition of the right way to raise a child.

The reason for the rapid and widespread acceptance of this new definition should already be clear: it was consistent with the parenting interests of the mothers who embraced it. Unlike the pre-World War II generation of American mothers, post-World War II mothers no longer experienced a conflict between this maternal interest and their obligatory deference to male authority. This authority, newly feminized, now served to legitimate their indulgent inclinations. I will take the liberty of ending this section with a personal note that nicely captures this change. Referring to the disciplinary practices prescribed for her first child by her pediatrician in the mid-1930s, my mother confessed: "I didn't like it, but what could I do, I did what the doctor told me. But by the time you were born [nine years later], I had a new pediatrician, and nothing could stop me from giving you as much love as I wanted to give."

VI. Conclusion

I have argued in this presentation that post-World War II, child-centered child-rearing practices were the result of a gender struggle in the course of which women gained greater control over the child-rearing decisions that they alone have always and everywhere been obliged to carry out. In *Marxism and Domination* I suggested that these indulgent child-rearing practices, in turn, may well have procured the psychological possibility of finally ending this exclusively maternal obligation. The men who encountered these practices as boys, I reasoned, would be far more mother identified, and thus far more emotionally open to "mothering" their own children, than their pre-World War II predecessors. Hence they could be expected to be more receptive to contemporary feminist demands that they share in the care of the very young. Spockean boys, in short, are more likely to become coparenting men.

And coparenting men, I argued in *Marxism and Domination*, are necessary to the overcoming of patriarchy. When boys and girls are more or less equally nurtured and frustrated by both their mothers and their fathers, the rage that results from their frustration will no longer be disproportionately directed first at their mothers and then at all the women they represent. Moreover, since coparented boys and girls will both have a same-sex and an opposite-sex primary "love object," we can anticipate that gender-based differences in their object relations will disappear along with their misogyny. Thus when they become parents there should no longer exist a gender-based opposition in their parenting interests. In this way coparenting would ensure the obsolescence of the gender struggle to which human history has hitherto been held hostage.

If (a) coparenting would ensure the obsolescence of gender struggle, and (b) coparenting would not have been possible without Spockean practices, and (c) Spockean practices would not have been possible without the twentieth-century gender struggle that preceded them, then perhaps one day we will be able to remember that gender struggle as the gender struggle to end all gender struggles.

chapter four

. Grandiosity .

So I did not make a fool of myself in public. But in private it was a different matter. There I was a complete fool, a fool in love with Shayla. She was blonde, blue-eyed, and beautiful. Already at six months it was clear that she would be a "knockout," as the men who stopped me on the street to stare at her would say. I loved to wheel her down the aisle of my favorite supermarket and listen to the Jewish grandmothers kvell over her charms. "You'll have to keep the boys away from her." "She'll be a real heartbreaker." Music to my ears. Of course, it wasn't supposed to be. Looks weren't supposed to matter, and it was especially important that girls were noticed for other things. But feminist scruples were easily swept aside by looks that were impossible not to notice. The fact is that I was proud to be seen with Shayla. Especially when people told me that she looked like me. . . .

Until November the physical affection had pretty much gone one way, from me to her. But now she was able to hold on to me as I held on to her and to return my kisses with (what I persuaded myself were) kisses of her own. So we spent a lot of time hugging and kissing. And dancing. She loved the raucous rhythms of Tina Turner. But later in the evening I would let Smokey work his miracles and help wind her down for the night: "ooh-ooh, baby, baby." And baby would slip her hand under my shirt, and fall asleep touching my breasts. They couldn't give her food, but at least they could give her some comfort.

And at least I could look forward to feeding her soon. Ever since Shayla was five months old I had been bugging Dotty about getting her started on solid food. Now that she was seven months, it was high time. Dotty disagreed. She had been doing fine and would continue to do fine on breast milk alone. I could scarcely object to the first half of her argument: Shayla was smack in the middle of the charts for height and weight and had never even been sick. But the second half really bothered me. I had recently learned of Dotty's decision to nurse Shayla "for at least a year." Did she plan to keep her off everything but her milk until her first birthday? "Of course not." "Then when?" "When she's ready." "She's ready *now*—every other kid on the block her age has already been on solids for a long time."

This was but the first skirmish in what was to be a protracted gender struggle in our household. The dynamics of this struggle were both different from and similar to the one on which I had theoretically expounded. The difference was that part of me wanted Shayla to be dependent, only on her father as well as her mother. The concerns I had earlier expressed about the consequences of Dotty's nursing had intensified when I learned that it would last much longer than I had originally anticipated. If we could get Shayla started on some solid food—the first time I composed that phrase I inadvertently substituted "*my*" for "*some*"—at least I could get in on the (satisf)action while Dotty continued to nurse. And I would introduce Shayla to gastronomical delights that more than matched what her mother had to offer. We would see how breast milk would stack up against Häagen-Dazs vanilla! And if she had the good sense (of taste) to prefer the latter to the former, perhaps Shayla would lose interest in nursing and Dotty would stop sooner rather than later. That was my secret plan.

But that was only part of the story. The other part is that, however much I loved my baby, I also wanted her to grow up. Beginning to eat solid foods was a natural part of this process. So was learning to walk and talk. I often told Dotty that I couldn't wait to see Shayla six months from now when she would be able to do both. Dotty told me that she liked her just the way she was. When I told Dotty that I was worried about a recent decline in Shayla's rate of growth and that I was (admittedly quite irrationally) afraid that she wouldn't get any bigger, she (only half) joked that that would be fine with her. It seemed to Dotty that I was (just like any man!) too much in a hurry for Shayla to grow up. It seemed to me that Dotty (just like any woman!) didn't want her to grow up at all.

The standoff ended just before Thanksgiving when Shayla swallowed a single bean sprout at—you guessed it—one of our favorite Thai restaurants. That Dotty allowed this to happen was no doubt less the result of my persistent pressure than the fortuitous presence of a faithful female friend of the breast who felt nonetheless that one little sprout couldn't hurt our little sprout. I was silently triumphant. Soon I would have her eating out of the palm of my hand! A week or so later I fed Shayla mashed sweet potatoes at Thanksgiving dinner. She liked them. Sweet potatoes were only the beginning. From now on I would be able to feed her all kinds of things. Round one of the gender struggle was mine.

I won that battle but I was losing the war. Over the next few months it slowly dawned on me that Shayla's growing interest in my culinary concoctions would not be accompanied by a corresponding decline in her interest in Dotty's breasts. She liked them as much as ever. This was clearly not the zero-sum game I thought we were playing. Except when Shayla was really upset: those were the times that only the breast would do. Those were the times that tried my soul. Not to be able to console a child in pain was bad enough, but to have to hand her over to her mother for a sweet soporific suck was a public defeat that was just too humiliating to bear. For half of my waking hours I was still Shayla's constant companion, but when it came down to the crunch I was obliged to do what the average father who spends less than twenty minutes a day relating to his one-year-old is only too happy to do: hand the kid over to mommy.[1]

Every time people watched me do this I knew I was reproducing the taken-for-grantedness of the very division—the age-old division—between the involved mother and the uninvolved father that I so desperately wanted to overcome. Silently I screamed: I am not like all the others. But I *was*, at least in this one, all-too-important respect. I couldn't give what my baby wanted most.

This was the reason, I persuaded myself, that Shayla seemed generally to prefer the presence of her mother to her father. When the three of us were together it often seemed to me that there was a lot more going on between Dotty and her than between Shayla and me. When I returned from work Shayla was usually less excited to see me than she was to see her mother when she got back. And, although she wasn't experiencing a great deal of separation anxiety, she was normally more perturbed by Dotty's departures than mine. This was exactly what I had feared: Shayla loved Dotty more than me. I had hoped to overcome the effects of the breast by performing all the other tasks of mothering as well and as lovingly as Dotty. But I had been kidding myself. You can't beat the breast. And there was no end to it in sight. As Shayla approached her first birthday, Dotty announced that now she wasn't sure *when* she would stop. The beginning had been so painful. It was important that the end be as painless as possible.

I was pissed. At Dotty for calling the shots. At Shayla for breaking my heart. At the world for not recognizing that my heart was breaking. And at myself for getting myself into this mess in the first place. For the first time I really *felt* the temptation to backslide that I had anticipated intellectually some years earlier when I wrote the last chapter of *Marxism and Domination*.

There I had warned (after reading Diane Ehrensaft's provocative article "When Women and Men Mother"[2]) that the emotional insecurities of the coparenting man might well encourage him to "compensate for his failures in child rearing by becoming more emotionally involved in his work" and less emotionally involved with his child.[3] More recently I had learned of a study that seemed to confirm this warning: Graeme Russell found that an alarmingly high proportion (forty-one percent) of the Australian couples who were coparenting when he first interviewed them had reverted to a traditional division of labor by the time of his follow-up study two years later.[4] So I had been aware that my task would not be an easy one. Yet I never expected it to be as gut-wrenchingly difficult as it turned out to be.

Not getting as much recognition as I wanted from Shayla would have been bad enough. The fact that Dotty seemed to resent the recognition I did receive made it even worse. She was clearly less than pleased when our wakeful daughter would cry out for "papa" rather than "mama" during the middle of the night. Nor was she happy when Shayla would reach for my breast, not hers, as a source of comfort during the day. The Ehrensaft piece had prepared me theoretically for the possibility that even women who were deeply committed to coparenting might be reluctant to relinquish their traditionally preeminent place in their children's hearts.[5] But somehow it had never occurred to me that this might apply to my wife. Unfortunately it did. Dotty obviously needed to be number one.

First place with Shayla left second place for me. Since I worked days and Dotty worked nights, we never did have a whole lot of time together to begin with. Now most of that time was spent with Shayla. Very little was spent alone. Certainly not enough to make love all morning on the weekends as we used to. Now we tried to be home and fit it in during Shayla's relatively brief naps. Late nights were a total loss. I considered myself lucky to stay up long enough to get Shayla down. By the time Dotty came home from rehearsal, I was long gone.

But I had been prepared for less time to make love, and less time alone in general. All our friends had warned us that it came with the territory. What I hadn't been prepared for was how much of the time the three of us spent together would be devoted to Shayla, how rarely we could relate directly to each other, and how often instead we would relate to each other through our daughter. Dotty felt strongly that Shayla's needs came first; after all, Shayla was the infant, and I was the adult. *I* could wait. So Shayla got Dotty's attention whenever she wanted it. Even in the middle of my sentences. "She needs to learn she's not the only person in the world," I would object. But for Dotty she was, or so it seemed to me. Now that my wife had become a mother, I felt like I had lost my wife. An old story, but one no less painful for the millions of times it has been repeated.

The fear of losing Dotty made me hang on to her more tightly than ever. I had always had to fight the terrible temptation to take charge of her life. Now I was losing the battle. The demon that drove me to teach her how to eat, dress, and talk—in short, to live—was back in the saddle again. I was more "helpful" than ever and more angry at Dotty when she refused my help. Dotty responded in kind. The intensification of my paternalism was matched by a dramatic decline in her willingness to tolerate it. More ominously, she seemed increasingly unable to distinguish the manipulation from the many measures of simple, pure concern that remained. It seemed like half my time was spent trying to persuade her that she mistook the genuine article for the counterfeit as often as I presented the fake in the guise of the real and that this mistake was the result of expectations of control she had internalized long before she had ever met me.

The time spent was time wasted. Dotty refused to concede that her *mishegas** was part of the problem. If she occasionally mistook concern for control, it was only because there was so much of the latter and so little of the former. How could she be blamed for being defensive when there was so much shit to defend against? So we disagreed over the source of our disagree-

---

*Yiddish for "craziness"

ments. About the only thing we agreed on was that Dotty's pessimistic prediction had proved to be correct: our wars over time and space had gotten much, much worse.

My work wasn't exactly a safe harbor from this domestic storm. In fact it wasn't providing much comfort at all. I was troubled by the fact that I had written nothing on my book since the paper I had presented in early November. Two weeks were lost to a Christmas vacation in Arizona. Dotty, Ike, and Shayla at the Grand Canyon: Its majesty was lost on a still only eight-month old Shayla, but she worked her wonders on the starstruck guests inside the lodge.

At the end of March I left our magical child for a conference on "Women and Moral Theory" at Stony Brook. It was the first time since her birth eleven months earlier that we had spent even one day apart. Shortly after my arrival, I got sick to my stomach; Shayla, I learned from Dotty, was simultaneously puking her guts up back in Chicago. Hmm. Perhaps the bond between us was stronger than I realized. More likely we had both caught the same bug just before I left.

On the flight back I realized I was afraid Shayla wouldn't recognize me when I returned. But after about a minute of pretending not to notice me, she noticed me with a great big hug.

Back home there was another diversion. I was one of the featured speakers at a conference on Foucault sponsored by the institute that was scheduled for the beginning of May. I had agreed to do this in the fall because I had been certain that by the spring I would have one of my two principal theoretical adversaries down cold. But knowing Foucault well enough to demonstrate that the Spockean transformation couldn't be explained on the basis of his assumptions was a far cry from knowing him well enough to subject these assumptions to the full-scale feminist critique that conference participants had been promised. I would have a lot of catching up to do, and fast.

Dotty made this possible by agreeing to extra child care until I was done. It took me about three weeks to reread the relevant sections of Foucault's voluminous writings as well as the equally enormous outpouring of both appreciative and critical commentaries. It took another week to figure out that Foucault had hoisted himself on his own petard and that he could only get down with feminist theoretical help.

On the morning of April 22 I learned that some feminist practical help was needed at home. The labor of a good friend whom Dotty had promised to assist had begun, and Dotty would probably have to be at the hospital well into the night. This meant that I would have to prepare for, and that Dotty would not be present at, Shayla's first birthday party. Bad timing. I felt sad for Dotty and Shayla. But I felt scared for myself. This was the perfect occasion for a monumental public embarrassment. Shayla would cry for her mommy and have a generally rotten time. Dotty's relatives would kill me softly with their kindness, sympathizing with the plight of a father who had to take care of a child who wanted her mother. And I would feel like crawling under a rock.

None of this nightmare came to pass. Shayla wasn't at her exuberant best, but she didn't cry for Dotty and—judging from her dark-brown smile—she liked the chocolate cake into which she had submerged the entire front side of her head. A momentary loss of face for Shayla but none for her much-relieved father.

Over the next two weeks I wrote and typed up what I had figured out about feminism and Foucault. A close call. I had two days left to reread my talk the dozens of times it would take to be able to deliver it so that I could look at my audience and not at my notes. On the big day Dotty and Shayla were part of that audience. By all accounts, they and everyone else saw a good show. A couple of weeks later I took the show on the road to U-Mass Amherst. It felt good to be back in circulation. And to earn a journal article—that would subsequently be reprinted in two different anthologies—from the work that I had done on Foucault.[6] But it was the end of May, the academic year was over, in four months I would have to start teaching again, and I was no closer to finishing my book than I had been back in November.

At that time, you will recall, I had decided to expand my focus to include a number of child-rearing regimes that had preceded the reign of Dr. Spock. Since then I had, in fact, learned a great deal more about the concerns of the theoretical proponents of the repressive regime of the late-nineteenth to early twentieth century. A close reading of John Watson's *The Psychological Care of Infant and Child* helped me to understand the impetus for his fierce—even fanatical—opposition to maternal indulgence. Starting from the assumption that "parents build in [their children] everything that is later to appear," Watson warned that coddling, or "over-conditioning" in love, builds in an overdependence on parents that robs "the child of its opportunity for conquering the world." So maternal indulgence endangered the capacity of men to "conquer the world"! Just like the attacks of the cultural conservatives on the maternal "permissiveness" that emotionally fueled the sixties counterculture, Watson's war against "too much mother love" was informed by fears about the future of industrial civilization itself:

> Mothers just don't know when they kiss their children and pick them up and rock them, caress them and jiggle them upon their knee, that they are slowly building up a human being totally unable to cope with the world it must later live in.

The mother who would, in contrast, properly condition her child to cope with the modern world, "functions as a professional woman and not as a sentimentalist," and therefore observes the following rules:

> Treat [children] as though they were young adults. Let your behavior always be objective and kindly firm. Never hug and kiss them, never let them sit in your lap. If you must, kiss them once on the forehead when they say good night. Shake hands with them in the morning.

Mothers who follow these rules for treating their child "perfectly objectively" will succeed in creating a "child as *free as possible of sensitivities to people* [my emphasis] and one who, almost from birth, is relatively independent of the family situation [and is prepared] above all [for] problem-solving." This "problem-solving" child will also be a "happy child . . . who never cries unless actually stuck by a pin . . . and who finally enters manhood so bulwarked with stable work and emotional habits that no adversity can . . . overwhelm him."

Watson worried, however, that mothers might never be equal to the awesome task of preparing men for modernity. Thus (like Plato before him) he questions "whether there should be individual homes for children . . . or even whether children should know their own parents." But the home, he regretfully concluded, would always be with us, along with the mother. And, therefore, the following problem: how can you get a *woman* to raise a modern *man?* Apparently the behaviorist would just have to teach her.[7]

Watson's teachings, I had learned, approvingly echoed the earlier, less theoretically informed but equally stern, recommendations of the attending physician to New York Babies Hospital, Luther Emmet Holt, whose best-selling *The Care and Feeding of Children* (at least thirteen editions between 1894 and 1929) made him "as famous in his day as Dr. Spock in ours."[8] Holt's model for the home was the hospital: regularity was as important in the former as the latter. Infants should be fed precise quantities of milk at invariant intervals. They should be toilet trained virtually from birth; placing them on a pot "at exactly the same time every day" should enable them to be regular "by the second month." They should never sleep with or be kissed by their mothers. Neither should they by played with, especially if they are under six months old. If an infant cries to be "indulged" in these ways, it "should simply be allowed to cry it out."[9]

Thus both Holt and Watson transformed a specifically male parenting orientation into the best possible way to raise children. The interest of men both in breaking the ties between their children and their mothers and controlling their children once these ties were broken was secured through practical advice that was based on the theoretical assumption (of behaviorism or protobehaviorism) that no human relationships other than instrumental ones are possible and/or desirable. This assumption conveniently transformed the man who was as "free as possible of sensitivities to people" into the ideal child.

In my institute lecture, I had argued that the hegemony of this "masculinist" definition of legitimate child-rearing practices reflected male control of the public sphere from the end of the nineteenth century through the first three decades of the twentieth century. The Marxist (apparently unmoved by my argument) objects: "Aren't we really talking about a bourgeois definition of legitimate child-rearing practices that reflects capitalist control of the public sphere? After all, wasn't the doctrine of Holt and his ilk simply the application of Frederick Taylor's principles of 'scientific management' to the child, and weren't these principles originally elaborated in an effort to maximize the boss's control over, and thus his ability to extract profits from, the worker?" Balbus responds: To begin with, there is no evidence that the principles of "scientific management" were first developed in the factory and then extended to the home; in fact Holt's *Care and Feeding of Children* was published nine years before Taylor's first well-known effort, "Shop Management," and a full seventeen years before his most popular work, "The Principles of Scientific Management."[10] Even if, as Harry Braverman writes, Taylor "began to lecture, read papers and publish results [in] the 1890s,"[11] then at best we are talking about the contemporaneous development of, and presumably a mutually reinforcing relationship between, two doctrines and not a temporal and causal priority of one over the other.

Second, and more importantly, there is nothing specifically capitalist about the hierarchical relationship legitimated and (supposedly) perfected by Taylor; the domination of the manager over the worker is just as necessary to the fulfillment of the Central Plan as it is to the quenching of the capitalist's thirst for surplus value. That's why Lenin liked Taylorism: "We must organize in Russia the study and teaching of the Taylor system and systematically try it out and adapt it to our ends."[12] Thus Taylorism is not a specifically economic doctrine but rather a theory of how to maximize the power of one set of individuals over another set of individuals. So is the Holt et al. theory of child rearing. Power to the boss over the worker or power to the parent over the child: two versions of the same disciplinary solution to the problem of human governance.

"My point exactly," the unrepentant Foucauldian interjects. "Taylorism and Holtianism are merely two parts of the whole called the disciplinary society, a society in which power is exercised over individuals not by preventing them from getting what they want (repressive power, the law) but by ensuring that what they want is to conform (positive power, discipline).[13] The precisely scheduled conditioning to which the body of the Holtian infant is subjected is but one example of the 'meticulous control of the operations of the body' in contemporary society, one among many 'political technologies' that produce 'docile,' that is, simultaneously productive and obedient, bodies.[14]

Productive: the child who has been obliged from birth to subordinate the internal signals of his or her body to the signals imposed on him or her from the outside, the child who has thus learned to conquer his or her body, is the child who, as Watson advertised, will take full advantage of 'its opportunity for conquering the world.' Obedient: the child who has learned from infancy the necessity of postponing pleasure can have no brief against, and will in fact happily adapt to, a civilization in which deferred gratification is the general order of the day. It is the imperatives of this distinctively modern, disciplinary society, and not those of 'masculinity,' that are reflected in the harsh childrearing regime of late nineteenth-to-mid-twentieth century America."

My rejoinder: this is a false opposition. There is, as Simmel was perhaps the first to recognize, a sense in which "modern society" is a peculiarly masculine civilization: "There is an essential connection between the process of objectification and the male character."[15] The definition of the other as an object over which control must be exercised is, as I argued in my institute lecture, a conceptual expression of the object relations of men. "Mind over matter" comes naturally to men, who, more than women, are compelled to try to prove that their mothers don't matter.

But if objectification is an expression of the object relations of men and male domination has been culturally universal, why haven't all cultures been equally committed to objectification? How, in other words, is it possible to reconcile Simmel's claim of an "essential connection between objectification and the male character" with the specifically modern, European obsession with objectification?

This is precisely the problem I explored in the ninth chapter of *Marxism and Domination*. I tried to specify the precise historical conditions under which a culturally universal domination of women is transformed into the culturally specific, Western domination of nature. My point of departure was the depth-psychological connection uncovered by Dorothy Dinnerstein between the fact that women have always taken care of young children and the fact that adults have always symbolized the earth as a woman. Because every infant depends on a woman for its survival, it is she who becomes the world to which the infant is symbiotically related and from which he or she will eventually be obliged to separate. Thus it is that the child comes to conceive the natural world that is both the source of his or her being, and the "other" in relationship to which this being is defined, in feminine terms: woman becomes the representative of nature because our childhood relationship with our mothers is paradigmatic of our subsequent relationship with our natural surround. The earth, in short, becomes "mother nature" because it is by a mother that we have all been nurtured.

It follows that our intense ambivalence toward our mothers will be projected onto nature: "she" is both the mother whom we love and on whom we wish to remain dependent and the mother whom we hate because that wish cannot be fulfilled. Thus our love-hate relationship with our mother becomes a love-hate relationship with nature; nature will be symbolized both as the loving woman to whom we owe our life and as the dreaded, dangerous woman who must be dominated or even destroyed. Dinnerstein acknowledges that the balance between "respect, concern, awe" and "hostility and rapacity" varies "from culture to culture" and that it "need not always be tipped in the same direction for woman and for nature."[16] But she does not attempt to explain the changing character of that balance, and why, in particular, it has been "tipped" dramatically in the direction of "hostility and rapacity" toward nature since the early modern era in the West.

Enter Balbus. My idea was that child-rearing practices that were considerably harsher (even during relatively indulgent periods) in modern societies than traditional societies were responsible for the peculiarly pernicious Western conception of nature. A cross-cultural comparison revealed that Western mothers not only typically touch their children much less but also frustrate them much more, and much earlier, than non-Western mothers. The Western (or westernized) child has normally been nursed for a much shorter period, sometimes (as we have seen) on schedule rather than on demand, has been toilet trained earlier, and probably more severely, and has been genitally more repressed.[17] He or she—especially he—is therefore likely to experience a much less intense primary identification with the mother than the traditional child. At the same time, the resentments that inevitably accompany separation from the mother will necessarily accumulate much sooner within the Western than the traditional child, since separations from her have likewise been imposed much earlier on the former than the latter.

Thus we can assume that the Western child's symbolization of nature, in contrast to his or her traditional counterpart, is established during a period of intensely ambivalent feelings toward the mother, with the mother serving as an object of both love and hate. This balance will tilt more toward hate in the case of the male child, whose "normal" masculine development demands that he define himself in active opposition to his mother. Since his masculinity also demands that he define himself against the world that represents her, we should expect that his unconscious emotional balance will be tipped even more than his sister's in the direction of "hostile and rapacious" feelings toward nature.

After completing *Marxism and Domination* I discovered that there is cognitive developmental, and not only psychoanalytic, support for this hypothesis. Piaget has argued that a child's feelings of "participation" and "communion" with the world result from a "continual response of the [maternal] environment," and thus from a "complete continuity between its parents' activities and its own." Consistent maternal gratification ensures an "absence of differentiation between the world and the self." This sense of differentiation—for Piaget the *disappearance* of feelings of participation and communion—only develops with the child's "liberation from the bond that ties him . . . to his parents."[18] Since this bond can only be broken by the frustrations imposed on the child by his or her mother, Piaget's argument is consistent with the claim that maternal deprivation is the foundation for the modern sense of separation between self and world. (Except that Piaget wouldn't call it deprivation since he treats the sense of separation that results from it as the culmination of the child's cognitive development, crowning the West as the Best in the process.)

It was not until the seventeenth century that this "realistic," modern worldview came to replace the more participatory, medieval worldview that had prevailed for centuries within the West. From the cross-culturally fertilized feminist psychoanalytic theory of *Marxism and Domination* it was therefore possible to infer that (what Max Weber called) this "disenchantment of the world" must have been preceded by an unprecedented increase in the severity of Western child rearing. In fact I had drawn exactly this inference shortly after completing that book. But I had never understood why this hypothesized hardening of child-rearing practices had happened.

Now I thought I did. From my gender-struggle theory the hypothesis could be derived that this hypothetically unprecedented increase in the severity of child-rearing practices must have been the result of a correspondingly unprecedented increase in the power of fathers over the mode of child rearing during this time. Now that would be a hypothesis that was really worth testing!

And so I began to toy with the idea of expanding my book in order to verify it.

To do so I would have to write a new first historical chapter that would be devoted to a description and explanation of the (hypothesized) transformation from late medieval to early modern child-rearing practices. Of course this expansion of my temporal horizons would also require an expansion of my spatial horizons. Once I pushed things back to the Middle Ages, I would no longer be able to focus exclusively on America. So I would not only be adding centuries but also countries to my study. I knew I would be facing a shitload of additional work.

This would mean a long delay in the completion of my project. But the results might be worth the wait. If all went well, perhaps I would be able to make a memorable contribution to the perennial problem of the origins of the Western industrial worldview. My gender-struggle theory offered a solution to that problem that no one else who had tackled it—not Marx, not Weber, not Durkheim, not Freud—had been able to invent. If I could show that modernization was, even in part, a result of the masculinization of the mode of child rearing, these master thinkers would have to make room for me.

chapter five

. Separation Anxiety .

$\mathcal{W}$hat chutzpah! But beneath this bravado I was barely breathing. The fact was that I was scared by the scope of my subject. Five centuries of child-rearing changes was a lot to take on, and I wondered if my theoretical assumptions were strong enough to carry so much historical weight. I decided to look for additional sources of support for those assumptions.

I found to my satisfaction that my theoretically derived notion of a gender-based opposition in parenting interests was consistent with the perceptions of contemporary boys and girls, at least within the West. James Walters's and Nick Stinnet's extensive 1971 summary of ten years of research on the way children perceive their parents concludes that "children [of both genders] experience their fathers as colder . . . and less nurturant than they do their mothers" and their mothers as "being less restrictive and punitive than [their] fathers."[1]

So much for the recent past. But what about earlier times? Leafing through a half-dozen exhaustive reviews of child-rearing manuals from the sixteenth through the twentieth centuries, I discovered that the authors of those manuals invariably expected (and, in both the Calvinist and behaviorist periods, deplored) that women would be more indulgent parents than men. Similarly, studies of the diaries of parents during this five hundred-year period revealed that husbands consistently condemned, and sought to prevent, the spoiling of their children by their wives, and that wives regularly resented, and attempted to mitigate, the harshness of their husbands. Nowhere did I find a single reference to the reverse.[2] So I was persuaded that my psychodynamic explanation for a gender-based opposition in parenting interests was an explanation for what was, in fact, a widely shared, long-standing cultural expectation.

But was it a culturally universal expectation? I discovered to my delight that it was. Morris Zelditch's study of "role differentiation in the nuclear family" of seventy-five different societies found no unambiguous exceptions to the general rule that the "male adult will play the role of instrumental leader [discipline and control] and the female adult will play the role of expressive leader [security and comfort]."[3] Similarly, Stephens's survey of 250 societies concludes that "in contrast to the father, the mother tends not to receive deference, demands less in the way of 'formality' and respect, and is less strict. . . . No ethnographer describes the mother as stricter than the father."[4]

Stephens also shows that when mothers clearly have more control over child-rearing decisions than fathers—as they do in those societies in which polygamy, long postpartum sex taboos, and separate mother-child households combine to create a "diluted marriage complex" that weakens the influence of the father over his children—they tend to be more "attentive and succorant" than mothers who do not. "Societies high on all the diluted marriage variables . . . tend strongly to be high on 'initial indulgence of dependency.'"[5]

This connection between maternal power over child rearing and maternal "indulgence" of children is exactly what my theory would have predicted. The expectation of a gender-based opposition in parenting interests that I had deduced from feminist psychoanalytic theory was confirmed cross-culturally not only by ethnographic reconstructions of the perceptions of indigenous informants but also by the behavior of indigenous parents themselves. So much for the claim that the theory was "culture-bound." Even though I was only trying to explain a pattern of child-rearing transformations in the West, I was pleased to be able to conclude that there was nothing ethnocentric about the theory on which that explanation would be based and that no one would justly be able to accuse me of a parochialism that betrayed the old assumption that the West is Best.

But there was nevertheless a difference between the West and the Rest. If a gender-based opposition in parenting interests is culturally universal, it was clear to me that the form of gender struggle that grew out of that opposition was not. There were many—perhaps most—non-Western societies in which conflicting parenting orientations did not seem to manifest themselves in recurrent, everyday conflict between parents over child-rearing practices. The extreme sex segregation characteristic of Stephens's "diluted marriage complex" societies, for example, effectively excludes the father from any responsibility for early child care and thus precludes from the outset any ongoing conflict between him and his spouse(s) over the nature of that care.

The opposition in their parenting interests assumes instead the form of the following structural compromise: everything happens as if fathers agree that both their daughters and their sons are the exclusive responsibility of their mother (and her kin) until their sons are old enough to become the responsibility of their fathers (and other men). Thus mothers keep their daughters and prepare them for motherhood, while men take their sons in order to break their tenacious ties with their mothers and turn them into "self-sufficient" men. Under these circumstances we should expect gender struggle between fathers and mothers to occur at the boundary of the female and male worlds through which the boy must pass, that is, over the timing and severity of the male initiation he is obliged to endure.

Lacking a gender-struggle theoretical lens, most anthropologists have not seen fit to record such conflicts. One prominent exception is Kenneth Read's vivid, moving depiction of the simultaneously sorrowful and vengeful collective resistance of the women of the Gahuku tribes of New Guinea to the effort of the men to initiate their sons.[6] And, more recently, Gilbert Herdt has described the sometimes forcible separation of Sambian boys from their mothers and the ritualized maternal mourning that follows it.[7] I had discovered two ethnographies that confirmed my theoretically based expectations concerning the form of gender struggle over child rearing in highly sex-segregated societies. Surely there were others either waiting to be uncovered or to be written in the first place. If there were, perhaps it might even be possible to demonstrate that the gender struggles they described were a principal source of change within Lévi-Strauss's misleadingly labelled societies "without history."

My historical and cross-cultural research had increased my confidence in the soundness of my theoretical assumptions. But I was still plagued by doubts about my project. It was already mid-July, and I had been working on my book for almost a full year. It would probably take at least two more years to complete it. Was it sufficiently important to justify the time and energy I would have to devote to it? Just what was so important about a gender-struggle explanation of the history of Western child rearing, anyway?

I reminded myself that this explanation was an effort to make good on the claim I made in my last book concerning the determining power of the mode of child rearing. I could always defend my project on the grounds that it was necessary for the defense of that theoretical claim. But why was it so important to defend that theoretical claim? Surely not just to prove that I had been right.

I was not just a theorist, I was a critical theorist, which meant that I believed that theory was only as important as its contribution to the practice of human emancipation. The particular emancipatory practice to which I was currently committed was coparenting. Thus my gender-struggle theory would ultimately have to be justified in terms of its contribution to coparenting practice.

On further reflection I remembered that it was precisely this theory-practice connection that had sparked my interest in Spock in the first place. In *Marxism and Domination* I had hypothesized that the contemporary commitment of men to coparenting was emotionally rooted in the Spockean practices they had encountered as boys, and it was this hypothesis that was in large part responsible for my selection of the Spockean transformation—rather than any other—as the initial object of my theoretical explanation. I had reiterated that hypothesis at the very end of my first effort to outline this explanation in my Humanities Institute lecture. So all along that hypothesis had served as the link between my theory and my practice.

But this meant that this link was only as strong as that hypothesis. The problem was that I was not at all sure of its strength. Was it really the case that Spockean boys were more likely to become mothering men?

There was yet another problem. If the ultimate justification for my theoretically informed history of practices within (what I now decided to call) the maternal mode of child rearing was that it would help me understand the roots of—and thus contribute to—the contemporary struggle to replace that mode of child rearing with coparenting, then there was no good reason to end my history around 1950. Although Spockean practices achieved ascendence among the educated middle classes around that time, they did not win the allegiance of working-class parents until much later, if at all. Moreover, even if by the mid-1980s the commitment to these practices was far more widespread than it was three or four decades ago, there was no reason to assume that this commitment was any more irreversible than the commitment to the indulgent practices of the early to mid-nineteenth century.

To the contrary: my assumption that Spockean practices express the parenting orientations of women leads us to anticipate male resistance to Spockean practices and thus to the universalization of what, according to my hypothesis, were the psychological preconditions to the commitment to coparent. An effort to assess the prospects of coparenting would, therefore, have to in-

clude an account of the forms and strength of that masculine resistance.

These reflections seemed to shed new light on the increasing
influence of cognitive developmental psychology both inside and
outside the academic world. Since the late 1970s, child-rearing
manuals infused with this psychology had been competing for
parental favor with those that were informed by the neo-Freudianism that preceded it.[8] I hadn't yet read these manuals, so I
didn't know how their advice compared with the advice of Spock
and his cohorts. But the mere fact that the new advice was a practical application of a theory based on an equation between mental
development and human development led me to suspect that this
advice might be a contemporary form of masculine resistance to
the prevailing feminine regime.

From Plato to Piaget, the subordination of the body to the
mind implicit in the equation of the cognitive and the human has
always been one characteristic expression of the emotional man-
date of men to repudiate their eminently embodied identification
with their mothers. As Carol Gilligan has argued, cognitive psychology's explicit account of development merely reproduces
this male flight from the mother and the world she represents in
the guise of a supposedly invariant, gender-neutral sequence
through which all minds ideally progress. The "fully developed"
child reaches exactly that place where men have always wanted
their children (especially their male children) to be: independent
of their (m)others.[9] This outcome, moreover, requires neither
coercion nor conditioning but only an intellectual environment
that is conducive to the optimal unfolding of an ostensibly universal developmental process. Who could blame parents if they
tried to push this process?

The idea that cognitive developmental psychology was the latest entry in a long line of legitimations of the parenting orientations of men had intriguing implications. There was a curious
affinity between the historical sequence from Calvinism to behaviorism to developmentalism and what developmentalist
Lawrence Kohlberg claimed was a cross-culturally invariant se-

quence in the development of individual moral reasoning. Kohlberg's thesis is that *if* moral development takes place, it *must* follow a path in which first the self-regarding consequences of individual action (the preconventional level), then particular societal norms (the conventional level), and finally universal principles (the postconventional level) are the criteria by means of which "morally relevant" conflicts are resolved.[10]

At the preconventional level, the individual identifies "right action" with action that maximizes his or her pleasure and minimizes his or her pain. The seventeenth- or eighteenth-century Calvinist effort to break the will of the child—to enforce obedience with physical punishment—would seem both to presuppose and reinforce precisely such a moral economy within the child. The late-nineteenth-century to early-twentieth-century emphasis on conditioning—on will-training rather than will-breaking—looked like the collective historical analogue of the conventional level, at which individual moral decisions are based on the internalization of norms whose violation would define individuals as "deviant." And the individual at the postconventional level who subordinates both self-interest and societal conventions to abstract principles of justice would appear to be the likely result of a child-rearing regime for which the optimal development of formal thinking was the overarching ideal. (Perhaps this is why Kohlberg and his colleagues have found so few individuals who reason at this "level"; insufficiently institutionalized, their theory has yet to become a self-fulfilling prophesy.[11]) Thus alongside Kohlberg's allegedly universal sequence of preconventional, conventional, and postconventional forms of individual moral reasoning I had identified what appeared to be a parallel historical sequence of preconventional, conventional, and postconventional forms of masculine parenting ideology.

I wasn't sure what this meant. Anthropologists and psychologists alike have argued that Kohlberg's theory is ethnocentric, that what he assumes to be a universally human sequence of individual moral development is really only the sequence of the moral "development" of individuals in the West.[12] (Yet another

West-is-Best theory.) If they are right, could they be right because (a) the stages of individual moral reasoning identified by Kohlberg are disproportionately associated with the specific child-rearing regimes that I had identified and (b) these child-rearing regimes are normally not found in non-Western societies? Was this a case of Western ontogeny (individual development) recapitulating Western phylogeny (the development of civilization)?

This implied that the historical sequence of masculine parenting ideologies that I had identified could justifiably be described as a developmental sequence. Kohlberg claims that his sequence of individual moral reasoning entails development because each successive stage is defined by a type of thinking that enables the individual to resolve problems for which the individual at the preceding stage could find no solution. Could the same be said of the sequence that ran from the Calvinist to the behaviorist to the developmentalist "stages" of the effort of men to solve their twin problems of severing the ties between their children and their mothers and controlling their children once these ties (or so they believed) had been broken? Was cognitive/moral development a more effective solution to these problems than conditioning, and conditioning a more effective solution than coercion? Had a historical learning process taken place within the framework of the psychodynamically governed "object relations" of men? If so, how could this learning process be explained?

I tried not to think about these questions as I slathered Shayla's skin with the number 15 sunblock that was supposed to protect it from the burning brightness of Blacks' Beach. In late July the family had taken off on a two-week trip to California. California. Too many Chicago winters and too few professional prospects had persuaded both Dotty and myself that this is where we wanted to wind up. So west we went, both to check in with an old friend and to check out the intellectual and artistic scene. An offer from a university in or near the Los Angeles area would put me where Dotty felt she needed to be. But full professors are not normally "marketable" unless a heavyweight reputation precedes them. So I knew that my new book would have to be a big hit in order to increase my mobility.

Shayla's mobility had been increasing by literal leaps and bounds. Now fifteen months old, she was running us ragged, at least until her still not entirely corrected feet tripped her up. I worried about the frequency of her falls. But not Shayla. No matter how hard she hit the ground, she picked herself up with scarcely a complaint and continued on her merry way. I learned to suppress my urge to console her, and even to appreciate her multiple bruises as the mark of an unusually resilient little girl.

But right now my barefooted little girl was heading, hatless and upwind, straight for a large pool of ice-cold water that had formed on the beach directly below Big Sur. I wanted her out of that water. California or not, it was fucking freezing. Dotty disagreed. You didn't get colds from being cold, you got them from viruses. This, I thought, was bullshit. I *knew* from years of experience that you catch a cold from catching a chill, that sneezes follow shivers like night follows day. Maybe my mother had been overprotective, but on this one she was surely right.

We were rehearsing one of our standard arguments, but now it was our daughter's health, and not Dotty's, that was at stake. We decided to compromise and let Shayla stay in the water, and then in a more protected spot on the beach, a little longer. I was sure she would get sick.

A day and a half later Shayla's temperature climbed past 103. That meant not only a cold but probably an ear infection as well (she had been getting them frequently over the past few months). And that meant a ten-day course of antibiotics. So after dinner we left my cousins' home in La Jolla and headed with their help to the nearest clinic. An ear infection it was. Oh shit, there goes the five days of sun and fun on Blacks' Beach.

But Dotty reminded me that our pediatrician had told us that there is no harm in a kid with a fever being on a beach. I was dubious. The next morning Dotty called her long distance and confirmed her recollection: no problem. I remained dubious. This was certainly not what my mother had taught me. But I tried to shut out her voice and let in the latest in modern medical opinion. After all, I wanted to spend a week on the beach too.

The scorching sun might not be making Shayla's ear any worse, but it could still give her a hell of a burn. And the same doctors who allowed her on the beach with a temperature also warned that one outbreak of blisters was all it took significantly to increase her subsequent risk of cancer. I was determined that not a single blister would ever form on her precious alabaster skin. Hence the care I took to ensure that every inch of her beautiful little body was covered with heavy-duty sunblock. And this precaution, I felt, was still insufficient. This might be a "clothing-optional" beach, but there was no option for Shayla. After two hours of *frei korper kultur** it was time for a head-to-toe cover-up. So for the better part of the day Shayla meandered midst the naturists dressed in Dotty's antinuke T-shirt, neckerchief, and "little slugger" baseball hat, drawing attention as far as the naked eye could see.

In between the cover-ups we managed to have a magnificent time. Earlier in the summer I had taken her for swimming lessons at the Y, hoping that by the time California dreaming became a reality she would greet the water as the old friend that it was. She did. Shayla loved me to hold her tightly as a wave approached, commanding me to lift her quickly out of the water so it would harmlessly pass her by. Waves of laughter followed until her next "Up!" and my next response. I marvelled at her persistent bravado.

When she finally got tired I would walk her on my shoulder until she fell asleep, then put her down on our blanket for a much needed nap. Covering her with a towel, I made sure that nothing but shade fell on her face. Now Dotty and I would have our one chance of the day to spend some time alone in the water (without however ever taking our eyes off Shayla).

Alone-time was something that I still felt was lacking in our life. Yet Dotty could correctly point out that for some time now

---

*free body culture

we had been leaving Shayla with a sitter on Friday or Saturday evenings (sometimes both), and that we were, in fact, going out almost as often as before her birth. And it was also true that we had started to rotate responsibility for Saturday afternoon play dates with the parents of Shayla's best friend Emma, which made it possible for us to be together for several hours during the day once every two weeks.

But somehow it wasn't enough. I seemed to need more time with Dotty now that Shayla was such a big part of our lives. However much time Dotty and I actually spent together, I found myself frequently fighting the feeling that I was losing her, or that she was already gone. Now that I had just about everything I had ever wanted, everything seemed to be completely out of my control.

Control was definitely something I was seeking in my home. I did not like a messy apartment. It didn't have to be as squeaky-clean as the one in which I grew up, where clean ashtrays myste-riously replaced dirty ones before my father could even light up his next Pall Mall. But it had to be orderly. Everything in its place. But Shayla was a one-person wrecking crew, displacing if not destroying everything that was unlucky enough to find itself in her path. My recognition that these pathbreaking forays were harmless, even necessary, explorations of the effects of au-tonomous action didn't make me like them any better. They were driving me nuts.

I tried to vary my tactics for the restoration of order. At times I would try to turn "cleanup" into a game, hoping that she would learn to take as much pleasure putting things back together as she did taking them apart. Fat chance. At other times I took a tougher tack, demanding in a firm but still friendly voice that she straighten up the mess she had made. All this did was to help make *no* one of her favorite words. At my worst times I simply screamed. That tactic didn't work any better than the others.

Nothing worked. The result was that I spent what seemed like hours cleaning up after her. Not just at the end of the day, when it would have made sense. At least to someone sane enough to tolerate a house that looked like it had been hit by a tornado. That someone was certainly not me. So on the days that I was home with Shayla, I became her full-time, live-in maid.

I was also becoming her expert on etiquette, especially at the dinner table. I wanted her to use her fork instead of her fingers. And to not throw her food. Or get it all over the dresses which, for reasons that I was sure could only be genetic, she increasingly preferred to her jeans. Of course the theoretical Ike was well aware that an "advance in the threshold of shame and revulsion" with respect to behaviors that were once considered perfectly normal was the terrible price of what Norbert Elias has called this "civilizing process."[13] But the paternal Ike was more than happy to have Shayla pay it. It was pitiful. The theorist of the "postinstrumental" society had turned into a partisan of the practice of Emily Post.

Emily would not have appreciated the following scene. Back home from our vacation, Shayla has just awakened from her nap. She sits on the floor next to her bed, on top of a large pile of shit. Shit covers her entire body: her legs, her stomach, even her mouth. Her unperturbed demeanor suggests that her poopy paint job has left her feeling neither shame nor revulsion. Only a bit puzzled, judging from the "Dis?, Dis?" (short, we have learned, for "What's this?") that greets her astonished parent. Acting unfazed, parent wraps child in a large towel, brings her downstairs, and gives her a bath. Fortunately the parent is not me. I was only too happy to learn about this secondhand from Dotty. It was then that I first started to think about toilet training.

chapter six

. Shayla .

*i*t was September, and the shit was about to hit the fan. I was heading back to the classroom. It had always been difficult if not impossible for me to make much progress on my writing while I was teaching full-time. And now I would be close to a full-time father as well.

I had arranged my teaching schedule to enable me to be as involved with Shayla during the second academic year of her life as I was during the first. My lower-division undergraduate courses would be held twice a week for two hours (instead of the usual four times a week for one hour) and my upper-division undergraduate and graduate seminars would be taught for three hours in the evening of one of the two days I would be teaching during the day. This would mean one hell of a hard Monday, but it would allow me to spend all day Tuesday and Friday with my daughter. Thursday was, in principle, available for writing, but I knew from past experience that other work-related responsibilities—seeing students, grading papers, attending meetings—would absorb much of that day as well.

So day-time writing was for all practical purposes out of the question. And the evenings didn't look good either, since I would have to be "on" for Shayla three of the four evenings during the work week when I wasn't teaching. Half of me hoped I would have sufficient strength to put paper to pen after I put Shayla to bed. But the other half figured I would be lucky to get through the day with body and mind intact and that my book would just have to wait until next summer. The first half was freaked at the prospect of a prolonged delay in my project, but the other half secretly welcomed a break from the problems with which the project continued to be plagued. I didn't want to admit it, but I was looking for a respite from my research.

But *respite* was hardly the right word to describe what I got from Shayla. She was a high-energy handful. She loved to run and roughhouse. Her legs were still covered with bruises from the frequent falls from which she would promptly and uncomplainingly pick herself up. My face was now covered with scratches from the nails of the little fingers that flailed wildly as we tickled and tumbled together on the floor. Already at seventeen months she was displaying the gross motor skills and tackling the large muscle tasks that are typical of boys, but not girls at that age. And her muscles showed it: Shayla was strong.

She was, I learned from Dotty, easily a match for the bigger boy bruisers with whom she had been in a weekly playgroup for almost a year. (When Dotty had informed me that this group would meet on Thursdays, when I would be at school, I did not protest. I feared that a male would not be entirely welcome at an otherwise entirely female affair. This was "women's space" into which I was not inclined to intrude. The one time I substituted for an ailing Dotty persuaded me that my inclinations had been correct. I was received cordially, but it seemed to me that there was little, if anything, to talk about. Perhaps it was difficult for the mothers to talk about "them" when one of them was there.) Shayla did not back down from, but responded in kind, to their aggressive assaults. And sometimes she initiated some of her own. No timid toddler she. She was tough.

I liked that. One of the points of coparenting was to raise a girl who was every bit as assertive as a boy. So far so good. Shayla was not hiding behind mommy's skirts (or daddy's pants); she was learning to stand up for herself. Maybe she would even learn the long throw from third-to-first, the pump-fake, the overhead smash. I looked forward to teaching her all the sports that had always been such a big part of my life. I wanted her to experience the pure joy of effortless athletic effort, those magical moments when mastery of the game accompanies a complete surrender to its demands.

My sense was that such moments were already hers. Every Tuesday morning I took her to the Y for "swim and gym." The swim she enjoyed, but the gym was really her forte. She was the first child her age successfully to negotiate the metal monkey bars to which she was immediately attracted. She was the only girl her age who even tried. Fearlessly she would climb up, scamper across, and climb down again, repeating this sequence over and over again until it was time for a swim. The mothers were amazed. The teacher told me she was a Mary Lou Retton in the making. I was proud of my daring daughter.

Entering the men's locker room, I felt a little daring myself. This was where I had to get Shayla into her swimsuit. But this was classical masculine territory, one of the last bastions of male bonding in an increasingly sex-integrated society. I wondered how the jocks would react to our invasion of their patriarchal preserve, to the sight of a man changing a little girl amidst their smelly sweat or taking her into the shower where they lathered up to lose it. And Shayla was not shy. Running (my protests notwithstanding) half-naked from one end of the room to the other, she made it impossible for them not to notice. To my surprise, most of them were enchanted by her presence. Somehow I had forgotten that many of the musclemen were also fathers and that some of them had kids her age. So we talked about our kids in the men's locker room! And I learned that on Saturday morning (mom's morning off) this room was filled with fathers and their toddlers who were, like Shayla and I, making the passage from gym to swim. This warmed my hopeful heart.

So did the sleepy face in my rearview mirror that I couldn't not watch as I drove us from swim to lunch. God, what a precious punum.* How could such a tough cookie be such a little angel? She was a remarkably caring little creature. She seemed genuinely concerned about the welfare of the other, less-hardy kids in her class, helping them back to their feet after their frightening falls. And she was so sweet to her best friend Emma. Just after Shayla turned eighteen months, Dotty recounted this story to me: Emma was over at our house and having a hard time; she couldn't stop crying. Shayla seemed pained by Emma's pain and tried to cheer her up. To no avail. Then Shayla walked out of the room, returned with a Kleenex which she handed to Emma, and uttered the word "eyes" as she motioned to her to dry them. Shayla's tenderness tamed the tears of her friend but moistened the eyes of her mother.

That was Shayla: tough but tender. Empathic yet assertive. She was a decidedly different being from both the boys and the girls her age. According to feminist psychoanalytic theory, you will recall, more-or-less exclusively mother-raised girls are normally more "relational" than boys because their intimate early relationship with their mother is unconsciously experienced as the source of, rather than an obstacle to, their gendered sense of self. Yet the very identification with the mother that is so essential to the female self prevents its unambivalent assertion: the girl transforms the powerful grudge that all (mother-raised) children hold against their mother into a grudge against herself, resentfully repudiating the authority of mommy by undermining the authority of mommy within. Thus most women wind up relational but submissive, emotionally prepared to defer to the others—especially the male others—on whom they have learned to depend.

This should no longer be true of the coparented girl. Having also, and more or less equally, submitted to the authority of her father, she would no longer hold a special grudge against her mother, and thus against herself. Her need for the other would

_____
*Yiddish for "face"

no longer be poisoned by hatred of herself. The withering of the roots of self-abnegation, moreover, would be accompanied by the growth of new shoots of self-assertion. Now that the girl was also intensely identified with her father, she would have (as the boy has always had) an opposite-sex love object against whom to establish her female identity. Her self would, in part (but only in part, since she would still be closely identified with her mother), have to be defined by her difference from daddy. Thus she would gain self-assertion without losing relationality.

Ever since Shayla's birth I had worried that she would be less identified with me than with her mother and that the results of our practice would, therefore, fall short of this theoretical pre-diction. But at eighteen months she was precisely the happy syn-thesis of traditionally masculine and feminine attributes that co-parenting was supposed to produce. Even if the bond between Shayla and me wasn't strong enough to satisfy the conditions of my ego, it was apparently sufficiently strong to satisfy the condi-tions for my theory. How else could her remarkable realization of its promise be explained?

There were other, related respects in which my year-and-a-half-old daughter was the best possible "proof" (that one child could ever be) of coparenting theory. Right on Stoller's schedule, she was beginning to discover that she was a girl and not a boy.[1] But that discovery, as far as I could tell, produced none of the dis-appointment that traditionally accompanies it. On the one hand, she was as preoccupied as her conventionally raised cohorts with her core gender identity; she made use of genital and other cues to determine that her gender was the same as her mother's and different from her father's. Guessing the gender of the people she saw on the street, on TV, or on the pages of the daily newspaper became one of her favorite games. It was a game she quickly mas-tered. I was amazed at her sensitivity to the subtlest of sex-specif-ic signals. It was one thing to be able to distinguish a man from a woman by type of clothes or length of hair but quite another to make accurate distinctions on the basis of facial features alone. Yet almost without exception Shayla correctly identified the faces in the photos that she scanned. An understandable exception: she thought Michael Jackson was a girl.

On the other hand, the fact that Shayla was increasingly aware that boys were different from girls did not seem to mean that she thought they were any better. She was burdened by none of the manifestations of "castration anxiety" that first Anna Freud and then Herman Roiphe and Elanor Galenson found to be so typical of female toddlers her age. I witnessed neither a "loss of zest and enthusiasm" nor an "upsurge in hostile aggression" disproportionately directed at her mother during this period.[2] Shayla was as full of life as ever, and when she was angry she was every bit as angry at me as at Dotty. Nor did she seem to suffer from the "penis envy" to which a girl's castration anxiety is supposed to give rise.

To the contrary. Consider the following scene: Shayla is twenty-one months old. I am giving her a bath, and we are seated face-to-face in the tub. Pointing to my penis, she does not confess longingly her desire to have one or angrily demand that I give her mine. What she says, with a smile, is "Take it off!" Whatever discomfort accompanies her awareness of the anatomical difference between us is resolved not by a wish that she become more like me but by a wish that I become more like her. From this I conclude that she values her vulva.*

Of course this is merely my interpretation of Shayla's words. But it is an interpretation whose plausibility is confirmed by her

---

*A little more than two years later I asked my then four-year-old daughter whether she remembered her bathtub request. Unhesitatingly she responded that she did (which was consistent with her many spontaneous, unsolicited recollections of other events during the second year of her life). Then I asked her, "Shayla, why did you ask me to take off my penis?" Equally unhesitatingly, and with great animation, she replied, "Because I wanted you to have a vulva!" "And why did you want me to have a vulva?" "Because I wanted you to be a girl!" There is, of course, no way to be certain that Shayla's retrospective interpretation of something that happened two years earlier was identical to her original understanding of the event. The feeling-tone of her responses to my questions suggests that it was.

behavior. She shows none of the "signs of [bodily] shame and embarrassment," that, according to Roiphe and Galenson, many mother-raised girls her age display.[3] Quite the opposite. Shayla is something of an exhibitionist. Disrobing at the drop of a hat, she proudly parades her pulchritude in front of anyone who happens to be home. Her parents are pleased. Her grandparents seem bemused. Her great-grandmother is aghast. And Shayla is having the time of her life.

I have noticed other ways in which she upsets traditional ideas about how girls are supposed to play. She has started to play with dolls, learning to take care of herself as she takes care of them. But she also hammers away at her workbench, learning to work on the world by pridefully pounding pegs into their proper place. She has just begun to play with blocks, and her first constructions do not conform to Erikson's expectations. Erikson found that there were gender-based differences in the block play of the ten-to twelve-year-old children he observed: boys erected towers and walled-off structures while girls built interiors of houses and enclosures with openings to the outside world. The "intrusive" tower represented the thrusting, external penis of the boy; the "inclusive" home symbolized the receptive, internal vagina of the girl. The difference in their "spatial modalities" both corresponded to and was an outgrowth of the difference in their sexual organs. Thus Erikson believed that there was a biological basis for the gender differences he observed.[4]

Roiphe and Galenson claim to have observed the same "sex differences in block play" among children of Shayla's age: eighteen-month-old "girls were now building largely enclosed structures while boys began to pile tall towers as a projection onto the inanimate world of the sense of their own genital body image."[5]

But even if her interpretation was a reconstruction that was mediated by meanings that she only subsequently came to associate with the words *vulva* and *penis*, the fact is that no girl who was suffering from penis envy could have produced a reconstruction in which the former term was given such positive valence.

But Shayla was building towers as often as she was building rooms, and she wasn't hermaphroditic. I concluded from this that gender-based differences in play and the sense of space they entail might well have more to do with nurture than with nature. Perhaps mother-raised boys build towers in order to assert themselves against their (m)others, and mother-raised girls build rooms in order to relate to them. Perhaps the equally assertive and relational, coparented boys and girls of the future would build both. Or so the current constructions of my girl-of-the-moment would seem to suggest.

There was another important way in which Shayla's relationship with her widening world of material objects differed dramatically from her conventionally raised peers. She never had the "security blanket," special doll, teddy bear, or toy that is so important to the typical toddler, especially during the second year of its life. Margaret Mahler and her associates have described this as a period marked by the young child's progressive realization of the full extent of his or her separation from the mother. Thus its earlier euphoric exploration of its autonomy from her is threatened by, and often gives way to, heightened anxiety about the loss of her love.

The objects to which children of this age are so ardently attached enable them to "work through" this intensified contradiction between dependence and independence that characterizes their so-called "rapprochement phase."[6] According to Donald Winnicott's by-now classical interpretation, these objects simultaneously symbolize the "union of the baby and the mother" and the separation between them.[7] On the one hand, by representing the presence of the mother they diminish the child's anxiety over her absence; they enable the child to retain a sense of connection with the mother (and the world for which she stands) on whom his or her dependence has been so complete. On the other hand, precisely because these objects symbolize his or her connection with the mother, the manipulations that the child performs on these objects enable the child to develop its independence from her—and from the world—unburdened by the fear of losing her—and it—entirely. Thus Winnicott calls these objects "transitional" because they "represent the infant's transition from a state of being merged with the mother to a state of being in relation to the mother as something outside and separate."[8]

If "transitional objects" were so important to the two-year-old toddler, how was Shayla able to do without them? How was she able to resolve the conflict between autonomy and dependence without the objects that were, according to Winnicott, indispensable for the resolution of that conflict? Since these objects serve as defenses against separation anxiety, I inferred from their absence that Shayla had less separation anxiety against which to defend. Less separation anxiety meant more autonomy. More autonomy could only mean that she had already overcome complete dependence on her mother—the "state of being merged with" her—in favor of the only kind of connection with her mother—a "state of being in relation to [her] as something . . . separate"— that is consistent with the development of her autonomy. But somehow she had done this without the "transitional objects" that are supposed to be essential to this kind of connection.

My inclination, of course, was to conclude that coparenting had made this possible. Why should this be the case? My first thought was that a child who was dependent on two "mothers" would be more autonomous because he or she would be less threatened by the prospect of losing either one. Perhaps having one's emotional eggs in two baskets rather than one leaves one rather less worried that they will break. But this would only be true, I realized, if both baskets seemed secure. The problem with my first thought, in other words, is that a child might well be equally (doubly?) threatened by the prospect of losing either parent unless the child was confident that acting autonomously from that parent did not endanger his or her relationship with that parent. So we are back to the problem of how this sense of "being in relation with [someone] as something separate" is more easily nurtured by two mothers rather than one.

Two "mothers" rather than one. But one of them was male and the other female. Each of us was both the same as, and different from, the other. All of a sudden, I was reminded of Winnicott's description of the "transitional object" as both the same as, and different from, the mother. No wonder Shayla didn't need a teddy bear or a blanket. She already had two transitional objects in the person of her parents! For the better part of Shayla's life, Dotty and I had been shuttling back and forth between home and work. Our "hi-by-here's the kid" lifestyle had accustomed Shayla at an early age to daily transitions from one parent to another. Separation from Dotty almost always (except for weekend nights out together when we relied on a sitter) meant the return of Ike and vice versa. Since I was both Shayla's substitute Dotty and someone who was separate from her, my presence could forestall the pain of Dotty's absence by simultaneously symbolizing Shayla's connection with, and independence from, her mother. And Dotty could do the same thing for Shayla when I left. Vis-à-vis Dotty, I was Shayla's transitional object, and Dotty was Shayla's transitional object vis-à-vis me. Thus it was possible for her to achieve a "state of being in relation" to each of us "as something separate."

And she really did seem to have achieved that state. Even between the age of eighteen and twenty-one months she showed few of the symptoms of the separation anxiety that is, according to Mahler and her colleagues, at its peak during this period. During the child's so-called "rapprochement crisis," "fear of losing the love of the [mother] becomes increasingly evident" and the child "employs all kinds of mechanisms in order to resist" that loss. These mechanisms range from the child "refusing to let the mother out of [its] sight" when she is at home to desperately clinging to her when she tries to leave. Girls are supposed to be even more "engrossed" with the mother, and to try even harder to hold on to her, than boys.[9]

But Shayla rarely cried when we left her with her sitter (and then, we would later learn, only as long as it would take us to get down the stairs) and almost never "shadowed" us when we were in the house. Instead of following our every move she seemed to do whatever moved her. I could do the dishes in the kitchen while she worked on a puzzle in another room. She was unfazed when I told her that next I would have to take the laundry to the basement. And when I got back a few minutes later she would still be working on the same puzzle, in the same place. I was amazed by her ability to be with herself without worrying where anyone else was.

In fact she was a lot better at this than me. It was hard for me not to take her self-reliance for indifference. Often it was I who would "shadow" her, trying to get her to pay more attention to me. Sometimes it seemed as if I needed her recognition more than she needed mine. And I didn't like it when I didn't get it.

Not getting it would have been bad enough. But having to watch Dotty get more of it than me made it even worse. Even a toddler as self-sufficient as Shayla regularly requests the attention and comfort of a parent. More often than not, that parent was Dotty rather than me. That had been true for a long time. The difference was that Shayla was now able to verbalize her preference for her mother. It was no longer necessary to infer that preference from her behavior; her words made it all too clear. When your daughter awakens from a nap and grumpily greets you with "I want Mamma!" there is no room for doubt.

I hated those three words more than any other I had ever heard. Especially when I heard them in public, like when the three of us went out to eat together. Why did Shayla have to announce to family and friends alike that she wanted to sit next to her mother? Why did she have to let everyone in the restaurant know that she wanted Dotty and not Ike to take her to the toilet? Probably no one else gave it a minute's thought: it was just the way things were. But it was not the way I wanted them to be. So I thought about it a lot. And one of the things I thought was that I liked it a lot better when Shayla and I ate out by ourselves.

If I wasn't getting enough of Shayla's love, I was certainly getting my fill of her rage. One thing that coparenting did not undo were the tempestuous trials of the (misleadingly named) terrible twos. The fact that by the age of a year and a half Shayla was unusually sanguine about her separation from her parents didn't mean that she was resigned to the exercise of their authority. Far from it. Like any kid her age, she wanted her way, and when she didn't get it she got pissed. The difference was she got pissed at her father at least as often as her mother.

I had theorized that a toddler who was disciplined as much by her father as her mother would not find in her father the blameless refuge from the authority of her mother to which conventionally raised toddlers are able to turn. Yet somehow I never realized until I became a father what this would mean. What it meant is that I would have to hear how much she hated me. I was getting less of the early love that conventional mothers usually get in return for less of the later love on which conventional fathers can count. Some bargain.

I tried to be a big boy about this and concentrate on Shayla's needs instead of mine. And I knew that what she needed was enough victories to confirm her power and enough defeats to reduce it to realistic dimensions. The psychoanalytic experts describe this as providing the "optimal frustrations" by means of which narcissistic "infantile omnipotence" can be replaced by a healthy "secondary narcissism."[10] The lay translation: you have to know when to pick your fights. Give way when it doesn't really matter but stand firm when it does. Sometimes I got this right. But sometimes I let Shayla get her way against my better judgment, because I didn't want to hear how much she hated me. At other times I denied her when I didn't really have to, because I was angry at her for having heard it so many times. The net result was that the one who was optimally frustrated was me.

chapter seven

. Wife-Mother .

*f*rustration breeds aggression, so I renewed the battle of the breasts. Dotty was still nursing, although by October she was down to two or three times a day. As far as I was concerned, this was two or three times too often. A year ago I had wanted Dotty to stop because I was afraid that Shayla would love her more than me. Witnessing precisely that effect over the past year had made me painfully aware that it was too late to overcome it. Yet I was more anxious than ever to untie the special knot that bound Dotty to our baby.

For one thing, she wasn't really a baby anymore; she was only four months shy of her second birthday. There was something strange, even unseemly, about a child ambling up to her mother and indicating that she would like to nurse. Weaning, I thought, went together with walking and talking. Besides, I was tired of sharing Dotty's body with Shayla. Weaning would end her claim on the breasts that I had monopolized before her birth. If it was too late to get Shayla back from her mother, it was high time to get my wife back from Shayla.

I realized that I was as threatened by Dotty's love for Shayla as

I was threatened by Shayla's love for Dotty. This didn't appear to be the case with Dotty. She seemed to be a lot more bothered by the attention that Shayla gave me than she was by the attention that I gave Shayla. Of course this asymmetry only confirmed my fears that she loved Shayla more than me. I was feeling like a jealous husband. Why didn't Dotty feel like a jealous wife?

I mastered this mystery when I remembered the feminist psychoanalytic explanation for why men are usually far more sexually possessive than women: the woman whom the man wants to monopolize is not only his wife but also his mother. Intimate bodily contact with someone whose sex is the same as the mother is, as Dinnerstein has argued, a much more direct and evocative reminder of the earliest, eminently embodied relationship with the mother than comparable contact with someone of the opposite sex.[1] Sexual intercourse does not provide the wife the kind of emotional access to the mother that it affords her husband. He is far more likely to represent her father, whose place in her emotional life is, according to Chodorow, normally far less central than her mother's:

> girls [during their oedipal period] . . . do not "reject" their mothers in favor of their father and men. . . . They usually make a sexual resolution in favor of men and their fathers, but retain an internal emotional triangle [within which] men tend to remain *emotionally* secondary.[2]

So the man is far less likely to serve as a mother substitute for the woman than the woman is for the man. The woman typically finds her mother-substitute instead in the person of her child, with whom she relives the primitive passions of preoedipal merger.

On the deepest possible emotional level, then, women are simply more important to men than men are to women. (This is why men—their protestations of greater "independence" notwithstanding—usually do a lot worse after the deaths of their wives than women do after the deaths of their husbands.) It follows that men are far more emotionally threatened by the infidelities of their wives than women are by the infidelities of their husbands (and that the penalties imposed on unfaithful women will be far harsher than those imposed on unfaithful men).[3]

Thus a man will also be much more threatened by the affection lavished on his child by his wife than his wife will be threatened by the attention he devotes to her child. Whereas the birth of the child "recreates the desired mother-child exclusivity for a woman [it] interrupts it for a man."[4] No longer will he be able to monopolize his wife-mother's attention. The child, in short, "robs him of his wife."[5] The man had already been obliged as a child to relinquish his oedipal claim on his mother in return for the promise that one day he too—like his father—would be able to possess a woman like her. The arrival of his child signals the betrayal of that promise and the reluctant recognition that he must, once again, give up his mother, this time in the person of his wife. As Dotty pithily put it to me, the man is a "two-time loser."

But he is not likely to take this loss lightly. He will respond, instead, by redoubling his efforts to monopolize his wife's attention and thus to limit his child's claim upon it. He tries, in short, to get back his wife by "getting rid" of his child, by attempting to break as quickly and thoroughly as possible the intimate bond between them. His wife, in turn, will find that his intensified possessiveness leaves him even less able than before to satisfy her emotional needs, and thus she is likely (if permitted) to intensify her already intense emotional involvement with her child. Which only serves further to intensify his possessiveness. And so on. . . .

This was precisely the vicious circle within which Dotty and I were trapped. Now that I understood its origins, perhaps I would be able to do the emotional work necessary to help extricate us from it. In the meantime there was theoretical work to be done. I realized I would have to reformulate my gender-struggle theory in order to take into account the father's oedipal stake in practices that frustrate rather than gratify the needs of his young child. Fathers are as resentful of their wives' dependence on their children as they are afraid of their childrens' dependence on their mothers. Jealousy of his children combines with a concern for their autonomy to make the father a more punitive parent than his spouse.

From the very beginning I had worried that my derivation of the father's parenting interest from his preoedipal relationship with his mother did not adequately explain his insistence on "instant obedience" and his anger at its absence. An "oppositional" orientation didn't quite seem to capture the roots of this rage. But now I understood that this rage had oedipal as well as pre-oedipal origins. The father resented his child—perhaps especially his male child—because he experienced his child as a sexual rival! No wonder he would attempt so angrily to assert his dominance over him.

This reformulation of the foundations of my theory made it possible for me to solve two additional problems for which there was previously no solution. The first problem was the thesis of "maternal indifference" propounded by Edward Shorter in *The Making of the Modern Family* and then modified by Elisabeth Badinter in *Mother Love*. Shorter's thesis was that "good mothering is an invention of modernization. In traditional society, mothers viewed the development and happiness of infants younger than two with indifference."[6] This thesis was an obvious challenge to my assumption that women of all cultures have always had a psychodynamically determined interest in the welfare of their young children.

So was Badinter's "correction" of Shorter. Although she found no evidence of maternal indifference in France prior to the sixteenth century, she agreed with Shorter that there was little or no "mother love" to be found in that country from that century through the eighteenth.[7] Even if this three-century absence of maternal affection was "exceptional," it was an exception that clearly violated my theoretical rule.

The case for "maternal indifference" was based largely on the prevalence of wet-nursing in England, Germany, and France during this period. Badinter and Shorter have shown that infants of upper- and middle-class urban families were suckled not by their mothers but by paid nurses to whose homes they were habitually exiled. This was an exile from which many were never to return. Since their wet-nurses were typically recruited from the poorest sectors of rural society, the conditions under which they were "nursed" were often hazardous to their health. Many nurses were obliged to share the milk intended for their urban charges with their own children. Many apparently never fed them milk at all. Those children who were fortunate enough to survive such circumstances were often shunted from one nurse to another. The lucky few who became attached to one reliable nurse were unlucky enough to have to return to a mother whom they did not know. That mothers who could afford to do otherwise would consign their children to such physical and emotional debility was surely a sign of their indifference to their welfare.[8]

But what if it was not mothers but fathers who were responsible for their childrens' unhappy fate? What if wet-nursing was imposed on wives by their upper- and middle-class husbands? My reformulated gender-struggle theory led me to hypothesize that paternal preference rather than maternal indifference was the reason for the reliance on wet-nursing among these classes. I found historical evidence that was consistent with this hypothesis. Sixteenth- and seventeenth-century observers testified to the widespread resistance of husbands during this period to their wives' nursing their children. The prevailing assumption that sexual intercourse spoiled the mother's milk led the doctors of that day to prescribe sexual abstinence during nursing in order to ensure the child's health.[9] Thus the husband of a nursing mother would lose the sexual services of his wife. How to avert this loss but keep his child alive was the cruel dilemma with which he was confronted. Wet-nursing was the only possible solution to this dilemma.*

I discovered that there were historians who agreed with this

---

*Except of course in polygynous societies, where the displaced husband can always rely on the sexual services of other wives.

interpretation. Lawrence Stone argued that "it was the insistence of the husbands rather than the desire of the wives which was the main reason for the employment of wet-nurses."[10] And David Hunt spelled out the emotional roots of this insistence in terms that were identical to my own: by banishing the infant from the home, the husband "buys a clear oedipal triumph, keeping the mother to himself . . . [wet-nursing] was a sexual triumph for the father."[11] Of course a complete explanation for wet-nursing would require an explanation for that triumph, that is, an answer to the question of why the father was powerful enough during this period (but not before or after) to prevail over his wife. But for now I was content to conclude that Western wet-nursing was not only not a problem for my newly "oedipalized" theory, but that this theory was the basis for the solution to the problem of Western wet-nursing.

The addition of an oedipal dimension also enabled me to account for the much more indulgent practices characteristic of "traditional," non-Western societies. In *Marxism and Domination* I had reported that a review of some fifty cross-cultural studies concluded that

> In spite of a great deal of cultural diversity, all the infants
> drawn from pre-industrial communities shared certain ex-
> periences during the first year: membership in an extended
> family with many caretakers, breast-feeding on demand,
> day and night; constant tactile stimulation by the body of
> the adult caretaker who carried the infant on her back or
> side, and slept with him [and] lack of set routines for feed-
> ing, sleeping, and toileting.[12]

In these communities responsibility for, and authority over, children is normally shared between their biological parents and their grandparents. In many of these communities it is the grandfather to whom both the mother and the father are ultimately obliged to defer. My preoedipal theory was unable to explain why child-rearing policy that was controlled by a grandfather should be any more indulgent than child-rearing policy that was controlled by a father: if all men privileged independence over dependence, there was no reason to expect that old men would be more willing than young men to encourage the dependence of their children.

But there was every reason to expect that this would be the case if there were an oedipal as well as preoedipal basis for the punitive parenting orientation of men. A man is far less likely to be jealous of a mother's attachment to her child if that mother is his daughter than if that mother is his wife. Thus a grandfather will be correspondingly less emotionally inclined to destroy that attachment than a father and more inclined to protect his grandchildren from the rivalrous feelings of his son (or son-in-law). So we should expect that child-rearing practices would be less harsh in the traditional societies in which grandfathers are the authorities than in modern societies during those periods when fathers are in command.

The oedipalization of my gender-struggle theory had enabled me to solve two puzzles for which there had earlier been no solution. But it was now January and I still hadn't gotten around to applying that theory to the history of child rearing from the late Middle Ages to the present. In fact between November and January I hadn't written a single word. It was now more than two years since I had first made a commitment to what I had then called my "Spock book," and I had yet to make good on that commitment. Although my January reflections had increased my confidence in the explanatory power of my theory, they had done nothing to increase my appetite for the tedious task of its historical application.

"Tedious task." That about summed up how I was feeling about my project. But it was difficult for me to admit it. I nearly chewed Dotty's head off when she suggested that I might have bitten off more than I could chew. I even snapped at her when she asked, gingerly, if I really wanted to write my book. My defensiveness betrayed the ambivalence I denied. I had always had a great deal of emotional energy for my work. The truth was that it was no longer there.

My energy level was generally lower than it had been in years. My body was lifeless, bound up as tightly as it had been before the years of dance therapy that had helped to unbind it. I was tired all the time, in part because I was still waking up in the middle of the night. Sleep deprivation left me even more hyper and less patient than usual. I was displaying both the "loss of zest and enthusiasm" and the "upsurge in hostile aggression" of Roiphe and Galenson's terrified two-year-old.

I was hoping that getting "mommy" back would relieve these symptoms. Dotty had finally decided that the time for weaning was at hand. For twenty-one months she had relied on her breasts to put Shayla down for the night or for naps, when I wasn't home to walk her to sleep on my shoulder. Because a chronic wrist problem made it impossible for Dotty to avail herself of this somnambulistic solution she was afraid that a breastless Shayla would have to cry herself to sleep. For a few days Dotty did have to endure fifteen to thirty minutes of heart-rending reactions, but then the crying stopped, and Shayla unfailingly fell out without the comfort to which she had become accustomed. Her protests against its absence during the day were similarly short-lived. And she even went straight from the breast to a training cup, bypassing the bottle entirely. It was all so much easier than Dotty had feared. Shayla was doing fine.

Not so her father. The day for which I had waited for three months short of two years had arrived. Shayla was no longer any more physically dependent on Dotty than on me. No longer did I have to share Dotty's body with Shayla. We even celebrated its release with our first romantic out-of-town weekend without her. But my anxiety did not abate. I was as listless and crabby as ever. And I still couldn't—or wouldn't—write. I decided that it was time to swallow my pride and get my ass back into therapy. It was time for more emotional meetings with my imaginary-mother-within.

Four days before my first session Shayla and I met her in the flesh as she emerged from the plane that had flown her from New York to Chicago. My mother beamed. Shayla squealed with delight, then hopped on her lap as the attendant wheeled them over to the baggage area. Already the giggles had begun.

My mother had waited a long time for her first grandchild. Since the death of my father in 1979 she had been living alone in the Queens apartment they had shared for more than forty years. I had hoped that when her grieving for him was over she would actually be able to see all the places she had only been able to visit in her mind because of her ties to the man-who-never-wanted-to-go-anywhere. She had even allowed Dotty and I to sign her up for a cruise halfway around the world. But at the last minute she had gotten cold feet. Our ideas for more modest trips were also rebuffed. So she never got to spread her wounded wings. In fact, she was having more and more trouble just walking. Her arthritis was getting worse and worse. She considered herself lucky just to be able to get to the store.

Shayla's birth was the only bright spot in my mother's otherwise increasingly dark, insular existence, so Dotty and I decided that she should see her granddaughter as often as possible. During Shayla's first year we took frequent trips to New York. Now we were sending my mother tickets to visit us every three or four months. They were good visits. Shayla really did seem to brighten up my mother's life. She would actually forget her troubles and let out the playful little girl inside her. I had never seen her so silly. Her silliness was infectious. Shayla caught it and gave it back to her. And got more in return. Together they filled the house with gales of laughter.

Shayla absolutely adored her "Banya" (her first try at "grandma" had stuck). As soon as she woke up she would beg me to let her wake Banya up. Then she would climb into bed with her, and the two of them would cuddle under the covers while my mother sang to her and told her stories. When it was time for my mother to get up, Shayla would find her cane and help her on with her slippers. Then they would join me for bagels and lox. When it was time to take Banya to the airport, the two saddened soulmates would hug each other as hard as they could. But Shayla didn't cry. She knew her Banya would be back soon. She also knew she would talk to her on the phone between trips. Together they would laugh long distance about the things they had last laughed about in person. And Banya couldn't stop talking to me about the "fresh face" of the most "bew-tee-ful" child she had ever seen.

Shayla made my mother happy. This is what I had spent much of my childhood trying to do. But somehow my ministrations never seemed to mitigate her misery. So I spent much of my childhood being miserable as well. Even now it was hard for me to be happy when she was unhappy; it seemed selfish to let myself feel good when I knew that she felt bad. This mother-knot had proven far tighter than I had anticipated. I thought I had untied it many years ago, but now it was choking me to death.

Or so my therapist and I concluded. For many years I had dared to be different from my mother and had achieved a measure of success and acclaim in the very public world of which first she, and then I, had been so terribly afraid. Then I had allowed myself to become similar to my mother; I got in touch with my need to take care of my daughter as my mother had taken care of me. Now I was faced with the challenge of being simultaneously similar to and different from my mother, of being a mothering man and an intellectual at one and the same time. I was failing this challenge because it was particularly difficult for me to identify with my mother without becoming identical to her, to maintain the boundaries between my mother and myself when I was doing the same thing as she.

Not being able to maintain these boundaries meant taking on her fears of the outside world. Taking on her fears of the outside world, in turn, meant being terrified of public reaction, which meant not being able—or not wanting—to write. This is why I was having so many problems with my work—and life—at this particular point in time.

So I danced out the boundaries between my mother and myself. My therapy became a moving reminder of the right of Ike-separate-person-Balbus to be happy even if Selma was not, and that the way for me to be happy was to write. I decided that the link I had mandated between my historical/theoretical project and my personal parenting project was an excuse not to write and that I should therefore sever that link. I would write my book on gender struggle and the history of child rearing whether or not there was any connection between that history and the contemporary commitment to coparent. I liked doing grand social theory, and I liked the recognition that comes from doing it well. What was wrong with that? Why shouldn't Marx et al. have to make room for me?

I was ready to do intellectual battle. Its high stakes meant that I would have to plan my attack carefully. It was already the end of the spring quarter. My project for the summer would be my first historical chapter, the one on the transition from the late-medieval to the early modern child-rearing regime. Then it would be back to teaching once again. I knew I would be lucky to write another historical chapter—on the transition from the early modern to the mid-nineteenth-century regime—before the end of the next academic year. That would leave two more historical chapters and a concluding chapter to go. These could be completed during the two-quarter sabbatical (and the summer that followed it) for which I would qualify during the academic year 1987–88. My book could be finished when Shayla was still only four years old.

Right now it seemed that she was two going on fourteen. "Dress up" had become her favorite game. She preferred to dress up, in her words, "like a teenager." A teenage girl, to be precise. In pink. God help the feminist father whose daughter prefers pink. She also loved her mother's high heels. So did I, but not on *her*. Precocity is one thing, but a two-year-old vamp is a bit much. The Jewish grandmothers in Treasure Island had been right: we would have to keep the boys away from her. But one day we wouldn't be able to keep her away from the boys. How would I ever be able to give my little girl away?

Of course she was half-gone already. She was fast becoming her own person. When, after your daughter does something wonderfully weird, you teasingly ask her, "What kind of person

are you, anyway?" and she answers "I'm a *woman!*", what is there
to do but stand in awe of her miraculous little mind? And when
you warn her of the dire consequences of disobedience and she
responds haughtily, hands on hips, with an "I just don't care!",
what is there to do but laugh? What a blithe spirit! Even the toilet training I have begun is unable to dampen it. To call it *training*
is actually something of a joke. Shayla has decided that she would
like to stop wearing diapers, so she allows me to take her to the
potty and wipe her little tush. It is clear that she will no longer
need my help by the time she begins preschool in the fall.

Shayla's preschool runs a (half)day camp in the summer. Even
though the kids are supposed to be at least two and a half, a just-
past-two Shayla wants to go. Fortunately I have been able to persuade a somewhat skeptical Dotty that she is ready. I drive her to
her first day of summer fun-in-the-sun on the very day that I am
supposed to start my summer-in-the-stacks. How fitting. Shayla
has reached the age of camp, and I have reached my middle ages.

chapter eight

. The Article .

i would rather have been in camp. By all ac-
counts, Shayla was having a lot better time there than I was here.
Dotty and I had been warned at a precamp orientation session
that one of us might have to stay with her during the first few
weeks to facilitate a graceful acceptance of our eventual absence.
But Shayla had "separated" so easily that by the second day she
was frolicking under the sprinkler and digging in the sandbox
under the watchful eyes of her counselors instead of her parents.

Meanwhile I was mired in the muck of medievalism. Combing
the library for material on Western child rearing from the tenth
through the fifteenth centuries wasn't exactly my idea of a great
way to start the summer, especially since I wasn't finding much of
what I was looking for. There were problems, moreover, with the
material that I did find. Like the material on early modern practices I had already gathered, the descriptions of medieval practices were based mainly on sources that were written for, or by,
the parents of that time. Thus any inferences about practices that
could be drawn from these sources would only apply to the liter-
ate, upper-class minority of the population. Then there was the

even more fundamental problem of the legitimacy of such inferences in the first place. Could one conclude that medieval prescriptions for proper child rearing were actually followed by
medieval mothers?

Historians of this as well as other periods were divided on this
question. Established scholars like Philippe Aries had routinely
relied on medieval discourse about children to paint their picture
of what medieval childhood was really like.[1] But a younger generation of revisionists were now calling into question this uncritical
assumption of a one-to-one relationship between theory and
practice. Jay Melching even went so far as to deny the existence of
any necessary relationship between them. This denial threatened
the integrity of my entire project. The reconstructions of child-
rearing practices in three of my four historical chapters would
have to rely heavily (although not exclusively) on child-rearing
advice. If Melching was right, my entire account could be wrong.

Melching argued that the reliance on child-rearing manuals as
indicators of child-rearing practices was based on two inferences
that were unlikely to be correct: (1) that the child-rearing values
of the experts were the same as the child-rearing values of the
parents and (2) that the child-rearing behavior of the parents was
consistent with their child-rearing values. The first inference is
unwarranted, according to Melching, because parents absorb the
child-rearing values of the culture as a whole, and there is no
good reason to assume that the particular values of the child-
rearing experts are identical to, or even consistent with, these
general cultural values. The second is unacceptable because the
actual behavior of parents was learned when they were children,
"primarily through interaction with *their* parents," and is relatively impervious to both the "secondary socialization" into a
culture's child-rearing values and the "direct instruction" into
the values of the child-rearing experts. Thus Melching proposed
the possibility that "official advice has nothing at all to do with
actual child-rearing behavior."[2]

If parents treat their children as they were treated by their parents, whether or not this treatment is mandated by the messages

they receive about how children should be treated, then (Melching concluded) "the very process by which the parent role is learned favors a basic consistency in this role across generations." This was precisely the conclusion that had led Lawrence Stone to reject out of hand the "psychological explanation" on which it was based. Convinced of the reality of change, Stone dismissed the theory that appeared to rule it out. Convinced of the truth of his theory, Melching asks us to "reexamine [the] principle . . . that parents do, in fact, change their behavior across generations."[3] Their positions were merely two sides of the same coin: they shared the assumption that there was an inherent opposition between "psychological explanation" and "historical change." Thus Melching's "no change" position was as vulnerable as Stone's "no psychological explanation" position to the gender struggle through which that opposition was transcended.

So was Melching's "no congruence" position on the relationship between child-rearing advice and child-rearing practice. According to my theoretical assumptions, child-rearing advice was an intellectual (be it scientific or religious) expression of either the parenting orientation of women or the parenting orientation of men. The authors of child-rearing manuals speak not merely for themselves but also for the gender whose unconsciously governed approach to child rearing these authors transform into the right way to raise children. Child-rearing advice, according to my interpretation, is a weapon in the struggle between the sexes to control the mode of child rearing.

It follows that the relationship between the dominant advice and the prevailing practice will depend on the state of that struggle. When the hegemonic advice is masculine, then mothers will be torn between what is supposed to be good for their children and what they would "naturally" prefer to do, between patriarchal authority and their inclination to resist it. The extent of that resistance, in turn, will depend on the capacity of their husbands and other representatives of masculine authority to oppose it.

I already knew that during the late-nineteenth- to early twentieth-century period the separation between the "female" home and the "male" workplace made it impossible for husbands directly and regularly to supervise the child-rearing practices of their wives and that the severity of those practices therefore fell considerably short of the behaviorist ideal to which these and other men were committed. I also knew that early modern mothers, in contrast, were obliged to care for their children under the watchful eyes of husbands who headed the family farm or workshop. Under these circumstances it would seem that mothers had little choice but to grit their teeth and heed the Calvinist advice to "break the will" of their children. Thus it was reasonable to suppose that the austere child-rearing advice of the early modern era was a generally accurate indicator of the actual practices that prevailed during that time.

But I needed to show not only that these practices were harsh but also that they were much harsher than the medieval practices that preceded them. What conclusions could I come to about medieval child rearing from the medieval discourse on child rearing with which I was beginning to become familiar? So far it did seem that medieval prescriptions were significantly softer, or more feminine, than their early modern counterparts. According to the assumptions underlying my theory, if the hegemonic advice is feminine, then mothers (or mother substitutes) will experience no conflict between what is defined as the right way and the way they actually want to raise their children. The legitimation of their indulgent orientation enables mothers freely to express it. Under these circumstances, we should expect a more or less one-to-one relationship between theory and practice.

My project had survived Melching's methodological assault. Our "debate" had convinced me that it was possible to draw legitimate inferences about the relationship between child-rearing advice and child-rearing practice. A clearly demonstrated difference between medieval and early modern advice could stand as a sign of a definite difference between medieval and early modern practice.

But our debate had also culminated in the seemingly paradoxical conclusion that this inference about the "facts" of child rearing during these two periods presupposed the truth of the very theory that these facts were "designed" to test. My inference was based on the assumption of a gender-based opposition in parenting orientations (as well as some preliminary information about the conditions favoring the implementation of these orientations). If my assumption about these orientations was not correct, then neither were my conclusions about the practices that (I assumed) were their outgrowth. But how could I know if this theoretical assumption was correct prior to a successful explanation of the facts I had described? To put it the other way around: to explain the facts it would seem that I needed independent access to those facts, but the facts did not exist independently of the theory through which they were constructed.

Of course it never is any different. My "problem" was merely one example of the inevitable interpenetration of theory and fact, explanation and description, whole and parts, that philosophers call the hermeneutic circle.[4] You have to know the whole in order to know the parts, but you have to know the parts in order to know the whole. At first this looks like a vicious circle that makes it impossible ever to know anything, yet it is the only possible route that learning can take. At any given point in time, we possess necessarily incomplete knowledge of both an organized pattern—or gestalt—and the particular elements of its organization. A previously unknown part of reality becomes a "fact" when we recognize it as an element of the gestalt, when we are able to figure out its place within the overall pattern of which we already have (partial) knowledge. Figuring this out simultaneously enriches our understanding of the overall pattern, which enhances our ability to identify and comprehend additional facts, and so on. Our knowledge becomes more complete the more we are able to assimilate the part to the whole and accommodate the whole to the parts. This sounds like arcane epistemology, but any kid who has ever put together a jigsaw puzzle knows the secret.

These methodological reflections increased my confidence in my conceptual solution to my particular parenting puzzle. And after about five weeks of searching I was finally able to find enough material on medieval and early modern child rearing to fit together one big part of this puzzle: my first historical chapter.

Gender Struggle and the Transformation of Western Child Rearing
Chapter One: From the Middle Ages to the Early Modern Era

I. Introduction

In *Marxism and Domination* I propose a theory of the determining power of (what might be called) the mode of nurture over the way in which we conceive of and relate to nature. More specifically, I argue that the "disenchantment of the world"[5] and the industrial civilization that it made possible owe their existence to child-rearing practices that are significantly more severe than those that typically prevail in nonindustrial societies. These austere practices enforce an unusually early, even premature dissolution of the primary identification between the child and its mother and thus establish the libidinal foundation for the symbolization of the earth she represents[6] as a pure object with which the human subject can experience no sense of connection and to which he can only instrumentally relate.[7]

From this argument it is possible to infer the hypothesis that this uniquely Western objectification of nature was preceded by a sharp increase in the severity of child-rearing practices over those practices that must have long been in place in the West prior to the triumph of objectification.[8] But nowhere in *Marxism and Domination* do I attempt to verify this hypothesis.[9]

In the first part of this essay I make good on this omission. Within the limits of the available evidence, I demonstrate that children of a variety of different classes in Western Europe and the American colonies were subjected from the sixteenth through the eighteenth centuries to a form of (what was then called) "family government" that was substantially more strict than the regime that children of those classes typically experienced during the Middle Ages. First I argue that it is reasonable to conclude from the existing studies of child-rearing advice, the personal diaries of parents, and the memoirs of those who recounted their childhoods during the two periods in question that early modern practices were, indeed, much harsher than medieval practices. Second, and more briefly, to confirm this conclusion I rely on Norbert Elias's simultaneously entertaining and persuasive demonstration that the early modern period was marked by a dramatic increase in the level of shame associated with the bodily processes of adults.

In the remaining parts of this essay I develop an explanation of the transformation in child-rearing practices to whose description the first part is devoted. This explanation entails a historical specification of what I call a gender-struggle theory of transformations in the mode of child rearing. The fundamental assumption on which this theory is based is that the hitherto culturally universal fact of "mother-monopolized" child rearing necessarily engenders a gender-based conflict in parenting interests, with fathers (or father substitutes) favoring more repressive, and mothers (or mother substitutes) favoring more nurturant, child-rearing practices. It follows from this assumption that transformations in the direction of more repressive practices—such as the one in question—result from fathers gaining greater control over (but not necessarily direct participation in) the mode of child rearing, thus increasing their capacity to enforce their repressive parenting interest.

This hypothesis, I show, is validated by historians who have unambiguously demonstrated that the transition from the late medieval to the early modern period was punctuated by a pronounced increase in the father's power within the home. It was this capture of paternal—and corresponding loss of maternal—control over the mode of child rearing that accounts for the harsh child-rearing practices that—according to the thesis proposed in *Marxism and Domination*—account, in turn, for the disenchantment and domination of nature. Industrial civilization, I conclude, was made possible by an early modern masculinization of the mode of child rearing.

II. *Medieval versus Early Modern*
Child Rearing

A. Feeding and Care

It is between the blissful presence and the dreaded absence of the breast that the "psychological birth of the human infant" occurs.[10] More prosaically, we can say that the child's symbolization of the mother—and thus of the world—is shaped by the mixture of gratification and deprivation that inevitably accompanies nursing. Whereas the gratification is the source of a sense of oneness or identity, the deprivation is the basis for a sense of separation, between self and world.[11] Thus indulgent nursing will be associated with a holistic or organic conception of nature, while niggardly nursing will be associated with an objectified or instrumental conception of nature.[12] We should expect to find, then, that early modern nursing practices were significantly less indulgent than the medieval practices they superseded.

Such indeed appears to be the case. The data on nursing in the Middle Ages are admittedly both ambiguous and incomplete, and selective emphasis on different aspects of these data has led to considerable disagreement among historians concerning the actual duration of nursing. Philippe Aries refers in his magisterial *Centuries of Childhood* to the "tardy weaning" of children of all classes during this epoch and estimates that it occurred "about the age of seven."[13] Hunt argues that this estimate is a "substantial exaggeration," but agrees nonetheless that weaning was "relatively late by our standards."[14] Ross suggests that weaning at about the age of two was typical for the middle-class child in the urban Italy of the late Middle Ages but cites an instance of a child being suckled until he was three.[15] The most thoroughgoing study of medieval feeding practices of which I am aware concludes that "what little can be discovered about the time of weaning in these centuries [ninth through thirteenth] suggests a variability between one and three years," a variability confirmed by DeMause in his survey of Western feeding practices from antiquity through the nineteenth century.[16]

Despite both the imprecision of, and conflict among, these accounts of medieval feeding practices, all differ dramatically from the available—and far more detailed and reliable—accounts of early modern nursing. DeMause locates only two cases of nursing beyond the age of a year and a half following the sixteenth century in England, Germany, and the United States, and demonstrates that in these countries nursing for a year or less became common after that time.[17] Pollack's more recent and systematic study of the diaries of British and American parents revealed an average age of weaning of 13.6, 13.2, and 9.5 months for the sixteenth, seventeenth, and eighteenth centuries, respectively.[18]

Country- and century-specific histories of child rearing confirm the results of these two longitudinal, cross-cultural surveys. Tucker cites evidence of sixteenth-century upper-class English children being weaned at one year, and Stone argues that children "at the upper levels of society" during the sixteenth and seventeenth centuries were nursed "until a year or eighteen months." He speculates that in these circles the age of weaning may have declined to well under a year by the middle of the eighteenth century, in which case it would have been consistent with the late-eighteenth-century insistence of John Wesley—the founder of Methodism—that "a thousand experiments shew [that weaning] is most safely and easily done at the seventh month."[19] Illick's review of the child rearing of seventeenth-century New Englanders mentions instances of weaning at fourteen and eighteen months, but concludes that "weaning at one year appears to have been the practice" early in that century.[20] Demos concurs that the normal length of breast-feeding in seventeenth-century Plymouth Colony was "about twelve months."[21] All of these studies confirm DeMause's conclusion that "by early modern times . . . very long nursing was becoming less common."[22]

The duration of nursing says nothing, of course, about its quality. But an additional consideration suggests that the latter and not merely the former declined precipitously from the medieval to the early modern period. The practice of wet-nursing was by no means unknown to the Middle Ages, but all the available evidence indicates that it was almost always confined to the children of noblewomen or prosperous burghers, and that it normally took place inside, rather than outside, their households.[23] This meant that the services of wet-nurses were purchased by parents who could afford reliable ones and who were in a position to supervise them. Thus there is no reason to assume that the relatively small proportion of children who were wet-nursed during the Middle Ages suffered greatly from this experience.

There is, in contrast, every reason to assume such suffering in the case of the far larger numbers of children wet-nursed during the early modern period. Badinter and Stone have shown that by the seventeenth century this custom had become common among the bourgeoisie and that by the eighteenth century (at least in France) "it had expanded to all segments of urban society."[24] During this period, moreover, the child was typically sent away to live with the wet-nurse rather than nursed at home. Since the expense—and presumably the reliability—of wet-nurses varied inversely with the distance of the residence from which infants were exiled, the parents with the greatest need to supervise their practices were generally the least able to do so. Their wetnurses were typically recruited from the poorest sectors of rural society, and many were obliged to share the milk intended for their urban charges with their own children. Horror stories abound concerning the mortality rates of urban children nursed under these conditions, and those who were fortunate enough to survive were often shunted from one nurse to another.[25] Thus it is reasonable to assume that deprivation rather than gratification was the predominant experience of large numbers of nursing children during the early modern era.

B. Cutaneous Contact

There is also evidence—albeit more impressionistic—that other forms of sensory deprivation during infancy were more pronounced in this period than in the Middle Ages. By all accounts, there was little or no sexual repression of children during the latter period. DeMause cites evidence indicating that childhood masturbation was not only tolerated, but encouraged, during the Middle Ages. Both he and Aries suggest, moreover, that parents and other caretakers actually sought sexually to stimulate their children by fondling and licking them in the course of their daily interactions.[26] Finally, Norbert Elias has shown that it was "natural" during the Middle Ages "for children and adults to share a bed. . . ."[27] Thus Morris Berman concludes, on the basis of these and other accounts, that during this period "body stimulation was a large part of early life."[28]

Religious manifestations of intense and prolonged mother identification in the Middle Ages tend to confirm this picture of indulgent contact between children and their primary caretakers. Herlihy suggests that medieval veneration of the Virgin Mary— not only the mother of Jesus but also the spiritual mother of the entire Christian family—reflects a peculiarly intense identification of children with their actual mothers, and that the parallel cult of Baby Jesus, in which "women were especially prominent and passionate," similarly expressed the devotion and libidinal attachment of mothers to their children.[29]

The early modern period, in contrast, was marked by what Berman calls the "desensualization of childhood."[30] Aries, De-Mause, Stone, and Ryerson have all emphasized the imposition of the hitherto unknown prohibition on childhood masturbation in France, England, and the American colonies.[31] They also show that this prohibition on the child's freedom to gratify herself sexually was complemented by a progressively strict, generalized taboo on sexual stimulation from whatever source. Previously normal forms of bodily contact between children and their parents, as well as among children themselves, were redefined as "abnormal": children who had earlier slept with their parents were now relegated to separate beds, parents were discouraged from "handling and dandling" their children, and children were "taught to conceal their bodies from others."[32]

It appears, then, that child-rearing practices during the early modern period reflected the insistence of John Wesley that "a wise and truly kind parent will take the utmost care not to cherish in her children the desire of the flesh, their natural propensity to seek happiness in gratifying the outward senses."[33] By discouraging an embodied attachment between children and their mothers, Wesley as well as many other Protestant theologians during this period helped to ensure a "profound alienation of individuals from their own bodies."[34]

The early modern desensualization of childhood can also be inferred from the Protestant assault on the cults of the Virgin and Baby Jesus. If these cults can be interpreted as signs of a particularly intense attachment between infants and their mothers, then the decline of these cults—and the corresponding increase in the importance of an exclusive relationship with a patriarchal God—can be seen as a sign of a dilution in the intensity of that maternal attachment. Less intense maternal attachment suggests, in turn, a comparable decline in the bodily contact between mother and child on which that attachment is based.

C. Discipline

The suppression of the oral and tactile demands of infants is by no means the only way in which the identification between child and mother—and thus between self and world—is suppressed. Any frustration of their spontaneous activities will tend to enforce a sense of separation between young children and their parents.[35] Thus strict and early discipline is likely to help establish the emotional foundations for an objectified conception of nature. We should expect, then, that such discipline would be far more common in the early modern than in the medieval era.

All the available evidence points to precisely that conclusion. Early modern children were not merely loved less, they were disciplined more than their medieval predecessors. There are, to begin with, clear indications of a hitherto unprecedented commitment to exercise control over the urination and defecation of young children at the beginning of the early modern period. Although most historians agree that the strict and early toilet training classically associated with the formation of the "anal compulsive" personality type probably did not predominate until the eighteenth century, some of the same historians have shown that parental efforts to enforce continence during the second year of the child's life were common in England, France, and the American colonies in the sixteenth and seventeenth centuries.[36]

There is, in contrast, no evidence of such efforts during the Middle Ages. Toilet training was apparently unknown in a society in which urination and even defecation by adults in public places was a familiar scene.[37]

The early modern emergence of toilet training was only one indication of a more general commitment—also apparently absent in the Middle Ages[38]—to ensure an early and complete submission to parental authority. This commitment was clearest in those societies—England, Holland, and the American colonies—in which the Reformation had the greatest influence. Here most child-rearing advice was offered by evangelicals for whom the self-assertion of infants and young children was an unmistakable sign of their innate depravity and the systematic suppression of this self-assertion was the indispensable condition for their salvation.[39] Thus mothers were morally mandated by Puritan preachers like John Wesley to "break their wills that you may save their souls."[40]

Wesley's advice was only one example of a common theme that echoed across more than two centuries of the English and Dutch speaking world:

> Give him no liberty in his youth, and wink not at his follies. . . . Bow down his neck while he is young . . . lest he wax stubborn, and be disobedient unto thee, and so bring sorrow to thine heart. (Becon, 1560, England)

> And surely there is in all children . . . a stubbornness . . . of mind arising from natural pride, which must be broken and beaten down. . . . This fruit of natural corruption and root of actual rebellion both against God and Man must be destroyed. Children should not know . . . that they have a will of their own, but in their parents' keeping; neither should these words be heard from them, save by way of consent, "I

will" or "I will not." (John Robinson, 1628, Holland)

[T]is a folly for [children] to pretend unto any Witt and Will of their own; they must resign all to [their father], who will be sure to do what is best; [his] word must be their Law. (Cotton Mather, 1706, Massachusetts)

In order to form the minds of children, the first thing to be done is to conquer their will and bring them to an obedient temper. . . . [W]hen the will of the child is totally subdued, and it is brought to stand in awe of the parents, then a great many childish follies and inadvertencies may be passed by. (Susanna Wesley, 1732, England)

A wise parent . . . should begin to break their will, the first moment it appears. In the whole of Christian education there is nothing more important than this. The will of a parent is to a little child in the place of the will of God. Therefore, studiously teach them to submit to this while they are children, that they may be ready to submit to his will, when they are men. (John Wesley, ca. 1783, England)

You should establish, as soon as possible, an entire and absolute authority. (John Witherspoon, 1797, Scotland)

These passages, as well as many others that could be cited, entail nothing less than what John Demos has aptly described as a "blanket indictment of the child's strivings toward self-assertion, and particularly of any impulses of direct aggression."[41] Since these strivings emerge most forcefully in the second year of life, we can assume that will-breaking usually started shortly after the child's first birthday. But there was some evidence, marshalled by Philip Greven, that in some Puritan families during the early modern period it began as early as "the first months of life."[42]

The general consensus among historians is that until the beginning of the nineteenth century the child-rearing practices of evangelical families generally reflected the advice I have just cited.[43] Even Pollack, who dissents from this consensus, acknowl edges that the diaries of the Puritan parents she inspected reveal the "rise of the training aspect of parental care—that of moulding a child into shape"[44]—during the early modern era.

There is good reason to believe, moreover, that this newfound disciplinary commitment was by no means restricted to evangelical families. Greven denies the existence of a "single consistent set of beliefs . . . characteristic of Protestants" in the American colonies in favor of the thesis that there was an important doctrinal division between a probable majority of evangelical and minority of "moderate" families. But he acknowledges that there was nonetheless a fundamental agreement in the child-rearing advice to which both moderates and evangelicals were attracted. Although moderates "preferred to bend rather than break their childrens' wills . . . in the end moderates were as intent as evangelicals upon ensuring the obedience of their children."[45] Thus John S. C. Abott, whose child-rearing advice, according to Greven, "epitomizes the moderate views of the early 19th century evangelicals," insisted that "obedience is absolutely essential to proper family government," and John Locke, whose extraordinarily influential secular child-rearing advice is classified by Greven as moderate, warned that "those . . . that intend ever to govern their children should begin it whilst they are very little, and look that they perfectly comply with the will of their parents."[46] Greven is ultimately obliged to admit that the views of moderate Enlightenment thinkers like Locke "were almost as repressive" as the views of evangelicals like Susanna Wesley and to agree with Peter Slater that the "specific tactics of restraint advanced by Enlightenment writers were the same as the ones presented . . . by the Calvinists: the child's mental habits remained the battleground."[47]

It would be wrong, finally, to assume that this disciplinary consensus was limited to Protestant families or to countries in which the Reformation was triumphant. Hunt shows that seventeenth-century French parents were equally wary of the child's will and every bit as determined to subdue it.[48] Aries claims that the first two principles of seventeenth-century French child rearing were that "children must never be left alone" and "children must not be pampered and must be accustomed to strict discipline early in life," and Ozment concludes that "preoccupation with . . . discipline was a pervasive feature of [child rearing] in the sixteenth and seventeenth centuries" throughout Western Europe as a whole.[49]

D. Prohibitions on Adults

The case I have made for an increase in the severity of child-rearing practices during the early modern era is vulnerable to the objection that much—although not all—of this case rests on a demonstrated increase in the severity of child-rearing *advice*—advice that may or may not have actually been followed. In the absence of more direct evidence of child-rearing practices, no definitive rejoinder to this objection is possible. But the following consideration lends additional strength to my case.

Norbert Elias has shown that an entire range of adult bodily behaviors that have long since been culturally proscribed were considered perfectly normal, and in fact were regularly witnessed, during the Middle Ages. He demonstrates, moreover, that it was precisely during the early modern period that a dramatic "advance in the threshold of shame and revulsion"[50] over these behaviors occurred. If we assume, with psychoanalysis, that the shame and revulsion that adults feel for their bodies is rooted in the bodily deprivations they experienced as children, then the early modern "take-off" of what Elias calls the civilizing process compellingly confirms the case for a significant increase in the repressiveness of child-rearing practices—and not just advice—during this period.[51]

In the Middle Ages, Elias tells us,

> the control and restraint to which the instinctual life of adults was subjected was considerably less than in the following phase of civilization [and] people gave way to drives and feelings incomparably more easily, quickly, spontaneously, and openly than today.[52]

"From the late Middle Ages and the early Renaissance on,"[53] however, the following cultural constraints on bodily functions and impulses were imposed:

1. *Taboos on Eating* Elias shows that early modern etiquette manuals increasingly proscribe as "uncivilized" any direct contact between food and the person consuming it. This transformation from "finger to fork" can be understood as an imposition of a prohibition on immediate oral gratification that reflects—and reinforces in turn—what I have argued were the increasingly less indulgent infant feeding practices of the early modern era.

2. *Taboos on Bodily Exposure and Contact* Cultural prohibitions on a "nakedness that was the everyday rule up to the 16th century" are progressively enforced after that time. Bodily contact— from touching during the day to sharing the same bed at night— that was previously common becomes a "general offense."[54] The increasingly evident shame surrounding bodily exposure and contact is consistent with—and can be interpreted as the result of—the dramatic decline in cutaneous contact between infants and their mothers that, I have argued, occurred on the eve of modernity.

3. *Taboos on Bodily Emissions* During the early modern era farting, nose blowing, spitting, and eliminating all reach the threshold of shame and embarrassment below which they had passed in medieval times. The cough as disguise, the handkerchief, the spittoon, and the private privy all come into prominence during this period. There is, in short, an increasing preoccupation with gaining control over bodily secretions that are now, for the first time, thought to be "disgusting." Would these bodily functions have become disgusting if not for the early child-rearing practices that suppressed them?

4. *Taboos on Aggression* Aggressive behavior that was accepted in the Middle Ages is accepted no longer. Fighting is increasing-

ly frowned upon. Taking pleasure at the suffering of others becomes "abnormal." The knife is never passed unless the blade is
pointed away from the person to whom it is passed. Aggression,
in sum, "is confined and tamed by innumerable rules and prohibitions that . . . become self-constraints."[55] These increasingly internalized constraints against the willfulness of adults confirm
my contention that this was a period during which there were intensified efforts on the part of parents to subdue the wills of their
children.

III. A Gender-Struggle Theory of Transformations in Child Rearing

The results of our comparison of medieval and early modern
child rearing are consistent with the hypothesis of an increase in
the severity of practices preceding the disenchantment of nature
and the industrial civilization that it made possible. In this section I derive an explanation for this change in child-rearing practices from the assumptions of the feminist psychoanalytic theories of Dorothy Dinnerstein and Nancy Chodorow. I will preface
this explanation by confronting the familiar objection that psychoanalytic explanations of child rearing are inherently unable to
account for such changes.

The eminent historian Lawrence Stone argues, for example,
that psychological explanation "blocks off any possibility of
change, since each generation is automatically obliged, by the
very fact of its own childhood experience, to impose the same experience on its children."[56] Vivian Fox and Martin Quitt are less
persuaded than Stone that a psychological explanation requires
the prediction of an intergenerational reproduction in child-
rearing practices but agree with him that no such explanation has
been able to specify the "psychological process [that] enables
children to mature into different kinds of parents from the ones
that they had been reared by."[57]

Both Stone and Fox and Quitt assume that a commitment to
psychological explanation entails a commitment to define the

problem of a transformation in child-rearing practices as a problem of the transformation of child-rearing orientations: they assume, in other words, that if the children of one generation are raised differently from the children of the previous generation, this can only be because the parents of the younger generation have become different kinds of parents than the parents who raised them—a possibility that Stone believes is ruled out and Fox and Quitt believe is at best unclarified by psychological theory.

That assumption, in turn, is based on the tacit assumption that mothers and fathers share the same parenting orientation. If we assume the existence of a single, gender-neutral parenting predisposition, it is of course true that the fundamental psychoanalytic assumption that child-rearing practices are governed by unconsciously motivated parenting predispositions leads to the conclusion that change in the latter is a prerequisite for change in the former. If, however, we abandon the first assumption in favor of the assumption of two different, gender-based parenting predispositions, we can retain the assumption that child-rearing practices are governed by unconsciously motivated predispositions—and thus remain on psychoanalytic terrain—without having to assume that a change in those practices requires a change in these predispositions. We can assume, instead, that changes in child-rearing practices result from changes in the balance of power between unchanging maternal and paternal parenting predispositions, i.e., on a gender shift in control over the mode of child rearing. If, moreover, we assume that there is not only a difference but an *opposition* between the parenting interests of mothers and fathers, we can also assume that such gender shifts result from gender struggle over the mode of child rearing. Both of these assumptions can, in turn, be derived from the basic assumptions of feminist psychoanalytic theory.

All past and present modes of child rearing can be described as maternal in the sense that mothers (or female mother substitutes) have been far more responsible than fathers (or male father substitutes) for the care of infants and very young children.[58] Thus, while it is true that "any current interaction between parent and child is motivated by the parent's past relationship with both of his [or her] parents,"[59] it is the parent's childhood relationship with his or her mother that more decisively determines the nature of the current interaction between parent and child. Both the nature of that relationship with the mother, and the way in which it informs this interaction between parent and child, are likely to differ dramatically according to the gender of the parent.

The development of the identity of children of both sexes depends on a period of "primary identification"—of symbiotic union—with the mother that results from her nurturant responses to their imperious infantile needs and on a subsequent separation from her that can only be enforced through maternal frustration of these very same needs. The universal dilemma of childhood is that emotional fusion with the mother is essential for, yet eventually an obstacle to, the formation of the self. Thus both boys and girls will be inescapably torn between a desire for and fear of the mother that will continue to reverberate throughout their lives. On the one hand, we all seek to recapture the "lost feeling of oneness"[60] that was the primordial source of our sentient selfhood; on the other, this very search cannot but evoke the terror of engulfment—of the possible loss of self—within the matrix from which we have so painfully and precariously emerged. We are all—women and men alike—fated to experience the "maternal tug" with profound ambivalence.

There is good reason to believe, however, that this ambivalence will be far more intense in the case of men. The boy is likely to have a much stronger fear of maternal engulfment than the girl, because identification with the mother is a threat to his gender identity but not to hers. He necessarily experiences a conflict between his initial feminine identification and his emergent masculinity, a conflict that is characteristically resolved by the suppression of that identification and the exaggeration of this masculinity.[61] The demands of masculine development dictate, in other words, that the need to separate from the mother in order to establish an independent self will be reinforced dramatically by the need of the male child to deny the female within him and thus to repudiate his attachment to his mother.

This repudiation is typically facilitated by the boy's identification with the authority of adult males—fathers or father figures—who encourage "dis-identification" from the mother by denigrating everything she represents and glorifying everything she does not.[62] This glorification of the world of men is typically accompanied by a variety of mechanisms—including residential segregation, pollution taboos, and male initiation rites—designed to enforce a physical and emotional separation from the world of women, the extent and starkness of which depend on the intensity and persistence of the male child's mother identification.[63] Thus boys ward off the threat of maternal engulfment that intimacy with a woman represents by learning to define women as simultaneously dangerous and inferior to men. As men they will attempt to reconcile the conflict between their need for, and fear of, their mothers by attempting to control the women who represent them.

Things are very different for the girl. Since the female child's identification with the mother is not an obstacle to, but rather a source of, her femininity, the development of her gendered sense of self is based not on a repudiation but on an affirmation of her relationship with her mother. "For girls and women, issues of femininity or female identity do not depend on the achievement of separation from the mother or the progress of individuation."[64] Thus the girl's eventual separation from her mother is not destructive of, but instead builds on, her emotional attachment to her mother. This emotional attachment persists, moreover, even in the face of the girl's "turn to the father"—or father figure—by means of which her heterosexuality is consolidated:

> Girls [during their oedipal period] . . . do not "reject" their mothers in favor of their fathers and men. . . . They usually make a sexual resolution in favor of men and their fathers, but retain an internal emotional triangle [within which] men tend to remain *emotionally* secondary.[65]

Thus the girl learns through her initial encounters with her mother that close relationships with others are essential to the development of her feminine sense of self. According to Chodorow, girls

> emerge from this period with a basis for empathy built into their primary definition of self in a way that boys do not. . . . [They] emerge with a stronger basis for experiencing another's needs or feelings as one's own.[66]

The asymmetry between the girl's and boy's relationship with the mother produces an asymmetry in their subsequent choice of "love objects." Both will reproduce the dynamics of their relationship with their mothers, but the mother substitute for the woman will be a person with whom she can relive the primitive joys of infantile merger, while the mother substitute for the man will be someone with whom these "oceanic feelings"[67] can be kept at bay. And there is yet another asymmetry: The man will be able, and the woman unable, to find their respective mother substitutes in the person of their heterosexual partner. He, not she, is fated to relive the maternal relationship with his mate.

There are two reasons why the woman is far more likely to serve as a mother substitute for the man than the man can serve as a mother substitute for the woman. First, and most obviously, intimate bodily contact with someone whose sex is the same as the mother is a much more direct and evocative reminder of the earliest, eminently embodied relationship with her than comparable contact with someone of the opposite sex.[68] Sexual intercourse does not offer the wife the kind of unconscious emotional access to the mother that it offers to her husband. He is far more likely to represent her father, whose place in her emotional life is, as we have seen, normally far less central than her mother's. Second, the man's fear of intimacy typically leaves him far less willing to play the role of the mother than the woman; even if she did look to him in order to reexperience merger with her mother, he would ordinarily not allow himself to be found. Thus she must look elsewhere for the oneness with the mother that she craves.

She characteristically finds that oneness in her relationship with her child. "The empathy of the mother for her child originates in the experiences of her early infancy which are reanimated by the emotions of the current experience of motherhood."[69] The child's complete dependence on her reproduces her initially complete dependence on her mother; its need for constant solicitude reawakens in her the memory of a time when her needs for nurture were similarly voracious. In nurturing the needs of her infant she simultaneously nurtures her own; in mothering her child she mothers the child within her. Her preoedipal identification with her mother has, in other words, left her with a powerful unconscious stake in the physical and emotional well-being of her offspring, in the "total concern for [her] infant's welfare" for which "maternal instinct" is the conventionally, but inadequately, invoked explanation.[70] Thus Chodorow concludes that

> As a result of having been parented by a woman, women are . . . likely . . . to seek to be mothers, that is, to relocate themselves in a primary mother-child relationship, to get gratification from the mothering relationship, and to have psychological and relational capacities for mothering.[71]

As a result of also having been parented by a woman, none of this will be true of the father. We have seen that his preoedipal experience has left him with an intensely ambivalent mixture of need for, and fear of, his mother, and that he will attempt to resolve this ambivalence with a combination of distance from, and domination over, the spouse who unavoidably represents her.[72] When he cannot avoid her he must control her: any manifestation of independence on her part evokes the twin terrors that "mommy" will leave him and that "mommy" will engulf him, and must, therefore, be suppressed. Threatened by the subjectivity of "their" women, men typically transform them into objects over which they can exercise control. As Dinnerstein has stressed,

> What is reflected in man's unilateral possessiveness . . . is not only the original, monolithic infant wish for ownership

of a woman but also a second, more equivocal feeling, rooted in early boyhood: that attachment to a woman is emotionally bearable, consistent with the solidarity among men
which is part of maleness, only if she, and one's feelings toward her, remain under safe control.[73]

Thus men are, cross-culturally, far more likely to be sexually possessive than women, for whom intimacy with a man is neither an
evocative reminder of her mother nor a threat to her gender
identity.[74]

It follows that men are also far more likely than their mates to
experience their child as a threat to their heterosexual relationship. Whereas the birth of the child "recreates the desired mother-child relationship for a woman [it] interrupts it for a man."[75]
The affection that she lavishes on her newborn is received by her
spouse as an all-too-clear signal that he will no longer be able to
monopolize his wife-mother's attention. The child, in short,
"robs him of his wife."[76] He had already been obliged, as a child,
to give up his claim to his mother in return for the promise that
one day he, too, would be able to possess someone like her. The
arrival of his child, however, betokens the betrayal of this
promise and the reluctant recognition that he must, once again,
relinquish his mother, this time in the person of his wife.

He is not likely to take this loss lightly. Instead he can be expected to redouble his efforts to monopolize her attention and
thus to limit his child's claim upon it. (His wife, in turn, will find
that his intensified possessiveness leaves him even less able than
before to satisfy her emotional needs and is thus likely to intensify her already intense emotional involvement with her child.
This, of course, will only serve further to intensify his possessiveness. And so on.) He tries, in short, to get back his wife by getting
rid of his child, i.e., by attempting to interrupt as quickly and
thoroughly as possible the intimate bond between them.[77]

Jealousy of his children thus gives the father an emotional
stake in child-rearing practices that frustrate, rather than gratify,

their oral and tactile needs. His resentment is also likely to surface in the form of an insistence on obedience and an intolerance of its absence. The internalization of the authority of his father by means of which his own oedipal crisis was resolved prepares him for an authoritarian response to the demands of his youthful oedipal rival; in disciplining his child—especially his male child—the father reenacts the discipline to which he, himself, was earlier subjected.[78]

The father's oedipally based stake in repressive practices, moreover, only reinforces an equally strong preoedipally based predisposition to these practices. Having learned as a boy to experience dependence as a threat to his autonomy, he will project his own fears of dependence onto his children—perhaps especially onto his male children—and push prematurely for their independence. In short, to defend against his own fears of dependence the father will try to break his children's dependence on their mother.

I assume, then, that the maternal mode of child rearing gives rise to a gender-based opposition in parenting interests, with women favoring relatively indulgent, and men favoring relatively repressive, child-rearing practices.[79] It follows that the child-rearing practices that are adopted in any given society will depend on which of these interests prevails, i.e., on whether child-rearing policy is set by women or by men. *The severity of child-rearing practices will vary directly with the extent to which men, and inversely with the extent to which women, exercise control over the mode of child rearing.* From this hypothesis we can derive the corollary that the sharp increase in the severity of child-rearing practices from the medieval to the early modern era was the consequence of an equally sharp increase in the power of fathers over the mode of child rearing during this time. The next section of this essay will attempt to verify this hypothesis.[80]

IV. Gender Control Over the Mode of Child Rearing: the Middle Ages versus the Early Modern Era

According to our theory, relatively indulgent child-rearing practices reflect relatively high maternal, as compared to paternal, control over the mode of child rearing. We should expect to find, then, that mothers had more power than fathers over the critical decisions that affected the lives of infants and very young children during the medieval period. A number of interrelated considerations point precisely to just that conclusion.

Medieval society was, to begin with, a military society: feudalism "is domination by the few who are skilled in war."[81] The members of this warrior class were expected to provide military service to their lord in return for their fief, "a complex of rights over the land which theoretically remained the legal possession of the lord."[82] This service occupied a considerable proportion of their time and energy. Thus the obligations of thirteenth century English vassals included:

> not only the prescribed military duty, *ost* or host, commonly forty days with complete equipment . . . but a less onerous duty, *chevauchee* or cavalcade, which might mean a minor expedition, or simply escort duty, for example, when the lord moved from one castle to another. In addition there was often the important duty of castle guard.[83]

Thus the ordinary military obligations of feudal noblemen took them away from their homes for protracted periods of time. Crusades and other full-scale wars greatly extended these periods,[84] and the military games (or tournaments) that were a "serious and important aspect of [the] life"[85] of the knightly strata likewise diverted their attention from the affairs of the household.

A life devoted to the preparation for, and the practice of, warfare was not a life that could be devoted to the supervision of the domestic domain, including child rearing. Such a life, moreover, was likely to be short: the "life expectancy of noblemen was . . .

low," and "many children lost their fathers at an early age."[86] Protracted father absence, in short, often became permanent father absence. In all these ways, "feudal militancy . . . subordinated [the] family life [of noblemen] to the affairs of war."[87]

Father absence, moreover, was not restricted to the nobility. Prosperous burghers were also absent from their homes for long periods of time. "Men travelled away from home in the service of the monarch or seigneur, and many travelled for commercial and financial reasons."[88] And, although prolonged father absence was far less common among the far more numerous peasantry, the obligation of serfs to provide labor services on the demesne of their lord regularly took them away from their family farm.[89] Like aristocratic fathers, neither burghers nor peasants were in a position closely and consistently to supervise the rearing of their children by their wives. Relatively free from the scrutiny of their husbands, medieval wives were in a position to raise their children as they saw fit.

Other features of medieval society diluted the father's, and enhanced the mother's, control over the medieval mode of child rearing. One such feature was the presence of numerous rela-tives within the household of the conjugal pair.[90] Although most medieval households were probably patrilocal—the wife taking up residence in the home of her husband's family—matrilocal arrangements were by no means uncommon.[91] Under these arrangements, husbands joined the households of their brides and were obliged to defer to the advice of her kin, who might be expected to take the side of his wife in the event of any conflict between them. Even the more familiar patrilocal arrangements were likely to be relatively favorable to the parenting interests of the wife. Although family authority under these arrangements is exercised by the father's, rather than the mother's, male elder, we should not expect that the parenting orientation of either male elder would be as repressive as the father's: lacking the oedipally based jealousy of the child, which, we have seen is, an important source of the punitive paternal predisposition, each was likely to be far more sympathetic than he to the indulgent orientation of its mother. Thus the subordination of the "family of procreation" to the "family of descent" that characterized both matrilocal and patrilocal households subordinated the father to his elders and impeded his capacity to enforce his parenting interest against the competing interest of his wife.

Feudal religion also made it more likely for the mother's parenting interest to prevail. If, as I have suggested, the medieval cult of the Virgin Mary was a religious expression of the intense mother identification that resulted from relatively indulgent medieval child-rearing practices, this veneration of the "spiritual mother of the . . . Christian family" also functioned to legitimate—and thus to reproduce—the very maternal control over child rearing from which these practices flowed. The same function could be attributed to the adoration of the female saints who attracted so many followers during the late Middle Ages.[92] The religious instruction offered by these "spiritual mothers" reinforced the religious role of the earthly mothers within the home. Herhily notes that an early fifteenth-century tract on family care that includes advice on the religious education of children is addressed to a woman, on the assumption that she bears the chief responsibility for that education, and argues that this was a common assumption of the late medieval period.[93]

Medieval law, finally, was relatively supportive of the power of women within the home. Noblewomen had the right to inherit fiefs along with the authority that accompanied them and to bequeath them to their heirs.[94] Townswomen typically retained rights to their own property, and widows were "entitled to enjoy the fruits of the dower for life." Although there was great regional variation in the inheritance rights of peasant daughters, "generally speaking, it may be said that in most regions daughters too inherited . . . [although] almost without exception the rights of sons took precedence."[95] Women were, in other respects, legal persons in the full sense of the term. As Maitland mentioned in his *History of English Law*, a woman in thirteenth-century England could "make a will, make a contract . . . sue and be sued."[96]

The same is true elsewhere in medieval europe. In sum, the exclusion of medieval women from the exercise of authority outside the family was not accompanied by their "rightlessness" within the domestic domain. In that domain, Mount claimed, "women had clearly established legal and customary rights and exercised these rights vigorously."[97]

The mother's domestic presence, her alliance with the elders with whom she lived, her religious responsibilities, and her legal status all left her in a favorable position to exercise power within the home and over child rearing in particular. This power was especially evident in the case of the noblewoman, who "comes to play an extraordinary role in the management of family property in the Middle Ages."[98] In the absence of her husband, she "ran the estate, direct[ed] the staff [including the ladies who acted as nurses for her children, and ma[de] the financial and legal decisions."[99] But female domestic power was by no means restricted to the aristocracy. According to Herhily, the mother had "prestige and influence within the household[s]" of all classes of the population and was far more "deeply involved in socializing the young" than her mate. Shahar agrees: "there can be no doubt that the mother fulfilled a more important function than the father in the life of a small child."[100] Thus the available evidence points compellingly to the conclusion that it was she, rather than he, who was able to exercise control over the mode of child rearing.

This is no longer the case during the early modern era. A number of interrelated, mutually reinforcing factors facilitated the father's capture of control over the mode of child-rearing control at this time.

The first was simply his presence within the home. The elimination of the fief in favor of private ownership eliminated the obligation to perform military services in return for the rights connected to control over landed property. Regular and protracted absence from their homes was no longer required of the male members of the early modern aristocracy, who were thus in a far better position than their feudal counterparts to supervise their domestic affairs. The same could be said for the (far more numerous) men of the less privileged classes. No longer obliged to divide their time between working their own land and working the land of their lord, peasant fathers were now in a better position to exercise control over the activity of their wives within their homes. Artisans working in their homes were in a similar position.

Thus the economic foundations for enhanced patriarchal authority were established with the consolidation of the domestic economy.[101] When the home became the principal site of production, husbands were obliged to spend far more time within it and thus to interact far more regularly with their wives. This meant, among other things, that wives were increasingly obliged to rear their children under the watchful eyes of their husbands.

The dissolution of the power of kinship during the early modern era also enhanced the domestic power of the father. Historians now agree that the extended family disappeared in Western Europe long before the rise of the industrialization that was formerly—and wrongly—assumed to be the principal cause of its disappearance.[102] Laslett, Stone, Houlbrooke, and MacFarlane have all demonstrated that by the sixteenth century the predominant family form in England was nuclear, with households comprised exclusively of parents, their children, and (if they could be afforded) servants.[103] Elsewhere in Western Europe this family form develops somewhat later but is firmly in place well before the industrialization that marked the end of the early modern period.[104] Thus early modern parents no longer live with, and are no longer obliged to defer to the wishes of, their older kin. The elimination of these kin from the home deprives the wife of the "natural allies" she was formerly able to find among them:

> Wives maltreated by their husbands were now less able to turn to their kin for support and defense. Intervention by the elders of the kin to settle marital quarrels was now less easy and less welcome. The kin could no longer so readily serve as mediators between the parents and the children.[105]

Thus the liberation of the family of procreation from the family of descent contributes significantly to the subordination of the wife to her husband.[106]

The Reformation plays a similar role. Luther's doctrine of the "priesthood of all believers" elevated the importance of the family as a site of religious worship and instruction; the family becomes, in effect, a "little church." It is a little church, moreover, within which the father came to exercise "semi-priestly functions." The Protestant elimination of the role of the Virgin and the saints in favor of the role of "God the father" simultaneously undermined the religious authority of the mother within the home and enhanced the authority of the father, in whose harsh image the Calvinist God is conceived. It is he, rather than she, whom Protestant theologians charged with the responsibility for the "moral welfare of [the] household,"[107] and thus he rather than she to whom child-rearing tracts were increasingly addressed.[108] By enhancing the importance of the father within the home, Protestant theology also enhanced the wife's dependence on her husband: "He for God only, she for God in him."[109] Thus the "reformation, by reducing the authority of the priest in society, simultaneously elevated the authority of lay heads of households."[110] In countries where it was influential, paternal control over the mode of child rearing was religiously reinforced.

The early modern process of "statification" also served to legitimate paternal power over child rearing. The patriarchal political theory of the sixteenth and seventeenth centuries sought to justify the absolute power of the monarch by drawing an analogy between his relationship to his subjects and the father's relationship to his dependents: the king "being *pater patriae* as the master is *pater familias*,"[111] the power of the former over his subjects is properly as unlimited as the power of the latter is over his children. This appeal to paternal authority as the legitimate basis for political authority reinforced, in turn, the legitimacy of the father's power within the home.

This ideological elevation of men was accompanied by the legal subordination of women. The early modern period witnessed a precipitous decline in the legal status of married women. The Western European "married woman . . . was largely subsumed under the legal personality of her husband; she was virtually without rights to own property, make contracts, or sue for damages on her own account."[112] At the same time, "royal legislation from the sixteenth century on took care to strengthen the father's power with regard to . . . his children."[113] The result was that the father "became the family despot . . . lording it over his wife and children."[114]

None of the factors I have mentioned operated in isolation from the others. Statification hastened the advent of the nuclear family by replacing loyalty to the "community of cousins" with loyalty to the ruler of a political community composed of relatives and nonrelatives alike, and the rise of the nuclear family reinforced the process of statification.[115] The Protestant emphasis on the preeminent role of the head of the family of procreation, on the one hand, and the decline in the role of the family of descent, on the other, similarly reinforced each other. The Reformation and statification were also reciprocally related, as each worked to undermine the small-scale organizations that mediated between "Man" and either God or state.[116] The domestic economy, finally, was simultaneously cause and effect of statification, the Reformation, and the decline of kinship.[117]

All of these factors worked in concert to facilitate an unprecedented increase in the power of the father within the home, making the early modern period the period *par excellence* of the patriarchal family in Western Europe. The father was now working in or near the home, was "less hampered by interference from the kin, [and] both Church and State were unanimous in reinforcing his authority and pressing new duties on him."[118] Thus the evidence amply sustains Stone's claim that the "powers of fathers over children and of husbands over wives . . . became greater than they had been in the middle ages."[119]

The results of our comparison of paternal power during the medieval and early modern periods are consistent with the hypothesis that a shift from female to male control over the mode of child rearing was responsible for the increase in the severity of child-rearing practices from the earlier to the later period. Deference to near-absolute patriarchal authority obliged early modern wives to subordinate their "soft" parenting orientations to the "hard" orientations of their husbands, and children who had earlier been mercifully shielded from were now obliged to bear the full brunt of their fathers' furies. This subordination of maternal to paternal power is confirmed by Schucking's account of the sixteenth- and seventeenth-century English Puritan family, whose "iron [paternal] strictness . . . made it impossible for true motherliness to have any appreciable influence and hindered its expression at every turn."[120] It is also confirmed by the literary testimony of early modern mothers, who lament the strictness of their husbands and its unfortunate consequences for their children, as well as of early modern fathers, who bemoan the (usually vain) attempts of their wives to mitigate that strictness.[121]

There is other direct evidence of the effort of early modern husbands to impose their harsh parenting interests on their wives and through them on their children. Sixteenth- and seventeenth-century Puritan authors testify to the widespread resistance of husbands during this time to their children being nursed by their wives.[122] The prevailing assumption that sexual intercourse spoiled the mother's milk led the doctors of the day to prescribe sexual abstinence during nursing in order to ensure the health of the child.[123] Thus the husband of a nursing mother would lose the sexual services of his wife, and his dilemma was how to avert this loss yet secure his child's survival.

The wet-nursing that was pervasive during this period was his solution to this dilemma. "It was the insistence of the husbands rather than the desire of the wives which was the main reason for the employment of wet-nurses";[124] not "maternal indifference" but paternal preference was responsible for this practice.[125] Early modern observers of wet-nursing were aware that this was the case: "many a tender mother," lamented William Gouge, "is prevented [from nursing] by the misplaced authority of a husband."[126] Through the exercise of this "misplaced authority" the husband banishes the infant from his home and thus "buys a clear oedipal victory, keeping the mother to himself . . . [Wet-nursing] was a sexual triumph for the father."[127]

Another observation about wet-nursing lends additional support to the hypothesis that this and other harsh early modern practices were the consequence of the father's enhanced power within the home. If this hypothesis is correct, then the sequence in the emergence of widespread wet-nursing across different Western European societies should match the sequence of the rise of paternal power in these societies. Unfortunately I have been unable to determine the former sequence and cannot therefore directly test this proposition. But data exist that enable us to test its corollary: the sequence in the elimination of wet-nursing across Western European societies should correspond to the sequence in the decline of paternal power within their families. DeMause, Stone, and Robertson demonstrate that wet-nursing was abandoned in England in the eighteenth century, did not die out in France until the late nineteenth century, and survived until the early twentieth century in Germany.[128] The available evidence also suggests that the decline of the classical patriarchal family follows the same curve: it is eliminated first in England, then in France, and finally in Germany.[129]

Our hypothesis also receives support from Philip Greven's comparison of child-rearing practices in the American colonies. He finds that families that practiced "moderate" and even "genteel" child rearing were typically more extended than the (more numerous) nucleated, evangelical families in which strict Calvinist practices prevailed. Moderate parents "still owed some degree of deference and obedience to the grandparents," who "could and did interfere with and influence the rearing of grandchildren." In genteel families, "much of the actual work associated with the care, feeding and discipline of children was done by people employed for the purpose: nurses, servants or slaves." Thus in moderate or genteel families "parental [hence paternal] power was rarely total because of the presence of other influential adults within the household." In evangelical families, in contrast, children were isolated "from the influence of grandparents and others," and thus "parental [hence paternal] authority was absolute."[130] Greven's within-country comparison yields the following result: the less the power of the father was limited by the "natural allies" of the mother, the more severe were the prevailing child-rearing practices that prevailed. This result is exactly what our theory would lead us to expect.

V. Conclusion

The assumption that the (maternal) mode of child rearing engenders a fundamental opposition between the parenting interests of women and the parenting interests of men leads us to expect that gender struggle over child-rearing practices will be exactly as universal, and last exactly as long, as that mode of child rearing itself.[131] The gender that lacks control over the mode of child rearing will have a psychodynamically based interest in challenging the parental hegemony of the other gender, while the latter will have a psychodynamically based interest in resisting the challenge to its hegemony. Thus the potential for gender shifts in control over the mode of child rearing—and for the transformations in child-rearing practices that follow in their wake—is endemic to the maternal mode of child rearing.

In locating the source of child-rearing transformations in the internal dynamics of the mode of child rearing,[132] our theory insists that the mode of child rearing contains the seeds of its own destruction. These seeds will only germinate, however, if the capacity of one gender to enforce its parenting interest increases at the expense of the other. We have seen that this is precisely what happened during the transition from the medieval to the early modern era. A number of interrelated, extrafamilial processes—the dissolution of the ties of kinship, the development of the domestic economy, statification, and patriarchal Protestantism—combined to produce a dramatic increase in the capacity of the father—at the expense of the capacity of the mother—to enforce his parenting predisposition and thus to produce an equally dramatic increase in the severity of child-rearing practices.

This transformation in child-rearing practices would not have occurred if the permanent[133] "contradiction" between maternal and paternal parenting interests had not been "over-determined" by the mutually reinforcing extrafamilial factors that helped to "explode" that gender-based contradiction.[134] That contradiction, in other words, must be understood as a necessary but insufficient cause of the early modern—or any other—transformation in the mode of child rearing.

It is important, however, to underscore its necessity. Although the social, economic, political, and religious forces to which I have referred were responsible for the dramatic increase in the power of the early modern father over child rearing, none of these factors—nor any combination thereof—can properly be said to have required or "called forth" the equally marked increase in the severity of child-rearing practices that was associated with that increase in paternal power. Child-rearing practices did not become harsher because harsh practices were necessary for, or even the direct consequence of, the operation of the nuclear family, the domestic economy, the centralized state, or evangelical Protestantism. Rather, they became harsher because the enhanced paternal power within the home for which these social, economic, political, and religious forces were responsible "unleashed" a paternal parenting predisposition the existence of which does not depend on these extrafamilial forces. The determining role of these cultural and historical factors, in short, was decisively mediated by the transcultural, transhistorical force of gender.

The same point can be made about the ultimate origins of the "disenchantment of the world" for which—to return for a final time to the thesis of *Marxism and Domination*—the harsh child-rearing practices of the early modern era were immediately responsible. To the extent that the nuclear family, the domestic economy, statification, and the Reformation helped make these child-rearing practices possible, they must be understood as important determinants of the modern industrial worldview. This point would appear to sustain the claim of a variety of different—including Marxian, Weberian, and Durkheimian—theoretical traditions concerning the contribution of these social, economic, political, and religious forces to a modernity that was uniquely Western in its origin. But only in part. Neither the founders nor the followers of any of these theoretical traditions have grasped that the contribution of these culturally and historically specific factors to modernization was contingent on their contribution to the unprecedented hegemony of the culturally universal parenting predispositions of men. None has recognized, in sum, that modernity was made possible by the triumph of the paternal over the maternal interest in the rearing of children. I believe that this conclusion enables us to clarify the sense in which it is possible to speak, with Philippe Aries, of the "essentially masculine civilization of modern times."[135]

chapter nine

. Tripping .

$p$rivately I was dissatisfied with this public conclusion. Although it was true that there would have been no
modernization without the triumph of the masculine approach
to child rearing, it was also true that there would have been no
triumph of the masculine approach to child rearing without the
transformations in kinship, economy, polity, and religion I had
described. If these extrafamilial transformations were insufficient, they were also necessary for the making of modernity. And
I had not really explained *them*.

I had argued that these social, economic, political, and religious transformations were interrelated and mutually reinforcing. They seemed to form an historical whole, or what Hegelians
like to call a "totality." But this formulation only posed the problem of the origins of that totality. This was a problem for which I
had no real solution. Prior to writing the chapter my assumption
had been that changes in the balance of power between men and
women within the home reflected changes in the outcome of the
contest between masculine and feminine values throughout the
society as a whole. This assumption obliged me to interpret the
new totality as the triumph of masculine over feminine culture.

But I didn't know if this was a plausible interpretation. Certainly the Reformation can be, and has been, viewed as a tough, masculine attack on the softer, more feminine side of Christianity.[1] But what about the decline in the authority of elders? The development of the domestic economy? The centralized state? Despite my closing citation of Aries, I really didn't understand the sense in which these dimensions of early modern civilization were "essentially [more] masculine" than the dimensions of medieval civilization they replaced.

There was another, perhaps related, problem. The totality I had described was unique to the West. Long ago Max Weber noted that in non-Western agrarian societies, like traditional India and China, the domestic economy, statification, and patriarchal religion did not undermine but were obliged to accommodate the persistent influence of the family of descent over the family of procreation.* This suggested that these economic, political, and religious forces were able to erode the influence of Western kinship—and with it the child's protection from the untrammeled exercise of paternal power—only because this influence had already been attenuated prior to the early modern era. Weber speculated that kinship had long been weakened in the West by the commitment of Christianity to the priority of universal moral principles over particularistic family ties, to "a common ethical way of life in opposition to the community of blood."[2]

So there was a sense in which the contribution of the nuclear family—the primacy of the family of procreation over the family of descent—was greater than the contribution of the domestic economy, statification, and patriarchal religion to the early modern masculinization of the mode of child rearing and the mod-

---

*The result was that in those societies infants and very young children were never left as vulnerable to the harsh parenting orientation of their fathers as were their counterparts in the early modern West. This would account for the fact that child-rearing practices in non-Western societies are generally less severe than in Western societies. See my *Marxism and Domination*, p. 330, 341.

ernization that followed in its wake. If Weber was right, this disproportionate contribution of the nuclear family was connected to the rise of Christianity in the West. This was a connection I chose not to explore. I had already pushed things back to the Middle Ages. I was not about to begin with the birth of Christ!

Besides, the pursuit of this connection might just undo all the others I thought I had established. I had argued that maternal control over the mode of child rearing was fostered by the subordination of the family of procreation to the family of descent during the Middle Ages. But Weber's argument implied that the influence of the family of descent was already in descent by that time. If his argument was right, it was difficult to avoid the conclusion that mine was wrong. If the medieval conjugal pair was not in fact subject to the control of the kin—if the family was already "nuclearized"—then either maternal control of the mode of child rearing did not depend on the influence of the kin or maternal control of the mode of child rearing did not exist. If maternal control did not depend on the influence of the kin, then it was implausible even partly to attribute the shift to paternal control to the waning of that influence. If maternal control did not exist, then either indulgent practices did not depend on maternal control or medieval child rearing was not in fact indulgent. And so on. Pulling the Weberian thread threatened to unravel my entire theoretical fabric. Better to ignore it, even at the cost of a few loose historical ends.

My review of the logical possibilities reminded me of just how little I really knew about the Middle Ages. One hundred and thirty-one endnotes following a fifty-two page text could not disguise—and perhaps only served to reveal—that one can't become a medievalist in a month! My descriptions of medieval child rearing, kinship, economy, polity, and religion were certain to encounter the objections of people who had devoted years to the study of any *one* of these areas. I knew that my tapestry was too big, and its weave too coarse, to display the details that were so dear to their hearts.

So I had my doubts about my chapter. Despite these doubts, I decided that I would try to get it published as an article in an academic journal. The trick was to send it out to a journal whose editors would be sympathetic to its basic thrust. I decided on a well-known journal of feminist history and theory. The editors of this journal would be more likely to be seduced by the sweep of my scholarship, and less likely to be disturbed by its dubious details, than the more orthodox medievalists and early modernists who would review it for a "straight" academic journal. I would have plenty of time to work on those details after my piece was accepted for publication.

I also decided that over the next two years I would submit the three other historical chapters for publication as separate articles. I hoped that a series of small success stories during this time would help me sustain the commitment necessary for completing The Book on schedule. They would also alert at least part of my audience to its eventual existence. And they would help me make some much-needed money.

My department had recently voted to double the percentage of our total salary pool that would be allotted for "merit" (as compared to across-the-board) increases. Academic Reaganism: if I wanted decent raises over the next two years, I would have to increase my "productivity." And, if I wanted to qualify for the first of these raises, I would have to be quick about it. My first article would have to be accepted for publication by next spring. If I deferred submitting my chapter to a journal until I received—and digested—the comments of my typically overcommitted colleagues, it would be impossible to meet that deadline. So I decided to send it out without first showing it to my friends.

I worried a bit about this. But only a bit. After all, I had been teaching for fifteen years and had never had an article rejected. Surely the worst that could happen is I would be asked to "revise and resubmit." I would write the revisions then. Not now. Now I needed a break. I had worked nonstop on my piece for almost three months. It had not come easily. To tell the truth, it had been something of a drag. I was tired of wrestling with what I had written. I wanted it off my back. . . .

My back still hurt. Therapy had unblocked my writing but not yet my body. It was still tight as a drum. A hit on a joint was about the only way I could loosen it up. All summer long I had slept no more than four to five hours a night. And I was starting to sneak the cigarettes from which I had worked so hard to unhook myself almost ten years ago. It seemed that I needed at least one of those little suckers to get me though the day. Of course they made me even more nervous than I otherwise would have been.

Right now I was nervous about the first week of school. Dotty was leaving town to peddle her tapes to producers in L.A. During the summer she had spent more time with Shayla so I could spend more time with my book. Now it was my turn to help out. Shayla had started preschool, but only for two hours, three mornings a week. There were two afternoons and one evening during the first week of school when I would have to be in class when she would have to be at home. A couple of friends volunteered to solve that problem. But what really worried me was how Shayla and I would do during the time we were together. This would be the first time since her birth that her mother was away while I stayed home. For five days. Five days that followed six weeks during which Shayla had gotten used to spending more time with Dotty than with me. I did not look forward to five miserable days of her missing her mother.

Fortunately my fears were unfounded. Dotty left on the Sunday before the start of school. On Monday morning I awakened to the tears of a two-and-a-half-year-old who wanted her mamma. Ten minutes later Shayla dried her eyes, looked up, and announced, "I'm better now." For the rest of the week she hardly mentioned her mother. She didn't even get very sad when she talked to her on the phone. In fact she was her usual happy self. And we did all our usual things together: talked, went on walks, took baths and bike rides, danced, shopped, and cuddled. Everything went as well while her mother was away as when she was at home. This was just the way it was supposed to be.

Shayla did have one scare later in the week. A friend of ours called to see how she was doing and invited her to see her daughter. Shayla demurred. Apparently she remembered that she had stayed at their house in February when Dotty and I were away for our post-weaning weekend. Hanging up the phone with a sigh, she told me that "I don't want to see Sonja. . . . I'm afraid you're going to go away." My assurance that I had no such intention quickly assuaged her fears. Her fears reassured me that when we did go away, Dotty was not the only one who was missed. This kid really *does* love me. I must be doing something right.

Of course I was getting more than a little help from my little friend. Shayla's remarkable awareness of her needs made it so much easier for me to meet them. "I'm better now." "I'm afraid you're going to go away." My God, she was more able to express her feelings at two-and-a-half than I had been at twenty. She was already so adult.

Which is why she was also so funny. Shayla was simultaneously very smart and very short, a less-than-three-foot model of maturity. The incongruity constantly cracked people up. Especially since she sounded a lot like Elmer Fudd. I worried that she would "chasthe wabbits" for the rest of her life. I knew that it was much too early to try to correct her. But she was already so stubborn I doubted that she would listen to me even when the time was wipe.

"That's not my style!" she would scream as I tried calmly to explain for the umpteenth time why her skirt should be worn above, not below, the apex of her rather ample tummy. Shayla had about as much patience for my sartorial suggestions as her mother. It seemed like neither of the women in my life would ever listen to me about anything.

At least I had my students. But precious few of them were really *my* students, students who had come here because they wanted to work with me. I would never know exactly how many others had been scared off by a combination of the limited prestige and limited theory offerings of my department. Whatever the reasons, the sad fact was that I was now chairing my first dissertation committee in the ten years I had been one of its member. My first doctoral student in a decade! I envied my colleagues at other institutions who complained that they had more than they could handle.

I especially envied the superstars among them, the academic popes to whom their faithful followers would annually flock. I was about to get a small taste of what that would be like. At the end of October I would be visited by Miriam Dixson, an Australian feminist historian who was at Harvard for the semester. Miriam had written of her great respect for my work and requested a visit to discuss it. I was only too happy to put her up for a long weekend. This was the first time that a colleague had ever come halfway across the country to talk to me.

Miriam was also the first historian with whom I chose to speak about my book. She greeted my thesis of an early modern decline in the quality of Western child care with the skepticism befitting a feminist who was more of a modernist than me. Several hours of discussion persuaded her that I was on to something important to which, she promised, she would respond in detail after she had read my manuscript. I was pleased that my project had survived its first real-life encounter with a historian. And I was delighted to learn about the work and life of a woman who had bravely refused to knuckle Down Under.

Miriam and I talked freely about the relationship between our personal and academic lives. Our conversations reminded me of how much I missed the dizzying dance of intimate theoretical discourse. How much, in particular, I missed Rob. He had been the one friend in Chicago with whom I could simultaneously discuss Marx and my marriage, Freud and our friendship. Our discussions were labors of love that helped us maintain our sanity in a society that vainly—and insanely—tries to enforce their separation. Back in June Rob had split for the greener grasses of the Pacific Northwest. I had lost my best friend in Chicago. Shayla had lost her "Uncle Rob." I promised her—and myself—that we would visit him as soon as we could.

As soon as we could was after I finished grading my final exams. The fall quarter had been the washout for my work that I had expected it to be. Nor would I be able to make any progress on my project during the winter break. Banya would be joining the family for a two-week vacation in Jamaica. Dotty and I had decided that the only way my mother would ever take a trip was if we took her along with us. I had been to the Caribbean ten times over the past twenty years and she had never in her life been south of the New Jersey shore. I knew from the first seven summers of my life that we spent there just how much she loved the sea. I remembered how happy she had been for me to hold her up as the waves washed harmlessly against her half-broken body.

Forty years later I longed to be her life preserver once again. Banya was almost eighty and increasingly immobile. Our offer was probably her last chance to ever smell the salt air, or feel the sand beneath her feet, again. I was thrilled when she accepted it.

Of course I was also afraid that she would ruin our trip. It wasn't exactly easy for Banya to have a good time, especially in a new and different place. And even if she was able to let go of her fears of the world, I knew it wouldn't be easy for me to let go of my need to protect her from it. Dividing my time and energy between my mother, my wife, and my daughter would be a tricky emotional task. The weaker part of me secretly hoped she would experience her usual preflight freak-out and refuse to go.

Boarding the plane to Seattle, I was having a bit of a preflight freak-out of my own. A litany of potential disasters raced through my mind. This was going to be a four-hour flight. What if Shayla cried the whole time? What if there was a long line for the bathroom and my diaperless daughter just couldn't wait? Rob's cabin was in the middle of a rain forest on the Olympic Peninsula. What if it rained the entire time we were there? How long could we color with crayons without going crazy? This was also the first time that she would be both away from home and away from Dotty. What if she missed her mamma more than she had in the fall?

Shayla never cried once on the plane. Nor did she pee in her pants. Most of the time she either slept on my lap or cavorted with the other kids. The flight went just fine. So did our time with Uncle Rob. It *did* rain almost the entire weekend, but the rain didn't dampen our spirits. We put on our ponchos and boots and marched merrily through the muddy meadows. Sometimes the "mud" turned out to be shit. A curious Shayla asked Rob about its origins. "Elk poop" was the answer that left us laughing until we almost split our sides. "Watch out for the elk poop!" became our wacky weekend watchword. The beautiful bond between Shayla and Rob had survived their six-month separation. And while Shayla napped Rob and I were able to talk as if he had never left. . . .

Back home I barely had time to unpack our bags before I had to pack them up again. But this time they were filled with sunwear instead of raingear. My mother had called to confirm her commitment to our trip despite the problems she was having with her stomach. I chalked these problems up to her anxiety about travelling and persuaded myself that she would be fine once we got to Jamaica.

To Negril, to be precise. Seven miles of narrow white sand beach covered with every conceivable kind of accommodation, from palace to pup tent. And every conceivable kind of person as well. Negril was definitely not one of your typical Caribbean tourist ghettos where the only local color is carefully covered by the uniforms of the hotel. Negril was funky. You went there to be with the people, to rub elbows with the Rastas.

We had explained this to my mother; she said that would be fine by her. And indeed it seemed to be. We started slowly. The first night we drove her to a restaurant at a respectable hotel. The next morning I helped her walk the one hundred-or-so feet from our adjoining rooms to the gentle, warm water that awaited us. Tears filled my eyes as I helped her lower herself into it for a fleeting float.

For lunch we sampled authentic island fare at a highly recommended, hot and dirty dive. After dinner Shayla played on the swings while a local band played on the beach. The sweet smell of Sensimillan filled the air as black brothers and white sisters rocked back and forth to the syncopated rhythms of reggae. Banya kept time with her cane. She was all smiles.

The smiles vanished in the morning. My mother woke up with a terrible case of the touristas. Poor Banya. For the next seventy-two hours she stayed in her room, unable to move from her bed except when Dotty or I helped her to the bathroom. I tried to convince myself that having to help Banya didn't have to stop me from having a good time. I could take care of her in her room and take care of myself on the beach. This was just a particularly extreme form of the test with which I was always faced, the test of maintaining the boundaries between my mother and myself.

I failed miserably. I was unable to have fun with Dotty and Shayla. How could I take pleasure with them on the beach when my mother was doubled over in pain in her room? After three days of shuttling back and forth between the two I was at my wit's end. Dotty's patience with a nervous nursemaid was wearing thin. And Banya wasn't getting any better. In fact she wanted to go home. "Do you really want to, or are you just saying that because you don't want to be a burden?" "I really want to." "Really?" "Really." I called my sister in Connecticut, who agreed to meet my mother at the airport. The next morning I drove Selma to Montego Bay and put her on a plane back to Queens. A sad Jamaica farewell for Banya. And a sad drive back to Negril for her son.

My spirits were lifted when I caught sight of Shayla bobbing up and down in the water in front of our hotel. "Look, Papa, I'm swimming!" I pretended not to notice the bright blue and yellow inner tube that was keeping her afloat. I couldn't not notice the hot little blue and black bikini that Dotty was wearing as she swam over to join us. The three of us stayed in the water, sucking on the sticks of sugar cane I had bought on the way back. Five days late, our vacation had begun.

Dotty and I used our common sense to slow down and mellow out. Shayla took in our good vibes and sent out more of her own. A group of older children picked up on them and more or less adopted her for the week, granting her grateful parents plenty of time on the beach, and even a little time in our bed, together. The sun and fun readied us for Shayla when she was ready for us.

When she was done downing milk shakes at the bar or cracking open coconuts with the kids the three of us took warm, lazy late-afternoon walks in the water. It was the best week we had ever spent together. And it was harder to leave Negril than any other place I had ever been.

It would have been ever harder had I realized what was in store back home. When I sent my manuscript to Miriam in the fall I had also decided to show it to a number of other faculty friends. The first to respond was a colleague at the University of Chicago on whom I could always count to go straight to the heart of an intellectual issue. David did not disappoint. He asked me some of the same troubling questions I had earlier asked myself, questions for which I still had no answers. And he also asked me this: did I really think that the parenting orientation of a seventeenth- or eighteenth-century female Puritan believer was less harsh than the parenting orientation of a twentieth-century, middle-class, secularly educated man?

The question implied the possibility—for David, the probability—that the "hegemonic" parenting ideology did not merely affect the capacity of mothers and fathers to impose their respective parenting preferences but that it helped to create those preferences in the first place. Culture did not "legitimate" but rather helped constitute the attitudes of parents toward their children.

This possibility was entirely inconsistent with my non-Marxist but nevertheless still materialist explanation of child rearing. My premises were that (a) the attitudes of parents were determined by their simultaneously physical and emotional, early experience with their own parents and (b) this experience differed dramatically according to the gender of the parent. My conclusion, therefore, was that there was a dramatic, gender-based difference in the attitudes of parents. David did not deny the second premise. But he disagreed with the first: the primacy of the preoedipal experience of parents. His claim was that this experience was less determinative of their attitudes than their subsequent socialization and that their subsequent socialization differed dramatically according to the culture (or epoch) in question.

In the case of Puritan culture, mothers were taught, and really came to believe, that severity was essential for their children's salvation. Thus it was misleading to argue, as I had, that early modern mothers were torn between what they thought and what men thought was good for their children, and that their actual practice reflected a (male-biased) balance between the two. Rather it would be more accurate to say that they were divided between what they and their husbands both thought was good for their children and their own gender-based feeling for them, and that these feelings inclined them to be somewhat softer (in their own eyes somewhat worse) parents than their husbands. But they were certainly harsher parents than twentieth-century fathers who believe that will breaking is barbaric. Generalizing from this example, David was prepared to acknowledge that, *within* the context of a particular culture, women were generally more indulgent parents than men. But he refused to concede that most women were cross-culturally (or transhistorically) more indulgent than most men. That would concede too much to gender psychology and too little to culture.

I hardly had time to think about David's objection when I heard it again. Or rather read it in a letter that explained why my manuscript was "not appropriate" for the journal to which it had been sent. "Not appropriate." I could barely believe my eyes. A letter of rejection was the last thing I had expected. My disbelief turned to anger when I read the explanation. Although I was assured that all the editors had found my piece "quite interesting—very stimulating and forcefully argued," I was also informed that some of them had "problems" with its "ahistorical positioning of women as the more nurturant parent." And I was reminded that "we have always rejected the historical method . . . of moving from the individual/psychic to the broadly political or intellectual, without any discussion of the many social realms that lie in between."

Like David, they were taking issue with my feminist psychoanalytic assumptions, but unlike him they didn't even take the trouble to tell me what was wrong—or even incomplete—about the explanation I had erected on those foundations. Instead they simply dismissed them out of hand. I sent my manuscript off to another journal where I thought it would have a better chance for a fair hearing and fired off a letter to the editor of the first journal protesting the fact that it hadn't received one. I assured her that I was writing not to express my "personal pique" but rather my objections to an apparent methodological orthodoxy that was particularly inappropriate for a "feminist/left journal ostensibly committed to the rejection of orthodoxy in all its forms." But it was hard for me not to take their political rejection personally.

The next week I read something that was just as hard to take. An ad in the independent socialist newsweekly *In These Times* announced in bold type that the theme of this year's Socialist Scholars Conference would be "Against Domination: State, Class, Race, Gender." The ad listed the names of two dozen of the "usual suspects" who had been invited to participate. My name was not among them. This omission was particularly galling. *Marxism and Domination* had been a call for the Left to overcome its obsession with class and to pay equal attention to other forms of domination like gender and the state. Unlike a number of similar post-Marxist appeals I had also offered a unified explanation of the origins and persistence of these forms of domination that simultaneously revealed the necessity for, and the obstacles to, the unification of the different "new social movements" that struggled against them. Five years later the official guardians of academic leftism were singing my song and they didn't even have the decency to invite me to their party. I was pissed. And hurt, as I discovered as I started to sob as I tried to talk about it over the phone to Rob and (my dearest other friend) Ron.

They agreed there was no way I shouldn't have been invited. Then we talked about why I wasn't. Ron reminded me that it was a largely inbred affair, that the great majority of speakers were self-selected members of a New York left intellectual circle in which I had never been included. Rob reminded me that most of them still considered themselves Marxists and that they were politically indisposed to invite someone for whom Marx was part of the problem rather than part of the solution. And he noted that the only feminist theorists who had been invited were women. The male Marxist Left wasn't looking for any non-Marxists and the female feminist Left wasn't looking for any men. That didn't leave much room for a non-Marxist male feminist theorist like me.

It was true that I was bumping up against some pretty formidable political obstacles, but it was also true that I had been doing little or nothing to overcome them. For many years Dotty had urged me to do more to make myself known: to arrange speaking engagements at other universities, to find out about conferences in order to get invited to them, perhaps even to organize conferences of my own. But I was very skeptical of anything that smacked of self-promotion. I couldn't help remembering how often my father's sarcasm had taken the wind out of my youthful sails: "Blessed be he who bloweth his own trumpet." I had absorbed his disdain for what he—and my mother—considered to be pushy people. I was proud that I had never sucked up to anyone in my entire academic life. Yet I also knew that there was something self-defeating about wanting recognition but not being prepared to do the things that were necessary to get it. I wanted it on my terms, not theirs. I wanted them to come to me.

But they weren't. A few weeks later I learned of another conference on gender, scheduled for the spring, to which I hadn't been invited to speak. And this one was at Northwestern, not in New York. It was the same story: male feminist theorists need not apply. It was only natural that the newly influential academic women who had long been obliged to defer to men were now unwilling to share the spotlight with even the most sympathetic among them. So it was not surprising that the same female feminists who privately shared with me their great admiration for my work would never even think to mention my name in their public presentations. The rule of the new game was: don't give the men any credit.

Understanding the reasons for this rule didn't make it rankle

any less. Especially since it was, I was certain, at least partly responsible for the fact that I hadn't gotten any interviews for the
feminist theory positions at the California schools to which I had
applied in the fall. I was going nowhere.

And I was more ambivalent than ever about the vehicle that
was supposed to take me where I wanted to go. My friend
Moishe had some of the same problems with my manuscript as
David. He was also very dubious about some of my descriptions
of medieval society. Perhaps taking on the Middle Ages had been
a huge mistake. Perhaps the entire project was a huge mistake. It
was starting to feel like an academic albatross.

It was still around my neck the second time around in Negril.
Dotty and I had loved it so much in December that we decided to
do it again in March. But this time without Shayla. We hadn't
had more than two days together since her birth. Now that Shayla was almost three we were sure she could handle an entire week.
Shortly before our departure she said so herself. I told her that I
was really going to miss her next week. She told me, "That's OK.
You'll be back, and then you'll be glad to see me." I was blown
away by the sensitivity of this confidently connected kid. I
thought I was trying to reassure her. But she picked up on my in-
security and wound up reassuring me. I sensed that I would have
more difficulty with our separation than she.

I was right. For the first two days in Negril I was unable to let
go of my darling little daughter. A scheduled phone call on the
second evening convinced me that she was doing just fine. But
my anxiety did not abate. No longer worried about Shayla, I worried about my work. I couldn't stay in one place for more than
ten minutes at a time. Dotty was not pleased. We had come for
closeness, and I was about as far away as I could be. We fought
our way through most of the week. Our paradise was lost.

So was my emotional equilibrium. A dark gray cloud moved in
on me and decided to stay for the spring. I was not only deeply
disappointed by, but also very angry about, the series of rejections I had suffered in the winter. I was much bossier with Shayla

than I needed to be. My impatience spilled over whenever she spilled her milk. "But I'm just a teeny little child" was her pathetically enlightened lament.

Apparently my anger was taking its toll. I learned from Dotty that Shayla had complained to her that "Papa's mad all the time." "How does that make you feel?" Dotty had asked. "It makes my heart broken" was her heart-breaking reply.

Dotty was also a target for my rage. I stepped up my effort to run her life. Predictably, she beat a steady retreat. The same old war over time and space. Only worse. Now our arguments were punctuated by Dotty's threats of divorce. These threats only made me more afraid and more angry. We were having more and more trouble keeping our fights behind closed doors. Shayla witnessed more screaming matches than we cared to remember. She reacted to them by turning away and tuning out. We worried about the long-term effects. So far her teachers had nothing but praise for her behavior:

> Shayla is a leader. She knows what she wants to do and how she wants to do it. She works hard at what she does and is often very proud of her accomplishments. More often than not, Shayla plays beautifully with the other children. Her sense of humor is terrific. Her enthusiasm is contagious. She really is a pleasure to have in the room.

We were proud of this sunny report. But there were clouds on the horizon. Dotty overheard Shayla tell a friend that "I don't like it when my parents fight because nobody pays any attention to me." Maybe our furious focus on ourselves explained what seemed to me to be her inordinate need to make her friends pay attention to her. Perhaps her habit of tuning out during the heat of battle explained why she sometimes seemed to tune me out long after the battles were over. I was worried about my daughter.

Not to mention my marriage. Or my work. Or my sleep. I was waking up in the middle of the night, was unable to nap in the afternoon, and was wasted by early evening. Ever more tired, I was ever less patient. Tired of my tirades, Dotty insisted that I get some help for my insomnia. I contacted a psychiatrist specializing in sleep disorders who determined after two sessions that my problem probably wasn't physiological. Worries about my aging mother and my ailing work were what was waking me up. For this I should have to pay $160? He invited me to come back to discuss these worries whenever I wanted. I never did. I had already left dance therapy three months earlier because I felt that I had already learned everything I needed to know about my relationship with my mother. And I thought the only way to improve my relationship with my work was to work. So I wasn't about to start therapy all over again with someone else. But I wasn't about to start sleeping, either.

Dotty also demanded that we see a marriage counselor. We had been at each other's throats for many months, and we didn't seem to be able to let go. She was right; we needed help. I told her I would go if she would take the time to find the counselor. Right now I didn't have any. It was almost mid-June, and I would have little more than two months to write my second historical chapter. The three weeks between the last week in July and the middle of August would be lost to a trip to Turkey. My plan was to write my description of the transformation from early modern to mid-nineteenth century child rearing before we left, then complete my explanation of this transformation in the month after we got back.

This seemed feasible. I had already written up my early modern material, and two years ago I had collected at least part of what I needed on child rearing in the early to mid-nineteenth century in the course of preparing for my Humanities Institute lecture in the fall of 1984. And in that lecture I had already sketched out an explanation for this transformation. Starting from the assumption that the early to mid-nineteenth-century increase in indulgence was a consequence of an increase in the power of mothers over the mode of child rearing, I had argued that a number of interrelated, mutually reinforcing factors were responsible for that increase in maternal power. The commercial market destroyed the domestic economy, separated the father

from the home, and left the economically "disenfranchised" middle-class mother at home in charge of the kids. The ideology of
"separate spheres" and the "moral mother" that justified the
mother's exclusion from the public sphere simultaneously undermined the father's, and celebrated the mother's, authority within
the private sphere. The mother's nurturant orientation was also
legitimated by the birth of a far more benign, anti-Calvinist concept of the child, a concept that was an expression of what historians have called the "feminization of American religion." All I
needed to add was some remarks on the way in which the mother's emotional inclination to represent the interests of her child
was politically reinforced by the decline of political absolutism
and the development of representative democracy.

Of course I hadn't yet figured out the precise nature of the in-
terrelationships among these economic, ideological, religious,
and political factors. Or the sense in which their emergence was a
manifestation and/or result of "gender struggle." But once I did,
I would dazzle the world with the following dialectical discovery:

> The economic and political modernization of the early to
> mid-nineteenth century, and the ideological and religious
> transformations with which it was connected, made it pos-
> sible for maternal control to supplant paternal control over
> the mode of child rearing. Weber has shown that the pre-
> condition for that political-economic modernization was
> the modernization of the mind—the triumph of rational
> calculation over magical thought—that he dubbed the "dis-
> enchantment of the world." I have shown (in the previous
> chapter), in turn, that the emotional foundations for the
> disenchantment of the world had been prepared by pater-
> nal control over the early modern mode of child rearing
> and the harsh practices it produced. This compels the con-
> clusion that the early modern masculization of the mode of
> child rearing engendered a modernization that culminated
> in the early to mid-nineteenth-century feminization of the
> mode of child rearing. Thus did the early modern, father-

controlled mode of child rearing contain the seeds of its own destruction.

Two thirds of the way through my descriptive section I received a letter that contained some destructive news of its own. My article had been rejected once again. But this time I had no political defense against intellectual rejection. The editor included copies of the readers' reviews. The first reader had some reservations but was impressed by the "bold speculative sweep" of my article. The second was more critical of my theoretical assumptions but still found my discussion "clear, well-organized, and very stimulating." But the third and deciding reader found "its scholarship [to be] very poor," and "strongly urge[d] rejection." Apparently a medievalist, he or she accused me of relying on historical sources that had been "superseded by later work" in order to construct a "ludicrous" picture of life in the Middle Ages. I was "dead wrong" about medieval land and labor, households, and law. Most peasant fathers were not required to leave their homes for labor services, most medieval households were neo-local* and nuclear, and only *un*married women had the right to "inherit and hold property." My descriptions of early modern Europe were "as problematical as those [of] the Middle Ages." Then came the coup de grâce: "Balbus doesn't know enough about medieval and early modern Europe to be writing an article on this subject."

Unkind but true. The reader was right. I had been crazy to think that in just five weeks I could learn enough about medieval and early modern history to write about it authoritatively. You can't become a medievalist in a month! I told myself I would just have to work harder and learn more. In September I would show my manuscript to the medievalist in our history department, who would let me know if it really was as bad as the third reader thought. Perhaps my colleague would even refer me to the sources I had neglected that the reader had neglected to mention.

---

*The husband and wife set up their own separate household.

In the meantime, there was writing to be done. I grit my teeth and ground out the last part of my descriptive section on schedule. I vowed that I would finish the rest of the article as planned when I got back from my trip. I was not going to let this blow keep me on the canvas. But I knew it would be hard getting up from this one. My work had always been controversial, but it had never absorbed such a total trashing. I'd been down, but not like this before. I was feeling down . . . and out.

chapter ten

. The Crash .

*t*he Turkish trip was no delight. Four years ago Dotty and I had fallen in love with a staggeringly beautiful stretch of mountain-backed beaches where the Aegean and the Mediterranean meet. Now we were back to share our special place with Shayla. Olu Deniz was as magnificent as we had remembered it. But the second time around there was no better than the repeat performance at Negril.

We arrived in the middle of a horrendous heat wave. The blistering sun was just too much for me to take. Or so I told myself. I spent most of my time in the shade while Dotty spent almost all of her time in the water. Shayla spent much of her time fending off the phalanx of local kids who repeatedly converged on what must have been the first blue-eyed blonde child they had ever seen. Shayla was not amused by their unceasing efforts to touch her hair or stare into her baby blues. By the second day she screamed at the mere sight of their approach. It wasn't until the last few days of our stay that she managed to find some kids who spoke her own language.

By that time Dotty and I were barely speaking. Normally I

sleep much better when I'm on vacation. But on this trip I got no more rest than I had been getting at home.

Three days after our return I begged my doctor for some relief. She agreed that two milligrams of Ativan before bed was better than four hours of sleeplessness after it. I came to count on these little friends for my first uninterrupted visits to the land of Nod in more than three years. But I wasn't feeling much better when I got back to earth. During the day there was no way to avoid the problems that I had finally been able to block out during the night.

I was having a much harder time than I had anticipated working out the complex connections between the economic and political modernization of the early to mid-nineteenth century and the gender struggle that (according to my theory) ultimately determined it. And I was running out of time to work them out. In one week I would be back in the classroom. Not only hadn't I finished the second chapter of my new book, I still hadn't revised the one that had twice been rejected.

This was only one of the many dilemmas I discussed with Rob along the lush trails surrounding Lake Quinault. I had decided that I desperately needed to talk to him about the problems of my project. I did not hide my ambivalence about completing it. I confided that I was close to concluding that the problems I had posed were too complex to resolve, that the project was clearly unmanageable, and that, most importantly, if I did not seem to want to complete it, I should just forget it and move on to something that really turned me on.

But how could I just "forget" the intellectual problems with which I had wrestled for three full years? Besides, the start-up time for a new project would undoubtedly absorb my entire winter and spring sabbatical, and when it was over I would have nothing written to show for it. Then I would be faced with the full-time teaching schedule that would prevent me from making much progress on that project. If I wanted to win the race for academic recognition—or even just a merit raise—I could scarcely afford such a prolonged postponement.

It was already more than five years since my last book had been published. For a long time I had been fighting the feeling that even those who had loved it were wondering: "what has he done for us lately?" *Gender Struggle and the Transformation of Child Rearing in the West* was supposed to be their answer. It was my ticket to the top. How could I abandon it without hitting rock bottom?

I also talked to Rob about the fact that Dotty and I weren't talking. For many months I had been reluctant to raise even the slightest complaint because I knew that it would only serve to launch a litany of her own. Twice before our trip to Turkey we had met with a counselor that had been recommended to Dotty. Twice he listened to us berate each other to no apparent end. We had decided on our vacation to find another counselor when we got back. I tried to persuade Dotty that my former therapist, with whom we had both worked before we decided to have a child, would be a good bet. Dotty was reluctant to work with someone whom she considered more my therapist than hers but finally agreed to give it a try.

Two days after my return from Quinault we had our first session. It was unproductive. So was the next. And the next. Privately I complained to Dotty that she seemed closed to the possibility of making any progress. She complained to me that she would be crazy to confide in a therapist who was clearly on my side. I tried to convince her that this reaction was merely one example of her more general paranoia. She tried to convince me that her problem was simply that she stayed too long in unhealthy situations. Now we were fighting about the therapy that was supposed to help us stop fighting. The fighting ended just before Thanksgiving when Dotty informed our therapist that she wasn't coming back. Getting this off her chest seemed to make Dotty feel a little better. It made me feel that we had just lost our last chance.

The chances of completing my project were also growing more dismal by the day. The fall quarter was lost to the usual combination of committees and classes. Actually I was thankful for my teaching, which was about the only thing in my life that was going well. Just before Thanksgiving the campus historian to whom I had given my manuscript gently and carefully confirmed the relentless critique it had already absorbed. He also gave me a long list of books on the Middle Ages that I knew I should, but feared I never would, read. A few days later my friend Moishe recommended that I defer my gender-struggle explanation of the transition from one period to another until after I had worked out a separate analysis of all four periods. I took this as an invitation to surrender. I was very, very close to doing just that. Three years of painful struggle had left me with as many questions as answers about my book. And in less than a month I would be face-to-face with the two-quarter sabbatical during which I was supposed to complete it.

My mood was darker than ever, a heavy cloud that was always ready to burst. Dotty couldn't stand the storm, and I was afraid that Shayla was increasingly feeling its effects. One day her teacher found her at the top of the jungle gym teaching her classmates to shout "stupid asshole!" at the top of her lungs. The teacher gently reprimanded me when she learned that Shayla was merely copying her father's by-now favorite greeting to the drivers of every car but his own. More importantly, Shayla's second evaluation was not quite as glowing as the first. She received many of the same rave reviews, but it was also noted that there were times when "she couldn't stand to listen and shouted for attention." Dotty and I also observed that she was going through what Dotty called a "real mommy stage": she was more clingy and crybabyish than ever before. Dotty thought it was sweet. But it seemed to me that Shayla was emotionally and intellectually stalled.

It also seemed to me that Dotty was holding her back. All too often she was protecting Shayla from the very risks that I was encouraging her to take. Of course this was merely the continuation of a pattern that had been in place ever since the second year of Shayla's life. I was always the one who tried to teach Shayla to take care of herself: to feed her self, to wipe her self, to go to day camp by her self, and now, to tie her shoes by her self. And my efforts to support her self-reliance had always encountered the resistance of a mother who thought I was pushing her daughter too far too fast.

The assumptions underlying my gender-struggle theory had led me to interpret this resistance as the result of a mother's greater tolerance for the dependence that a father feared. But it was increasingly obvious that Dotty was at least as afraid of Shayla's independence as I was of her dependence. I had never really believed that my support for my daughter's autonomy was merely the expression of a "repressive" paternal parenting interest. Now it was also clear to me that my assumption of a "nurturant," or even "indulgent," maternal parenting interest was an overly euphemistic description of the ways in which Dotty subverted that autonomy. Thus I was persuaded that the opposition between an indulgent and a repressive parenting interest did not adequately capture the opposition between us.

Perhaps it didn't adequately capture the opposition between other parents, either. Maybe most mothers were as overprotective as Dotty. This was a disturbing theoretical possibility. I had derived the assumption of an "indulgent" maternal parenting interest directly from the feminist mothering theory of Nancy Chodorow. If "overprotective" more accurately described that parenting interest than "indulgent," then either there was something wrong with my derivation or there was something wrong with her theory. So I decided that I had better take another look—a very close look—at *The Reproduction of Mothering.*

It did not take me long to locate the passages from which my assumption had been derived. I noted Chodorow's claim on page 167 that "girls emerge from [their preoedipal period] with a basis for 'empathy' built into their primary definition of self . . . a basis for experiencing another's needs . . . as one's own," as well as the conclusion on page 206 that "women are more likely [than men] to get gratification from the mothering relationship, and to have psychological and relational capacities for mothering," that was based on that claim. But I also noticed something that had hitherto entirely escaped my attention. Just one page prior to her conclusion on page 206 Chodorow warned that

The preoccupation with issues of separation and primary identification, the ability to recall their early relationship to their mother—precisely those capacities which enable mothering—are also those which may lead to over-identification and pseduo-empathy based on maternal projection rather than any real perception or understanding of their infant's needs. . . . Capacities which enable mothering are also precisely those which can make mothering problematic.

This was not an isolated warning. It was repeated, for example, on page 211, where Chodorow avers that "a mother's sense of continuity with her infant may shade into too much connection and not enough separateness," and again on page 212, where she argues that

[M]othering is invested with a mother's often conflictual, ambivalent, yet powerful need for her own mother. That women turn to children to fulfill emotional . . . desires unmet by men or other women means that a mother expects from infants what only another adult should be expected to give.

I don't know how I had missed it, but there it was! Chodorow was clearly claiming that a mother's insufficient sense of separation from her children would likely predispose her to prolong their merger at the expense of their autonomy. Thus the assumption of an overprotective maternal parenting interest could as easily and as correctly be derived from her argument as the assumption of a nurturant or indulgent maternal parenting interest. The problem was that Chodorow's argument was divided against itself: she wavered between the claim that a mother's early relationship with her own mother enables her to be, and the claim that this relationship prevents her from being, empathic with her own child.

On reflection I realized that Dorothy Dinnerstein could help me resolve Nancy Chodorow's ambivalence. Dinnerstein focused far more forcefully than Chodorow on the fateful transformation of the girl's grudge against her mother into a grudge against herself. For Dinnerstein the girl's sense of self was inevitably burdened by a strong streak of self-denigration. This emphasis on female self-denigration enabled me to correct what I could now identify as Chodorow's idealization of the parenting predisposition of women. A mother who cannot empathize with the mother-within-her—a mother who, in Chodorow's own words on page 205, "remain[s] in conflict with [her] internal mother"—will scarcely be in an emotional position consistently to empathize with the needs of a child who evokes her mother.

Rather we should expect that a mother who suffers, in effect, from low self-esteem will be unable to resist the psychological pressure to rely on her child to relieve her suffering. Thus a properly critical feminist psychoanalysis tells us that the conscious inclination of mothers to sacrifice their own needs on the altar of their children's is merely the surface manifestation of their unconscious need to be needed by them. And mothers who are emotionally dependent on their children will inevitably encourage their children to be emotionally dependent on them.

I discovered that there was, in fact, a body of literature devoted to such mothers. This literature typically cited a number of culturally and historically specific forces—including small, isolated families, father absence, and maternal unemployment—as sources for what David Levy called "maternal overprotection."[1] But my derivation from Dinnerstein taught me that these forces only swelled a current of maternal overprotection that was as old and as wide as the maternal mode of child rearing itself.[2]

Dinnerstein and Chodorow had also taught me to appreciate the tenacity of the overprotective mother's ties to her children. Anything that threatens her merger with them will be unconsciously experienced as the loss of herself and will therefore trigger clinging responses designed to forestall that loss. A mother who desperately fears the flights of her fledglings will do what she can to prevent them from leaving the nest; in protecting her children from the dangers of the world, she protects herself from the loss of her children.

But the suppression of their steps toward separation is not likely to be the only means by which the mother maintains the merger between her self and her children. Once these steps have been taken she will also want to spare her children the burden of bumping into the boundaries between themselves and their world. Setting firm boundaries between her children and their world requires a willingness to say "no" to their inevitably grandiose efforts to treat the world as an extension of themselves. But denying her dependents means risking their rage and with it the end of their merger. This is a risk that a mother-who-needs-merger will be reluctant to take. The safer emotional path is to protect her children from pain in order to protect herself from that risk.

I was persuaded by these reflections that when my sabbatical started I would have to reformulate my central assumption of a gender-based opposition in parenting interests as an opposition between an overprotective maternal interest and what I now decided to describe as an underprotective paternal interest. The struggle between women and men to control the mode of child rearing, I now realized, was not a struggle between a good (or "child-centered") maternal and a bad (or "adult-centered") paternal way to raise children but was rather a contest between two antithetical but equally problematical parenting predispositions. Thus the parents of each gender had equally good reason to fear that the victory of the other gender would amount to a defeat for their children.

I was ambivalent about this theoretical revision. On the one hand, the assumptions underlying my gender-struggle theory were now much more consistent with Dinnerstein's analysis— echoed in *Marxism and Domination*—of the pernicious consequences of *any* form of the maternal mode of child rearing. My assumption that the parenting interests of women were more in tune with the interests of children than the parenting interests of men had never really squared with the feminist psychoanalytic claim that more or less exclusively mother-raised boys and girls will inevitably grow up to be men who need to dominate women and women who need to acquiesce in that domination. My reformulation of the parenting interests of women from "indulgent" to "overprotective" would eliminate this inconsistency.

It would also give me some much needed ammunition with which to combat the overprotectiveness of my wife. Perhaps Dotty would let Shayla take more chances if she realized—and worked through—just how afraid she was of losing her. Maybe she would be more willing to discipline her daughter once she recognized that she was bending over backwards to spare Shayla the pain that *she* had endured as a child. But even if I couldn't persuade Dotty that in protecting Shayla she was protecting herself, at least I would be able to persuade myself that I should stick to my parenting guns. I was pleased that there was a practical advantage to my theoretical revision.

On the other hand, I was frightened by the fact that this revision would bring me back to the theoretical beginning of my book just when I was supposed to be bringing it to conclusion. With my sabbatical about to start it felt like I was starting from scratch. Pressure drop. I was terrified that I would succumb to it and that I wouldn't be able to write at all. The few halting steps that I had taken in this direction during the last week in November were swamped by an anxiety that had refused to abate. Right now writing seemed impossible.

So right now I was looking for diversions. On December 4 Dotty and I dropped Shayla off for a sleepover with some friends. We were heading for our first movie, and then our first evening in bed, in a long time. As usual we were late. As usual I was angry. I didn't want to miss a minute of the sexy, scary movie that was the hottest smash of the season. I stepped on the gas, ignored the changing light, and sped through the open intersection. Only it wasn't open. Slamming on my brakes, I braced myself for the collision with the now-visible car that had crossed my path. The next thing I heard were Dotty's screams. Five of the longest minutes of my life later, they were joined by the siren sounds of an arriving police ambulance.

The paramedics were pretty sure that Dotty would be okay: no broken neck, no serious internal injuries. Probably "just" a few broken ribs. It could have been much, much worse. The movie that had driven me to distraction could easily have lived up to its name.

chapter eleven

. Separation-
Individuation .

$t$he nearly fatal attraction of a second-rate film prompted some pretty serious second thoughts about the emotional race I had been running. I decided to take the accident as a sign that I needed to slow down before it was too late. How else could I live with the fact that my frantic trip had almost cost my wife her life?

Besides, Dotty made it crystal clear that she would only stick around if I did everything possible to lower the level of stress in my life. "Everything possible," as far as she was concerned, included the exploration of pharmacological options. A half-dozen sessions with a shrink who neither opposed drugs on principle nor dispensed them casually to all comers culminated in the conclusion that they were "not indicated." Psychoanalysis was. But who could afford four hours a week for ninety dollars a throw on top of what I would be paying for the additional marital therapy to which I had already made a commitment? So Dotty and I agreed to look for a couples therapist who was psychoanalytically prepared for in-depth individual work whenever it was necessary. And I decided to enroll in a yoga class for some immediate relief.

I also realized that to reduce my stress I would have to come to terms with the book that had become such a burden. But I was no closer to closure than I had been at Quinault. In fact I was still stuck: I couldn't write it but I couldn't let it go. For the first two weeks of my sabbatical I nearly drove myself nuts circling back and forth between this impossible either/or. By mid-January I was fit to be tied. How the hell did I ever get myself into such a mess? Why did I have to write the book that I couldn't write? Why couldn't I write the book that I had to write? Suddenly it occurred to me that the only way to get unstuck was to try to answer those questions. Of course! The way to escape my double bind was to figure out how I got into it in the first place! I decided I would devote my sabbatical to writing about my (not) writing.

The knots loosened around my neck. For the first time in many, many months I felt hopeful about my work. At least I would be able to start putting pen to paper. And maybe I would actually be able to enjoy writing once again. I told myself that that would be enough. But I also harbored hopes that something more might come of it. Perhaps I would eventually be able to transform a book in which I theorized about the child-rearing experiences of others into a book that was about my experience of theorizing about child rearing. Perhaps I could change its focus from the product to the process of theoretical production.

This personal change in focus would parallel a collective shift in social-scientific sensibility with which I was already sympathetic. Husserl's once-lonely lament against a positivist science in which the scientist "never appears in the process of scientific investigation"[1] had long since become a chorus of complaints against the methodological barriers that safely separate the social scientist (the subject) from the object of his study. By now there was a common cry to do battle against those barriers. Joining this battle would enable me to unwrite an unsuccessful theoretical history of Western child rearing into a successful history of my unsuccessful effort to write a theoretical history of Western child rearing. Thus could phenomenological victory be snatched from the jaws of theoretical defeat.

I knew that this victory would not come cheaply. A change in the content of my book would also require a change in its form. A declarative voice that concealed would have to be replaced by a first-person narrative that revealed the presence of this subject in his theoretical object. This move from declarative to narrative would allow me to transform my theoretical strategy and its accompanying tactics from merely private preliminaries to the public story into part of the public story itself. And this story would have to include all the false starts, reroutings, and dead-ends that the declarative voice denies. Along the way the reader would still learn a lot about the history of child rearing and different efforts to explain it. But anyone who looked for the Truth at the end of this road was bound to be disappointed. What they would encounter, instead, would be a description of what it was like to be preoccupied with finding it.

This sounded very postmodern. But my task, as I understood it, was not merely to "deconstruct" my discourse but rather also to plumb its emotional depths. I would try to figure out how my *life* was implicated in my *thought*. Of course I was afraid that subjecting myself to the social-scientific scrutiny normally reserved for others would be an uncomfortable exercise. Transgressing the boundary between myself and the people I studied would inevitably evoke the very anxiety that, according to George Devereux, that boundary is designed to dispel. If the effort to draw this line between observer and observed might be described, following Devereux, as a movement from anxiety to method, then my effort to erase it could just as well be characterized as a movement from method to anxiety.[2]

But if I could make this move I would be able to heed the call of Alvin Gouldner for social scientists to cultivate "the ingrained *habit* of viewing our beliefs as we now view those held by others" in order to "recognize the depth of our kinship with those whom we study."[3] In fact, this was a call to which I had already committed myself at another lecture I had given at the Institute for the Humanities a couple of years ago. I had argued that a self-reflexive social science was the only way to avoid the implication that the social scientist was a special, privileged subject to whom his explanations of ordinary human "objects" did not apply. Now I could make good on that commitment.

I was persuaded that it was both personally and politically important to write what, in my more optimistic moments, I allowed myself to think of as my new book. I even toyed with tentative titles. The one I liked best was *Men and the Art of Mothering*. It was intended to convey both a certain kinship with, and distance from, the immensely popular work of Robert Pirsig that I hoped it would evoke.[4] Like Pirsig, I would describe a theoretical journey that was motivated by intensely personal concerns. But Pirsig's personal concerns were largely divorced from his relationship with his son, and his theoretical concerns were correspondingly detached from the problems of intimate interpersonal involvements. His emotionally solitary trip across America struck me as a metaphor for the masculine experience, and the range of theoretical problems with which he dealt, and the solution for these problems to which he was driven, remained almost entirely within the horizons of masculine assumptions about the world.

Unlike Pirsig, my theoretical and personal trips had taken me to the domestic domain. Thus my book would explore the relationship between my child-rearing theory and my child-rearing practice. It would clarify the connection between the fact that I had devoted the last four years of my intellectual life to writing the definitive history of Western child rearing and the fact that during the same time I had devoted the better part of my personal life to taking care of my daughter. When I hadn't been at school working my way back from the 1950s to the Middle Ages I had been at home helping Shayla work her way through the first four years of her life. As my daughter grew older and bigger so did my book. But my book collapsed under its own weight while Shayla was still pulling her own. What was the relationship between her development and my descent?

To answer this question I would have to reconstruct as much as I could remember about my relationship with my daughter. I expected that the therapy I was about to begin in February would help evoke those memories. Writing about my relationship with Shayla, in turn, might help me excavate the buried memories of my own childhood with which that relationship had been burdened. And this might prove to be a useful adjunct to my therapy. So my therapy would help my writing and my writing would help my therapy. I was pleased at this promise of intellectual and emotional integration.

But right now integration seemed a distant prospect. In fact my marriage seemed to be coming apart at the seams. During January things between Dotty and me had gone from bad to worse. She was angry at me for the accident, during which she had banged up an already bad knee. I did not exactly win points with her when I suggested, defensively, that she should have been wearing her seat belt. For Dotty this suggestion seemed to be the last straw. Up to this point we had always made love—or at least had sex—even in the midst of our misery. In fact, "fight hard, fuck hard" had always been Dotty's motto. But now we were fighting hard—harder than ever—and fucking not at all.

Nor were we talking, not even in the therapy that we had just started. After several screaming matches our therapist suggested that we might do better in individual sessions. I was ambivalent about this suggestion. On the one hand, I knew that I needed help with my problems, and I also knew that these problems were partly responsible for the distorted dynamics between my wife and myself. But only partly. Dotty had her problems too. It was, I was convinced, the interaction between her shit and my shit that had made our marriage such a mess. How could we clean it up if we didn't work on it together? If we did therapy separately how could I trust that we wouldn't go our separate ways?

This was the fear with which I began to work in my first individual session with Alisa. "Just why *are* you so afraid of losing Dotty?" Alisa's question took me aback. "Isn't it obvious that someone who had already gone through one divorce wouldn't want to endure a second?" "But what would be so bad about a second divorce?" she asked. "Well, I would look like a two-time loser to the omnipresent Them." "Anyone among Them you're particularly worried about?" "My mother, it would be hard for my mother to take. I don't want to disappoint her again." "How did she deal with your first divorce?" "She was fine, very support-ive." "What makes you think she wouldn't be this time?" "Well, this time there's a child involved."

The floodgates opened. I began to sob . . . and sob. For almost twenty minutes. Just before the end of the session I blurted out: "I'm afraid that Shayla won't be OK." We agreed that next time we would talk about these fears.

In the meantime I thought a lot about them. I knew that it would be difficult for Shayla to deal with her mother and father breaking up. But it was already hard for her to hear our shouting. Lately she had taken to knocking on the door and begging us to stop. Surely breaking up with Dotty would be better than Shayla breaking up our fights. Besides, Shayla was a strong and confi-dent kid. I should trust that she would be able to weather the storm of a separation, especially since I would be there to help her.

But who would be there to help me? A separation from Dotty would mean a partial separation from Shayla as well. It would cut in half the time that I would be able to be with my near-constant companion for the past four years. No longer would I be able to see her every day or sing her to sleep every night. More sobs. My tears told me that it would be hard as hell for me to handle this. I seemed to need Shayla even more than she needed me.

I talked about this need with Alisa during my next session. "I just don't know if I can stand not seeing her every day," I wailed. "It sounds like you're the child and she's the mother," she replied. All of a sudden, I remembered my reflections from three years earlier on the virtues of a psychoanalytic approach to child rearing: "it makes good psychological sense," I had told myself, to assume that "nothing is more likely to evoke, and reanimate the determining role of, a person's past relationship with his par-ents than a person's present relationship with his child." Some-how I never realized that this would apply to me. But of course it did. In mothering my daughter I had been reliving my relationship with my own mother.

It followed that I could treat the dynamics of my current relationship with Shayla as a clue to the dynamics of my early relationship with Selma. If I sometimes let my need to be recognized by Shayla interfere with her need to be recognized by me, this could only mean that my mother must have similarly suppressed my struggle to separate from her. And if I was all-too-often angry at Shayla for not fulfilling my need for recognition, I must still be angry at my mother for not adequately mirroring me. In short, mothering Shayla had reawakened both my unsatisfied childhood needs for mothering and my defensive reactions against them.

Shayla was not the only one who was suffering from this cycle. Dotty was too. Now I understood better why I had been so demanding of her attention ever since Shayla's birth. Shayla didn't merely rob me of my wife/mother, she also made me need my wife/mother more than ever. My neediness, in turn, was so great that Dotty could not possibly satisfy it. This left me feeling angry and rejected much of the time. And much of the time I defended against this rejection by trying to control her behavior. This was (my contribution to) the deadly emotional dialectic that was poisoning my marriage.

So I was reproducing what must have been the dynamics of my relationship with my mother not only with my daughter but also with my wife. Perhaps the same could be said of my relationship with my work. It too seemed to be ruled by a self-defeating race for recognition. In the course of the first two years of my daughter's life my book had ballooned from a modest effort to explain the Spockean transformation of American child rearing into the grandiose project of explaining the history of child rearing in the West since the Middle Ages. Although that project could be intellectually justified as an effort to answer large and important questions that were left unanswered by my previous work, it had been emotionally fueled by an effort to ensure a place for myself alongside Marx, Weber, and Durkheim in the pantheon of the master thinkers of modernity. The enormity of this need for intellectual recognition, in turn, virtually guaranteed that it would not be satisfied. It fostered the illusion that in a couple of years I could complete a book that would have required a good part of a lifetime to complete, or that in a couple of months I could learn enough about the difference between medieval and early modern child rearing, religion, work, and politics to write a publishable article devoted to the transition from one to the other. And so great was my rush for recognition that I refused even to consult my colleagues before sending that article out.

Retrospectively I recognized that I had set myself up for rejection and thus for the anger and the depression that accompanied its inevitable arrival. Demanding too much recognition ensured that I wouldn't receive it, and staking so much of my self on winning it led to my defeat when I didn't. Thus my relationship with my work had been dominated by the same overdependence on the other as my relationship with my daughter and my wife. So I must have been reproducing the dynamics of my relationship with my mother in my professional as well as my personal life.

To straighten both out I would therefore have to learn more about those dynamics, more about the "deficits" in the way I had been mothered as well as my currently exaggerated mechanisms for defending against those deficits. Neither my feminist mothering theory nor my previous therapy had taught me enough about my early pain, its source, and my manner of responding to it. Learning more about this would be my therapeutic and my intellectual task for the next seven months.

I was confident that my therapist could help me tackle that task. Alisa was sympathetic but smart, both as warm and as psychoanalytically sophisticated as I had hoped. She certainly knew a transference reaction when she saw one. She watched me transform her into a mother whose approval I needed in order to exist. And myself into a little boy who was so good he would be guaranteed (or so he thought) to get it. Or into the little boy who was terrified that if he wasn't good he wouldn't get it. Or, finally, the little boy who was enraged that he didn't get it no matter how good he was. Little by little, I learned how my overly inflated expectations as well as my inauthentic strategy for fulfilling them set myself up for repeated rejections at the hands of my wife/mother and how these rejections instantly elicited defensive, angry withdrawals and rejections of my own.

In the process I discovered just how limited my previous therapy had been. I had gotten to know the "good boy" and the "frightened boy," the boy who thought it was selfish to speak up for himself. I had worked hard to express my own needs rather than to satisfy the anticipated needs of my (m)others. But I never understood that what I really needed most was a perfect mother, someone who would make me feel that I existed by devoting her existence entirely to me. Nor had I understood how angry I was that I had never found her. The depths of my neediness as well as the rage that followed its inevitable frustration had entirely escaped me.

Narcissism was the name of my neurosis, or "character disorder," to be more clinically correct.* I had always wanted to read the psychoanalytic literature on narcissism, but somehow I had never gotten around to it. Now I had a personal stake in reading that literature. During the spring I immersed myself in the writings of Masterson, Kernberg, and Kohut.[5] Their clinical descriptions of narcissism pretty much matched the description that my therapist had derived from our own clinical setting. But they disagreed among themselves on the etiology of that disorder.

---

*There is actually no psychoanalytic consensus on the meaning of this clinical category. Some analysts—like Heinz Kohut and Alice Miller—define narcissism broadly to include both a grandiose devaluation and an overdependent idealization of the other, while others—like Otto Kernberg and James Masterson—define narcissism more narrowly as grandiosity and use other terms, such as "borderline," to refer to the patient for whom idealization is the predominant defense. Thus my own character disorder could only be described as narcissistic on a broad definition of that term. For these and other terminological issues, see Otto Kernberg, *Borderline Conditions and Pathological Narcissism* (New York: Jason Aronsen, 1975) and James Masterson, *The Narcissistic and Borderline Disorders* (New York: Brunner/Mazel, 1981).

It seemed to me that Masterson's mastery of the problem was superior to Kernberg's or Kohut's. He connected narcissism much more clearly than his colleagues to the mother's failure to adequately respond to the rapprochement crisis of her child. "Good-enough-mothering," to use Winnicott's term, occurs when the mother is able to serve both as the all-embracing, predictable presence with which the infant can merge *and* as the responsive mirror for its emerging exhibitionism without which the need for merger cannot give way to the "sense of being connected as something separate."[6]

Infants whose needs for (what Kohut calls) an "ideal object" and a "grandiose self" have not been satisfied by their mothers will become "adults" who oscillate between overdependence on the other (connection without a sense of separation: the pole of the "ideal object") and a falsely self-sufficient denial of any need for the very others on whom they are overly dependent (separation without a sense of connection: the pole of the "grandiose self").[7] But the predominance of either pole in their personality (I inferred from Masterson's account) will depend on whether their mothers have overrewarded or underrewarded their separation-individuation. The dominant defense of the child whose mother has overrewarded separation and rejected merger will be regression to the infantile omnipotence of the grandiose self. The principal defense of the child whose mother has overrewarded merger and rejected separation will be regression to the infantile need for the ideal object.

Since I seemed to be more the second child than the first, I paid particular attention to Masterson's account of the links between narcissism and "maternal overprotection." According to that account, the overprotective mother unconsciously experiences the self-expression of her child as an obstacle to her (narcissistic) effort to "shape him or her as an object essential to maintain her own [sense of self]." This effort requires that she systematically suppress her child's self-expression, which leads inexorably to the child's "abandonment depression, an essential part of which is rage." The child defends him or herself against this depression with "regressive compliance with the mother's projections," that is, with clinging behavior that satisfies her own clinging and thus relieves her anxiety. This internalization of the "intrapsychic system" of the mother—what Winnicott calls the "false self"—is then "projected [back] onto the environment and constantly reactivated."[8] This means that the child can only experience the others that he or she encounters (or might encounter) as mothers who reject self-expression and reward self-sacrifice and that he or she will "choose" self-sacrifice in order to relieve the anxiety and depression connected with self-expression. Thus does one type of narcissistic mother produce the same type of narcissistic child.

I tried Masterson's analysis on for size. It seemed to fit. My mother had always been so terrified of the world, so anxious in the company—or even the proximity—of other people. (From Masterson's account I could infer that this anxiety was a result of a regressive identification with her own overprotective, rejecting mother, projected back onto the environment.) This meant that she must have been anxious in my company as well, and that her overprotectiveness must have been her way to alleviate that anxiety.

This defense must have been magnified, moreover, by the culturally and historically specific factors stressed by the students of maternal overprotection. In fact my mother fit their profile to a T. She was never employed outside the home, she had only one other child (who was nine years older than I), and her husband worked six days a week for the first five or six years of my life. Thus during that time there was very little going on in her life besides her relationship with me. And she did not hesitate to let me know it: more than once I would hear that the only thing that mattered to her was that *I* was happy. The message from my mother, in short, was that I was the most important egg in her very small basket.

No wonder she was so afraid that I would break. "Easy, easy, easy" was the maternal mantra that echoed throughout the apartment whenever I was feeling feisty. "Be careful!" was the warning

that dampened my spirits whenever I ventured into her closely
guarded kitchen. Evidently danger lurked behind every door. Especially the front door of our apartment, which so rarely opened
out to the surrounding world. When it did, my mother and I
would almost always walk through it together. She would typically take me to places to which my friends were already flying solo.
She went with me to buy my clothes until I was halfway through
high school. She never left me with a baby-sitter. In fact she
never really left me alone at all. Even the closed door of my own
bedroom was insufficient protection from her intrusions. Or so it
must have seemed to the little boy who dreamed recurrently of
his room being invaded by a witch who looked suspiciously like
his mother and moved menacingly along tracks that joined that
room to the rest of the apartment.

Masterson helped me understand that the overprotected son
was the son whose self-expression had been squelched, that the
boy who dreaded his mother's surveillance was the same boy who
had been abandoned by her. Contrary to my mother's self-per-
ception, she had not indulged my needs but rather her own, projected onto me. *My* needs had been neglected. The empathy of
my therapist helped me relive the terrible trio of helplessness,
fear, and rage that was the result of that neglect. I began to empathize with the little boy whose only defense against anxiety and
depression had been to attempt to alleviate the anxiety and depression of his mother, the boy who learned that love meant having to take care of the (always infirm) mother who was supposed
to take care of him. I remembered how she would turn my tears
into her own: "Don't cry, it hurts me too much." So I learned to
suppress my pain in order to soothe my mother's.

Becoming the perfect mother of my mother was a grotesquely
high price to have to pay to be treated as a good boy. It not only
meant the sacrifice of my self-expression but also a life filled with
the very anxiety that self-sacrifice was supposed to allay. My
mother's message was: if you don't take care of them they will reject you. That would have been enough to worry about. The
problem was compounded when I discovered, much to my cha-

grin, that my efforts to take care of "them" were rather more resented than appreciated. So they would reject me if I tried to help them and reject me if I didn't. No wonder I had always been so afraid of other people.

And angry as well. If they refused to accept—not to mention reciprocate—the gifts that I gave them that could only mean they were less gifted than I. Gradually I came to understand that this defense against rejection by the other was a displacement of the rage that my mother had never allowed me to vent against her. How many times had I heard that "you catch more flies with honey than you do with vinegar"? And there had been many variations on the same theme: good boys don't get angry. If these warnings weren't enough to teach me that anger was unacceptable, then my mother's few but furious outbursts certainly were.

Thus I must have never had the opportunity to destroy my mother in fantasy that is, according to Winnicott, the necessary condition for being able to experience her as separate in reality. Unless the child discovers that the real mother is able to survive its aggressive assaults, he or she will never learn the difference between the mother as a "projective entity" and the mother as "an entity in [her] own right."[9] If the mother remains a "projective entity," then the child has no way of knowing that its rage will not, in fact, destroy her.

Idealization of the mother is the child's typical defense against this terrifying fantasy: the child transforms her into a mother who is far too good ever to become the object of his or her aggression. Once suppressed, the aggression is turned against the self, and then split off and displaced onto others, who become the unwitting targets for the child's unrecognized rage against the mother.

This account helped me understand why I had always had a sense of my mother's perfection that was so impervious to the actual way she treated me. That sense was an idealization of my mother that defended me against a rage that was simply too dangerous directly to express. Now I knew why I was so rarely angry at my mother but often so angry at others.

My idealization of my mother, moreover, had always served to justify the sacrifices I had made on her—or my—behalf. I had to be perfect for my mother because my mother was perfect for me. This was the vicious cycle of my merger with my mother.

This was the cycle I was reproducing with my daughter. All too frequently I treated her as my "projective entity" rather than as an "entity in her own right," that is to say, as my mother instead of my daughter. The adult in me recognized, of course, that Shayla was a child who had been merged with, and was struggling to separate from, her father. Sometimes I successfully supported that struggle. But the needy little child in me, for whom our first year together had been a merger with my mother, could only experience Shayla's separation from me as a frightening form of maternal abandonment.

The terror of that abandonment, in turn, had evoked my characteristic defense mechanisms against it. If I took perfect care of her, then surely she would take perfect care of me; she would never fail to show how much she needed me. I expected her to be a mirror that would repeatedly reflect back loving reassurances that her separation would not mean the end to our connection. "Look, Mommy, look!" When Mommy didn't look, Daddy got depressed.

Then I would get angry at her for having abandoned me and would try to control her. When she got angry at me for trying to control her I felt even more abandoned. No wonder I felt so lifeless: I was losing my mother all over again. And, since I had never successfully separated from her—since she remained my "projective entity" rather than an "entity in her own right"—the loss of my mother felt like the loss of myself.

These reflections on the narcissistic dimensions of my parenting practice brought me back to my long-deferred question of the emotional origins of my coparenting commitment. Before Shayla was born I had speculated that that commitment was an expression of an intensified maternal identification that resulted from my encounter with the indulgent, child-centered practices popularized by Dr. Benjamin Spock. But I did not understand why my plausibly more intense mother identification did not eventually evoke the mother-denying defense against it by means of which "normal" masculine identity is forged. Thus I didn't *really* know why a Spockean boy would become a mothering man.

I could not answer that question because it was badly put. It was based, to begin with, on the assumption that the child-rearing practices I experienced in my earliest years were "indulgent" and "child-centered." But they were anything but. My introduction to narcissism theory taught me that those descriptions of my mother's practices were idealizing denials of their deficits. The fact was that my mother didn't know the difference between her son and her self. Under these circumstances "child-centered" theory cannot but culminate in "parent-centered" practice. Thus Spockean advice can just as easily legitimate the inclinations of a narcissistic mother as those of a good-enough mother.

I also learned that the concept of mother identification masks a profound difference between a boy's identification with the former and his identification with the latter. Edith Jacobson was one of the first to recognize that "a helpless child with either a hostile, rejecting or smothering mother will do his best to accept and submit to his powerful, aggressive love object, and even give up his own self rather than give up the love object entirely."[10] The maternal identification of the son of a narcissistic mother, in other words, is already a defense against the fear of losing her. It is a defense that any subsequent "dis-identification" from her is unlikely to displace.

Thus the message of narcissism theory is that boys with "smothering mothers" like mine tend to become "smothering men." Smothering men try to control their (m)others by taking care of them. I could not escape the conclusion that it was precisely this peculiar combination of care and control that had fueled my fathering fires.

I didn't know whether this combination was common to other men who were committed to coparenting. Diane Ehrensaft's study of coparenting couples confirms the strong maternal identification of highly involved fathers but also describes the quality of their involvement as being less narcissistically overprotective than my own.[11] So the jury is out on the question of the connection between the "new narcissism" and the "new fathering." Perhaps one day I would pursue that question. But right now the point was not to interpret my practice but rather to change it: it was high time to take better care of Shayla. To take better care of Shayla, I now understood, I would have to learn to take better care of myself.

Learning to take better care of myself meant that I would have to start listening to, rather than neglecting, the needy, frightened little boy inside myself. I would have to treat his anxiety as a symptom of a wound that I needed to heal instead of a signal to soothe somebody else's. But to heal my wounds I would first have to feel their pain.

And feel them I did. Sometimes it was so bad I could barely get out of bed. Suspended between the self I was leaving behind and the self I had yet to find, the simplest tasks of everyday life suddenly seemed like sisyphean struggles. I was terrorized by the very teaching on which I had always relied for reassurance. Every few days I would choke, almost to the point of puking, on the awful anxiety that gripped my chest and throat. It would only let go when I would force myself to cry.

I cried everywhere. In and out of therapy. In my home, my office, my car, and even in restaurants. For many months my days were punctuated by the same pattern: I choked, I cried, and I tried to comfort myself. There were times that I despaired that it ever would be different. Alisa reassured me that the only way over was through and that I *would* get over. But I wasn't convinced. The only thing I was sure about was that learning to take care of myself was a far tougher task than I had ever imagined. No wonder so many people preferred to take care of others!

No wonder that I sometimes felt that I was selfishly spending too much time on me and too little on them. Sometimes I lost the fight against this feeling and fell back into the pattern of trying to be perfect for others rather than good enough for myself. But gradually I came to understood that I was falling back into an

old way of being rather than being the only way that it was possible to be. At least I knew that there was another way. And I knew
how to get there: feel my pain and soothe myself. More crying
and more comfort. Little by little, the new way became more and
more familiar, and the old way became increasingly . . . old. I was
starting to like taking care of myself.

In the process I discovered that I was having a better time taking care of my daughter. The more attention I paid to my little
boy the less abandoned I felt when my little girl didn't pay attention to me. The less abandoned I felt, the fewer reassurances I
needed from her that her separation did not mean the end to our
connection. The more confident I was about our connection, the
less afraid I was that I would lose it unless I took perfect care of
her. The less anxious I was about being a perfect mother, the
more I was able to relax and enjoy being with Shayla. The more I
was able to enjoy being with her, the more she seemed to enjoy
being with me. In short, the less I tried to win Shayla's love, the
more she was able to give it. Zen and the art of mothering. . . .

There were times, of course, when her master would just have
to lay down the law, and Shayla sometimes still got angry when I
did. But somehow her anger no longer hurt me as much as it had.
I was increasingly able to show her that I could calmly withstand
her rage. Hopefully this would help her deal with, rather than
deny, her inevitable ambivalence toward her daddy.

We even invented a game to facilitate this process. Shayla
would tell me that she hated me, and I would pretend to cry. As
soon as I started to "cry," she would tell me that she loved me,
and I would smile and tell her how happy that made me. At
which point she would immediately insist that she hated me,
leading to more of her father's fake tears. "I love you, I hate you."
"I love you, I hate you." And so on, until we were both splitting
our sides. It was neither too soon for my daughter nor too late for
her father to learn this little lesson in not splitting ourselves.

Especially since it looked more and more that Dotty and I
would be splitting up. An icy distance had settled in between us
that capped a mountain of unspoken recriminations and regret.

212   . Emotional Rescue .

My efforts to melt this distance and deal with these feelings were rebuffed as unwelcome intrusions into Dotty's private space. Dotty was clearly shoring up her boundaries. Consider the following scene: Dotty and Shayla are sitting next to each other, about three feet apart, at the edge of the pool where we had rented a cabana for the summer. I emerge from the pool and sit down between them, extending my arms to embrace their shoulders. Dotty jumps up and moves away, daggers in her eyes.

It was then that I realized that we were no longer really a family. The separation that I once dreaded had already happened. So when Dotty asked me in September to make it formal I did not protest. . . .

We decided that Shayla should not have to leave her home unless—or until—we decided to make it final. In the meantime we would rent a small apartment not far from our house, in which each of us would live when the other was caring for Shayla. That way we could live separately but continue to share equally in her care.

I agreed to find and furnish the apartment by October 1. We also agreed that on that day we would sit down together with Shayla and tell her what we had decided. We also rehearsed what we would say and how we would say it. Dotty asked me if I would explain our decision, after which she would explain the logistics.

On October 1 I woke up sweating and shaking. It was time to talk to Shayla. I took some deep breaths, and here is what I said:

> Shaylie, we need to talk to you about something important. Mama and I have decided—we both feel the same way— that we need to live apart—separately—for a while. But each of us will still take care of you, neither of us is leaving you. We've been fighting too much for too long and it's not good for us—or you—and we haven't been able to stop. So we need to see if we can learn to get along better by having more time to be alone. We hope more than anything that we'll learn to do this and that we'll be able to come back together again. But in the meantime we've worked out a way

that each of us can continue to be with you here, in your house, and also live separately in a small apartment not far from here. Mama, do you want to explain how it will work?

Before Dotty could say anything Shayla let out a long, loud "Noooooo!" Then she threw a thirty-second fit, flailing her arms and kicking her feet, knocking over the small bookcase by the side of our bed. And then she cried for a few minutes, during which we took turns holding her. When she finally stopped, Dotty explained how it would work. Shayla would be with each of us separately every other day, and with both of us for a few hours on Sunday, which would be "family day." Since today was Sunday, we asked Shayla if she would like to come with us to the park, and then see the apartment. She agreed.

It was off to Oz Park and the newly constructed playground we had heard so much about. As soon as Shayla got a glimpse of it, she waved goodbye and ran to join what seemed like the hundreds of kids who were already fighting in the fort. As I watched her disappear from view, I told myself that my brave little scout would be just fine. And that her father would be, too.

chapter twelve

. Development .

i was right. It was a couple of months into the separation, and so far Shayla didn't seem to be suffering any ill effects. She was still excited about the nursery school she had started in September, she still loved playing with Emma and her other close friends, and she and I were getting along great. Although I missed her on the days that I lived in the coach house, I was able to do just fine without her. In fact I was enjoying being alone. There were actually times when I would turn down dates with friends in order to be just with me. Sometimes I would even eat out in a restaurant by myself without feeling like I had to hide behind a book.

Being alone every other night also gave me a lot of time to work on my new book. In fact writing the narrative proved surprisingly easy. Describing my relationship with Shayla was nothing less than a labor of love. Making the connection between my personal life and my intellectual life felt like a long overdue liberation from the academic discipline that insists on their separation. And the narrative form gave me the freedom to indulge my love of alliteration and penchant for puns with which you are, by now, probably all too familiar. In short, I was having fun. So the story practically wrote itself. By the end of 1988 I had written over two hundred pages and had taken the reader on a road that went as far as the separation between Dotty and myself.

But then I reached an impasse. I simply didn't know how to end my story. Or rather I knew what I needed to do but I didn't know how to do it. Let me explain.

My effort both inside and outside therapy to put psychoanalytic theories of narcissism into practice had enabled me to take better care of Shayla and better care of myself. As a result I had been persuaded of the truth of narcissism theory and became one of its partisans. But my problem was that the defining assumptions of this theory were not only different from, but in important respects opposed to, the feminist psychoanalytic theory on which my gender-struggle theory had been based. Thus my encounter with narcissism theory had shaken the very theoretical foundations of my original book. The encounter that had helped me through my emotional crisis had brought me face-to-face with an intellectual crisis that I knew I needed to resolve.

In order to resolve it I would have to confront, and attempt to overcome, the opposition between the assumptions of the two theories to which I was now committed. Whereas feminist mothering theory assumes that there is a *gender-based* sense of self that is engendered by the (mother-monopolized) *structure* within which early parenting takes place, narcissism theory assumes that there is a *gender-neutral* sense of self that is produced by the particular quality of early maternal *practice*. It seemed to me that each of these assumptions could help explain aspects of my own experience as a parent for which the other could not account.

On the one hand, feminist mothering theory could explain certain crucial aspects of my daughter's development that must remain a mystery for psychoanalytic theories of narcissism. The assumptions of feminist mothering theory lead us to expect that a transformation in the structure of parenting would produce a transformation in the gendered sense of self. More specifically, they yield the hypothesis that a coparented girl will develop a simultaneously relational and assertive sense of self. I considered Shayla's remarkable combination of strength and sensitivity to be as compelling a confirmation of this hypothesis as one case could ever be. Because narcissism theory takes the maternal mode of child rearing for granted, it could neither anticipate nor explain this effect of its elimination.

Nor could it explain why I was (at least in certain respects) a less overprotective parent than Dotty. Its assumption that a narcissistically overprotective mother produces a narcissistic child who becomes a narcissistically overprotective parent did not help explain why Shayla's father was consistently more likely than her mother to encourage her to rely on herself instead of her parents. But this paternal preference for, and maternal opposition to, risk-taking is exactly what feminist mothering theory would lead us to expect.

On the other hand, the gender-based opposition in parenting interests that I derived from feminist mothering theory could not account for what *were* the narcissistically overprotective aspects of my own parenting practice. The hypothesis that "underprotective" fathers will discourage the merger—and overreward the separation—of their children cannot be squared with the ways in which I overrewarded Shayla's merger and discouraged her separation. Thus the problem in my parenting practice was exactly the opposite of what feminist mothering theory would lead us to anticipate. But visiting my mother's overprotectiveness on my daughter is precisely the problem that narcissism theory would predict.

Feminist mothering theory would also be blind to the effects of this overprotectiveness on Shayla. By focusing all its attention on the need to transform the mother-dominated structure of child rearing, it necessarily ignores differences in the quality of parenting practice that outlive that structure and with it the problem of the effects of these differences on coparented children. Because I had often demanded that Shayla recognize me instead of simply recognizing her, she sometimes demanded more attention than she deserved. If I had continued to convey the message that she needed to take care of me in the course of taking care of herself, the mere fact that her gender was different from her daddy's would not have prevented her from having serious problems with separation. She, too, would have learned to equate separation with abandonment and to experience the anxiety that accompanies this equation. My coparented daughter might not have learned to defend against this anxiety in precisely the same way as her mother-raised father, but she would have been every bit as burdened by it as me. In short, it took narcissism theory to help me understand the difference between coparenting and "good-enough" coparenting.

Since each theory could explain what the other could not, a synthesis between them seemed not only necessary but possible. A new theory that preserved the merits and overcame the limits of the two theories that it transcended would be just what the doctor ordered. So I decided that developing this theory should be my intellectual prescription for the next few months. Then I would be able to complete my story.

"Then" turned out to be much, much further away than I thought. It was not a few months but many years before I was able to work out even the broad outlines of my theoretical synthesis. The reasons why are as complicated as my life between 1989 and 1996.

On the last day of 1988 I asked Dotty for a divorce. Within twenty-four hours we agreed that she would keep the house, that Shayla would live there for roughly half the week and in a new apartment with me for the other half, and that this arrangement would begin on March 1, 1989. But there was very little else on which we agreed. Our differences were not resolved until the end of 1989, when the divorce was finally granted. Until that time I was far too preoccupied with those differences and with making a new home for Shayla to think about writing.

Neither did I write between 1990 and 1991. The loss of my marriage—the loss of my *family*—triggered more of the same debilitating anxiety that I suffered before the separation. Once again, it was all I could do just to teach my classes and take care of my daughter. And then—in March 1991—I fell in love with Mary. We saw each other regularly for the next year until she moved in with me and Shayla at the end of the summer of 1992. By that time I was feeling much stronger but I still did not—could not—return to my manuscript. Dwelling on the death of my relationship with Dotty just when I was really starting to live with Mary was about the last thing I wanted to do.

In fact I decided that this time I really would have to let my manuscript go. This decision was based not only on my commitment to Mary but also on my concern for Shayla. Now eight years old, Shayla was doing as well as any child of divorce could ever do. She loved school and got great evaluations from her teachers, even though she regularly challenged their authority when she felt it was exercised unfairly. She had a virtual army of friends, many of them very close, and our relationship was better than ever. But she definitely did not like even the slightest hint of animosity between her mother and me. And sometimes there were more than mere hints. I knew that the times that Dotty and I could not keep our criticisms to ourselves were deeply distressing to our daughter. But there was no way I could publish my story without airing at least some of my complaints about her mother. So I concluded that I just shouldn't publish it.

I felt that I could live with this conclusion because I had discovered a new project. My tentative title for the book that would come out of that project was *Mourning and Modernity*. The thesis of that book would be that modernity simultaneously maximizes the need and minimizes the opportunity to mourn, driving us crazy and making us sick in the process. By the end of 1992 I had immersed myself in the vast sea of psychoanalytic literature on mourning from Freud through Klein and Bowlby and beyond, as well as in the slowly swelling stream of writings that applied their theories to the problem of contemporary culture.

Once again I was pleased to have selected an intellectual project that was informed by, and could in turn inform, my personal project. The consensus of the psychoanalytic literature was that grieving our losses is essential to our emotional and intellectual growth. Grieving my losses—both the loss of my (intrapsychic) mother and the loss of my wife—is exactly what I had been doing over the past few years. Letting go of my book about my daughter and myself now seemed like a natural extension of that process. Thus my new project not only gave me something else to do but also helped persuade me that dropping my old one was the psychologically right thing to do.

So I had some good cries and said goodbye to my manuscript. Between the end of 1992 and the summer of 1994 I read just about everything there was left to read about mourning in preparation for another sabbatical in the fall of 1994, during which I would begin writing *Mourning and Modernity*. But by the time the sabbatical was half over I had only a fifteen-page lecture to show for it. Every time I tried to start the book I was stopped by the thought that there was more that I just *had* to read. 1994 was almost history, and I was no closer to publishing a third book than I had been in 1984.

But then, in December, I got a request from the sociologist Art Shostak to contribute to a book of essays he was editing with the tentative title *Very Personal Sociology*.* Shostak had learned of my mothering manuscript and thought that a selection from it would fit in nicely with his format. I was very ambivalent about his request. On the one hand, I was worried about the emotional consequences of returning to the work with which I had—or so I thought—already made my peace. Was I secure enough about my present to rehash my painful past? Could I do so without putting Shayla at risk? On the other hand, it had been more than a decade since I had published anything that was based on my own research. Could I afford to throw that opportunity away? It was an opportunity, moreover, to make something good come of all those years when I had tried, but failed, to write a book, first on the history of Western child rearing and then on the history

---

*Eventually published as *Private Sociology: Unsparing Reflections, Uncommon Gains* (Dix Hills, NY: General Hall, Inc., 1996).

of my effort to write that history. There would never be a book, but at least there could be an article on the relationship between my theory and my practice.

In early 1995, and with Mary's enthusiastic support, I decided to give it a try. Since Shostak wanted the emphasis to be on the personal rather than the theoretical, I could avoid the problem of the synthesis between feminist psychoanalytic theory and narcissism theory on which my mothering manuscript had foundered. Instead I merely condensed the narrative I had already written into a thirty-page essay. And I took care not to mention any of my misgivings about Shayla's mother.

It all went very smoothly. I didn't get depressed, I finished the essay before the end of winter, and Shostak very much liked what I sent him. I could look forward to a book chapter sometime in 1996! At long last I would be able to fulfill my promise to publish something on the relationship between my work and my life.

In May 1996 I fulfilled another promise. Mary and I were married in a ceremony that took place in the great room of the loft that we had purchased the previous year. Then we took off for a week in Saint Vincent, after which it was back to teaching, first in the summer and then in the fall.

During the fall I chaired a search committee for a junior position in political theory for which my department had been authorized to interview. Among the more than two hundred applicants were four bright young scholars who made the final cut. Among the four who made the final cut was a man named Marc Stier. It turned out that Marc was also a committed coparent of a daughter to whom he was deeply devoted. Over drinks we talked about our kids, and I talked about my essay and the larger manuscript of which it was an excerpt. We agreed that I would give him a copy of that essay before he left town and that he would soon let me know what he thought.

Several weeks later I received an enormously enthusiastic letter from Marc. He not only loved the essay but encouraged me to make one more effort to turn my manuscript into a book. For many weeks I pondered this possibility. Once again Mary encouraged me to embrace it. But before I could embrace it I knew that I would have to talk with Shayla.

I explained to my daughter that my manuscript included descriptions of disagreements—often strongly expressed—between her mother and her father. How would she feel if she read about those disagreements or, perhaps more to the point, if her friends brought them to her attention? Shayla—who was fast approaching her twelfth birthday—replied that everyone knows that people who get divorced have deep differences and that she thought she could handle my making them public. In January I finally decided that I would give it one last shot. I would try to work out the synthesis I had abandoned in 1989.

I also decided that I needed to change the mode of presentation of my manuscript. If the manuscript was going to culminate in a theoretical argument—a claim not just about myself but also about the world—then that argument should be presented in a way that the world could evaluate it. And if that argument was supposed to be a synthesis of earlier theoretical arguments, then those earlier arguments should also be allowed to speak for themselves. But a purely narrative presentation conveyed the impression that those arguments were merely signs of their private emotional origins. So I decided I would have to unwrite my narrative to make it alternate with declarative presentations of both my original theory and its eventual *aufhebung*.*

I rewrote two hundred pages by the end of the spring. By the summer I was ready to tackle the task that I had for so long deferred. In six weeks I was able to work out the broad outlines of my theoretical synthesis. Here is what it looks like:

---

*A synthesis that negates, preserves, and overcomes the shared limitations of, the elements of which it is composed.

Self and (M)other: Toward a Synthesis of Feminist Mothering Theory and Psychoanalytic Theories of Narcissism

I. Introduction

In this essay I outline a partial synthesis of the feminist mothering theory of Dorothy Dinnerstein, Nancy Chodorow, and Jessica Benjamin, on the one hand, and the psychoanalytic theories of narcissism of Heinz Kohut, Otto Kernberg, and James Masterson, on the other. In the next section I summarize the competing assumptions of these two bodies of psychoanalytic theory and argue that it is both necessary and possible to resolve the opposition between them. Since each raises key questions about the sources of the self for which the other can provide no answer, a theoretical synthesis would enable us to answer more important questions about the self than either of the theories on which that synthesis was based. In the third section I work toward that synthesis by evaluating two recent reflections on the relationship between gender and narcissism. This evaluation sets the stage for my effort in the final section of this essay to set forth (the beginnings of) a synthesis that incorporates the merits, and overcomes the limits, of those recent reflections.

II. Structure or Practice: Feminist Mothering Theory versus Psychoanalytic Theories of Narcissism

Feminist mothering theory starts from the assumptions (a) that there is a gendered sense of self and (b) that this gendered sense of self is produced by the "mother-monopolized" structure within which parenting takes place. Dorothy Dinnerstein, Nancy Chodorow, and Jessica Benjamin all argue that under these conditions there are fundamental differences in the "object relations" of men and women—their sense of themselves in relation to others—and that these differences are the inevitable outcome of an inherent difference in their early relationship with the mother. Because boys must define themselves in opposition to their mothers in order to become men, mother-raised men will develop a disproportionately "oppositional" orientation within which connection with others will be sacrificed to separation from them. Because the relationship of girls with their mothers, in contrast, is not an obstacle to, but rather the source of, their feminine sense of self, mother-raised women will develop a "relational" orientation within which separation from others will be subordinated to connection with them.[1]

Thus neither men nor women will be able to combine connection with separation until the end of the female monopoly on mothering, i.e., until fathers join mothers as equal partners in the early care of their male and female children. Under coparenting boys would also be closely identified with a primary caregiver of the same sex and men would thus become less afraid of connection than exclusively mother-raised men. Under coparenting girls would also be closely identified with a primary caregiver of the opposite sex and thus coparented women would be less fearful of separation than exclusively mother-raised girls. In sum, the consequences of this transformation in the structure of child rearing would be that men would become more like women and women more like men, each absorbing the best that the other presently has to offer.

Thus feminist mothering theory ignores differences in the quality of parenting practice under the prevailing, mother-dominated structure of child rearing as well as differences in parenting that might outlive the transformation of that structure in the direction of coparenting.[2] It thereby also ignores the problem of the difference in the object relations of children of both genders that these differences in parenting might make.

These are precisely the differences with which psychoanalytic theories of narcissism are preoccupied. The defining assumptions of these theories are (a) that the sense of self is not gendered and (b) that the sense of self is produced by the quality of parenting practice. Kernberg, Kohut, and Masterson all assume that differences in the object relations of individuals result (at least in part) from differences in the quality of the maternal care they experience in their earliest years. Masterson connects those differences in object relations more clearly than Kernberg and Kohut to the way in which the mother responds to the "rapprochement crisis" of her child, i.e., to the way she handles his or her effort to negotiate the increasingly intense, conflicting claims of connection and separation during the second year of his or her life.[3]

If mothers suppress the separation and overreward the merger of their little boys and girls, then they will grow up to be men and women who privilege connection over separation. If mothers suppress the merger and overreward the separation of their little boys and girls, then they will grow up to become men and women who privilege separation over connection. Both men and women will be able to combine connection and separation if, in contrast, they have been fortunate enough to have had a mother—a "good-enough mother"—who was able to encourage each equally during their early period of rapprochement.

Thus narcissism theorists take for granted the mother-dominated structure of parenting and do not explore the way in which this structure inhibits the formation of "good-enough" object relations in both women and men. They likewise tend to ignore any connection between gender and sense of self that might result from that structure.[4] Consequently they neglect as well any changes in that connection that might result from the transformation of that structure.

Each of these theories, it should be clear, is the exact obverse of the other. Feminist mothering theory assumes the complete dominance of structure over practice and of gender over sense of self. It thereby ignores the relative autonomy of practice from structure and sense of self from gender. Narcissism theory, in contrast, insists on the complete autonomy of practice from structure and of sense of self from gender. It necessarily neglects in the process the influence of structure over practice and gender over sense of self. In order to preserve the merits and overcome the limits of both theories it is therefore necessary to grasp what neither theory is able to grasp, namely the *relationship of connec-*

tion and separation between structure and practice and between gender and sense of self.

This is what I shall attempt to do in the fourth and final section of this essay. But first I will take up two recent efforts to understand the relationship between narcissism and gender: one that privileges practice over structure and sense of self over gender, the other that privileges structure over practice and gender over sense of self. My critique of these efforts should serve to clarify some of the criteria that a more adequate understanding would have to satisfy.

III. Recent Reflections on Gender and Narcissism

A. Christopher Lasch's Critique of Feminist Mothering Theory

In *The Minimal Self* Christopher Lasch relies on Otto Kernberg, as well as other psychoanalytic theorists of narcissism for a depth-psychological diagnosis of the discontents of modern capitalism. He argues that capitalist culture "tends to favor regressive solutions . . . to the [universal] problem of separation"[5] of individuals from their maternal origin, viz, that it encourages omnipotent fantasies of either symbiotic fusion with, or grandiose independence from, the world that both reflect and reinforce the narcissistic defenses of children who have not been able to achieve a "state of being in relation to the mother as something outside and separate."[6] This is a provocative, and to my mind persuasive, argument about the reciprocal relationship between narcissism and contemporary capitalism.

Far less persuasive, however, is Lasch's bold claim that "narcissism has nothing to do with femininity or masculinity."[7] This claim is intended as a rejoinder to feminist mothering theorists like Nancy Chodorow, as well as other feminists, who have associated "relatedness" or "feminine mutuality" with a woman's never entirely renounced wish for merger with her mother, on the one hand, and a "radically autonomous" sense of self with a man's enduring denial of his dependence on his mother, on the other. According to Lasch, that kind of argument

> dissolves the contradiction held in tension by the psycho-
> analytic theory of narcissism: namely, that all of us, men
> and women alike, experience the pain of separation and si-
> multaneously long for a restoration of the original sense of
> union. Narcissism originates in the infant's symbiotic fu-
> sion with the mother, but the desire to return to this bliss-
> ful state cannot be identified with "feminine mutuality"
> without obscuring both its universality and the illusions of
> "radical autonomy" to which it also gives rise, in women as
> well as men. The desire for complete self-sufficiency is just
> as much a legacy of primary narcissism as the desire for
> mutuality and relatedness. Because narcissism knows no
> distinction between the self and others, it expresses itself in
> later life both in the desire for ecstatic union with others, as
> in romantic love, and in the desire for absolute indepen-
> dence from others, by means of which we seek to revive the
> original illusion of omnipotence and to deny our depen-
> dence on external sources of nourishment and gratification.
> . . . Since both [fantasies] spring from the same source . . . it
> can only cause confusion to call the dream of [absolute in-
> dependence] a masculine obsession, while extolling the
> hope of [ecstatic union] as a characteristically feminine pre-
> occupation.[8]

Thus Lasch's claim that "narcissism has nothing to do with femininity or masculinity" is based on the argument that the fan-tasies of absolute independence and absolute fusion cannot be considered gender-based since both these fantasies stem from the same source, namely the "pain of separation" from—and the longing for "the restoration of the original union" with—the mother that "all of us, men and women alike," have experienced. But this argument is simply a non sequitur. From the premise that the source of narcissistic fantasies is gender-neutral we cannot infer that the fantasies themselves are necessarily gender-neutral; although the pain of separation and the longing to undo it may be common to both male and female infants, the way in which boys and girls, and thus men and women, come to defend against this pain and longing may be very different. Lasch arbitrarily assumes, in other words, that the narcissistic fantasies that defend against the separation anxiety of boys and girls have nothing to do with the fantasies by means of which their gender identity is constructed. Consequently he is able to conclude, equally arbitrarily, that the differences in the boy's and the girl's preoedipal relationships with the mother, which shape their respective gender identities, have no effect on their narcissistic fantasies.

There are good reasons to reject this conclusion. Masterson argues, as we have seen, that narcissism is the child's defense against the mother's failure adequately to respond to his or her rapprochement crisis during the second year of his or her life. It is precisely at this point, according to Robert Stoller, that the child begins to become aware of his or her "core gender identity" as well as the identity or difference between that identity and the gender identity of his or her mother.[9] Thus the peak of children's "pain of separation" from their mother is likely to coincide with the onset of their concern about whether they are either the same as, or different from, her. Does it not seem probable that the way in which they come to defend against that pain will depend decisively on their answer to that question? More specifically, should we not expect that a child whose longing "for a restoration of [his] original union" with his mother is complicated by fear that this union threatens his emerging gender identity is particularly prone to fall prey to the "illusion of radical autonomy" and thus that—contrary to Lasch's claim—boys are far more likely than girls to succumb to the grandiose narcissism of "complete self-sufficiency"?

Essentially the same point can be made with respect to Kohut's account of the origins of the narcissism of the "grandiose self." According to this account, a child whose self-esteem is not confirmed by a mother who "mirrors [his or her] exhibitionistic display" will defend against this maternal deficit by "concentrating perfection and power upon the self . . . and turning away disdainfully from an outside to which all imperfections have been assigned."[10] This account, in other words, is based on the assumption that any child will feel affirmed if he or she is adequately mirrored by his or her mother. But this assumption is called into question by feminist mothering theory. As Jessica Benjamin has argued (echoing a similar, earlier argument of Dorothy Dinnerstein),

> The need to sever the identification with the mother in order to be confirmed both as a separate person and as a male person . . . often prevents the boy from recognizing his mother. She is not seen as an independent person (another subject) but as something other—as nature, as an instrument or an object, as less than human. The premise of this independence is to say, "I am nothing like the one who cares for me." In breaking this identification with . . . mother, the boy is in danger of losing his capacity for mutual recognition altogether.[11]

If, following Hegel, we assume that all self-affirming recognition must be mutual,[12] then the fact the boy is in "danger of losing his capacity for mutual recognition" means that there is no guarantee that he will feel self-affirmed by the recognition he receives from his mother. To the contrary, a boy who refuses to recognize a mother who mirrors him will be unable to recognize himself in her mirror and therefore will be unable to take pride in being recognized by her.[13] Thus he is likely to be far more vulnerable than his sister to omnipotent fantasies that unrealistically inflate his pride. In short, under the maternal mode of child rearing boys are more likely than girls to suffer from the narcissism of the "grandiose self."

Feminist mothering theory can also explain why girls are much more likely to suffer from what Kohut calls the narcissism of the "ideal object," or to defend against the anxiety of separation from the mother with what Lasch calls fantasies of "ecstatic union" with the other. Because the intimate preoedipal relationship with her mother is the source of, rather than an obstacle to, the girl's gendered sense of self, "girls [according to Chodorow] come to experience themselves as less separate than boys, as having more permeable ego boundaries . . . [and] come to define themselves more in relation to others." The others in relation to whom girls define their self often become others to whom that self is sacrificed: "there is a tendency in women toward boundary confusion and a lack of sense of separateness from the world." This tendency will be particularly pronounced in the case of women whose preoedipal relationship with their mothers was marked by the "prolonged symbiosis and narcissistic overidentification" that are often characteristic of that relationship.[14]

Chodorow's clinically based inferences are confirmed by empirical observations of the different ways in which boys and girls negotiate the difficulties of their rapprochement stage. Margaret Mahler and her colleagues report that just when boys were

> beginning to enjoy their functioning in the widening
> world, girls seemed to be more engrossed with mother . . .
> and were more persistently enmeshed in the ambivalent aspects of the relationship. . . . [T]he task of becoming a separate individual seemed . . . to be generally more difficult
> for girls than for boys.[15]

The girl's task of individuation is more difficult than the boy's, according to Chodorow, because she "does not have something different and desirable [a penis] with which to oppose maternal omnipotence."[16] Unlike the boy, the girl cannot rely on any obvious physical difference to help disentangle herself from a relationship with her mother that is even more overwhelming than his. What she can—and usually does—do (at least within intact nuclear families) is to "transfer to the father . . . much of the weight of her positive feelings [toward her mother], while leaving the negative ones mainly attached to their original object." In this way the girl "gains a less equivocal focus for her feeling of pure love, and feels freer to express her grievances against her mother without fear of being cut off altogether from . . . a magic, animally loved, parental being." But the price she eventually pays for this overidealization of her father is a "worshipful, dependent stance toward men"[17] to whom she will sacrifice her agency in order to repudiate her mother's.

According to Kohut, narcissists of the idealizing type defend against the loss of infantile omnipotence by "giving over the previous perfection to an admired, omnipotent . . . self-object: *the idealized parent imago*." Their central defense mechanism, in effect, is the fantasy that "you are perfect, but I am part of you."[18] This description of the narcissist who defends against separation by basking in the reflected glow of the overidealized other clearly dovetails with Chodorow's and Dinnerstein's descriptions of women who live their lives through the men with whom they seek "ecstatic union."

Their account of the origins of this tendency toward female self-subordination is also consistent with Kohut's (rather sparse) reflections on the etiology of this type of narcissism:

> [U]nder . . . favorable circumstances, the idealized parent imago . . . becomes integrated into the adult personality. Introjected as our idealized superego, it becomes an important component of our psychic organization by holding up to us the guiding leadership of its ideals. . . . If the child, however, *suffers . . . traumatic disappointments in the admired adult*, then the idealized parent imago . . . is retained in its unaltered form [and] is not transformed into a tension-regulating psychic structure.[19]

"Traumatic disappointments in the admired adult"—in the admired mother—are precisely what, according to feminist mothering theory, most mother-raised girls experience as they turn from their mothers to embrace their fathers. Thus feminist mothering theory is able to explain what neither Kohut nor Lasch is even able to recognize, namely the disproportionate tendency of women to defend against what Lasch calls the "pain of separation" and the longing for a "restoration of the original sense of union" by privileging "union" over "separation."

Thus from feminist mothering theory it is possible to derive the generalizations that (a) "grandiose" narcissists are more likely to be men than women and (b) "idealizing" narcissists are more likely to be women than men. These generalizations are confirmed by careful consideration of the case material that Kernberg, Kohut, and Masterson present in their major works. Ilene Philipson has noted that among the "29 cases presented as exemplary of . . . narcissistic disorders [of the grandiose variety]" in Kernberg's *Borderline Conditions and Pathological Narcissism,* and Kohut's *The Analysis of the Self* and *The Restoration of the Self,* "only five depict women."[20] My own count of the cases in Kernberg's book revealed an even stronger correlation between gender and type of narcissism: I found only one woman among the fourteen "grandiose" narcissists but sixteen women among the twenty-four "idealizing" narcissists (who are called "borderline" by Kernberg). My count of the cases in Masterson's *The Narcissistic and Borderline Disorders* revealed a strikingly similar result: all four grandiose narcissists were men and seventeen out of twenty-four idealizing narcissists (also called "borderline" by Masterson) were women.

Thus the gender composition of the clinical cases of the psychoanalytic theorists of narcissism on whom Christopher Lasch relies confirms the connections between gender and narcissism that feminist mothering theory would predict. We can conclude, then, that feminist mothering theory is well able to withstand his critique.

B. Ilene Philpson's "Gender and Narcissism"

But another look at the gender composition of Kernberg and Masterson's cases reveals something that feminist mothering theory is *not* able to explain. Although all but one of their grandiose narcissists were men, and although all but one of their female patients were idealizing narcissists, seven out of Masterson's twenty-four idealizing narcissists, and eight out of Kernberg's twenty-four idealizing narcissists, were men. To state these findings another way: whereas the combined ratio of male to female grandiose narcissists is seventeen to one, the combined ratio of female to male idealizing narcissist is barely more than two to one. These results are an anomaly for feminist mothering theory.

We have seen that from the assumptions of feminist mothering theory it is possible to derive the hypothesis that it is the daughter's difficulty of disentangling herself from her mother that accounts for the narcissistically idealizing woman. It would therefore seem to follow that we should expect that narcissistically idealizing men would have similar difficulties in extricating themselves from their preoedipal relationship with their mothers. But this inference is excluded by the assumptions of feminist mothering theory. This becomes clear when we examine a recent account of gender and narcissism that is based on those assumptions.

In "Gender and Narcissism" and "Heterosexual Antagonisms and the Politics of Mothering,"[21] Ilene Philipson draws on feminist mothering theory in order to criticize Kohut's gender-neutral account of narcissism and to claim that "it is men who are more likely [than women] to display feelings of grandiosity and extreme self-centeredness, and to need the admiration of others." She also argues that the way in which the female narcissist "deal[s] with low self-esteem appears to be quite different from the grandiosity . . . of men" and typically entails the fantasy that "male love partners [are] part of the woman's self."[22] The following passage nicely sums up her conclusions concerning the connection between gender and narcissism:

> For men . . . women partners do not become parts of the self; in fact, they are used to admire and esteem the defensively autonomous and tenuously maintained self. Women admire men's grandiosity, while male partners are constitutive of women's sense of worth. Women esteem men, while men are the vehicles through which women frequently attempt to find their self-esteem.[23]

To reach this conclusion Philipson relies on many of the same
Chodorowian arguments that I have independently adduced in
my critique of Christopher Lasch.[24] But she also emphasizes one
that I did not. Philipson argues that the asymmetries in the boy's
and girl's preoedipal relationships with the mother are compounded by the tendency of the mother to treat them differently:
"sons are most likely to be seen [by insufficiently empathic moth-
ers] as husbands, fathers, and brothers, while daughters are seen
as women's mothers or as extensions of themselves."[25] The passages from Chodorow's *The Reproduction of Mothering* that this
claim references are worth reproducing in detail:

> Because they are the same gender as their daughters and
> have been girls, mothers of daughters tend not to experi-
> ence [their] infant daughters as separate from them in the
> same way as do mothers of infant sons. In both cases, a
> mother is likely to experience a sense of oneness and conti-
> nuity with her infant. However, this sense is stronger, and
> lasts longer, vis-a-vis daughters. Primary identification and
> symbiosis with daughters tends to be stronger and cathexis
> of daughters is more likely to retain narcissistic elements,
> that is, to be based on experiencing a daughter as an exten-
> sion or double of a mother herself, with cathexis of the
> daughter as a sexual other usually remaining a weak, less
> significant theme.[26]

> Mothers tend to experience their daughters as more like,
> and continuous with, themselves. Correspondingly, girls
> tend to remain part of the dyadic primary mother-child re-
> lationship itself. This means that a girl continues to experi-
> ence herself as involved in issues of merging and separa-
> tion, and in an attachment characterized by primary
> identification and the fusion of identification and object-
> choice. By contrast, mothers experience their sons as a
> male opposite. Boys are more likely to have been pushed
> out of the preoedpial relationship, and to have had to cur-

tail their primary love and sense of empathic tie with their
mother. A boy has . . . been required to engage . . . in a
more emphatic individuation and a more defensive firming
of experienced ego boundaries.[27]

Thus Chodorow assumes that girls will find it difficult to separate from their mothers not only because they do not experience
themselves as different from their mothers but also because their
mothers do not experience them as different from themselves;
this identity leads mothers to treat their daughters as extensions
of themselves and thus to discourage their separation. Boys, in
contrast, will separate from their mothers far more easily, both
because of the internal pull toward separation that results from
the boy's experience of an opposition between his gender and
hers and because this internal pull will be complemented by an
external push toward separation that results from her experience
of him as a "male opposite." Thus it is Chodorow's assumption of
a necessarily complementary, mutually reinforcing push-pull toward separation that leads Philipson to her conclusion that "it is
men who are . . . likely to display feelings of grandiosity and extreme self-centeredness," i.e., to associate men exclusively with
narcissism of the grandiose self.

   It is precisely that assumption, then, that makes it impossible
to account for men who are idealizing narcissists. Such men, I
have suggested, must have difficulties with separation that are, at
least in certain respects, similar to the difficulties of narcissistically idealizing women. If these men have similar difficulties with
separation, this can only be because their separation was similarly discouraged by their mothers. But Chodorow's assumption
that mothers experience their sons as "opposites" and thus push
them toward separation effectively denies the existence of men
whose separation has been suppressed by their mothers.[28] To
make room for these men, it is therefore necessary to call that assumption into question. We must challenge the claim that mothers necessarily treat their little boys in a way that is fundamentally different from the way that they treat their little girls.

Miriam Johnson has already done so. In *Strong Mothers, Weak Wives* she summarizes an impressive array of empirical studies that contest Chodorow's claim of significant, gender-based differences in the maternal care of young children. According to Johnson, very "few of these [studies] find differences in the way in which mothers interact with male and female children." Most report that there are "no differences on the part of mothers in the amount of affectionate contact between mother and male and female infants" and that "the degree of early attachment to the mother appears to be remarkably the same for both genders." Thus she concludes that "mothers do not differentiate appreciably between males and females in the amount of nurturance they provide."[29]

Although Johnson's insistence on exonerating mothering from any blame leads her to interpret this evidence as a refutation of Chodorow's claim that many mothers are narcissistically overinvested in their daughters, a less idealist interpretation of this evidence would culminate in the conclusion that many (mother-raised) mothers are also likely to be narcissistically overinvested in their sons. Such mothers, *pace* Chodorow, will not "experience [their sons] as separate from them," will not "experience [them] as a male opposite," and will not "push them out of [their] pre-oedipal relationship." Instead we should expect that they will strive to suppress their sons' separation every bit as strenuously as they attempt to discourage their daughters'.

IV. Conclusion

Chodorow infers from the fact that their sons are in some sense their gender "opposites" the conclusion that mothers will necessarily *experience* their sons as "opposites" and act accordingly. But the evidence suggests that this inference is an unwarranted form of gender determinism. Mothers who, in the words of Donald Winnicott, treat their children as "projective entities" rather than as "entities in their own right"[30] may be just as likely to experience their sons as mothers who exist to take care of them as husbands who exist to fulfill them. If they experience their sons as mothers, they will treat them as mothers despite the "obvious" physical difference between them. The relative indifference of fantasy to reality thus makes it impossible directly to derive parenting practice from the structure of parenting.

Neither can the sense of self be directly derived from gender. If the structure of parenting does not guarantee that mothers will encourage the separation of their sons, it follows that it does not ensure, *pace* Chodorow once again, that "the basic masculine sense of self is separate."[31] This claim, it seems to me, only applies to the boy who has been both pushed and pulled away from his mother. Having received, as it were, a consistent set of messages about the dangers of connection, it is he who becomes a man who consistently privileges separation from over connection with the others he encounters. It is he, in other words, who will suffer from the narcissism of the grandiose self.

The boy who has, in contrast, been simultaneously pulled toward and away from his mother has received an inconsistent set of messages about the meaning of separation. He learns, in effect, that separation from the (m)other is both incompatible with and essential to the survival of his self.

Having been overprotected by his mother, he (like his overprotected sister) will defend against the anxiety he associates with separation by seeking out relationships with overidealized others to whom he can cling. In this respect his sense of self is anything but separate, and in this respect his narcissism duplicates the idealizing narcissism of his female counterpart.

But the very symbiosis he seeks necessarily negates the masculinity that he must maintain. In order to transcend this double bind the narcissistically idealizing man is likely to seek the safest possible connections with others, connections within which his need for others takes the form of a need to take care of them. Thus the idealizing man is both similar to and different from the grandiose man. Both need to control others to shore up their selves. But the grandiose man tries to control others by proving that he does not depend on them, while the idealizing man tries to control others by proving that they depend on him. Thus he differs from his narcissistically idealizing female counterpart by virtue of what might be considered his grandiose defense against an underlying overdependence on his others.[32]

I have argued that the problem with feminist mothering theory is that it overestimates the determining power of gender and that the problem with narcissism theory is that it underestimates the determining power of gender. Thus at first glance my argument appears to be divided against itself. But the gender determinism that I have called into question and the gender determinism that I have reaffirmed entail different kinds of claims. The former entails the claim that the practice of the mother will be determined by the identity or difference between her gender and the gender of her child. The latter entails the claim that the child's sense of self will (in part) be determined by the identity or difference between his or her gender and the gender of his or her mother. The coherence of my argument depends, therefore, on the assumption that gender is in some sense more salient for the (preoedipal) child than it is for his or her mother. This assumption is clearly counterintuitive. But so is psychoanalysis itself. It teaches both that the projections of adults with not-good-enough object relations are remarkably resistant to external reality—including the reality of gender—and that the object relations of children are formed during a period of maximum receptivity to all the salient signals—including the signals of gender—that shape their sentience.

chapter thirteen

. **Back to**
the Beginning .

i knew that this theoretical synthesis was far from complete. It was clear to me that the type of mothering that boys experience was a necessary but not sufficient explanation for the type of men they in fact become. A more comprehensive account of the variations on the theme of masculine identity would have to consider the kind of relationship that boys establish—or fail to establish—with their fathers.

In fact I had been thinking a lot lately about the kind of relationship I had established as a child with my own father. In the course of my therapy with Alisa I had uncovered many early memories of that relationship. I remembered how my father would take me for hikes in the woods behind my house, and how even in his mid-fifties he would help me hone my skills on the baseball diamond and the tennis court. Like many fathers, he had certainly played—sometimes *over*played—an important teaching role. But I also remembered his hugs. And I had vague recollections of being fed and bathed by him as well. So, within the limits of the paternal expectations of the 1950s, he must have played an important nurturing role as well.

Many years ago I had speculated that a relationship with a relatively warm father might explain why a strongly mother-identified boy would wind up straight rather than gay. My assumption, in other words, had been that the boy's identification with his father had everything to do with the consolidation of his heterosexuality and nothing to do with the persistence of his maternal identifications. But this assumption was undermined by my memories of my father's ministrations. Surely those ministrations had made it easier for me to think that I could mother without losing my manhood.

Recently I had read something that confirmed my speculation. John Munder Ross emphasized the crucial role of the father in "determining . . . a son's readiness or not to tender love" and thus whether his "urges towards generativity and the reality of his gender identity [will] coalesce."[1] According to Ross's account, "in their nurturing and teaching roles [fathers] may provide possibilities for their sons to include in their definitions of masculinity capacities first learned in identification with their mothers."[2] Thus a friendly father was necessary for the incorporation of maternal propensities into a masculine identity.

Ross's reasoning led to the conclusion that maternally overprotected boys who identify with relatively nurturing fathers will become different kinds of men from maternally overprotected boys who do not. My sense was that only the former will wind up to be narcissistically idealizing "good boys" who try to take care of others, while the latter will lean toward the nastier narcissism of a hypermasculine misogyny. Whereas the overprotected and father-identified boy can defend against his frighteningly powerful need for his mother by telling himself, "Because I am a man like my father who takes care of my mother, I will one day be able to take care of a woman who is like my mother," the overprotected boy with an absent or distant father is only able to defend against his fearsome fusion with his mother by trashing the women who represent her and thus assiduously avoiding long-term, emotionally intimate relationships with them.

Similarly, maternally underprotected boys who are able to

identify with their fathers will grow up to be different kinds of men from maternally underprotected boys who are not. Both boys will defend against premature separation from their mother with fantasies of exercising omnipotent control over her, but the grandiosity of the boy who confronts, and then internalizes, his father's prohibitions is repressed, while the grandiosity of the boy who does not encounter, and therefore never identifies with, paternal authority is given free reign. Only the latter become men "who feel they have the right to control and possess others and to exploit them without guilt feelings,"[3] while the former will develop the strong superego of the inhibited, "inner-directed" man. Although psychoanalysis typically contrasts the neurosis of the "Guilty Man" with the narcissism of "Tragic Man,"[4] Jessica Benjamin has argued, persuasively, that the repressed (and therefore never really relinquished) narcissism of Guilty Man inevitably returns in the form an "aspiration to omnipotence that is nowhere more clearly evident than in the rape of nature."[5] Thus it would be more accurate to distinguish between what might be called the neurotic narcissism of the underprotected but father-identified man and the grandiose narcissism of the underprotected and nonfather-identified man.

My synthesis had even less to say about variations on the theme of feminine identity. In treating idealizing narcissism as a disproportionately female phenomenon I had offered no explanation at all for the (apparently) relatively rare instances of grandiosely narcissistic girls. It would seem to follow from my theoretical assumptions that their preoedipal merger with their mothers must have been prematurely curtailed and that the combination of this external push away, and their internal (gender-based) pull toward, their mothers would lead them to defend grandiosely against their own tendency toward self-denigration. But I wasn't sure why they would have been pushed away from their mothers.

At first I thought that paternal control over maternal practices might be part of the answer. But I had learned from Miriam Johnson that "*fathers differentiate more than mothers* between their male and female children" and that we should not expect that a girl will be treated nearly as harshly by her father as a boy.[6] Even the most underprotective father will be far less threatened by the dependence of "daddy's little girl" than by the dependence of his "big strong boy." But if this is the case, then paternal control over maternal practices is not likely to be a satisfactory explanation for a mother's disdain for her daughter's dependence. What a satisfactory explanation would be remained, for me, an entirely open question.

So too was the question of the difference that daddy would make. Maternally underprotected girls who were able to identify with their fathers are likely to grow up to be very different women from the maternally underprotected girls who were not. Perhaps only the latter would become the cold female counterparts of guiltlessly grandiose men. It also followed that maternally overprotected girls who were father-identified should become different kinds of women from maternally overprotected girls who were not. Perhaps only the mother-fusion fantasies of the former culminate in an idealization of men, while the mother-fusion fantasies of the latter will be focused more exclusively on their children.

These were questions to which I would eventually have to return in order to complete my synthesis. But right now I was faced with a far more pressing problem, namely the implications of that synthesis for the gender-struggle theory with which I had struggled for so long. That theory had been an extrapolation from feminist mothering theory, but my encounter with narcissism theory had culminated in the conclusion that feminist mothering theory "overestimates the determining power of gender." Thus it would seem that I would be obliged to concede that my gender-struggle theory likewise overestimated the determining power of gender. Yet I had also concluded that "narcissism theory underestimates the determining power of gender." This suggested that I should soften, rather than abandon, my claim about the determining power of gender struggle.

This is precisely what I want to do. On the one hand, I no

longer think that it makes sense to claim that gender struggle is the single most important source of changes in parenting practices. This was a claim on which I was never really able to make good. My argument was that a change in parenting practices resulted from a shift in the balance of power between mothers and fathers, and that this shift in the balance of power within the family was the outcome of a shift in a number of extrafamilial, e.g., social, economic, ideological, and political, factors. But that argument would only be consistent with the claim of the determining power of gender struggle if it were possible to demonstrate that the shift in those extrafamilial factors was itself (mainly) the outcome of (extrafamilial) gender struggle. And that is exactly what I was never able to demonstrate.

I would not even have bothered to try if I knew then what I know now. It follows from the assumption that "the sense of self can not be directly derived from gender" that the social, economic, political, and ideological struggles of the self can never simply be reduced to gender struggles.[7] If the outcome of those struggles outside the home necessarily and profoundly affects the balance of power between mothers and fathers within it, then shifts in that balance of power can likewise never be understood as the exclusive result of gender struggle. Neither therefore can the changes in parenting practices that follow in their wake. Thus my synthesis rules out the claim that gender struggle is the dominant determinant of transformations in child-rearing changes.

But it in no way excludes the claim that gender struggle is an important determinant of these changes. In fact I believe that that claim can be derived from my synthesis. Although that synthesis assumes, as we have seen, that there will be important within-gender differences (and thus cross-gender convergences) in object relations that result from differences in parenting practice, it also assumes that there will be significant within-gender similarities (thus cross-gender differences) that result from the similarity of the (mother-monopolized) structure within which that practice takes place. Although it is true that overprotected boys are far more likely to become "caretaking" narcissists than underprotected boys, it is also true that *all* boys are likely to become men for whom dependence on their mothers and masculinity are a contradiction in terms. We have also seen that it makes sense to assume that most men will fantasize their wives as mothers whether their real mothers have been overprotective or not.

Similarly, girls who were underprotected by their mothers will undoubtedly grow up to be different from girls who were overprotected by their mothers, but *all* girls are likely to experience an identity rather than an opposition between their gendered sense of self and their dependence on their mothers. And they are *un*likely to treat their husbands as substitute mothers.

So my synthesis supposes that there remain both preoedipal and oedipal sources of a gender-based opposition in parenting interests. The parenting orientation of (father-identified) overprotected men will be more protective than the orientation of underprotected men, but overprotected men will (a) still be more ambivalent about the dependence of their children than most women and (b) still be more threatened by the ties between their wives and their children than their wives will be threatened by the ties between their children and their husbands. For both reasons both underprotected and overprotected men can be expected to contest the dependence of their children on their mothers. Thus it still makes sense to assume a fundamental opposition between a paternal and a maternal parenting interest.

This assumption, I would argue, remains indispensable to an adequate account of the history of child rearing in the West. It would take another book to sustain this argument, but perhaps the following thumbnail sketch will serve to establish its plausibility:

Under the early modern child-rearing regime (I have learned to keep my mouth shut about the Middle Ages!), mothers regularly resisted but were normally obliged to defer to the demands of their economically and politically far more powerful husbands for a swift and radical break in the bonds between their children and themselves. Those demands were justified by a theory of the innate depravity of the child that was both cause and consequence of the neurotic narcissism of early modern men. Boys who had been (preoedipally) denied by the mothers and (oedipally) repressed by their fathers defended against their unacceptably intense hatred of their parents first by turning it against themselves and later by projecting it onto their own children, whose (resulting) "depravity" demanded that they, in turn, be (preoedipally) denied and (oedipally) repressed.

But the repressed omnipotence of these early modern men returned in the form of the fantasy that nature was an object that must be possessed and dominated by a sovereign human subject. Thus what Weber dubbed the "disenchantment of the world" was in fact a fantastic defense against a swift and sudden separation of early modern men from their mothers. This magical "modernization of the mind," in turn, set the stage for the economic and political modernization that followed in its wake: once nature was reduced to fungible matter it became possible for the commodities made up of that matter to become formally equal objects of economic exchange and for the men who produced them to likewise become formally equal subjects of political representation.

So by the early nineteenth century men began to move out of the domestic domain and into the public world of work and politics. The ideology of separate spheres that justified and promoted this exodus of men from the family served simultaneously to legitimate the increasing power of the "moral mother" within it. Thus were early to mid-century mothers able to "take command" of the care of their children.

When they did they were able to rely on a parenting theory that repudiated the assumption of the innate depravity of the child in favor of the assumption of infantile innocence. This optimistic, post-Calvinist doctrine was clearly more consistent with a commitment to economic and political development than the profoundly pessimistic doctrine it replaced, and thus we can acknowledge that economic and political forces fueled its eventual hegemony. But the development of the new doctrine was also a result of a "feminization" of American Protestantism for which middle-class women were themselves in large part responsible.

Women who had been reared under the harsh "break-the-will" Calvinist regime helped to create, and were willing to support, a much gentler regime of "Christian nurture" because their parenting orientations remained far more protective than those of the men who were broken by that brutal regime. Unlike their husbands, they were able identify with the dependence of their children, both because their own dependence was not as summarily squelched by their fathers and because girls are rarely as afraid of dependence as boys. Thus when they gained control of the mode of child rearing the stage was set for a dramatic shift from the underprotective early modern practices to the overprotective practices that prevailed until the latter part of the nineteenth century.

From their very inception these practices encountered the resistance of an older generation of men who worried about the feminization of their younger brethren. And these worries were not entirely unfounded, as the overprotected sons of early to mid-nineteenth-century mothers were undoubtedly more likely to become "good boys" who wanted to take care of others than "neurotic narcissists" who wanted to conquer the world. The regime of Christian nurture engendered narcissistically overprotective men who were attracted to Transcendentalism as well as other Romantic doctrines whose glorification of nature bespoke their profound and persistent idealization of their mothers. It was not entirely accidental that Thoreau's Walden Pond was but a mile from his mother's home and that he is said to have visited her every day.[8]

But the parenting orientations of these overprotected sons of mid-nineteenth-century middle-class mothers nonetheless remained far less protective than the orientations of their wives. On the one hand, their need to disidentify from their mothers led them to repudiate the very unions they craved (in Transcendentalism this fear of dependence assumes the form of an exclusively individualistic concept of communion with nature); on the other hand, their need for their mothers returned in the form of intense jealously of the bond between their wife/mother and their children. Thus were the overprotected sons of the regime of Christian nurture emotionally primed to resist the regime that had raised them.

Behaviorism and its prototypes both fed off and reinforced that resistance. (It was also promoted by men who never experienced Christian nurture and who, like Watson, were reared under latter-day versions of the early modern Calvinist regime.) Men who feared maternal engulfment welcomed the doctrine that declared that mother love was the great danger against which "science" must defend. That science assured them that the way to defeat that danger was to "condition" the child to become a "problem-solver" who was "as free as possible of sensitivities to people" and who "almost from birth [was] relatively independent of the family situation." Thus behaviorism both expressed and encouraged a grandiose denial of dependence on the mother that culminated in the fantasy of total control of the other. Under its auspices the commitment to "control and possess" and to "exploit . . . without guilt feelings" was extended from nature to humans. In short, behaviorism was both the theory and the practice of the grandiose self.

Thus it was a disproportionately masculine philosophy, an outcome of, and a weapon in, the struggle of men against women. But it also justified the "Taylorist" production of "docile bodies" within both the factories and the bureaucracies of early twentieth-century capitalist (as well as twentieth-century state socialist) industrial societies, and the economic and political requirements of those societies therefore undoubtedly reinforced the hegemony of behaviorism.

Once it became hegemonic, behaviorism legitimated a child-rearing regime that produced a generation of grandiosely narcissistic men. But—as we have seen—this disciplinary regime was resisted by the very mothers who were obliged to enforce it. And even though they disciplined their daughters as well as their sons, their daughters—like the daughters of early modern mothers—

grew up to become mothers who were far more protective than their husbands. Thus they eagerly embraced the neo-Freudianism that supplanted behaviorism as the hegemonic parenting ideology following World War II.

As I argued in my Institute lecture, the rise of neo-Freudianism was the result of a successful struggle to feminize pediatrics, child psychology, and other child-related professions that was itself rooted in the effort of nineteenth-century middle-class women to overcome their exclusion from the public sphere by turning the ideology of the "moral mother" on its head. But there were also political and economic reasons for its subsequent success. The neo-Freudian commitment to "child-centered" child rearing was clearly more consonant with the democratic fight against fascism than the disciplinary doctrine it replaced.[9] And there is no doubt that demand for feeding "on demand" was also fed by the extraordinary expansion of consumer demand following the war.

The central message of Dr. Spock was that all would go well if mothers paid close attention to, and did their best to satisfy, the needs of their children. But mother-raised mothers are never likely to be entirely clear about the difference between their children's needs and their own. Mothers with only one or two children, who did not work outside the home, whose husbands were absent more often than not, and who were separated in the suburbs from kith and kin were particularly prone to project their needs for merger onto their kids. Thus post-War middle-class mothers raised a generation of overprotected middle-class sons who were far more likely to become idealizing narcissists than their fathers.[10]

This set the stage for the bitter battles of the sixties and seventies between an older generation of narcissistically underprotected and a younger generation of narcissistically overprotected men. Perhaps the so-called generation gap of that period was in large part an emotional gulf between narcissistically grandiose and narcissistically idealizing men. Perhaps they were truly poles apart.

We can therefore speculate that as the new generation gradually replaced the old, idealizing narcissism eventually supplanted grandiose narcissism as the modal male personality type of our time. If we assume that "codependence" is a generally accurate pop-psychological translation of "idealizing narcissism," then the veritable explosion in the 1980s and 1990s of self-help programs and therapies designed to combat codependence could be taken as support for that speculation.[11] If that speculation proved to be correct, then we would have to conclude that the seeds of the dominant character disorder of the end of the twentieth century were sown by the successful struggle of women following World War II to recapture the control of the mode of child rearing they had lost at the beginning of that century.

Three things stand out from this sketch. First, there is more room for Marx and Foucault in the history of Western child rearing than I realized when I so decisively dismissed them back in 1984. Changes in the balance of parenting power between mothers and fathers depend on changes in hegemonic parenting ideologies that are themselves the result not only of gender struggle but also of economic and political changes that cannot be reduced to it. Thus if I were to rewrite my Institute lecture today, I would not claim that "not Marx, not Foucault, but *Balbus* could explain the Spockean transformation." Instead I would make an important place for their respective contributions within my overall theoretical framework.

Second, my sketch suggests that the history of child rearing in the West can be understood as a history of different forms of Western narcissism. My synthesis of feminist mothering theory and psychoanalytic theories of narcissim culminates in the claim that the dominant form of narcissism during different periods of Western societies will be shaped by the contemporary outcome of the gender struggle to control the mode of child rearing of those societies.

To say this is to argue that dramatic within-gender differences in parenting orientations (e.g., the orientations of grandiose versus idealizing male narcissists) are not only consistent with, but are also partly the result of, persistent cross-gender differences in parenting orientations. We do not have to claim that cross-gender differences are more important than within-gender differences in order to reach this conclusion. This (third) point brings me back to my dialogue with my friend David.

David had argued that (a) there was rather more similarity between the parenting orientations of Puritan mothers and fathers than there was between Puritan fathers and Spockean fathers (rather more cross-gender convergence than within-gender similarity) and that (b) this suggested that culture did not legitimate but rather partly constituted the parenting orientations of women and men. At that time I assumed that if I wanted to resist (b) and thus to remain on psychoanalytic terrain I also had to reject (a). I thought that the only way to avoid "culturalist" conclusions was to try to make the (very difficult) case that the parenting orientation of Spockean fathers was indeed closer to the parenting orientation of Puritan fathers than it was to the parenting orientation of Spockean mothers, i.e., that within-gender differences (or cross-gender convergences) were less salient than within-gender similarities (or cross-gender differences). I thought this because I assumed at that time that *either* parenting orientations were a function of the (mother-monopolized) structure of child rearing *or* that they were the result of culture. But once we recognize that different parenting *practices* also determine parenting orientations we can explain the dramatic difference in, for example, the parenting orientations of Puritan men and Spockean men as a function of the fact that the mother merger of the former was suppressed too soon while the mother merger of the latter was encouraged too long. Similarly, we could explain the significant differences in the parenting orientations of Puritan women and either their mid-nineteenth-century or mid-twentieth-century counterparts as a function of the fact that the former were relatively underprotected, while the latter were relatively overprotected, by their parents. In sum, we can avoid culturalist conclusions by explaining within-gender differences (across different historical periods) as a consequence of the differences in the prevailing parenting practices during those periods. And we can explain those differences in parenting practices as the outcome of changes in the balance of power between mothers and fathers that is itself (partly) the result of a gender struggle between them that is based on an opposition in their parenting interests. That is what I would say to David if I were able to talk to him today.

Thus I was persuaded that my (admittedly now more modest) gender-struggle theory had not only survived my synthesis but had in fact been strengthened by it. This confirmed my sense that even though this synthesis was incomplete it was still an important intellectual development. So completing it seemed much less important than reflecting on the personal path that had made it possible. My task was to sum up my understanding of the relationship between my parenting theory and my parenting practice. Then my book would finally be finished.

chapter fourteen

. Postmodernist
Problems .

*O*r so I thought. But I barely had time to savor the success of my synthesis before I began to worry that it might just be superfluous. Twelve years had passed between my original derivation of the gender-struggle theory from the assumptions of feminist mothering theory and the partial critique of those assumptions on which my synthesis was based. Readers of the first draft of that synthesis reminded me that in 1996 feminist mothering theory was no longer what it was in 1984. There were definite differences between the position of Nancy Chodorow circa 1978 (the publication date of *The Reproduction of Mothering*) and the position of Nancy Chodorow circa 1996. Perhaps my critique no longer applied to her new position; perhaps that new position had even anticipated my own critique. To respond to these concerns I realized I would have to read the post-1978 Chodorow works that I had ignored until now.

Feminism and Psychoanalytic Theory was published in 1989 and included articles and essays written between 1979 and 1987. I discovered that in one of those essays Chodorow called for a "melding of object-relations feminism and recent psychoanalysis" that would treat the "self as . . . separate from but related to gender identity."[1] So it seemed that by 1987 she was already committed to the same kind of synthesis as mine. But a careful reading of *Feminism and Psychoanalytic Theory* revealed that she did not make good on that commitment.

On the one hand, Chodorow now relied on psychoanalysts like Winnicott to understand the way in which the child's sense of self is shaped by the quality of the practice of his or her parents:

> The integration of a "true self" that feels alive and whole . . . is fostered by caretakers who do not project experiences or feelings onto the child and who do not let the environment impinge indiscriminately. It is evoked by empathic caretakers who understand and validate the infant as a self in its own right, and the infant's experience as real.[2]

Thus I could no longer correctly claim that Chodorow "ignores differences in the *quality* of parenting practice under the . . . mother-dominated structure of child rearing [as well as] the problem of the difference in the object relations of children of both genders that these differences in parenting might make."

On the other hand, this newfound focus on the impact of parenting practice on the formation of the self was in no way integrated with her longstanding and once-again-reaffirmed recognition of the impact of parenting structure on the formation of gender. At one point, in fact, Chodorow appeared to preclude the very possibility of such an integration when she argued (in an essay originally published in 1979, to be fair) that "problems [in object relations] are [not] bound up with questions of gender; rather they are bound up with questions of self."[3] Here Chodorow seemed to reject her claim that "questions of self [are] separate from but related to gender identity" in favor of the claim that they are *entirely* separate. But this latter claim was an exact echo of Christopher Lasch's argument that narcisissim and gender are entirely unrelated and was therefore vulnerable to the critique of that argument that I developed en route to my synthesis.

At another point, however, Chodorow came to a diametrically opposed conclusion. In the same essay in which she insisted that questions of self and questions of gender are "separate but related," she also effectively eliminated the distinction between them, reiterating the structural claims of *The Reproduction of Mothering* that "as a result of being parented primarily by a woman . . . the basic feminine sense of self is connected to the world [while] the basic masculine sense of self is separate."[4] And in the same 1979 essay in which she insisted on the opposition between "questions of gender" and "questions of the self," she also reaffirmed her 1978 claim that one (of the two) reasons why the masculine sense of self is more separate than the feminine is that "a mother unconsciously and often consciously experiences her son as more of an 'other' than her daughter."[5] But that is exactly the claim, we have seen, that makes it impossible to account for the difference between the idealizing "good boy" and the grandiose "macho man" or, more generally, for any significant differences in the sense of self of different men.

So after a close reading of *Feminism and Psychoanalytic Theory* I came to the conclusion that Chodorow had not worked out a synthesis between structure and practice, or gender and sense of self, but rather wavered between an insistence on their absolute separation and a collapse of the difference between them. Caught between these contradictory claims, she was unable to grasp what (I had argued in the introduction to my synthesis) it was necessary to grasp, "namely *the relationship of connection and separation between structure and practice and gender and sense of self.*"

Nor, it seemed to me, did she come any closer to grasping this connection in her subsequent work. In *Femininities, Maculinities, Sexualities*, published in 1994, Chodorow was once again divided against herself. But this time the division was different. Whereas the question which confounded her in 1989 was "what is the relationship between gender-identity and the sense of self?" the problem that plagued her now was whether it was possible to speak of any (unitary) "gender identity" at all.

One answer seemed to be no. Embracing the postmodern

feminist "wariness . . . of generalizations about gender differences" (as well as what she had learned as a therapist about the particularity of her patients) Chodorow cautioned that "though each person's gender is centrally important to him or her, it does not follow that we can contrast all women, or most women, with all or most men."[6] Gender identity was, instead, as multiple as the plurals in her title proclaimed. Indeed, Chodorow concluded her book with the claim that "to understand femininity and masculinity . . . requires that we understand how any particular woman or man creates her or his own cultural and personal gender,"[7] which sounded very much like the claim that there could be as many different gender identities as there were different people.

Chodorow's conclusion that gender is an individual creation thus appeared to rule out the very possibility of a structural account and seemed instead to point in the direction of (an individualistic version of) what postmodernists like Judith Butler have called a "performative" account of gender. But Chodorow's concession to postmodernism was called into question by her reaffirmation of the utility of the very gender generalizations that were anathema to the postmodernist feminists. Chodorow argued that such narratives or "patterns help give meaning to and interpretively situate particularity" and reminded the reader that "I have written about gender differences, and I take the usefulness of these insights for granted."[8] Indeed, she recirculated exactly the same insights or gender generalizations that she first formulated in *The Reproduction of Mothering*. Whereas

> most girls seek to create in love relationships an internal
> emotional dialogue with the mother . . . those aspects of
> men's love that grow out of their relationship to their
> mothers are more likely . . . to be intertwined . . . with
> [their] sense of . . . masculinity. Subjective gendering for
> men means that such love defines itself negatively in
> relation to the mother as well as in terms of positive . . .
> attachment.[9]

There it was: mother-raised women are relational, while mother-raised men are oppositional. The more things change, the more they stay the same. And they remained the same in "Gender as a Personal and Cultural Construction," published in *Signs* in 1995, in which Chodorow not only repeats this generalization but also reiterates one of the reasons why it holds: "typically, mothers unconsciously as well as consciously experience . . . sons and daughters differently, because of their gender similarity or otherness."[10] Thus she reaffirms the very structural account of gender that the title of her article would appear to call into question.

In principle, of course, there is no inherent opposition between a structural and a constructionist theory of gender. It is always possible to argue that the structure accounts for the commonalities across different men and across different women and that the "construction" accounts for the differences within each gender. A generous reading of Chodorow's search for "patterns [that] help give meaning to and interpretively situate particularity" might suggest that this was exactly the case that she was trying to make. But the problem, as I saw it, was that she failed to make that case because her structural account of "patterns" eliminated rather than illuminated the "particularity" to which her constructionist account was committed. It does not seem possible simultaneously to sustain the claim that "the basic masculine sense of self is separate" and to make the case that the relational "good boy" and the oppositional "macho man" are two separate-but-equal variations on the theme of masculine identity.

To accommodate this particularity it would be necessary to contest rather than reaffirm Chodorow's gender generalization about "the basic masculine sense of self." And, as I showed in my synthesis, to contest that generalization it would be necessary as well to challenge the unwarranted gender determinism that underlies it, namely the assumption that mothers necessarily experience their sons as "others" rather than "mothers" and will therefore push them away rather than reel them back in. But Chodorow continued to chain herself to precisely that assumption.

It was not clear to me why she did. In *Feminism and Psychoana-lytic Theory* Chodorow approvingly cited Miriam Johnson's find-ing that fathers are far more likely to sex-type their children than mothers.[11] But her assumption that mothers treat their male in-fants fundamentally differently from the way they treat their fe-male infants was entirely inconsistent with that finding. It also seemed to me that that assumption was also inconsistent with Chodorow's emphasis in "Gender as a Personal and Cultural Construction" on the centrality of "processes of transference"— and the process of projection in particular—in the construction of gender identity. In "projection [she tells us in that essay] we accord an emotional and fantasy meaning to others . . . because of intrapsychic processes or we project fantasied or experienced as-pects of ourselves into aspects of these others."[12] But if projec-tion was so central to the formation of gender-identity then there was no reason to assume that a mother wouldn't fantasize her son as a mother to take care of her just because his body was "objec-tively" different from hers.

In short, my conclusion was that Chodorow still suffered from a literalism that prevented her from theorizing the difference be-tween the mother who encouraged and the mother who sup-pressed the separation of her son. The consequence of her inabil-ity to theorize this difference in parenting practice, in turn, was that rather too much of the variance in masculine identity was treated as a purely personal construction and rather too little as the result of that difference in parenting practice. Thus Chodor-ow's overly voluntaristic constructionist account of gender iden-tity and her overly deterministic structural account of gender identity were merely two sides of the same theoretical coin.

After reading Chodorow's most recent writings I was therefore confident that my synthesis was anything but superfluous. But it was still likely to encounter the objection that it relied on a num-ber of assumptions that had recently been called into question by the very postmodernists to whom Chodorow now claimed to be intellectually and politically indebted.

You will recall that I continued to claim that mother-raised boys (whether or not they have been pushed away by their mothers) must in some sense disidentify from their mothers in order to become men. This claim was based on the assumption of an inevitable opposition between a boy's "core gender identity" and an earlier "primary identification" with his mother that is normally resolved in favor of the former and against the latter. That assumption, in turn, was based both on the assumption of the inevitability of a male core gender identity and the assumption of the inevitability (under the maternal mode of child rearing) of a primary female identification that conflicts with it. Both of these assumptions were reaffirmed in Chodorow's latest work[13] and both remained central to my synthesis. So I decided that I had better revisit them.

The assumption of core gender identity entails the claim that children will normally develop "a cognitive sense of gendered self, the sense that one is [either] male or female" that corresponds to their anatomical sex.[14] They will make use of genital and other physiological markers to determine whether they are girls like their mothers and unlike their fathers or brothers, or boys unlike their mothers and like their fathers or brothers. Although Chodorow endorsed Stoller's claim that core gender identity is normally established during the second year of life and firmly and irreversibly consolidated by the end of the third,[15] the precise periodization of this process may in fact be subject to cultural variations. But the outcome of this process is not. To make use of a theory that was based on the assumption of core gender identity is to assume that the overwhelming majority of the members of any conceivable society—even a society in which all children are coparented—will be *gendered* in the elemental sense that they will be constrained by their embodiment to think of themselves as either male or female rather than both male and female, something in between, or something entirely different.

Notice that this assumption does not entail the claim that (what are sometimes called) "gender role identities"—shared expectations about "masculine" as compared to "feminine" attributes or actions—are culturally universal. To the contrary: we have seen that feminist mothering theory simultaneously relies on the assumption of core gender identity *and* hypothesizes that gender-based differences in the "role identities" of coparented children would be significantly attenuated if not entirely eliminated. It predicts that anatomically male and female coparented children would continue to think of themselves as either boys or girls, and then women and men, even as girls and women become more "oppositional," and boys and men become more "relational," than their conventionally raised counterparts.

This prediction, as we have seen, is based on the assumption that the "primary identification" of coparented boys and girls would no longer be exclusively female, since both boys and girls would have a same-sex and an opposite-sex pimary caregiver on whom they were dependent and with whom they were united. The coparented boy could tell himself "I am a male like the father-with-whom-I-am-one" just as the conventionally raised girl can tell herself "I am a female like the mother-with-whom-I-am-one." Thus the boy would no longer have to disidentify from his primary caregiver—to repudiate his primary identification—in order to prove that he was a man. In fact he wouldn't have to "prove" his manhood at all, since the source of his manhood would already be inside him.

Thus feminist mothering theory is as dependent on the assumption of a primary identification—of an "early, non-verbal, unconscious, almost somatic sense of primary oneness"[16]—with the first parent(s) as it is on the assumption of an anatomically based core gender identification. It argues that it is the conflict between these two identifications that creates the problem for/of the mother-raised boy and that it is the congruence between them that creates the solution for/of the coparented boy.

This argument is open to the familiar objection that neither conflict nor congruence between these two identifications can exist for the boy (or, for that matter, for the girl) because his sense of oneness with his primary parent(s) develops before his awareness of gender and is therefore not experienced as either a female or male identification. This objection, in turn, is vulnerable to the ready rejoinder that when gender awareness does develop that sense of oneness will be retrospectively redefined as a gendered identification that is either consistent or inconsistent with the consolidation of his emerging core gender identification as a male.[17] But postmodern feminists like Judith Butler have raised other, perhaps more powerful objections to these gender-identity assumptions. Since these assumptions were carried over into my synthesis of feminist mothering theory and narcissism theory, the defense of my synthesis required that I respond to those objections.

The targets of Butler's enormously influential critique of psychoanalysis included orthodox Freudian and Lacanian, as well as object-relational, accounts of gender identity. I had no quarrel with Butler's deconstruction of Freudian and Lacanian accounts. But these accounts relied neither on the assumption of a primary (now) feminine identification nor on the assumption of a core gender identification, and thus none of her criticisms of those accounts was really to the point of my position. What was to the point was a series of objections to object-relational accounts that she outlined in an essay entitled "Gender Trouble, Feminist Theory, and Psychoanalytic Discourse" that appeared in *Feminism/Postmodernism* in 1990, as well as a number of related arguments she made in *Gender Trouble: Feminism and the Subversion of Identity*, published in the same year, and in *Bodies That Matter: On the Discursive Limits of "Sex,"* published three years later.[18]

It turned out that my meeting with Butler would also be an opportunity to bid farewell to my old friend Foucault. I discovered that Butler's deconstruction of the psychoanalytic discourse on gender was deeply indebted to Foucault's critique of all true discourse. According to Foucault, true discourse constructs the very object that it purports to describe, thereby exercising and dissimulating power at one and the same time. Its innocent claim to reveal a preexisting truth about those of whom it speaks is betrayed by the equally inevitable normalization of those who happen to conform to this supposed truth and exclusion or marginalization of those who do not. Butler's claim was that this dominative discursive deception is exactly what is at work in the feminist object-relations discourse on gender.

Thus in *Gender Trouble* she counters Stoller's concept of core gender identity with the striking claim that "there is no gender identity behind the expressions of gender." Instead, "that identity is performatively constituted by the very 'expressions' that are said to be its results."[19] In other words, the performance of "masculine" and "feminine" roles is not the expression of some underlying, more essential sense of maleness and femaleness, but rather that which constitutes that sense of maleness and femaleness in the first place. By treating that sense as an essential cause rather than a contingent effect, the discourse of core gender identity disguises the constitution of that sense and thereby helps ensure its efficacy. Thus this discourse must itself be understood as one of the *"regulatory practices* of gender formation and division,"[20] i.e., as one of the practices that produce both masculinity and femininity and the illusion that they are expressions of a male and female core gender identity.

Moreover, in producing these oppositions object-relations theories "offer story lines about gender acquisition which effect a narrative closure on gender experience and a false stabilization of the category of woman [and the category of man]."[21] Consider the "story" that begins with the assumption that a "primary identification" with the mother is the source of the girl's gender identity but an obstacle to the boy's gender identity, and that culminates in the conclusion that women are "relational" and men are "oppositional." Even if this story is told by feminists like Chodorow and Benjamin, who remind us that it holds true only so long as women "mother" and men do not, it remains "effectively essentialist" because the assumption of unified and opposing masculine and feminine identities "forecloses convergences" across genders as well as "all manner of dissonance" within them.[22] Thus the "stabilization of the category of woman [and man]" effected by object-relations theory is not only false but "exclusionary."[23]

Object-relations theory can effect this stabilization only because it is based on the unwarranted assumption of "an orderly temporal development of identifications in which the first identifications serve to unify the later ones."[24] For example, unless we assume that the girl's initial identification with the mother is primary in the sense that her subsequent identifications with her father or with her brother "are easily assimilated under the already firmly established gender identification with women . . . we would lose the unifying thread of the narrative."[25] If "the temporal prioritization of primary identifications" were "fully contested," then we would "have . . . the gender equivalent of an interplay of attributes without an abiding or unifying substance."[26]

But then we would also be beyond "the regulation of sexuality within the obligatory frame of reproductive heterosexuality."[27] It is precisely the "heterosexualization of desire" that "requires . . . the production of discrete, asymmetrical oppositions between 'feminine' and 'masculine,' where these are understood as expressive aspects of 'male' and 'female.'"[28] (Or, as Butler puts it more pithily in *Bodies That Matter*, "'it's a girl!' anticipates the eventual arrival of the sanction, 'I pronounce you man and wife.'"[29]) Since, as we have seen, Butler claims that object-relations theory produces exactly those oppositions and exactly that understanding, it follows that object-relations theory must be considered one of the disciplinary practices that serve "the interests of the heterosexual construction and regulation of sexuality."[30] In short, object-relations theory necessarily normalizes heterosexuality and marginalizes homosexuality.

I do not believe that any of these claims can be sustained. Let me begin with the last, the claim that object-relations theory is inherently heterosexist. Butler's argument that a commitment to the categories of "women" and "men" and "feminine" and "masculine" necessarily culminates in a normalizing commitment to "feminine women" loving "masculine men" cannot in fact be squared with the object-relational understandings of the relationships among "core gender identity," "gender role identity," and "sexual identity." Although it is true that for both Freud and Lacan all three idenities are established in one fell oedipal swoop, so to speak, for Stoller and Chodorow core gender identity, as we have seen, is established during rapprochement and therefore well before the oedipal stage. Moreover, the object-relational concept of gender identity leans on Freud's claim in *Group Psychology and the Analysis of the Ego* that "identification is known to psychoanalysis as the earliest example of an emotional tie with another person" rather than his subsequent assertion in *The Ego and the Id* that "the ego is a precipitate of abandoned object-cathexes."[31] Identification for object-relations theory is not a substitute for object love but something prior to and separate from it. The theory is thefore vulnerable to the objection that this separation of identification and desire makes it difficult to explain *sexual* identity, and heterosexual identity in particular. But even if this objection is correct, there is a world of difference between an inability to explain heterosexuality and a normalizing presupposition of its existence.

That object-relations theory is not in fact wedded to this presupposition can be seen from what it has to say, or rather *does not* have to say, about homosexuality. If a commitment to the concept of "core gender identity" entailed a commitment to the "heterosexualization of desire," we would expect that relational psychoanalysts would argue that homosexuals typically suffer from gender identity disorder. But they do not. A recent report conludes that "most homosexual men have not experienced boyhood Gender Identity Disorder, which is relatively rare."[32] The fact that an overwhelming majority of gay men think of themselves as men (and that, presumably, the overwhelming majority of gay women think of themselves as women) is not an anomaly for, but is rather entirely consistent with, the assumptions of object-relations theory.[33]

So too is the possibility of widespread bisexuality in a future society of coparented children. In fact we can derive this prediction from the assumption of a primary identification with primary parents and the assumption of "core gender identity" as long as we are willing to add to the assumption of primary identification the additional asssumption that the relationship that gives rise to that identification is also an erotic relationship. If, in other words, we assume that sexual desire is born in the eminently embodied interaction with the primary caregiver, we can hypothesize that when female and male infants are caressed by their fathers as well as their mothers they will grow up to be women and men whose core gender identities are intact but whose love objects are as likely to be same-sex as opposite-sex. This hypothesis may turn out to be wrong, but the fact that it is in no way ruled out by the twin assumptions of primary identification and core gender identification means that object-relations theory can justifiably plead not guilty to the charge of enforcing "compulsory heterosexuality" and thereby marginalizing homosexuality.

I believe that is also innocent of the charge of imposing unified "gender role identities" on women and men that foreclose gender "convergences" and "dissonances" and exclude the women and men who enact them. To begin with, we have seen that feminist object-relations theory does not rule out but in fact predicts cross-gender convergences in the gender-role identities of co-parented women and men. But my synthesis has also shown that (far less positive) cross-gender convergences among exclusively mother-raised women and men are also consistent with object-relations theory. Once the assumptions of "primary identification" and "core gender identification" are no longer burdened by the Chodorowian assumption that mothers necessarily support the separation of their sons, object-relations theory can easily accommodate the fact that women and men sometimes suffer from essentially similar character disorders. It leads us to expect that if a man has been smothered by his mother his narcissism will tend to converge with the idealizing form of narcissism that is more frequently found among women. Here gender divergence goes hand in hand with care-taking convergence.

If the idealizing narcissism of the overprotected man is similar to the narcissism of many women then it must be decidedly different from the grandiose narcissism of the underprotected man. Cross-gender convergence implies within-gender dissonance. If object-relations theory can accommodate the former, it can also accommodate the latter. Thus I have shown that both the good boy and the macho man are consistent with the assumptions of primary identification and core gender identity (as well as the corollary of mandatory male disidentification from the mother). I have also suggested that if we factor in for the presence or absence of father identification we wind up not with two but with four different types of men—all of them consistent with the basic assumptions of object-relations gender theory. I have also argued that (if we are willing to abandon the corollary to Chodorow's assumption that the mother never subverts her son's separation, namely that the mother never suppresses her daughter's merger) four types of women are also consistent with those assumptions. So the point is that a good deal of difference can go hand in hand with an object-relational concept of gender identity and that far many more women and men can therefore find themselves in the gender generalizations of object-relations theory than Butler believes.

Of course at this point Butler is likely to object that it is only the unwarranted "assumption of an orderly temporal development in which the first identifications serve to unify the latter ones"[34] that enables me to continue to speak of four types of *women* and four types of *men*. Unless we assume, for example, that the subsequent identifications of physiologically male individuals are always assimilated to their prior core gender identification, there is no good reason to group the father-identified, physiologically male individual and the nonfather-identified physiologically male individual under the same gender category. But this objection merely reiterates Butler's opening argument against core gender identity, and the force of that argument depends entirely on the plausibility of her alternative, "performative" account of gender.

That account, I want to argue, is simply not plausible. To understand why, consider the following passage:

[A]cts, gestures, and desire produce the effect of an internal core or substance, but produce this *on the surface* of the body through the play of signifying absences that suggest, but never reveal, the organizing principle of identity as a cause. Such acts, gestures, enactments, generally construed, are *performative* in the sense that the essence or the entity that they otherwise purport to express are *fabrications* manufactured and sustained through corporeal signs and other discursive means. That the gendered body is performative suggests that it has no ontological status apart from the various acts which constitute its reality. . . . [W]ords, acts and gestures, articulated and enacted desires create the illusion of an interior and organizing gender core.[35]

According to this account, then, core gender identity is a "fabrication" in the two-fold sense that it is a manufactured illusion. The conviction that comes to almost all anatomically female and anatomically male children before the end of their second year of life that they are either girls or boys, and not both or something else entirely, reveals no "truth" about who or what they really are but rather only the power of the "words, acts and gestures"—the "corporeal signs and other discursive means"—that compel that conviction. It is not clear whether Butler wants us to construe these "words, acts and gestures" as those of the parent or those of the child, or both. But what is clear is that she treats these signs as arbitrary, "contingent acts that create the appearance of a naturalistic necessity."[36] For Butler anatomy functions not as destiny but as alibi. The illusion that the signifiers of core gender identity represent (re-present) our bodies is precisely what enables these signifiers to construct them.

But if the signifiers of "core gender identity" are body builders that are entirely unconstrained or "unmotivated" by the bodies they build, then it would seem that "gender itself becomes a free-floating artifice, with the consequence that *man* . . . might just as easily signify a female body as a male one, and *woman* . . . a male body as easily as a female one."[37] Although Butler considers this position to be problematical, it is not clear how she can avoid it. She insists that gender is not "a set of free-floating attributes" but is rather "compelled by the regulatory practices of gender coherence."[38] But this formulation merely reproduces the problem of voluntarism at the level of culture: although individuals are constrained by the "regulatory practices of gender coherence," these regimes themselves seem to "float freely" from the bodies they construct. So why couldn't there exist a regime that radically separates gender from anatomical sex? Why not the cultural construction of three, or four, or a hundred, genders rather than two? Why not, indeed, unless "gender" is constrained by the very bodies it "constructs"?

To her credit, Butler addressess this problem in *Bodies That Matter*. She tries to solve it with the notion of construction as "constitutive constraint."[39] That notion is designed to transcend what she describes as the "tired" opposition between a "radical constructivism" that dissolves the materiality of the body entirely into discourse and an "essentialism" for which the body is simply "prediscursive" and unconstructed.[40] The difficulty with radical constructivism is that it can be read (as I have read it above) as a linguistically deterministic denial "that there are, minimally, sexually differentiated parts, activities, hormonal and chromosomal differences that can be conceded without reference to 'construction.'"[41] To overcome this difficulty a concept of construction must be constructed that does not claim that discourse "originates, causes, or exhaustively composes that which it concedes."[42]

To do this we must "rethink . . . the meaning of construction" so that it is no longer understood as something "artificial and dispensable" that is opposed to something "natural and necessary."[43] A defensible "constructivism needs to take account of the domain of constraints without which a certain living and desiring being can not make its way."[44] It must recognize that there are "constructions without which we would not be able to think, to live, to make sense at all," without which "there [might] be no 'I', no 'we.'"[45]

Although this kind of constructivism denies the determinism of discourse, it still insists on its "formative" power. It thereby maintains its distance from an essentialism that fails to grasp that "there is no reference to a pure body which is not at the same time a *further formation* [my emphasis] of that body." Unlike essentialism, it understands that "the constative claim is always *to some degree* [my emphasis again] performative."[46]

It seems to me that this reformulation rescues Butler's performative account of gender from linguistic determinism at the exhorbitant price of virtually eliminating the distinction between her account and the very account of core gender identity that she contests. Is not the claim of the theorists of core gender identity precisely that physiologically male and female children are constrained by their physiology to construct an elementary sense of maleness or femaleness, without which they "can not make their way" in the world and which is inseparable from their sense of "I" or "we"? Doesn't this mean that there is now rather more "identity" than "difference" between Butler and Stoller?

Of course to keep her distance Butler might argue that Stoller and his followers continue to ignore the power of an always physiologically constrained but nonetheless "formative" gender discourse, the extent to which the discursive "reiteration of a . . . set of [gender] norms"[47] by the parents performatively constructs the gendered body of the child. But that is simply not the case. Stoller specifically argues that core gender identity is the result of an interaction between "biologic forces" on the one hand and the "sex assignment" made by, and the "attitudes" of, parents on the other.[48] Perhaps Butler would reply that Stoller grants rather too much to biology and rather too little to discourse. But then she would making an empirical claim about a difference of degree rather than a principled argument about a difference in kind. She would be making a gender point that mattered. But she would no longer be making gender trouble.

chapter fifteen

. Conclusion .

$\mathcal{M}$y dialogue with Chodorow and Butler convinced me that my synthesis of feminist mothering theory and narcissism theory was neither theoretically superfluous nor theoretically suspect. I was more confident than ever that it was a defensible theoretical development. Thus it was more important than ever to reflect on the path that had made it possible.

On the one hand, I do not think that the reconstruction of my *theory* would have been possible without the reconstruction of my *practice*. By the "reconstruction of my practice" I mean both my effort to transform a book in which I tried to explain others into a book in which I tried to explain my self and my effort inside and outside therapy to transform the self that I had begun to try to explain. It seems to me that each of these more or less simultaneous, mutually reinforcing practices of the self was essential to the work I was eventually able to do on my theory.

By January 1989 I had reached the point of not being able to do any work at all on that theory. The pounding that it had taken from friendly and not-so-friendly readers alike left me reeling between the equally unacceptable alteratives of defeat or defiance. I took their criticisms not as an opportunity to modify, but rather as a demand either to abandon or defend, my theory. In short, instead of being able to do new work on my theory I was repeating my old relationship with it.

The self-reflexive turn that I took in the middle of that month might be described as therapy for that theory. My decision to write publicly about not being able to write simultaneously "owned" my problem with my book and committed me to uncovering the private source of that problem. The search for that source enabled me to make a clear and direct, rather than doubtful and indirect, connection between my theory and the coparenting practice to which the other half of my life had been devoted. When I made this connection I released repressed emotional energy that eventually made it possible for me to overcome my compulsion to repeat. I discovered that in order to explain the relationship between my theory and my self I had to turn to an account of the self that was very different from the account in my theory. Narcissism theory helped me to understand what feminist mothering theory could not, namely that my alternatingly defeatist and defiant stance toward my theory reflected my overdependence on the other as well as my destructive defenses against it. In short, it helped me see that I was stuck in that stance because I was repeating my relationship with my mother.

The work I did on my relationship with my mother, in turn, increased my confidence in the power of narcissism theory to explain my self. The hypothesis that a narcissistic relationship between self and other—in which the other is treated as a projective entity rather than an entity in its own right—is a defense against maternal abandonment would likely have remained just another hypothesis had I not confirmed its power by gradually developing a less narcissistic relationship with my daughter as the result of a direct and painful confrontation with my fear of that abandonment. I might have eventually read the theories of Kohut, Kernberg, and Masterson, but in the absence of a personal practice that seemed to me to verify their respective truth claims, my response to their work would have probably been restricted—

like the response of Ilene Philipson summarized in Chapter Twelve—to a critique of their neglect of those features that are the focus of feminist mothering theory. In short, I might have simply subsumed narcissism theory under feminist mothering theory. But this theoretical option was obsolete once I become as much a partisan of narcissim theory as a partisan of feminist mothering theory. And I only became a partisan of narcissism theory because it helped me simultaneously to explain and transform my self.

Thus the relatively successful practice of narcissism theory created the conditions for a major modification of, rather than mere assimilation to, the feminist mothering theory with which I began. It left me equally committed to two theories between which there was an opposition that was impossible to ignore. For many years I remained suspended between these theories, but eventually I was able to build a bridge between them that enabled me to complete my theoretical trip. That I was able to complete that trip was contingent on all the twists and turns of my life between 1989 and 1996. But of one thing I am certain: I never would have even *tried* to build a bridge between my old and new theory if I had not also tried to to build a bridge between my old and new self. So there was no way I could have completed my theoretical trip without the emotional trip that accompanied it. The reconstruction of my theory was inseparable from the reconstruction of my self. Thus no emotional development, no theoretical development.

But the reverse also seems to me to be equally true. My emotional development was clearly contingent on the very theoretical development that it ultimately helped to call into question. That emotional development involved the resolution of a psychological crisis that resulted from reliving my earliest relationship with my mother in the course of attempting to "mother" my daughter. And I do not think I would have been in a position to mother Shayla so intensively—and thus to experience my own rapprochement crisis in the process of responding to hers—if I had not been committed to the truth of feminist mothering theory and thus to the effort to put it into practice.

Although it is likely that I would have tried my hand at coparenting without having read Dinnerstein and Chodorow, I am certain that my participation would have been both less extensive and less persistent if I had not already been persuaded by their psychoanalytically informed arguments for the necessity of that participation. In the absence of my psychoanalytically informed political commitment—without the conviction that coparenting was essential to ensure that Shayla would be as free as possible from submissive tendencies—even my considerable caretaking capacity would not have convinced me to devote so much time and energy to taking care of her during the first three years of her life. Without the intense connection I established during the first year, the separation I experienced during the second and third years would hardly have been as painful as it was. And without the emotional pain, there would have been no emotional gain.

Thus it seems that *the practice of one theory was the condition for the possibility of an emotional development involving the practice of a second theory that was, in turn, the condition for the possibility of a synthesis of the two theories that I had tried to practice.*

I do not know if this account of the reciprocal—dare I say dialectical?—relationship between my emotional and theoretical development applies to anyone else but me. But I do believe that the theoretical development that this particular path made possible enables us to shed more general light on the relationship between theoretical and emotional development. My synthesis suggests that the growth of knowledge about the world and the growth of knowledge about the self are two inseparably related parts of the same process.

Consider what my synthesis says about the psychological preconditions of the process of theoretical development as it is described by Imre Lakatos. I choose Lakatos's account not merely because of its enormous influence but also because it is phrased in terms that invite—even incite—psychoanalytic translation. Lakatos argues , on the one hand, that

The direction of science is determined primarily by human creative imagination and not by the universe of facts which surrounds us. . . . Scientists dream up phantasies and then pursue a highly selective hunt for new facts which fit these phantasies. This process may be described as "science creating its own universe."[1]

Thus scientific development depends on our capacity to fantasize a world that may not in fact exist as well as on our commitment to find the facts that confirm those fantasies. But Lakatos also tells us that scientific development ultimately depends on our willingess to pay attention, and respond creatively, to the way in which the world may resist our fantasies. The theory to which we are committed will inevitably encounter facts that appear to contradict it. Thus we will be compelled to adjust our theory in order to resolve its contradiction with those counterexamples. The nature of this resolution, in turn, determines whether the theoretical adjustment can be considered a genuine theoretical development:

If we put forward a theory to resolve a contradiction between a previous theory and a counterexample in such a way that the new theory, instead of offering a content-increasing (scientific) *explanation*, only offers a content-decreasing (linguistic) *reinterpretation*, the contradiction is resolved in a merely semantical, unscientific way. *A given fact is explained scientifically only if a new fact is also explained with it.*[2]

Scientific "explanations" resolve the contradiction between the original theory and the counterexample in a way that enables us to "predict . . . some novel, hitherto unexpected fact,"[3] whereas pseudoscientific "reinterpretations" rescue the old theory at the cost of preventing us from learning anything really new about the world. We might say that reinterpretations modify the world the better to fit our fantasies, whereas explanations modify our fantasies the better to fit with the world. Thus theoretical development depends as much on our capacity to call into question the fantasies to which we are committed as it does on our capacity to invent them in the first place.

Both capacities have psychological correlates. On the one hand, scientists will only be able to "dream up phantasies and then . . . hunt for facts which fit these phantasies" if they retain something of the illusion of infantile omnipotence on which all confidence in the ability to affect the world ultimately depends. Thus Winnicott argues that creative impulses originate in the infantile fantasy of creating the breast that results from the fact that the "good-enough" mother makes it appear whenever it is desired.[4] But he also argues that implementing those impulses requires an ability to recognize and tolerate the resistance of reality that only develops if the very mother who so perfectly gratifies her child eventually and optimally frustrates her child as well. Unless the mother both resists her child and calmly withstands the rage that results from that resistance, her child will never learn the distinction between self and world or between fantasy and reality. And if the child-scientist has never learned the distinction between fantasy and reality, she will never be in a position to respond creatively to any opposition between them. In fact this opposition will not be fully felt in the first place. Counterexamples will never really count.

They will only count for individuals who are emotionally equipped to endure the experience of an opposition between their projections and the world. When we call into question our projections we perforce perturb the security of the connection to the world that depends on them. Thus, as Evelyn Fox Keller has argued, the "pressure to delineate self from [world] . . . leaves us acutely vulnerable to anxiety about wishes or experiences that might threaten that delineation."[5] Problematizing our projections thus requires a willingness to acknowledge and work through, rather than defend against, the separation anxiety that inevitably accompanies the accumulation of counterexamples. A creative response to those counterexamples requires that we tolerate—even embrace—the feeling of not knowing rather than fight that feeling by redefining the world to fit with what we (think we) already know about it. Unless we are emotionally prepared to heed the objections of the world to our wishes, we will never be able to learn anything really new about it.

Of course the objections of the world to our wishes are not directly addressed to us by the world but rather indirectly through the interpretations of other scientists who evaluate the claims we make about it. The "context of justification" is always an intersubjective context. There are therefore certain relational requirements for a context of justification that is conducive to theoretical development. Unless the self is able to relate to the other as someone to whom one is connected, but from whom one is also separate, the respective claims of self and other (about the world) will never get a fair hearing. A fair hearing requires a self that is strong enough both to assert its own claims with confidence and to remain emotionally open to the claims of the other. Emotional openness to the claims of the other, in turn, presupposes an openness to the possibility that our resistance to those claims may reflect our emotional stake in our own. Thus the dialogue on which theoretical development depends must be a dialogue among partners whose commitment to evaluate truth-claims about the world is matched by a commitment to evaluate truth-claims about themselves.

Narcissism precludes this possibility. Individuals who either subordinate the other to the self or the self to the other will be neither willing nor able to hold both self and other psychologically accountable for their respective truth-claims. Thus narcissism negates not only our emotional development but our intellectual development as well. So too, therefore, do the structures and practices of parenting in which narcissism is nurtured.

It follows that good-enough coparenting is the only long-term remedy for the narcissism that distorts our intellectual development. Children who have been cared for by competent coparents will learn the difference between the other as a "projective entity" and the other as "an entity in his own right" and will therefore be psychologically prepared for an adult dialogue that asks them to own their projections and call them into question. But psychoanalysis is the remedy on which, it seems to me, the rest of us must rely in order to make good on that invitation. In the short term, a psychoanalytically informed, self-reflexive dialogue is the best possible antedote to the narcissism that simultaneously stunts our emotional and intellectual growth. I offer this book as a contribution to that dialogue.

notes

Introduction

1. Herbert Marcuse, *An Essay on Liberation* (Boston: Beacon Press, 1969), 37.
2. Ibid., 25, 31, 23, 21, 37.
3. Ibid., 29, 5, 37, 89.
4. In fact Marcuse's own description in his next work, *Counter-Revolution and Revolt* (Boston: Beacon Press, 1972), of the relationship between critical theory and political practice implies not a union of rationality and sensibility but rather the subordination of the latter to the former. See Isaac D. Balbus, "The Missing Dimension: Self-reflexivity and the 'New Sensibility,'" in John Bokina and Timothy J. Lukes, *Marcuse: From the New Left to the Next Left* (Lawrence: University Press of Kansas, 1994), 106–17.

Chapter One

1. Isaac D. Balbus, *Marxism and Domination: A Neo-Hegelian, Feminist, Psychoanalytic Theory of Sexual, Political and Technological Liberation* (Princeton, NJ: Princeton University Press, 1982).
2. Dorothy Dinnerstein, *The Mermaid and the Minotaur: Sexual Arrangements and Human Malaise* (New York: Harper & Row, 1976), 234.
3. Joseph H. Pleck, *Working Wives/Working Husbands* (Beverly Hills, CA: Sage Publications, 1985), 40.
4. Carl Philip Hwang, "The Changing Role of Swedish Fathers," in Michael E. Lamb, ed., *The Father's Role: Cross-Cultural Perspectives* (Hillsdale, NJ: Lawrence Erlbaum Associates, 1987), 127–28.
5. Nancy Chodorow, *The Reproduction of Mothering* (Berkeley: University of California Press, 1978), 206.
6. Sigmund Freud, *Three Essays on the Theory of Sexuality* (New York: Avon Books, 1962), 32; Irving Bieber et al., *Homosexuality: A Psychoanalytic Study of Male Homsexuality* (New York: Basic Books, 1962); Charles Socarides, *The Overt Homosexual* (New York: Grune & Stratton, 1968), and "Psychoanalytic Therapy of a Male Homosexual," *Psychoanalytic Quarterly*, 38, no. 2 (April 1969), 173–90.
7. Richard Flacks, "The Liberated Generation: An Exploration of the Roots of Student Protest," *The Journal of Social Issues*, 23 (July 1967), 52–75; Kenneth Kenniston, "The Sources of Student Dissent," *The Journal of Social Issues*, 23 (July 1967), 103–37.
8. Heinz Hartmann et al., "Comments on the Formation of Psychic Structure," *The Psychoanalytic Study of the Child*, vol. 2 (New York: International Universities Press, 1946), 20. See also Chodorow, *The Reproduction of Mothering*, and Dinnerstein, *The Mermaid and the Minotaur*.
9. Benjamin Spock, *The Common Sense Book of Baby and Child Care* (New York: Duell, Sloan and Pearce, 1945); Lynn Z. Bloom, *Doctor Spock: Biography of a Conservative Radical* (Indianapolis, IN: Bobbs-Merril, 1972), 84–85, 126–29; A. Michael Sulman, "The Humanization of the American Child: Benjamin

Spock as a Popularizer of Psychoanalytic Thought," *Journal of the History of the Behavioral Sciences*, 9, no. 3 (July 1973), 258–65; telephone interview with Benjamin Spock, May 6, 1983.

10. John Anderson, *The Young Child in the Home* (New York: D. Appleton-Century Co., 1936); Allison Davis and Robert J. Havighurst, "Social Class and Color Differences in Child-Rearing," *American Sociological Review*, 11, no. 6 (December 1946), 698–710; Orville Brim, *Education for Child Rearing* (New York: Russell Sage Foundation, 1959); Robert R. Sears et al., *Patterns of Child Rearing* (New York, Harper & Row, 1957); Urie Bronfenbrenner, "Socialization and Social Class Through Time and Space," in Theodore M. Newcomb, et al., *Readings in Social Psychology*, 3rd ed. (New York: Henry Holt and Co., 1958), 400–425.

11. Antonio Gramsci, *Prison Notebooks* (New York: International Publishers, 1971).

Chapter Two

1. Hartmann et al., "Comments on the Formation of Psychic Structure"; Melanie Klein, *Envy and Gratitude and Other Works, 1946–1963* (New York: The Free Press, 1984); Stephen Robinson, "The Parent to the Child," in Barry Richards, *Capitalism and Infancy* (London: Free Association Books, 1984), 167–206.

2. Therese Benedek, "Parenthood as a Developmental Phase," *Journal of the American Psychoanalytic Association*, 7, no. 3 (July, 1959), 410.

3. Lawrence Stone, *The Family, Sex and Marriage in England: 1500–1800* (New York: Harper & Row, 1977), 178.

4. Lloyd DeMause, "The Evolution of Childhood," in *Foundations of Psychohistory* (New York: Creative Roots, Inc., 1982), 3.

5. Ibid., 18.

6. David Bakan, "Behaviorism and American Urbanization," *Journal of the History of the Behavioral Sciences*, 2, no. 1 (January, 1976), 5–28; John C. Burnham, "On the Origins of Behaviorism," *Journal of the History of the Behavioral Sciences*, 4, no. 2 (April, 1968), 143–51; Lucille C. Birnbaum, "Behaviorism in the 1920s," *American Quarterly*, 7, no. 1 (Spring, 1955), 15–30; William I. Thomas and Dorothy Swaine Thomas, *The Child in America* (New York: Alfred A. Knopf, 1928).

7. Robert R. Sears, Elanor E. Maccoby, and Harry Levin, *Patterns of Child Rearing* (Evanston, IL: Row, Peterson and Co., 1957).

8. Ann Douglas, *The Feminization of American Culture* (New York: Alfred A. Knopf, 1977); Nancy Cott, *The Grounding of Modern Feminism* (New Haven: Yale University Press, 1987); William Leach, *True Love and Perfect Union* (New York: Basic Books, 1980).

9. Sigmund Freud, "On Narcissism: An Introduction" [1914], *Standard Edition of the Complete Psychological Works of Sigmund Freud*, vol. 14, ed. and trans. James Strachey (London: Hogarth Press, 1957, 91.) (Hereafter cited as *SE*.)

10. "Sigmund Freud, *New Introductory Lectures on Psycho-Analysis* [1933], *SE*, vol. 22 (London: Hogarth Press, 1964), 67.

11. Max Weber, "The Social Psychology of the World Religions," in Hans H. Gerth and C. Wright Mills, *From Max Weber* (New York: Oxford University

Press, 1958), 280; Reinhard Bendix, *Max Weber: An Intellectual Portrait* (Garden City, NY: Anchor Books, 1962), 46–47.

12. Mary McCarthy, *The Group* (New York: Harcourt, Brace & World, 1954), 224–47.

Chapter Three

1. Balbus, *Marxism and Domination*, 346.

2. Nancy Pottishman Weiss, "Mother, the Invention of Necessity: Dr. Benjamin Spock's *Baby and Child Care*," *American Quarterly* 29, no. 5 (Winter 1977), 519–46; Michael Zuckerman, "Dr. Spock: The Confidence Man," in Charles E. Rosenberg, ed., *The Family in History* (Philadelphia: University of Pennsylvania Press, 1975), 179–207. See also note 8, chap. 1, above.

3. See note 10, chap. 1.

4. See note 10, chap. 1.

5. See note 10, chap. 1.

6. Sigmund Freud, "'Civilized' Sexual Morality and Modern Nervous Illness" [1908], , *SE*, vol. 9 (London: Hogarth Press, 1951), 181–204.

7. Sigmund Freud, *Civilization and Its Discontents* (New York: W.W. Norton & Company, 1961).

8. Benjamin Spock and Mabel Huschka, "The Psychological Aspects of Pediatric Practice," in *The Practitioners Library of Medicine and Surgery* (New York: D. Appleton-Century Company, 1938), 757–808; Margaret Ribble, *The Rights of Infants* (New York: Oxford University Press, 1943). On the dominance of neo-Freudian pediatric advice following World War II, see Christina Hardyment, *Dream Babies* (New York: Harper & Row, 1983) 229–40 and n 9, chap. 1, above.

9. Historians tell us that this "permissive" transformation disproportionately affected middle-class families. But during the early national period, "middle-class people were a significant part of the population, probably as much as three-fifths, if commercial farm families are so denominated." Carl Degler, *At Odds: Women and the Family in America from the Revolution to the Present* (New York: Oxford University Press, 1980), 82.

10. There is considerable evidence that American mothers took the new advice to heart. Conservative Calvinists like Heman Humphrey lamented the "great laxness of family government which characterizes the present age," and European observers consistently remarked on the "indulgence . . . shown by parents . . . toward children in earliest youth." Cited in A. W. Calhoun, *Social History of the American Family*, vol. 2 (New York: Barnes & Noble, 1945), 63, 65.

A careful study of forty-two accounts of American society during the first half of the nineteenth century written by European travelers of "very different prejudices" concludes that "the most significant observation about American children was the permissive child-rearing patterns that apparently were widespread at this time." Frank R. Furstenberg, Jr., "Industrialization and the American Family: A Look Backward," *American Sociological Review*, 31, no. 3 (June, 1966), 328, 334–35.

11. This pattern has been reconstructed from all the works cited in this chapter that describe child-rearing practices in America since 1800.

12. For somewhat different variations on this theme, see Zuckerman, "Dr. Spock:

The Confidence Man"; Daniel R. Miller and Guy E. Swanson, *Inner Conflict and Defense* (New York: Henry Holt and Company, 1960); Christopher Lasch, *The Culture of Narcissism* (New York: W.W. Norton & Company, 1978), 169–70.

13. Paul A. Baran and Paul M. Sweezy, *Monopoly Capital* (New York: Monthly Review Press, 1966); Martin J. Sklar, "On the Proletarian Revolution and the End of Political-Economic Society," *Radical America*, 3, no. 3 (May–June 1969), 1–42; Stewart Ewen, *Captains of Consciousness; Advertising and the Social Roots of the Consumer Culture* (New York: McGraw Hill, 1976).

14. Ilene Philipson, "Child Rearing Literature and Capitalist Industrialization," *Berkeley Journal of Sociology*, 26 (1981), 64–65.

15. Michel Foucault, *The History of Sexuality*, vol. 1 (New York: Pantheon, 1978).

16. Robert Castel, *The Psychiatric Society* (New York: Columbia University Press, 1982).

17. Michel Foucault, *Power/Knowledge* (New York: Pantheon, 1980), 139–40.

18. Cited in Bernard Wishy, *The Child and the Republic* (Philadelphia: University of Pennsylvania Press, 1967), 129.

19. Michel Foucault, *Discipline and Punish* (New York: Pantheon, 1977).

20. Foucault, *Power/Knowledge*, 142; see also *The History of Sexuality*, 95–96.

21. Foucault, *The History of Sexuality*, 95.

22. Foucault, *Power/Knowledge*, 117. To Foucault's directive to "dispense with the constituent subject" we are, of course, entitled to respond that the one "subject" with which Foucault cannot "dispense" is Foucault himself. To account for the subjectivity that animates his own discourse he would have to exempt himself from his ban on the constituent subject. But then what grounds, other than an elitist exceptionalism, would there be for not *generally* revoking this ban?

23. Dorothy Dinnerstein, *The Mermaid and the Minotaur* (New York: Harper & Row, 1976).

24. Isaac D. Balbus, *Marxism and Domination* (Princeton, NJ: Princeton University Press, 1982), chap. 9.

25. Dinnerstein, *The Mermaid and the Minotaur*, 192.

26. Nancy Chodorow, *The Reproduction of Mothering* (Berkeley: The University of California Press, 1978), 206.

27. Margaret Mahler, *On Human Symbiosis and the Vicissitudes of Individuation* (New York: International Universities Press, 1968).

28. Anne L. Kuhn, *The Mother's Role in Childhood Education: New England Concepts, 1830–60* (New Haven: Yale University Press, 1947); Carroll Smith Rosenberg, "Beauty, the Beast, and the Militant Woman: A Case Study in Sex Roles and Social Stress in Jacksonian America," *American Quarterly*, 23, no. 4 (October 1971), 562–84; Daniel Scott Smith, "Family Limitation, Sexual Control and Domestic Feminism in Victorian America," *Feminist Studies*, 1, no. 3/4 (1973), 40–57; Ruth H. Bloch, "American Feminine Ideals in Transition: The Rise of the Moral Mother, 1785–1815," *Feminist Studies*, 4, no. 2 (June 1978), 101–26; Ruth H. Bloch, "Untangling the Roots of Modern Sex Roles: A Survey of Four Centuries of Change," *Signs*, 4, no. 2 (Winter 1978), 237–52; Barbara Welter, "The Cult of True Womanhood: 1820–1860," *American Quarterly*, 18, no. 2 (Summer 1966), 151–74.

29. Ann Douglas, *The Feminization of American Culture* (New York: Alfred A. Knopf, 1977).
30. Donald G. Matthews, "The Second Great Awakening as an Organizing Process, 1780–1830: An Hypothesis," *American Quarterly*, 21, no. 1 (Spring 1969), 23–43; Nancy F. Cott, "Young Women in the Second Great Awakening," *Feminist Studies*, 3, no. 1/2 (Fall 1975), 15–29; Douglas, *The Feminization of American Culture*, 97–99.
31. The term is from Horace Bushnell, *Views on Christian Nuture* (Hartford, CN: Edwin Hunt, 1848). On the early to mid-nineteenth-century decline of the doctrine of innate depravity, see Philip J. Greven, Jr., *Child-Rearing Concepts, 1628–1861* (Itasca, IL: F. E. Peacock, 1973); Hardyment, *Dream Babies*, 33–86; Wishy, *The Child and the Republic*, 11–49.
32. Smith, "Family Limitation, Sexual Control and Domestic Feminism in Victorian America." Smith points out that declining birth rates reflect an increased power of women within the family during this period. Declining birth rates would, in turn, tend to encourage a more intimate relationship between mothers and their children.
33. Linda A. Pollock, *Forgotten Children* (Cambridge: Cambridge University Press, 1983), 119; Peter Gregg Slater, "Views of Children During the Early National Period" (Ph.D. diss., University of California at Berkeley, August, 1970), 204.
34. Hardyment, *Dream Babies*, 33–86; Philipson, "Child Rearing Literature and Capitalist Industrialization," 61–2.
35. *Historical Statistics of the United States: Colonial Times to 1957* (Washington, DC: Bureau of the Census with the Cooperation of the Social Science Research Council, 1960), 14.
36. Estelle Freedman, "Separatism as Strategy: Female Institution Building and American Feminism, 1870–1930," *Feminist Studies* 5, no. 3 (Fall 1979), 512–39; William Leach, *True Love and Perfect Union* (New York: Basic Books, 1980); and see n 28, above.
37. John B. Watson, *Psychological Care of Infant and Child* (New York: W.W. Norton, 1928), 87. See also Terry Strathman, "From the Quotidian to the Utopian: Child Rearing Literature in America, 1926–1946," *Berkeley Journal of Sociology*, 29, (1984), 1–34.
38. Watson, *Psychological Care of Infant and Child*, 183, 7, 13.
39. Ibid., 38.
40. Balbus, *Marxism and Domination*, chap. 9; Susan R. Bordo, *The Flight to Objectivity* (Albany: State University of New York Press, 1987); Evelyn Fox Keller, *Reflections on Gender and Science* (New Haven: Yale University Press, 1985); Jane Flax, "Political Philosophy and the Patriarchal Unconscious: A Psychoanalytic Perspective on Epistemology and Metaphysics," in Sandra Harding and Merill B. Hintikka, eds., *Discovering Reality* (Boston: D. Reidel, 1983), 245–81.
41. Hardyment, *Dream Babies*, 173; Strathman, "From the Quotidian to the Utopian," 3–8; Lucille Birnbaum, "Behaviorism in the 1920s," *American Quarterly*, 7, no. 1 (Spring 1955), 29; Celia B. Stendler, "Sixty Years of Child Training Practices," *Journal of Pediatrics*, 36 (1950), 122–36.
42. Elizabeth Lomax, "The Laura Spelman Rockefeller Memorial: Some of Its

Contributions to Early Research in Child Development," *Journal of the History of the Behavioral Sciences*, 13 (1977), 283–93; Orville G. Brim, Jr., *Education for Child Rearing* (New York: Russell Sage Foundation, 1959), especially 328–35; Barbara Ehrenreich and Deirdre English, *For Her Own Good; 150 Years of the Experts' Advice to Women* (Garden City, NY: Anchor Books, 1979), 207–8.

43. Molly Ladd-Taylor, *Raising a Baby the Government Way* (New Brunswick, NJ: Rutgers University Press, 1986), 1–46; Nancy Pottishman Weiss, "Mother, the Invention of Necessity: Dr. Benjamin Spock's *Baby and Child Care*," *American Quarterly*, 29, no. 5 (Winter 1977), 519–46; Martha Wolfenstein, "Trends in Infant Care," *American Journal of Orthopsychiatry*, 23, no. 1 (January 1953), 120–30.

44. Mary McCarthy, *The Group* (New York: Harcourt, Brace & World, 1954), 224–47; interview with Selma Balbus, June 1984.

45. David Cohen, *J.B. Watson: The Founder of Behaviorism* (London: Routledge & Kegan Paul, 1979), 203; Hardyment, *Dream Babies*, 176.

46. *The Young Child in the Home: A Survey of Three Thousand American Families*, Report of the Committee on the Infant and Pre-School Child, John E. Anderson, Chairman (New York: D. Appleton-Century Company, 1936).

47. Christopher Lasch, *Haven in a Heartless World* (New York: Basic Books, 1979), 13–21; John Chynoweth Burnham, "Psychiatry, Psychology, and the Progressive Movement," *American Quarterly*, 12, no. 4 (1960), 457–65.

48. Nathan G. Hale, Jr., *Freud in America*, vol. 1 (New York: Oxford University Press, 1971), 398.

49. Burnham, "Psychiatry, Psychology, and the Progressive Movement."

50. Leach, *True Love and Perfect Union*, 344, 346.

51. The argument that child-centered post-World War II child-rearing practices were made possible by a pre-World War II softening of psychoanalytic theory that was itself inspired by the study of "primitive" child-rearing practices has intriguing implications. Consider that conservative critics—including Spiro Agnew—blamed the "sixties" counter-culture on precisely those "permissive" child-rearing practices for which they held the notorious Dr. Spock responsible. Suppose that a case could be made that these critics were correct, that counter-cultural sensibilities were indeed engendered by the early indulgence enjoyed by the members of the "love generation." (For speculations along these lines, see my *Marxism and Domination*, chap. 10.) Then a case could also be made that their "primitivist" repudiation of modernity was the fruit of a cross-cultural learning experience by means of which modern, masculine child-rearing practices were ultimately abandoned in favor of feminine practices that more closely approximated those that prevailed in the primitive world. If so, then we could say that it was through gender struggle that the West came to learn from (what it parochially dismisses as) the Rest.

52. Marvin Harris, *The Rise of Anthropological Theory* (New York: Crowell, 1968), 431.

53. Lasch, *Haven in a Heartless World*, 70.

54. Harris, *The Rise of Anthropological Theory*, 408; Lasch, *Haven in a Heartless World*, 70.

55. Benjamin Spock and Mabel Huschka, "The Psychological Aspects of Pediatric Practice"; Lawrence K. Frank, "Cultural Coercion and Individual Distor-

tion," *Psychiatry*, 2 (1939), 11–27, and "Freedom for the Personality," *Psychiatry*, 3 (1940), 341–49; Erik Homburger Erikson, "Childhood and Tradition in Two American Indian Tribes," *Psychoanalytic Study of the Child* vol. 1 (1945), 319–50; Margaret A. Ribble, "The Significance of Sucking for the Psychic Development of the Individual," *Journal of Nervous and Mental Diseases*, 90 (1939), 455–63.

Chapter Four

1. Joseph Pleck, *Men's New Roles in the Family: Housework and Child Care* (Ann Arbor, MI: Institute for Social Research, December 1976).
2. Diane Ehrensaft, "When Women and Men Mother," *Socialist Review*, 49 (January–February 1980), 37–73.
3. Balbus, *Marxism and Domination*, 383.
4. Graeme Russell, *The Changing Role of Fathers?* (London: University of Queensland Press, 1983), 184.
5. Ehrensaft, "When Women and Men Mother," 46–52.
6. Isaac D. Balbus, "Disciplining Women: Michel Foucault and the Power of Feminist Discourse," *Praxis International*, 5, no. 2 (January 1986), 466–83. Subsequently reprinted in Seyla Benhabib and Drucilla Cornell, *Feminism as Critique* (Cambridge: Polity Press, 1987), 110–27, and Jonathan Arac, *After Foucault* (New Brunswick, NJ: Rutgers University Press, 1988), 138–60.
7. *Psychological Care of Infant and Child*, 38, 79, 80; chap. 3, 44, 149, 81–82, 186, 5–6.
8. Hardyment, *Dream Babies*, 99–100. Hardyment refers (p. 100) to at least twelve revisions of Holt's book, whereas Watson refers in his *Psychological Care of Infant and Child* (p. 4) to "28 editions" of that work.
9. *The Care and Feeding of Children* (New York: D. Appleton & Co., 1914), 162–63, 176, 173, 170.
10. Richard Edwards, *Contested Terrain* (New York: Basic Books, 1979), 250.
11. Harry Braverman, *Labor and Monopoly Capitalism* (New York: Monthly Review Press, 1974), 91.
12. Cited in Braverman, *Labor and Monopoly Capitalism*, 12.
13. Foucault, *Power/Knowledge*, 78–108.
14. Foucault, *Discipline and Punish*, 137, 24, 135.
15. Guy Oakes, "Translator's Introduction" to Georg Simmel, *On Women, Sexuality, and Love* (New Haven, Yale University Press, 1984), 22.
16. Dinnerstein, *The Mermaid and the Minotaur*, 101.
17. Balbus, *Marxism and Domination*, 316–17.
18. All the quoted material is from Jean Piaget, *The Child's Conception of the World* (New York: The Humanities Press, 1951), 153, 246, 154–55, 236, 385.

Chapter Five

1. Larry B. Feldman, "Sex Roles and Family Dynamics," in F. Walsh, ed., *Normal Family Processes* (London: Guilford, 1982), 366. Feldman's summary of Walters's and Stinnet's findings is confirmed by "three more recent studies" that he cites on the same page. Walters's and Stinnet's findings were originally reported in their "Parent-Child Relationships: A Decade Review of Research," *Journal of Marriage and the Family*, 33, no. 1 (February 1971), 70–111.

2. John Cleverly and D.C. Phillips, *From Locke to Spock* (Hong Kong: Melbourne University Press, 1976); Hardyment, *Dream Babies*; Kuhn, *The Mother's Role in Childhood Education*; Pollack, *Forgotten Children;* Slater, "Views of Children during the Early National Period"; Stone, *The Family, Sex and Marriage in England: 1500–1800*; Wishy, *The Child and the Republic.*

3. Morris Zelditch, Jr., "Role Differentiation in the Nuclear Family: A Comparative Study," in Talcott Parsons and Robert F. Bales, *Family, Socialization and Interaction Process* (Glencoe, IL: The Free Press, 1955), 313–15. Linda Nicholson has pointed out to me that claims of cultural universality are vulnerable to the objection that "since there is no contemporary society which has not been affected by capitalism, we cannot merely use evidence from diverse contemporary societies as evidence for the universality of anything" (personal communication, January 24, 1997). But Zelditch's sample was drawn from the bibliographies of George Peter Murdock's *Social Structure* (New York: Macmillan Co., 1949) and Robert H. Lowie's *Social Organization* (Holt, Rinehart and Winston, 1948), both of which included ethnographies from the early decades of the twentieth century. The claim that what looks like cultural universals are nothing more than specifically capitalist commonalities does not seem plausible when it comes to commonalities that were discovered long before the advent of contemporary "globalization" and its homogenizing effects. Even today, moreover, the plausibility of this claim is called into question by the cultural diversity that persists even in the midst of globalization. If globalization has not been powerful enough to eliminate all cultural differences, then why should we assume that it is powerful enough to create all cultural commonalities?

4. William N. Stephens, *The Family in Cross-Cultural Perspective* (New York: Holt, Rinehart and Winston, 1963), 319.

5. William N. Stephens, *The Oedipus Complex: Cross Cultural Evidence* (Glencoe, IL: The Free Press, 1962), 10–12.

6. Kenneth Read, *The High Valley* (New York: Scribner, 1965), 170–72.

7. Gilbert H. Herdt, ed., *Rituals of Manhood: Male Initiation in Papua New Guinea* (Berkeley: University of California Press, 1982), 58–59.

8. Hardyment, *Dream Babies*, 240–46; 291.

9. Carol Gilligan, *In a Different Voice* (Cambridge, MA: Harvard University Press, 1982).

10. Lawrence Kohlberg, *The Philosophy of Moral Development: Moral Stages and the Idea of Justice* (New York: Harper & Row, 1981).

11. Kurt Bergling, *Moral Development: The Validity of Kohlberg's Theory* (Stockholm: Almqvist & Wiksell International, 1981), 63–66, 85–86; C. B. White, N. Bushnell, and J. L. Regnemer, "Moral Development in Bahamian School Children: A 3-Year Examination of Kohlberg's Stages of Moral Development," *Developmental Psychology*, 14, no. 1 (January 1978), 58–65.

12. Elizabeth Leonie Simpson, "Moral Development Research: A Case Study of Scientific Cultural Bias," *Human Development*, 17, no. 2 (1974), 81–106.

13. Norbert Elias, *The Civilizing Process: The History of Manners* (New York: Urizen Books, 1978), 224.

Chapter Six

1. Robert Stoller, *Presentations of Gender* (New Haven: Yale University Press, 1985), 10–24.
2. Herman Roiphe and Elanor Galenson, *Infantile Origins of Sexual Identity* (New York: International Universities Press, 1981), 258, 205.
3. Ibid., 256.
4. Erik H. Erikson, *Childhood and Society* (New York: Norton, 1950), 97–108.
5. Roiphe and Galenson, *Infantile Origins of Sexual Identity*, 96.
6. Margaret S. Mahler et al., *The Psychological Birth of the Human Infant* (New York: Basic Books, 1975).
7. Cited in Christopher Lasch, *The Minimal Self* (New York: W.W. Norton & Co., 1984), 194.
8. D. W. Winnicott, *Playing and Reality* (New York: Basic Books, 1971), 14–15.
9. Mahler et al., *The Psychological Birth of the Human Infant*, 77–78, 89, 99, 102, 106, 213.
10. Winnicott, *Playing and Reality*, 1–13.

Chapter Seven

1. Dinnerstein, *The Mermaid and the Minotaur*, 42.
2. Chodorow, *The Reproduction of Mothering*, 140, 167.
3. Dinnerstein, *The Mermaid and the Minotaur*, 38–75.
4. Chodorow, *The Reproduction of Mothering*, 201. See also Dinnerstein, *The Mermaid and the Minotaur*, 41.
5. Elisabeth Badinter, *Mother Love: Myth and Reality* (New York: Macmillan, 1981), 39.
6. Edward Shorter, *The Making of the Modern Family* (New York: Basic Books, 1975), 168.
7. Badinter, *Mother Love*, 72.
8. Shorter, *The Making of the Modern Family*, 175–90. Badinter, *Mother Love*, 39–52, 109–14.
9. Stone, *The Family, Sex and Marriage in England*, 427.
10. Ibid.
11. David Hunt, *Parents and Children in History* (New York: Harper & Row, 1972), 107–8.
12. Emmy E. Werner, "Infants Around the World: Cross-Cultural Studies of Psychomotor Development from Birth to Two Years," in Stella Chess and Alexander Thomas, *Annual Progress in Child Psychiatry and Infant Development*, vol. 6 (New York: Brunner/Mazel, 1973), 84–112.

Chapter Eight

1. Philippe Aries, *Centuries of Childhood* (New York: Vintage Books, 1962).
2. Jay Melching, "Advice to Historians on Advice to Mothers," *Journal of Social History*, 9 (1975), 49, 45.
3. Ibid., 50, 60 n 23.
4. Hans-Georg Gadamer, *Truth and Method* (New York: Continuum, 1993).
5. Max Weber, *The Sociology of Religion* (London: Methuen, 1965), chaps. 2–3.
6. Dinnerstein, *The Mermaid and the Minotaur*, chap. 7.

7. Balbus, *Marxism and Domination*, 334–44. See also the somewhat different but ultimately compatible formulation of Jane Flax in "Political Philosophy and the Patriarchal Unconscious," 245–81.

8. After completing *Marxism and Domination* I discovered that this hypothesis has also been advanced by Morris Berman in *The Reenchantment of the World* (Ithaca, NY: Cornell University Press, 1981), chap. 6.

9. Berman's case on behalf of this hypothesis—like mine in *Marxism and Domination*—rests largely on an inference drawn from a comparison of contemporary Western and non-Western societies: "Child-rearing practices among contemporary non-western cultures may be indicative of what was typical in the west down to the early Renaissance," (165–66). This essay attempts to ground this inference with empirical evidence.

10. Margaret Mahler et al., *The Psychological Birth of the Human Infant* (New York: Basic Books, 1975).

11. Heinz Hartmann et al., "Comments on the Formation of Psychic Structure," *The Psychoanalytic Study of the Child*, vol. 2 (New York: International Universities Press, 1946), 20.

12. There is cognitive developmental, as well as psychoanalytic, support for this proposition. Piaget argues in *The Child's Conception of the World* (New York: The Humanities Press, 1951) that the child's feelings of "participation" (153) and "communion" (256) result from a "continual response of the [maternal] environment" (154) and thus from a "complete continuity between its parents' activities and its own" (155). Consistent maternal gratification, in other words, "ensures an absence of differentiation between the world and the self" (236). This sense of differentiation—for Piaget the disappearance of feelings of participation and communion—only develops with the child's "liberation from the bond that ties him . . . to his parents" (385). Since the dissolution of this bond between mother and child is set in motion by the frustrations that the former imposes on the latter, Piaget's argument is consistent with the claim that maternal deprivation is the foundation for a sense of separation between self and world. Because Piaget treats the modern Western mix of maternal gratification and deprivation as the only possible mix, his conclusion is that the development of this sense of separation is both natural and inevitable. Thus he fails to acknowledge the possibility that a mix that was weighted more heavily in favor of gratification would produce persistent feelings of participation and communion that are not "outgrown." But this possibility can be inferred from his assumptions.

13. Philippe Aries, *Centuries of Childhood* (New York: Vintage Books, 1962), 411.

14. David Hunt, *Parents and Children in History* (New York, Basic Books, 1970), 48.

15. James Bruce Ross, "The Middle-Class Child in Urban Italy, Fourteenth to Early Sixteenth Century," in Lloyd DeMause, ed., *The History of Childhood* (New York: The Psychoanalytic Press, 1974), 195, 192.

16. Mary Martin McLaughlin, "Survivors and Surrogates: Children and Parents from the Ninth to the Thirteenth Centuries," in DeMause, *The History of Childhood*, 116; Lloyd DeMause, "The Evolution of Childhood," in DeMause, op. cit., 36.

17. DeMause, "The Evolution of Childhood," 36.

18. Linda Pollack, *Forgotten Children: Parent-Child Relations from 1500 to 1900* (Cambridge: Cambridge University Press, 1983), 220.
19. M. J. Tucker, "The Child as Beginning and End: Fifteenth and Sixteenth Century English Childhood," in DeMause, *The History of Childhood*, 244; Lawrence Stone, *The Family, Sex and Marriage in England, 1500–1800* (New York: Harper & Row, 1977), 151, 159, 426, 431.
20. Joseph E. Illick, "Child Rearing in Seventeenth Century England and America," in DeMause, *The History of Childhood*, 325–26.
21. John Demos, *A Little Commonwealth* (New York: Oxford University Press, 1970), 133.
22. DeMause, "The Evolution of Childhood," 35.
23. McLaughlin, "Survivors and Surrogates," 116; Aries, *Centuries of Childhood*, 374; Shulamith Shahar, *The Fourth Estate* (London: Methuen, 1983), 140. See also Elisabeth Badinter, *Mother Love* (New York: Macmillan, 1981), 41.
24. Badinter, *Mother Love*, 42; Stone, *The Family, Sex and Marriage in England*, 479. See also Elizabeth Wirth Marvick, "Nature versus Nurture: Patterns and Trends in Seventeenth Century Child-Rearing," in DeMause, *The History of Childhood*, 266. For evidence of wet-nursing in the American colonies, see John F. Walzer, "A Period of Ambivalence: Eighteenth Century American Childhood," in DeMause, *The History of Childhood*, 353–55.
25. Edward Shorter, *The Making of the Modern Family* (New York: Basic Books, 1975), chap. 5; Badinter, *Mother Love*, chap. 3; Stone, *The Family, Sex and Marriage in England*, 100.
26. DeMause, "The Evolution of Childhood," 19–20; Aries, *Centuries of Childhood*, 100–6.
27. Norbert Elias, *The Civilizing Process: The History of Manners* (New York: Urizen Books, 1978), 178. See also Aries, *Centuries of Childhood*, 107.
28. Berman, *The Reenchantment of the World*, 165.
29. David Herlihy, *Medieval Households* (Cambridge, MA: Harvard University Press, 1985), 121–22, 125–26. See also McLaughlin, "Survivors and Surrogates," 106, 109, 127, 133–34.
30. Berman, *The Reenchantment of the World*.
31. Aries, *Centuries of Childhood*, 107; DeMause, "The Evolution of Childhood," 43, 48; Stone, *The Family, Sex and Marriage in England*, 511–12; Alice Judson Ryerson, "Medical Advice on Child Rearing, 1500–1900," *Child & Family*, 13, no. 4 (1974), 326.
32. Elias, *The Civilizing Process*, 168; Ryerson, "Medical Advice on Child Rearing," 326.
33. Cited in Philip J. Greven, *Child-Rearing Concepts, 1828–1861* (Itasca, IL: F. E. Peacock, 1973), 63. Evangelicals like Wesley were not the only child-rearing "experts" to adopt this antisensual advice. John Locke, the foremost English exponent of secular, Enlightenment child-rearing advice, likewise advised parents in his *Some Thoughts on Education* that "the principle of virtue and excellency lies in a power of denying ourselves the satisfaction of all our desires, where reason does not authorize them." Cited in Greven, *Child-Rearing Concepts*, 24.
34. Philip J. Greven, *The Protestant Temperament* (New York: Alfred A. Knopf, 1977), 65.

35. Hartmann et al., "Comments on the Formation of Psyche Structure," 25.
36. Stone, *The Family, Sex and Marriage in England*, 159–60; DeMause, "The Evolution of Childhood," 39–40; Illick, "Child Rearing in Seventeenth Century England and America," 311; Ryerson, "Medical Advice on Child Rearing," 325. The consensus that very early toilet training did not begin until the eighteenth century is based largely on the absence of references to such training in the sixteenth- and seventeenth-century child-rearing manuals. It is possible, however, that this absence of toilet-training advice reflects not an absence of the practice but rather a reluctance—itself part of the early modern increase in shame and embarrassment about bodily functions—to speak about it. If this is so, then it is possible that intensive toilet training began earlier than most historians believe. See Abigail J. Stewart et al., "Coding Categories for the Study of Child-Rearing from Historical Sources," *Journal of Interdisciplinary History*, 4 (Spring 1975), 691–92.
37. Elias, *The Civilizing Process*, 129–42, especially 135.
38. Aries, *Centuries of Childhood*, 128, 411–12.
39. Stone, *The Family, Sex and Marriage in England*, 175; Peter Gregg Slater, "Views of Children and of Child Rearing during the Early National Period: A Study in the New England Intellect," Ph.D. diss., University of California at Berkeley, 1970, 3, 31; Hardyment, *Dream Babies*, 7; John Sommerville, *The Rise and Fall of Childhood* (Beverly Hills, CA: Sage Publications, 1982), 109.
40. Cited in Greven, *The Protestant Temperament*, 35.
41. Demos, *A Little Commonwealth*, 135.
42. Greven, *The Protestant Temperament*, 36–37.
43. Melching and Pollack are dissenters from this consensus. Both argue that (a) we cannot infer with confidence that the theories of the "experts" actually affected the attitudes of those who read them and (b) even if they did, we should not expect to find a one-to-one relationship between parental attitudes and parental behavior. Jay Melching, "Advice to Historians on Advice to Mothers," *Journal of Social History*, 9 (1975), 43–63; Pollack, *Forgotten Children*, 43–45. I will argue below that there are, to the contrary, good reasons to assume a generally close relationship between theory and practice.
44. Pollack, *Forgotten Children*, 113.
45. Greven, *The Protestant Temperament*, 17, 12, 152. Greven also suggests that there were "genteel" families committed to indulgent child-rearing practices but acknowledges that they were a small minority, restricted to "families of wealth, eminence, and power" (265).
46. Greven, *Child-Rearing Concepts*, 113, 119–20; Greven, *The Protestant Temperament*, 160.
47. Greven, *The Protestant Temperament*, 160, and Slater, "Views of Children and Child Rearing during the Early National Period," 195, 161, 193. Slater also argues (131) that in America the Enlightenment theories of child rearing did not gain widespread acceptance until after the Revolutionary War, i.e., toward the very end of the early modern period.
48. Hunt, *Parents and Children in History*, 139.
49. Aries, *Centuries of Childhood*, 114–15; Steven Ozment, *When Fathers Ruled* (Cambridge, MA: Harvard University Press, 1983), 135.
50. Elias, *The Civilizing Process*, 224.

51. Elias himself ignores (what I have hypothesized are) the early childhood roots of the process he describes, although in vol. 2 of *The Civilizing Process* (New York: Pantheon Books, 1982) he acknowledges in a footnote that an explanation of this process "demands . . . a general study of changes in the upbringing of children" (295), one that he does not, however, undertake.

52. Elias, *The Civilizing Process*, vol. 1, 140–41, 214.

53. Ibid., 257.

54. Ibid., 164, 139.

55. Ibid., 192.

56. Stone, *The Family, Sex and Marriage in England*, 178.

57. Vivian C. Fox and Martin H. Quitt, eds., *Living, Parenting, and Dying: The Family Cycle in England and America, Past and Present* (New York: Psychohistory Press, 1980), 275.

58. Dinnerstein, *The Mermaid and the Minotaur*; Balbus, *Marxism and Domination*, chap. 9; Chodorow, *The Reproduction of Mothering*.

59. Therese Benedek, "Parenthood as a Developmental Phase," *Journal of the American Psychoanalytic Association*, 7, no. 3 (July 1959), 410.

60. Chodorow, *The Reproduction of Mothering*, 79.

61. Homosexuality is, of course, another possible way for the boy to deal with this conflict.

62. On the concept of "dis-identification," see Ralph Greenson, "Dis-Identifying from Mother: Its Special Importance for the Boy," *International Journal of Psycho-Analysis*, 49 (1968), 370–74.

63. Balbus, *Marxism and Domination*, chap. 9.

64. Carol Gilligan, *In a Different Voice* (Cambridge, MA: Harvard University Press, 1982), 8.

65. Chodorow, *The Reproduction of Mothering*, 140, 167. Emphasis in the original.

66. Ibid., 167.

67. These are the feelings to which Freud refers at the outset of *Civilization and Its Discontents* (New York: W.W. Norton & Co., 1961), 11–13, but which, he (wrongly) believes, are not amenable to psychoanalytic investigation.

68. Chodorow, *The Reproduction of Mothering*, 194; Dinnerstein, *The Mermaid and the Minotaur*, 42.

69. Benedek, "Parenthood as a Developmental Phase," 395. See also Chodorow, *The Reproduction of Mothering*, 204.

70. Chodorow, *The Reproduction of Mothering*, 208. This psychodynamic explanation of the "reproduction of mothering" does not exclude the possibility that there may also be a physiological basis for maternal behavior. Pregnancy and lactation are exclusively female experiences that may well intensify the sense of oneness between mother and child and thus the willingness of the former to devote herself to the welfare of the latter. If this is so, even coparented men— men who, unlike all men until the present day, have been able to form an intense early identification with someone of their own sex—may prove to be less nurturant parents than their female counterparts. We shall see when the first generation of such men become fathers. For an interesting analysis of the possible interaction between physiological and psychological determinants of maternal behavior, see Benedek, "Parenthood as a Devlopmental Phase."

71. Chodorow, *The Reproduction of Mothering*, 206.

72. The precise nature of this combination is likely to depend on the intensity and persistence of the man's initial mother identification and thus on the child-rearing practices from which the quality and duration of that identification derive. Indulgent practices that produce an intense and protracted identification should result in greater fear of, than need for, the mother and thus in a masculine response that privileges avoidance over control, while strict practices that prematurely interrupt mother identification will tend to result in less fear and more need and thus in a reaction in which control takes precedence over avoidance. This hypothesis is consistent with the fact that intimacy between men and women is discouraged by sex segregation in preindustrial societies in which indulgent child-rearing practices typically prevail, while it is encouraged—but typically perverted by the need of men to be in control—in industrial societies in which child-rearing practices are usually far more strict. See Balbus, *Marxism and Domination*, chap. 9.

73. Dinnerstein, *The Mermaid and the Minotaur*, 49–50.

74. Ibid., chap. 4.

75. Chodorow, *The Reproduction of Mothering*, 201. See also Dinnerstein, 41.

76. Badinter, *Mother Love*, 39.

77. Except in polygynous societies, where a man who "loses" one wife to a child can always count on the devotion of another.

78. Benedeck, "Parenthood as a Developmental Phase," 413.

79. Anne Ferguson also argues, in "On Conceiving Motherhood and Sexuality," in Joyce Treblicot, ed., *Mothering: Essays in Feminist Theory* (Totowa, NJ: Rowman & Allanheld, 1983), that the fact that the woman mothers "tends to make her identify with the sex/affective interests of the child more than does the father" (162), but she rejects a psychoanalytic explanation of this identification. This rejection is based on her distaste for the "static, deterministic emphasis of feminist neo-Freudian analyses like those of Nancy Chodorow" (176). By now it should be clear, however, that such analyses can be liberated from a "static, deterministic emphasis" and that the price of a dynamic analysis of child rearing need not be the abandonment of the psychodynamic terrain and with it the inability to comprehend the power of the identifications to which child rearing gives rise.

80. Strictly speaking, of course, no hypothesis is ever "verified." The fact that one hypothesis is consistent with reality in no way precludes the possibility that competing hypotheses, derived from different theories, might be equally consistent with reality and thus equally worthy of being taken seriously. But in "Neither Marx nor Foucault: Gender Struggle and the Transformation of American Child Rearing," a lecture delivered at the Institute for the Humanities, University of Illinois at Chicago, 7 November 1984, I demonstrate that no other theory of which I am aware is able to explain the pattern of American child-rearing transformations from 1800 to the present as well as mine. [See chap. 3 above.]

81. Reinhard Bendix, *Max Weber: An Intellectual Portrait* (Garden City, NY: Anchor Books, 1962), 365.

82. Joseph and Frances Gies, *Life in a Medieval Castle* (New York: Thomas Y. Crowell Company, 1974), 45.

83. Ibid., 47.
84. Shahar, *The Fourth Estate*, 141; David Herlihy, "Land, Family, and Women in Continental Europe, 701–1200," in Susan Moshar Stuard, *Women in Medieval Society* (Philadelphia: University of Pennsylvania Press, 1976), 30, 34.
85. Bendix, *Max Weber*, 364.
86. Shahar, *The Fourth Estate*, 141. Shahar reports (129) that in England from 1330 to 1475 46 percent of the men from ducal families died violently after their fifteenth year, and that between 1350 and 1500 20 percent of the men in families of secular peers died violent deaths.
87. Arthur W. Calhoun, *A Social History of the American Family* (New York: Barnes & Noble, 1945), 22.
88. Shahar, *The Fourth Estate*, 187.
89. Ibid., 234; Herlihy, *Medieval Households*, 57.
90. Herlihy, *Medieval Households*, 70–72; Aries, *Centuries of Childhood*, 353; Stone, *The Family, Sex and Marriage in England*, 124, 133–35; William N. Stephens, *The Family in Cross-Cultural Perspective* (New York: Holt, Rinehart, and Winston, 1963), 319. As Stone points out (86), the influence of elders over the conjugal pair was not limited to coresidents: "Since the kin formed a community, marriage meant . . . entry into a new world of the spouse's relatives."
91. Herlihy, *Medieval Households*, 71.
92. Ibid., 122–23.
93. Ibid., 123–24.
94. Suzanne Fonay Wemple, *Women in Frankish Society* (Philadelphia: University of Pennsylvania Press, 1981), 195; Shahar, *The Fourth Estate*, 128–30.
95. Shahar, *The Fourth Estate*, 181–82, 222.
96. Cited in Ferdinand Mount, *The Subversive Family* (London: Jonathan Cape, 1982), 230.
97. Ibid., 238.
98. Herlihy, "Land, Family and Women in Continental Europe," 13.
99. Gies and Gies, *Life in a Medieval Castle*, 81. See also Shahar, *The Fourth Estate*, 145–52 and Herlihy, *Medieval Households*, 100.
100. Herlihy, *Medieval Households*, 129, 159; Shahar, *The Fourth Estate*, 141.
101. Christopher Hill, *Society and Puritanism in Pre-Revolutionary England* (London: Seker & Warburg, 1964), 449; Max Horkheimer, "Authority and the Family," in *Critical Theory* (NY: The Seabury Press, 1978), 47–128; Wilhelm Reich, *The Mass Psychology of Fascism* (New York: Farrar, Straus & Giroux, 1970), 48–54.
102. For an example of this by-now discredited thesis, see Shorter, *The Making of the Modern Family*.
103. Peter Laslett, *The World We Have Lost* (New York: Charles Scribner's Sons, 1983); Stone, *The Family, Sex and Marriage in England*; Ralph A. Houlbrooke, *The English Family 1450–1700* (London: Longman, 1983); Alan MacFarlane, *The Origins of English Individualism* (New York: Cambridge University Press, 1979); and *Marriage and Love in England 1300–1840* (Oxford: Basil Blackwell, 1986). MacFarlane claims that the nuclear family was in place in England as early as the thirteenth century, but the plausibility of this claim, it seems to me, rests on an overly broad definition of that term.

104. Aries, for example, specifies the eighteenth century as the era of the emergence of the nuclear household in France and Italy. *Centuries of Childhood*, 398–407.
105. Stone, *The Family, Sex and Marriage in England*, 150.
106. Ibid., 124–57.
107. Hill, *Society and Puritanism in Pre-Revolutionary England*, 458, 466, 450, 457. Stone agrees with Hill: "The principal result of the Reformation was the heavy responsibility placed . . . upon the head of the household to supervise the religious and moral conduct of its members." *The Family, Sex and Marriage in England*, 154. Gordon Rattray Taylor argues that Puritanism was not only a cause, but also a consequence, of the preeminent role of an authoritarian father: "Evidently Puritanism is, in part, an attempt to cope with the aggression evoked by a severe father." *Rethink* (New York: E. Dutton, 1973), 54.
108. Carl N. Degler, *At Odds: Women and the Family in America from the Revolution to the Present* (New York: Oxford University Press, 1980), 73.
109. John Milton, cited in Stone, *The Family, Sex and Marriage in England*, 154. See also Hill, *Society and Puritanism in Pre-Revolutionary England*, 457.
110. Hill, *Society and Puritanism in Pre-Revolutionary England*, 446.
111. Robert Sanderson, cited in Hill, *Society and Puritanism in Pre-Revolutionary England*, 461. Sanderson was echoed by King James I of England, for whom "kings are compared to fathers in families: for a king is truly *parens patriae*, the political father of his people." Cited in Stone, *The Family, Sex and Marriage in England*, 152.
112. Demos, *A Little Commonwealth*, 84. Demos notes that the legal status of married women was considerably higher in the American colonies.
113. Cited in Aries, *Centuries of Childhood*, 356. See also Badinter, *Mother Love*, 19–22.
114. Stone, *The Family, Sex and Marriage in England*, 158.
115. Ibid., 132–35.
116. Ibid., 135–42.
117. Hill, *Society and Puritanism in Pre-Revolutionary England*, 482–500.
118. Stone, *The Family, Sex and Marriage in England*, 216.
119. Ibid., 151. See also 216.
120. Levin L. Shucking, *The Puritan Family* (New York: Schocken Books, 1970), 88.
121. Ibid.; Stone, *The Family, Sex and Marriage in England*, 438; Pollack, *Forgotten Children*, 118, 163; Slater, "Views of Children and Child Rearing during the Early National Period," 203–4.
122. Robert Schnucker, "Views of Selected Puritans, 1560–1630, on Marriage and Human Sexuality," Ph.D. diss., University of Iowa, 1969, cited in Ozment, *When Fathers Ruled*, 118.
123. Stone, *The Family, Sex and Marriage in England*, 427; Ozment, *When Fathers Ruled*, 118.
124. Stone, *The Family, Sex and Marriage in England*, 427.
125. Even Elisabeth Badinter, a proponent of the "maternal indifference" thesis—the thesis that early modern mothers were largely indifferent to the welfare of their children—is obliged to acknowledge that "the child, particularly the infant, seems to have been an unbearable burden for the father—for it is the child who robs him of his wife," and to conclude that "since society placed the

greatest value on the man, thus the husband, it was normal for the wife to put his interest above the baby's." *Mother Love*, 39, 51.

126. William Gouge, *Of Domesticall Duties* (London, 1622), cited in Stone, *The Family, Sex and Marriage in England*, 427.

127. Hunt, *Parents and Children in History*, 107–8.

128. DeMause, "The Evolution of Childhood," 39; Robertson, "The Home as a Nest," in DeMause, ed., *The History of Childhood*, 410; Stone, *The Family, Sex and Marriage in England*, 432.

129. Stone, *The Family, Sex and Marriage in England*, 478; Reich, *The Mass Psychology of Fascism*, 48–54; Mark Poster, *Critical Theory of the Family* (New York: The Seabury Press, 1978), 51.

130. Greven, *The Protestant Temperament*, 155, 274, 153, 32.

131. Although this conflict is culturally universal, the way in which it is expressed or organized is not. In rigidly sex-segregated societies, for example, in which male children are raised exclusively by their mothers or female mother substitutes until they reach the age of initiation—after which they become the exclusive responsibility of their male elders—the conflict is likely to center over the nature and timing of the initiation. See Kenneth E. Read, *The High Valley* (New York: Charles Scribner's Sons, 1965), 152–77, and Gilbert H. Herdt, ed., *Rituals of Manhood* (Berkeley: University of California Press, 1982), 58–59. It is only in societies in which sex-segregation is less rigid and in which, as a consequence, both parents are considered responsible for infants and young children that their opposing parenting interests will be expressed in regular gender struggle over the way they are treated.

132. Elsewhere I demonstrate that an internal critique of economic and political accounts that ignore these internal dynamics reveals the need for a theory in which they are accorded a central place. Balbus, "Neither Marx nor Foucault: Gender Struggle and the Transformation of American Child Rearing," lecture delivered at the Institute for the Humanities, University of Illinois at Chicago, 7 November 1984.

133. "Permanent" at least under the conditions of what I have called the "maternal mode of child rearing".

134. On the concept of an "overdetermined" contradiction, see Louis Althusser, *For Marx* (New York: Vintage Books, 1970), 89–116.

135. Aries, *Centuries of Childhood*, 61.

Chapter Nine
1. Gordon Rattray Taylor, *Rethink*, 60–64.
2. Cited in Bendix, *Max Weber*, 139.

Chapter Ten
1. David M. Levy, *Maternal Overprotection* (New York: Columbia University Press, 1943), 112–60; Hans Sebald, *Momism: The Silent Disease* (Chicago: Nelson Hall, 1976), 19–83; Philip Slater, *The Glory of Hera* (Boston: Beacon Press, 1968), 410–66, and *The Pursuit of Loneliness* (Boston: Beacon Press, 1970), 53–80.
2. Long after I derived the assumption of an overprotective maternal parenting interest from Dinnerstein's account of the dynamics of mother-dominated

child rearing I learned that Evelyn Fox Keller had come to a similar conclusion: "[B]y inhibiting the development of autonomy in women, [it] serves to reproduce mothers who, because of their own underdeveloped sense of self, may feel the child's increasing autonomy as loss or rejection and may thus be unable to realize the full dyadic potential of the mothering relation. Mothers who rely on their children for the continuity on which they are socialized to depend, and which they are denied in the rest of their lives, are ill-prepared to foster the dynamic independence their children need." *Reflections on Gender and Science* (New Haven: Yale University Press, 1985), 107.

Chapter Eleven

1. This formulation of Husserl's complaint is from William Leiss, *The Domination of Nature* (New York: George Braziller, 1972), 132.
2. George Devereux, *From Anxiety to Method in the Behavioral Sciences* (The Hague: Mouton and Co., 1967).
3. Alvin Gouldner, *The Coming Crisis of Western Sociology* (New York: Basic Books, 1970), 490.
4. Robert M. Pirsig, *Zen and the Art of Motorcycle Maintenance* (New York: Bantam Books, 1981).
5. James F. Masterson, *The Narcissistic and Borderline Disorders: An Integrated Approach* (New York: Brunner/Mazel, 1981); Otto Kernberg, *Borderline Conditions and Pathological Narcissism*; Heinz Kohut, *The Analysis of the Self* (New York: International Universities Press, 1971).
6. Winnicott, *Playing and Reality*, 14–15. See also D. W. Winnicott, *The Maturational Process and the Facilitating Environment* (New York: International Universities Press, 1965), 57–58, 145–68.
7. Kohut, *The Analysis of the Self*.
8. Masterson, *The Narcissistic and Borderline Disorders*, 106, 187–88. For the concept of the "false sense" see Winnicott, *The Maturational Process and the Facilitating Environment*, 140–52, and Masterson, *The Narcissistic and Borderline Disorders*, 104–8.
9. D. W. Winnicott, *Playing and Reality*, 89.
10. Edith Jacobsen, *The Self and the Object World* (New York: International Universities Press, 1964), 103.
11. Diane Ehrensaft, *Parenting Together* (New York: The Free Press, 1987), 79–117.

Chapter Twelve

1. Chodorow, *The Reproduction of Mothering*, especially chap. 6; Jessica Benjamin, *The Bonds of Love* (New York: Pantheon, 1988), chaps. 2–3.
2. Strictly speaking, Chodorow does not entirely ignore differences in maternal practices under the prevailing structure, but these differences are treated—inadequately—as the automatic result of the structure. See section III B.
3. Masterson, *The Narcissistic and Borderline Disorders*, 12–14, 25–27, 102–7, 133.
4. Masterson is a partial exception to this generalization. He suggests that narcissistic disorders [of the "grandiose" type, in which separation is privileged over connection] may result from a "wholesale [transfer of] the symbiotic relationship with the mother onto the father in order to deal with [the child's] aban-

donment depression," and speculates that "since this turn to the father occurs earlier and more harmoniously in boys than in girls . . . narcissistic disorders [of the grandiose type] may be more common in boys than girls, which seems to agree with clinical experience" (*The Narcissistic and Borderline Disorders*, 13–14). But this passing, two-page reference to the connection between gender and narcissism is not developed further, and it is, in fact, the only such reference in a book of some 250 pages. References to this connection are entirely absent in Kernberg's *Borderline Conditions and Pathological Narcissism* and Kohut's *The Analysis of the Self* and *The Restoration of the Self*.

5. Lasch, *The Minimal Self*, 194.
6. Winnicott, *Playing and Reality*, 14.
7. Lasch, *The Minimal Self*, 20.
8. Ibid., 245–46. See also 20, 184.
9. Stoller, *Presentations of Gender*, 10–24. See also Mahler et al., *The Psychological Birth of the Human Infant*, 104–6.
10. Kohut, *The Analysis of the Self*, 116, 106.
11. Benjamin, *The Bonds of Love*, 76. Dinnerstein's earlier discussion of this same point appears in *The Mermaid and the Minotaur*, chap. 6.
12. G. W. F. Hegel, *The Phenomenology of Mind* (New York: Harper & Row, 1967), 229–31.
13. It makes a difference, of course, whether or not a mother adequately mirrors her son prior to the point at which he becomes aware of the opposition between her gender identity and his own, and thus prior to the point at which the boy repudiates his "mirror." The narcissism of the boy who is inadequately mirrored prior to this point is likely to be even more grandiose than the narcissism of the boy who is lucky enough to have a "good-enough" mother. But the point is that even this more fortunate son is likely to exhibit grandiose tendencies.
14. Chodorow, *The Reproduction of Mothering*, 93, 110, 104.
15. Mahler, et al., *The Psychological Birth of the Human Infant*, 102, 106. See also Ernest Abelin, "Triangulation, the Role of the Father and the Origins of Core Gender Identity during the Rapprochement Subphase," in Ruth F. Lax et al., *Rapprochement: The Critical Subphase of Separation-Individuation* (New York: Jason Aronsen, 1980), 151–69; Ricki Levenson, "Intimacy, Autonomy and Gender: Developmental Differences and Their Reflections in Adult Relationships," *Journal of the American Academy of Psychoanalysis*, 12 (1984), 529–544 and Jane Flax, "The Conflict between Nurturance and Autonomy in Mother-Daughter Relationships and within Feminism," *Feminist Studies*, 4 (June 1978), 171–89.
16. Chodorow, *The Reproduction of Mothering*, 122.
17. Dinnerstein, *The Mermaid and the Minotaur*, 51–53; see also ibid., 69, and Chodorow, *The Reproduction of Mothering*, 123.
18. Kohut, *The Analysis of the Self*, 25, 27.
19. Ibid., 28, emphasis added.
20. Ilene Philipson, "Gender and Narcissism," *Psychology of Women Quarterly*, 9 (1985), 213–28.
21. *Socialist Review*, 66 (November–December 1982), 55–77.
22. Philipson, "Gender and Narcissism," 224–25.

298 . Notes .

23. Philipson, "Heterosexual Antagonisms and the Politics of Mothering," 70.
24. Only after working out that critique did I encounter Philipson's articles.
25. Philipson, "Gender and Narcissism," 220.
26. Chodorow, *The Reproduction of Mothering*, 109.
27. Ibid., 166–67.
28. To avoid misunderstanding I want to stress that my claim is not that Chodorow is unaware of the existence of such boys. Indeed in *The Reproduction of Mothering* (184–89) she specifically refers to them. My claim is rather that their existence cannot be squared with her *assumption* that "mothers experience their sons as a male opposite" and that "boys are [therefore] more likely to have been pushed out of the preoedial relationship" than girls.
29. Miriam Johnson, *Strong Mothers, Weak Wives* (Berkeley: University of California Press, 1988), 136, 109.
30. Winnicott, *Playing and Reality*, 89.
31. Chodorow, *The Reproduction of Mothering*, 169.
32. On the concept of a (grandiosely) narcissistic defense against an idealizing overdependence on the other, see Masterson, *The Narcissistic and Borderline Disorders*, 32–37, and *The Emerging Self* (New York: Brunner/Mazel, 1993), 16–17.

Chapter Thirteen

1. John Munder Ross, "Towards Fatherhood: The Epigenesis of Paternal Identity during a Boy's First Decade," *International Review of Psycho-Analysis*, 4 (1977), 342, 345.
2. Irene Fast, *Gender Identity: A Diffentiation Model* (Hillsdale, NJ: Lawrence Erlbaum Associates, 1984), 101. Fast relies on Ross, among others, to buttress her claims that "it is not necessary . . . for the boy to dis-identify with the mother" (72) and that "'dis-identification' . . . signals failure in optimum development of masculinity" (73). It seems to me that the second claim is correct but that the first claim is not. Fast herself acknowledges that the fact that "boys [in contrast to girls] must recognize their differences from their primary caregiver . . . may make it more difficult for boys than girls to move from sharply dichotomous notions of what it is to be masculine and feminine" (104). This admission undermines her claim that the boy's "dis-identification" from his mother is unnecessary under the maternal mode of child rearing and suggests that the "optimum development of masculinity" to which she is committed is far more dependent on coparenting than she realizes.
3. Kernberg, *Borderline Conditions and Pathological Narcissism*, 228.
4. Heinz Kohut, *The Restoration of the Self* (New York: International Universities Press, 1977), 171–248.
5. Jessica Benjamin, "The Oedipal Riddle: Authority, Autonomy, and the New Narcissism," in John Diggens and Mark E. Kahn, *The Problem of Authority in America* (Philadelphia: Temple University Press, 1981), 216.
6. Johnson, *Strong Mothers, Weak Wives*, 128, emphasis in the original.
7. I actually argued this many years ago when I wrote (overoptimistically) in *Marxism and Domination* that the "feminist, participatory democratic, and ecology movements were "the reciprocally interacting, mutually interdependent elements of an emerging post-Instrumental mode of symbolization"

(384). With this formulation I tried to capture both the connection and the separation among all three movements. Thus my effort in my gender-struggle "book" to inflate the first to include the other two was only possible because I had forgotten what I once knew.

8. Dean Pinos, "The Rearing of a Revolution: Child-Rearing Pratices and the Rise of American Transcendentalism," senior honors thesis, Department of Political Science, University of Illinois at Chicago, May 1995.

9. Terry Strathman, "From the Quotidian to the Utopian: Child Rearing Literature in America, 1926–1946," *Berkeley Journal of Sociology*, 29 (1984), 25–26.

10. The claim that mother-controlled regimes are much more likely than father-controlled regimes to produce men who are idealizing narcissists does not contradict the claim in Chap. twelve that men raised under any child-rearing regime are more likely to be grandiose narcissists than women. But it does suggest that the very high ratio of grandiose to idealizing narcissists among the male patients of Kernberg, Kohut, and Masterson during the 1960s and 1970s no longer reflects the current ratio in the general male population.

11. Anthony Giddens, *Modernity and Self-Identity* (Stanford, CA: Stanford University Press, 1991).

Chapter Fourteen

1. Nancy J. Chodorow, *Feminism and Psychoanalytic Theory* (New Haven: Yale University Press, 1989), 197, 189.
2. Ibid., 106.
3. Ibid., 110.
4. Ibid., 184; Chodorow, *The Reproduction of Mothering*, 169.
5. Chodorow, *Feminism and Psychoanalytic Theory*, 110.
6. Nancy Chodorow, *Femininities, Masculinities, Sexualities: Freud and Beyond* (Lexington: University Press of Kentucky, 1994), 89–90.
7. Ibid., 92.
8. Ibid., 89.
9. Ibid., 82–84.
10. Nancy Chodorow, "Gender as a Personal and Cultural Construction," *Signs*, 20, no. 3 (Spring 1995), 522.
11. Chodorow, *Feminism and Psychoanalytic Theory*, 109.
12. Chodorow, "Gender as a Personal and Cultural Construction," 520.
13. Chodorow, *Feminism and Psychoanalytic Theory*, 109–110; Chodorow, *Femininities, Masculinities, Sexualities*, 82–84; Chodorow, "Gender as a Personal and Cultural Construction," 527.
14. Chodorow, *Feminism and Psychoanalytic Theory*, 109.
15. Chodorow, *The Reproduction of Mothering*, 150.
16. Chodorow, *Feminism and Psychoanalytic Theory*, 109.
17. Chodorow, *Femininities, Masculinities, Sexualities*, 83.
18. Judith Butler, "Gender Trouble, Feminist Theory, and Psychoanalytic Discourse," in Linda J. Nicholson, ed., *Feminism/Postmodernism* (New York: Routledge, 1990), 324–40; Judith Butler, *Gender Trouble: Feminism and the Subversion of Identity* (New York: Routledge, 1990); Judith Butler, *Bodies That Matter: On the Discursive Limits of "Sex"* (New York: Routledge, 1993).

19. Butler, *Gender Trouble*, 25.
20. Ibid., 16, emphases in the original.
21. Butler, "Gender Trouble, Feminist Theory, and Psychoanalytic Discourse," 329.
22. Ibid., 330, 339.
23. Ibid., 332.
24. Ibid., 331.
25. Ibid., 330–31.
26. Ibid., 331.
27. Ibid., 337.
28. Butler, *Gender Trouble*, 17.
29. Butler, *Bodies That Matter*, 232.
30. Butler, "Gender Trouble, Feminist Theory, and Psychoanalytic Discourse," 335.
31. Cited in Paul Ricoeur, *Freud and Philosophy* (New Haven: Yale University Press, 1970), 218, 223.
32. Paula Bernstein, "Gender Identity Disorder in Boys," *Journal of the American Psychoanalytic Association*, 41, no. 3 (1993), 739. See also Richard C. Friedman, *Male Homosexuality: A Contemporary Psychoanalytic Perspective* (New Haven: Yale University Press, 1988).
33. Object-relations theory can also accommodate the apparent independence of "gender-role identity" from sexual orientation. The fact that many gay men are, and many straight men are not, stereotypically "masculine" in their affect and demeanor is entirely consistent with object-relations theory, because for that theory "gender-role identity" is no more predictive of sexual identity than is core gender identity. The same can be said of the persistence of stereotypically masculine and feminine role identities within homosexual relationships, e.g., "butch" and "femme" members of lesbian couples. Thus there is no necessary connection between the object-relational assumption of masculine and feminine gender-role identities and the heterosexist assumption that the only normal love is between masculine men and feminine women.
34. Butler, "Gender Trouble, Feminist Theory, and Psychoanalytic Discourse," 330–31.
35. Butler, *Gender Trouble*, 136. Emphases in the original.
36. Ibid., 33.
37. Ibid., 6.
38. Ibid., 24.
39. Butler, *Bodies That Matter*, xi.
40. Ibid., 6, 10, 93–94.
41. Ibid., 10.
42. Ibid.
43. Ibid., xi.
44. Ibid., 94.
45. Ibid., xi.
46. Ibid., 10–11.
47. Ibid., 12.
48. Robert Stoller, *Presentations of Gender* (New Haven: Yale University Press, 1985), 11–14.

Chapter Fifteen

1. Imre Lakatos, "Falsification and the Methodology of Scientific Research Programmes," in Imre Lakatos and Alan Musgrave, eds., *Criticism and the Growth of Knowledge* (Cambridge: Cambridge University Press, 1970), 187.
2. Ibid., 119, emphases in the original.
3. Ibid., 118.
4. Winnicott, *Playing and Reality*, 11–12.
5. Evelyn Fox Keller, *Reflections on Gender and Science* (New Haven: Yale University Press, 1985), 148.

index